# QUEENS OF WOVEN FATES

## VESSELS OF THE GODS
## II

### KATERINA STEVENS

First Paperback Edition June 2025

Cover art by Tina @tcdesigns271 [Instagram]

Interior art done by Katerina Stevens

[Canva Pro & Inkarnate Commercial License]

ISBN Paperback: 979-8-9985657-2-4

ISBN E-book: 979-8-9985657-3-1

*To Mom & Dad – for always supporting my love of reading, for letting me name our family dog Pikachu, and for encouraging me to always follow my dreams. (I know we are all very thankful that I didn't become a lawyer or a marine biologist.)*

*Queens of Woven Fates* is a fast-paced and thrilling dark fantasy filled with morally grey characters, friendly-*ish* beasties, and kingdoms in peril. As such, this story includes elements that might not be suitable for all readers. Violence, gore, bodily injury, blood, murder, death (including the death of parents and siblings), imprisonment, dealing with loss and grief, seizures, perilous situations, sexual activities, alcohol, graphic language, manipulation, torture, and mentions of war are depicted. Readers who may be sensitive to these elements, please take note, and prepare to follow the woven threads that lead to an inevitable fate...

OBSIDIAN KINGDOM
OPAL KINGDOM
LARIMAR ISLANDS
IRRIDESSEN
THE SEVEN KINGDOMS OF
SLATE KINGDOM
TERRAMERE

INGOTHERIA
JADE KINGDOM
TOPAZ KINGDOM
RUBY KINGDOM

# PROLOGUE

The Dark Queen stood atop the dais carved from obsidian stone, glaring down the assembled court with quiet distaste.

She swept serpentine-green eyes through the first row of pews, her red lined lips flattening into a scowl. A smattering of fae shrank back as her gaze passed over them, but they remained warily silent. Tension hung in the air, thrumming like a beating heart and thick with apprehension.

The gargoyles in attendance watched their newly coronated Queen with quiet reverence, their attention fixated on her, entranced by her. Daughter of their beloved Queen Elera – rumored to be as ruthless as she was beautiful. All had gathered to witness this moment, though they questioned what brand of justice would be doled out. They knew her path to the throne had been fraught with peril and bathed in blood, but with her claim of succession sealed, her reign would now be scrutinized and critiqued by the very citizens she'd fought to protect.

Thin jewel-encrusted bands accentuated the Queen's lithe waist, glimmering faintly against her night-hued dress in the flickers of candle-light. Matching chains with dangling rubies highlighted the sharp talons at the apex of her black wings.

Next to the Dark Queen, the Golden Gargoyle leaned casually upon his own onyx throne, his glorious, metallic wings draped around him, absentmindedly running fingers through his reddish-brown beard - as if this entire scene bored him, and he was ready for the events of the day to be over. He stifled a yawn, bouncing his knee impatiently, as he cut his eyes to his mate.

Gold horns jutted from his curly hair, shining softly in the dim lighting thrown from the torches dotting the craggy walls. A circlet of sun-bleached bone adorned the Golden Gargoyle's brow, sibling to the one the Queen wore. But the smooth bones of her crown were fashioned into a curved diamond, nestled between the junctures of thick ram's horns that extended from the top of her head and curled around pointed ears pierced from lobe to tip with black gemstones.

Clinking shackles and shuffling footsteps echoed outside the throne room of the Obsidian Palace. The court seemed to hold in a collective breath as the doors creaked open.

Queen Absolute Esmeray smiled viciously as two royal guards entered, half dragging their prisoner between them. The court craned their necks and leaned across pews to catch a glimpse of the being brought before the throne for judgement.

Imprisonment had not done the disgraced Regent of the Obsidian Kingdom, Lord Magnamus, any favors. The start of a stringy beard did little to hide his hollow cheekbones and sallow skin, though the cold expression on his face cracked into a sneer as he beheld the Dark Queen. His black hair lay matted and scraggy, bits of grime caked through the thin strands - a far cry from the groomed and manicured male that used to sit upon the same dais he now approached in cuffs. A faint light pulsed from the bronze chains locked around his wrists and ankles, nullifying his fae magic.

Queen Esmeray gave a curt nod to the guards, and they halted, unceremoniously dropping the Regent onto the unnervingly glass floor. Lord Magnamus threw his bound hands out, catching himself at the last moment, before kneeling back on bare feet, narrowing his eyes to the dais.

"*You*," he snarled, baring his fangs in defiance. "Traitor Queen." Lord Magnamus attempted to stand, only for a guard to kick the ditch of his knee, forcing him to stay down.

"You will speak when spoken to, and you *will* watch your tone when you address the Queen Absolute," The Golden Gargoyle, King Consort of Irridessen, snapped, uncrossing his legs to lean forward and flash his teeth at the captive Regent.

Lord Magnamus spat, earning a jeer of disapproval from the gargoyles standing at attention behind him. "My *niece* is no more Queen in my eyes than you are King Consort, *Commander* Keerian."

"Be thankful you still have eyes, *Uncle*," Esmeray retorted - her voice soft, yet the weight of the words drew all attention to her once more. She shook her head, unaffected by the rage shining on the face of her late father's brother, and the heightened anger exuding from her mate, who stared down the prisoner before them like a threat that needed to be extinguished immediately. Lord Magnamus quieted, though a muscle feathered in his jaw.

Laying a calming hand against Keerian's forearm, a wicked gleam sparked in her eyes as she watched the Regent - a predator with their prey successfully cornered, debating the best way to eviscerate them. Esmeray surveyed the male intently until he shifted nervously and lowered his stare.

"Lord Magnamus, you are here because you conspired against the late King Scottrell and Queen Elera. You are *here* because you supported my sister, Adara, in her traitorous bid for *my* rightful throne." A hush blanketed the room, the fizzing and popping of candles the only sound. The court waited for judgement to fall, eyes darting between the dishonored Regent and the new Queen.

"How do you plead?" Keerian asked in a deadly calm voice, though his expression brimmed with the promise of violence.

Lord Magnamus gritted his teeth, his hands balling into fists as he raised his chin and locked eyes with the Dark Queen. "Your father was *weak*," he scoffed. "He *knew* how powerful Queen Adara was with that spell book. He could've used her to decimate any army, win any battle. He held all that power, yet he wasted it, fearful and jealous of the magic his daughter wielded. Queen Adara shouldn't be punished – she could take over Ingotheria, the Slate Kingdom, the Larimar Islands." Esmeray hissed. Dropping his voice low, he seethed, "Adara could've taken *everything*. But my brother was small-minded and easily swayed by his mate. Look where it got him in the end."

"Using fae spells is forbidden in Irridessen, and Adara cast those spells to *murder* the late King and Queen in cold blood, framing Queen Esmeray for their deaths. Do we really need to remind you of that?" Keerian shot out of the throne with a growl, his considerable size dwarfing the Queen next to him. But the room continued to watch her. Even Lord Magnamus flicked his focus from King Keerian back to Queen Esmeray, setting his jaw in a hard line.

"How do you plead?" Esmeray purred, laughing quietly to herself as she stepped back to sit on the onyx throne behind her. "It's such a nuanced question, *Uncle*, considering you've made your support for Adara *so* well known. But, the laws of Irridessen do dictate you deserve the right to a fair trial."

An icy smile slithered across the Dark Queen's face as she cocked her head. "And yet, we see *many* rules being rewritten these days - isn't that what you told the Oracle?"

The throne room trembled.

Lord Magnamus paled as a deep roar ricocheted from the caverns below. The assembled court flinched, though no one made any move to run.

A great black dragon with silver tipped wings launched from the rippling glass floor, a snarl tearing from his throat as he landed, claws raking across the glass, causing a shrill screech to echo through the space. His spiked tail thudded heavily against the steps leading to the matching rough-hewn thrones as he settled into a crouch, eye-level with the Dark Queen. She shot a smirk at the beast before turning back to face her prisoner. With a menacing rumble, the dragon snaked his head around to fix the Regent in place with a single, slitted, pupil.

"What are you doing?" Lord Magnamus demanded, his voice pitched, breathless.

"Giving you your fair trial," Esmeray replied simply.

With a bellow, the dragon opened his maw and enveloped Lord Magnamus in silver-edged flames, leaving nothing but charred bone behind.

The silence in the throne room was deafening, and the statement made to the court was simple.

The reputation of this new Queen would be built against the smoldering coals of her actions. Any challenges to her reign snuffed out - reduced to nothing more than ashes that she would rise from like a vengeful phoenix.

# Part One

---

## The ASHES

# CHAPTER ONE
# SPARROW

SPARROW JOLTED INTO CONSCIOUSNESS with a ragged sob. Heart hammering, with sticky sweat cooling against her face, she blinked through the disorienting darkness. Nightmares plagued her incessantly this week – emphasizing that recurring feeling of being hunted, of being watched. And like always, it ended with the sense she was freefalling through nothingness - landing in a tiny, isolated cage.

Even just thinking about the dream made her uneasy and cagey, the sheets on her bed suddenly too restrictive against her clammy skin.

Glancing over at the shadowed figure sleeping peacefully next to her, Sparrow silently eased out of the bedroom, padding across the hall to her quaint and cheery kitchen. The glass bulbs strung around the ceiling flared to life as she waved her hand, bathing the ivy green cabinets and pink walls in a soft glow. The light helped banish the echo of her nightmare into the corners of her mind.

She shuddered as she filled a kettle with water and set it on the stove, the feeling of being watched settling around her like a cloak, as if someone hovered just out of sight. But it was nothing more than paranoia, leftover anxiety dredged up from her dreams.

Recent events rattled traumatic memories back to the forefront of her mind – thoughts she desperately shoved away in favor of remembering the good times instead. Lost in her brooding, Sparrow jumped with a shrill gasp when ebony arms covered in swirling white tattoos wrapped gently around her waist.

"Hey," the deep voice soothed, "What's wrong? I woke up and you weren't in bed."

Sparrow blew out a deep breath, her heartrate steadying as she turned to nuzzle her face into Laurent's broad, bare chest. "I had a bad dream," she admitted, inhaling the fae's calming scent of lavender and cedar.

Laurent pressed a kiss to the top of her head, his brows scrunched with worry as she sighed and closed her eyes. Gently, he trailed a hand down her back, rubbing circles against the fabric of her still-damp-with-sweat shirt. "Is it...does it have to do with Merrick?"

"No... Well, I don't know. It's been *four months,* Laurent. And he...disappeared. I know he took his ring off. I try every morning to speak into his mind, but it's like shouting into a canyon with no echo back." Sparrow's voice broke, but she cleared her throat, turning from the bright emerald eyes of the handsome fae, her soul tied mate, to pull the whining kettle off the stove.

Moving effortlessly around her, Laurent plucked two mugs and a box of tea from the cabinet. Sparrow couldn't help the small smile that bloomed as her mate plopped a fat teabag into each mug before silently taking the kettle from her hands, pouring them both a cup.

Hopping up onto the counter, the oversized cotton shirt she'd stolen from Laurent rising with the movement, Sparrow murmured her thanks as she gripped her tea in both hands, welcoming the calming warmth seeping into her numb fingers. With the first sip of tea, she drank in the sight of shirtless, sleepy Laurent wearing nothing but loose, linen pants from above the rim of her mug.

His powerfully built frame was cut with deep abdominals from decades of service to the late King and Queen of Irridessen – muscles that Sparrow had taken her time getting acquainted with as they lay in bed tangled up with each other. As Sparrow locked her gaze with his, he shot her a heated wink before taking a swallow of his own tea, the kitchen lights twinkling against the silver studs travelling up both of his pointed ears. There were new additions to his collection of earrings - two delicate blue gems, matching her own eye color, that Laurent proudly wore on his lobes - a gift she'd given him last month.

Laurent leaned against the counter on the opposite side of the kitchen, one hand running through the short growth of hair he'd begun favoring over the smooth, clean-shaven look he'd had when they first met. "Do you want to talk about it?"

"Do I *want* to talk about how I'm soul tied to two males, yet only one of them seems okay with it?" Sparrow countered roughly, immediately hating the tone of the words she'd let out. With a mumbled apology, she leaned her head back against the cabinet. "Not particularly."

The night Esmeray rescued Keerian from Adara, the full moon hit its apex in the sky the moment Sparrow saved Merrick's life. When Merrick came to, they'd locked eyes and a soul tie clicked into place, surprising both of them as the faint glimmer sparked. Their hands had been intertwined on his chest, healing him – and cementing their connection.

During the battle with Adara, after she shifted into her ghastly Sentry, Sparrow caught Laurent's eye and another soul tie bloomed, twinkling through the dust and carnage – seconds before Sparrow was knocked into him. And as they fell together in a pile of limbs, their hands had touched.

Sealing her soul tie to Laurent as well.

It'd been chaos in the throne room, and both soul ties went unnoticed by everyone else as they fought to stay alive against an unnaturally formidable foe.

So, Sparrow left the Opal Palace with two mates. Which was utterly unheard of throughout history. And once Adara was contained in the dungeon below the Obsidian Palace, Sparrow, Merrick, and Laurent found themselves trying to sort out what happened.

Laurent's calm demeanor hadn't been ruffled in the slightest. When Sparrow asked him how he felt, he shrugged and replied that if this is what Carra, the Goddess of Soul Ties, decided – then he was happy.

Merrick, however, didn't take the revelation as well, and after they returned to Florra, the gargoyle stayed one night, sleeping on the couch, before flying back to the Obsidian Palace at first light – stating he needed space to figure out his emotions.

Laurent had been asked by Esmeray to oversee the Opal Palace while she dealt with Lord Magnamus, but once Esmeray relieved him of the duty, he'd come straight back to Florra and lived with Sparrow ever since. Sparrow hadn't told her best friend about either soul tie – she knew Esmeray's hands were full ruling Irridessen and wanted to give her and Keerian space to get back into the rhythm of their lives together as mates since they'd been forced apart for a year due to Adara's cruel reign.

Sparrow closed her eyes, inhaling the aroma of the honey and lemon tea. Laurent and Sparrow had been living in harmonious balance since that first day, falling into an easy routine, their feelings turning from intrigue to obsession quickly. And after a few days of the soul tie tugging and needling at her as she lay in bed alone, she gave in, throwing open her bedroom door to go to Laurent - only to find him standing at the threshold of her bedroom, hand raised as if he was about to knock.

She'd taken him to bed that night, and every night since.

Sparrow was thrilled to be mated with Laurent, she was falling in love with the smart, kind fae – but that piece of her soul tied to Merrick yearned for the gargoyle to be here, too. In addition, there was a new, lingering awareness inside her – an off-kilter feeling like she'd forgotten something but no amount of wracking her brain would remind her. It had Sparrow on edge, braced and defensive.

Causing an influx of intrusive thoughts to hiss through her mind.

*Was she a good enough mate to Laurent?*

*Would her soul ever stop feeling like a stranger to her?*

*What was she even doing with her life?*

"Do you think you should talk to Esmeray about it?" Laurent prodded gently, interrupting the loathsome questions fluttering wickedly through her thoughts. "I know this," he said gesturing from himself to her, "is really new. But we are mates – your soul is intertwined with mine. And I don't feel any less of a male to say my mate has two soul ties. I'm just thankful to be one of them."

Sparrow lowered her eyes, but the words made her smile. It was the way he spoke, so thoughtfully and eloquently, that originally piqued her interest in the famed Spy Master when he landed on her front porch. "Maybe I'll talk to Esmeray next time she comes to Florra - but for now..." Tingles flooded her core, that giddy feeling of her skin buzzing, wanting to be touched, vibrated through every nerve ending in her body.

Locking eyes with Laurent under her lashes, she gave her mate a sultry smile. With a throaty groan, Laurent crossed the small kitchen in one stride, fitting himself between Sparrow's knees, his hands gently tilting her face up to meet his lips to hers. Sparrow rolled her hips, feeling Laurent moan against her mouth as he realized she had nothing on under the soft shirt. Sparrow felt the hard length of him through his pants, his warm hands burying themselves under her shirt, calloused palms brushing over-sensitive skin, making her feel as if she'd erupt into flame if he didn't take her now.

The tea was forgotten along with the nightmare as Sparrow melted into his strong arms. Laurent tugged her off the counter, his hands cupping her bare backside and pulling her against his body. Sparrow wrapped her legs tightly around his hips, her fingers threading themselves through the short hair at the nape of his neck. "Please take me to bed," Sparrow whispered, her eyes brimming with all the emotions she couldn't say aloud.

"Anything you desire," Laurent murmured before carrying her to their bedroom, shutting the door behind them. The darkness of the room didn't seem as overwhelming when Laurent laid her against the cool sheets, his body following hers into blissful release.

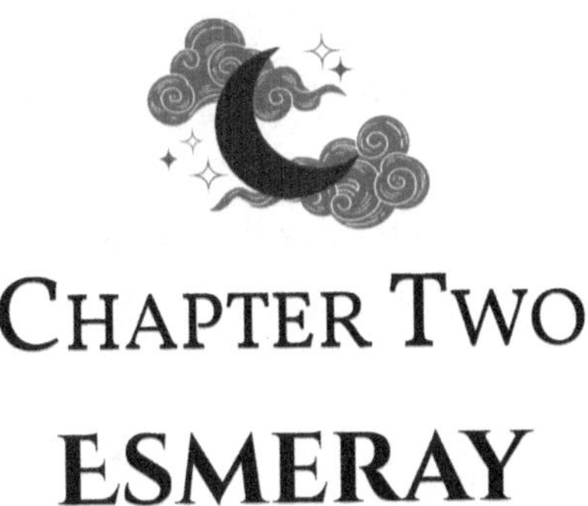

# CHAPTER TWO
# ESMERAY

I KICKED MY FOOT out as I entered the Queen's chambers, sighing in relief as the uncomfortable heel went flying, hitting the wall across the room with a *thunk*. The other followed suit as Keerian ambled up behind me, unclipping the sheath around his thigh where his dagger sat, tossing the weapon on the desk.

"Your parents had separate bed chambers, and that still blows my mind," he mused, gold wings shining in the soft sunset bleeding through the narrow window. Crossing the large foyer, he stretched, groaning and aiming for our bed.

I shoved aside the stress threatening to overwhelm me, instead turning to smirk at Keerian. "I don't think my mother was in her own room very often – if ever."

He snorted a laugh, the sound freeing me further from the nagging wave of brooding determined to overtake my headspace. I stood by my decision to carry out Lord Magnamus's death sentence, yet my council members filled my day with pointless arguing about how I could've done it better - how it made "*us*" look to outside Kingdoms.

I cut my last meeting short since my temper was fraying, my magic continuously bubbling beneath my skin, pushing me to a breaking point as they dissected every single one of my actions without providing any actual advice. The council had been my parents' idea to enact - to give those with noble blood a chance to get their own voices heard.

Did it make me a bad Queen to admit I hated it?

The council wasn't *all* bad – but the voices of old, stuffy lords and tittering, empty-headed ladies drowned out those few advisors that *did* have good feedback.

Dismantling the bastards from power was on my never-ending list of things to do, but I had to be smart. It was normal for a new ruler to change their advisors out, weeding through who they could and couldn't work with, but after decades of actively avoiding the council meetings my father invited me to, I now had to bite my tongue, spend time feeling them out for myself, to see who I truly needed on my side and who could kick rocks.

Keerian sprawled onto the bed, propping his arms under his head to watch me untangle my hair and horns from the silver and opal crown I wore today.

My mate was my life-compass these days. He'd been to countless council meetings in the past, though he went from standing guard on the outskirts of the room to sitting in the chair closest to the head of the table.

Which was *another* thing a few of the advisors had a bitch of a time wrapping their heads around – that a lowly, albeit high ranking, Commander snatched my coveted soul tie and the King Consort title.

Keerian knew the quirks and personalities of each of the six council members. He knew who was speaking up for selfish gain and who was providing actual, helpful, advice to be considered. He was brilliant and strategic, with his quiet contemplation and even temper, yet quick to defend my actions, call an advisor out on bullshit. To me, Keerian's opinion was more valuable than diamonds – an anchor that helped me stay grounded and level-headed when the world became too tumultuous.

I snuck a peek at my mate in time to see Keerian's green eyes heat at the sight of me undoing the hidden clasps down the bodice of my dress. I felt his gaze rove my body, sending thrills shimmying down my spine. "Come here, my Queen." His voice turned husky, deep, simmering with desire.

I *almost* gave in - hovering right out of reach, a smile tugging at the corners of my lips as I silently dared him to get me. He bared his teeth at me in a feral grin before lunging forward and swiping his fingers out - missing the fabric of my skirt by millimeters as I darted out of his grasp, sticking my tongue out at him playfully. With a low growl, he scooted himself up on his elbow, his wings curled tight to his back.

"What do *you* want?" I questioned innocently, taking a half step back as I unlaced the skirt and let it pool to the floor. Stepping out of the filmy material, Keerian's eyes never leaving mine, I chanced a toe closer. Quicker than I was prepared for, his hand snapped out, grabbing me around the waist and hauling me on top of him. I shrieked, the sound turning into a giggle as he grasped my face in his hands and kissed me.

This male - I loved him, horns and all. Almost losing him four months ago was the most difficult thing I'd ever faced. Having him here, at my side, as we ruled over Irridessen made my heart flutter and leap. My amazing mate. The other half of my soul. Kissing him deeply, I rubbed my palms over his broad chest, undoing the buttons on his black shirt as I went.

These last two weeks residing solely in the Obsidian Palace had taken its toll on us – the long meetings with the residing lords at court, the debates on if a Regent will be placed in one Kingdom, or if Keerian and

I would split our time between both Palaces, the overwhelming feeling of doing all of this without my parent's guidance...

I stilled, my mind growing dark as I thought of the dungeons below this palace, where my twin sister squatted in her cell. I only visited her sparingly. And every time I stormed out of the dungeon wanting to slit her throat. She showed no remorse, no empathy, no.... nothing. She sat. In that cold, dank cell. Dirty and disheveled. And leered at me.

She gave no mention of what she'd done while on the throne, clamming up when I prodded, argued, screamed at her. There was a list of missing beings that now numbered in the hundreds that disappeared while she ruled. Adara refused to utter a word about their whereabouts, resorting to stupid fucking riddles and half-truths that made me see red.

The overwhelming sense of panic that'd been bearing down on me teetered on a precipice. I didn't want to be in this palace for another second.

"Let's go someplace," I said against Keerian's lips.

"Opal Palace?" Keerian asked, pulling away slightly to meet my eyes. I saw the concern flick across his face for a half second as he surveyed my expression.

The Opal Palace held its own bad memories. Adara locked Keerian in a warded room for a year while she cut Irridessen off from outside contact, murdering whomever she fancied and pinning it on me. The throne room and the great hall were still in shambles from our battle, though, thankfully, Merrick leapt at the chance to oversee the renovations, promising it would look like nothing happened by the time he finished. I hoped he was right, though I never expected "master designer" to be a talent in the gargoyle's repertoire.

I crinkled my nose at him. "No. I'm over royal duties. Let's go pop by Florra and surprise Sparrow and Lenna."

My best friend had been distant lately. I wondered if something happened behind closed doors between her and Merrick, but I didn't have any clues to go off of aside from remembering how flirty they'd been around each other before the fight against Adara. And I knew Lenna was still adjusting to living in a land of magic since we talked through our mind speak rings a few times a week. But now, Sparrow kept to herself in Florra, Merrick spent his time ignoring everyone and training a new elite aerial unit, Lenna was busy with her new life, and Gods only knew where Laurent was - the Spy Master had his own agenda that he shared only when directly asked.

We were spread out, and I missed the close-knit feeling of having friends nearby. I knew Keerian did, too, though having time alone to reconnect with my mate was a gift unto itself.

The only one of us that didn't seem to be feeling the same way was Merrick. I allowed Merrick to go to the Opal Palace – to distance himself from us – because I trusted the gargoyle, and knew he needed to work out whatever aggression and fear he bottled up.

Coming back from the dead probably dredged up those emotions.

I gave Keerian another quick kiss before hopping off him, crossing our room to the massive closet carved from the mountain itself. The Obsidian Palace was half the size of the Opal Palace, not counting the sprawling gardens surrounding the latter, or the monstrous mountains nestled around the former. But I never discounted the allure or power of the Obsidian Palace, or its worth, as Adara had. Which – in the end – cost her dearly.

Throwing on my favorite comfy sweater and grey pants that tapered in at the ankles, I threw Keerian a black shirt and matching slacks. He caught them in one hand, blowing me a kiss before changing quickly.

Just knowing that we could spend a day in Florra as Keerian and Esmeray and not King and Queen, made me feel lighter. This weight of the Kingdoms was one I would gladly bear, but even Queens need a damn day off. The decision to go to Florra stopped my stress in its tracks, the babble in my head dimming.

I threw my hair up into a messy bun and stretched out my wings. The ache to fly outweighed the convenience of waning straight into Sparrow's living room. Though it was beneficial to disappear in a flash of light, reappearing miles away a split second later, the air called to me, and I wanted to swoop into it, carry myself off and embrace a couple hours of flying to get my mind together.

Standing along the rim of the balcony, breathing in the crisp evening breeze, the chill from the snowcapped mountain peaks sang through my veins. The drop to the ground was over two hundred feet, but up here, gazing out to the mountains beyond, made me feel invincible.

Keerian strode up to my right, flexing his golden wings that were much thicker and larger than mine. I bumped his wing with my own affectionately, and he shot me a wicked grin before he jumped, falling about twenty feet before ripping through an updraft and soaring between the spires of the Palace. I pumped my wings, reveling in the bite of the frozen wind, before joining him, the weight of the Kingdoms left on the balcony below.

# CHAPTER THREE
# ORLA

STANDING RIGIDLY IN FRONT of the floor to ceiling window, Orla narrowed her gaze to the sea beyond. The water looked calm now, with teal blue waves lapping softly against the coast, seafoam billowing across the black sand beach like a veil before receding...

But she knew better.

The sea was a monster - a cold, unfeeling entity with no remorse.

It had been years since she felt anything other than anger and resentment, and the past four months merely stoked those emotions further, until she felt hollow, empty. A shell that lashed out in fury, that hid behind walls of rage, coated in an impenetrable armor of despair.

She'd run with the sugary sweet promises of freedom on her tongue, only to learn the outside world was larger than she thought.

And much more dangerous.

That tiny sliver of hope died on her tongue, leaving only the bitter taste of blood behind.

She thought back to Doortan as if the memories were from a lifetime ago. The crumpled piece of parchment in her fist crinkled pitifully as she crushed it further, the edges warping under the pressure. The dull yellow of the note was water damaged and fraying at the corners, the ink splotchy, but after painstakingly drying it in the heat of the summer sun, Orla had been able to peel off the seal and read the parts where water hadn't completely destroyed the words.

*Orla is a dear friend, but she is young and headstrong.*

*Orla needs something to do that will keep her mind off her past.*

*Orla is afraid.*

The words Lenna, Lady of Doortan, wrote to the Lady of Wilfur, who was supposed to take in two wayward servants sailing off the coast of the Slate Kingdom on the wings of a dream. Only for those wings to morph into a terrifying beast.

Orla knew Lenna wrote the note to help her. But the line '*Orla is afraid*' kept prowling around in the back of her mind, an incessant pest that buzzed in her face like the flies that swarmed the kitchens of the Doortan manor in the springtime.

With a sigh, she turned, stepping away from the window and crossing the small, sparsely furnished room to toss the note onto the simple wood desk, trying to keep the dark thoughts at bay.

Their ship departed the Doortan port and begun its run to Bardon in the early days of summer. Her travel companion, Marlo, had been asked by her cousin, Dollin, to help the sailors in exchange for free room and board. As Doortan women were rarely experienced with the workings of sea travel, Orla spent the first two days sequestered in their cramped cabin, poking at her sore face in a mottled-with-rust mirror, and sleeping as the ship rocked against the waves.

Lenna's husband, the Lord of Doortan, was the ass who gave her the assortment of bruises around her throat and face. At the time, Orla had been so grateful for that black eye – it became her ticket to getting the fuck out of the manor once Lenna caught wind of her husband's abuse and swore she would personally pay for Marlo and Orla to escape.

So different from her husband, Lenna was kind and caring, making sure she helped in whatever way she could, though she held little power in the estate. Doortan was hard on women, embracing antiquated values passed down from old-fashioned patriarchies and lordships held by nasty, cruel men.

A strong storm woke Orla on that third night, the yells of sailors fighting the sails and the plunging of the ship's stern making her heart lurch as much as her stomach. Marlo had run down the steps into their cabin, face pale, as he recanted what he'd learned - the ship was pushed off course by heavy gusts of wind that whipped off a brutal monsoon, and the crew was fighting to right their passage. Marlo's words had been cut off as the shouted orders on the deck above them turned to screams...and then a deafening, unearthly roar drowned out all other voices.

Marlo ran upstairs, towards the noise, Orla following on his heels, driven by instinct alone. On the deck, the rain lashed painfully against her sore skin, the icy water drenching her in seconds, causing her dark curls to plaster themselves across her face, and her clothes to adhere uncomfortably to her body. A sailor ran past, screaming about angering the gods, abandoning his post and the rope he'd been fighting to retie against the main sail. Marlo jumped forward, grabbing the rope, yelling over the wail of the storm to secure the tail end as it slashed back and forth in the heavy winds and pitching sea. She had just touched the rough twine when another bellow jarred her very bones, causing her to look up, squinting against the heavy rain pummeling them.

Between the angry green and black clouds, a glint of yellow scales was illuminated by a strike of lightning. Orla stood, petrified, as a beast from myth and legend became fully visible, flying through the thick rain before opening its massive maw, a blast of orange fire hitting the water beside their boat, hot steam erupting from the waves with a deafening hiss, filling her vision with stinging smoke. She fought to clear her eyes, her feet scrambling for purchase against the water-slick deck as terror slammed through her. The last thing she remembered was Marlo roaring at her to go back to their cabin and hide as the dragon turned its mighty wings towards the sail – a bright flash of fire - and then her whole world went black.

She awoke on a beach of black sand on the coast of the Ruby Kingdom, burning under the unrelenting sun, soaked to the bone, and coughing up gallons of saltwater, a thin rope tying her to a broken barrel.

A burning pain had snaked throughout her body, and she fainted. She didn't know how she got *here*, but she'd awoken in a panic driven fit of rage, in this room.

Blinking back tears, she chewed her lip, only stopping after a twinge of hurt and the metallic taste of blood filled her mouth.

"Orla." The masculine voice from the doorway made her jump as Marlo entered the bedroom with a small silver tray of pastries and tea. He tentatively sat it down on the desk next to her, his wary gaze immediately putting Orla on edge. But this is how it'd been since their arrival. For the first few hours after their reunion, they sobbed with relief and embraced each other. But that was short-lived, followed by months of difficult emotions and sheerly opposing views of their current situation.

Marlo was dressed in a muted red silk shirt, the ties undone at the top. He'd already adjusted to their new life, and Orla hated him for it. For his flexibility, his positive outlook, how he could adapt to anything thrown in his path.

With a concerned look on his face, he tilted her head up gently, eyeing the small cut on her lip that bled. "Do you want me to call the healer up here?"

Orla pulled away, her dove grey eyes lowering. She'd been in bad shape after the shipwreck and spent the majority of the last four months in this room, with healers setting her broken bones, using magic to repair her torn muscles and black eye, and completely freaking her the fuck out.

The whiplash from those first few days being in and out of consciousness made her curl inward. The healers were able to mend her physical wounds, but the emotional pain was too heavy, and she continued sinking deeper and deeper into depression, lashing out at anyone who got too close.

Which, with her self-isolation, was pretty much only Marlo.

She was woman enough to understand what she was doing. She'd set her jaw and sat quietly as the healers worked, as they calmly explained the existence of species such as the fae and gargoyles, explained how a godsdamned *dragon* attacked their ship, explained magic. Upon Orla's arrival, Marlo had already been found by a roving patrol of guards – and deemed the only other survivor from the attack of a wild dragon that roosted at the southernmost point of Ingotheria in the mountain range accurately and uncreatively named Dragon's Peak.

Orla watched as Marlo busied himself with filling a cup of tea and adding a delicious smelling strawberry tart to a plate, offering it to her before pouring his own cup. Taking the rickety chair across the room, Marlo stretched out his long legs, sighing as he took the first sip of his drink. Tipping her tea to her lips, Orla surveyed her companion in silence. His blonde hair had already begun growing floppy and untamed during their months here, and he'd put on a few pounds of muscle that complimented the deepening tan of his skin. Doortan rarely had a stretch of nice weather, opting instead to dump rain on them daily, and any rain-free days stayed perpetually overcast and humid. But here, rain rarely interrupted the day, and Marlo's skin held a healthy, sun-kissed glow.

In comparison, Orla had lost weight, her tawny skin stayed uncomfortably dry from the arid heat of the desert, and her curls rebelled in their own way that had her covering them with a head scarf more often than not. She barely had the energy to do anything more than get out of bed, and though the healers offered their assistance to bathe her or braid her hair, Orla hated feeling like a burden and dismissed them every time they tried.

"I got some news," Marlo started, carefully watching Orla as he continued, "King Eamon is on his way back from a diplomatic visit to the Topaz Kingdom, and I was told we'll have a chance to speak with him to hopefully be deemed citizens of the Ruby Kingdom."

"I don't want to stay here," Orla snapped, her control immediately slipping at the thought of being trapped in these foreign lands. "I *hate* this place. Marlo, we aren't supposed to *be* here. We're human, we belong in the Slate Kingdom - everything I *know* is in the Slate Kingdom."

"There are humans here! If you ever decided to leave this room, you'd be able to see them – meet them." Marlo gritted his teeth, his blue eyes flashing. "But you won't even try."

"Why would I?" Orla deadpanned, looking past Marlo to stare out of the window once more. This same conversation was an annoying recurrence between them. Marlo would beg her to venture out of the room, and Orla would downright refuse. If he pushed, she'd hurl insults his way until he got the hint to leave her the fuck alone.

The King had been away from the Palace these last few months, but now, with his return, an hourglass began counting down in Orla's mind, her restlessness gnawing at her from the inside. The healers had warned her that upon his Majesty's return, she would need to meet him to resolve the fact that she was basically a foreign intruder with no citizenship papers and no money. Apparently, arriving to the Ruby Kingdom by shipwreck wasn't a common occurrence, and no one really knew what to do with her. So, she'd been given a room, nursed back to health, and told to wait for the King.

"The King'll take one look at us and realize we aren't worth his time – or he'll lock us up. *Maybe* he will deem us perfectly boring and set us up with servant's quarters so we can become another nameless, faceless, human surrounded by people – *beings* - who look down on us. They have *magic* here, Marlo, does that not terrify you?"

"Well, whatever the King decides, I'm asking to stay." Marlo stood suddenly, his tall frame towering over Orla. She shut her mouth and glared at him, causing Marlo to huff in irritation and shake his head. "Do whatever you want," he growled. She knew the conversation was ultimately over, which left her as resigned as before.

Uttering a prayer under his breath, or it may have been a curse, Marlo turned on his heel and stomped out of the room. Orla felt a wave of guilt crash over her, deep in her soul, but she pushed it down, ignored it, until the sounds of Marlo's steps disappeared down the hall.

Orla slumped back into the chair, hissing out a curse of her own before shoving the plate with the half-eaten tart away. The anger she felt towards Marlo dissipated, replaced by a dull burn that began in her lungs and spread, like wildfire, through her blood.

# CHAPTER FOUR
# SPARROW

BY SPARROW'S COUNT, THE day was a massive success. *Three* of her exotic flowers bloomed with the help of her magic urging them on, their petals unfurling to reveal metallic sheens. She even spotted a *very* rare songbird in her birdbath, signifying the unique mix of seeds she carefully curated was well received by the flocks returning to Florra with the changing season.

After rinsing off the dirt from gardening, Sparrow set her evening plans in motion. With a smug amount of pride at her own craftiness, she slipped into her thinnest silk nightgown, pairing it with the fluffiest robe she owned that also happened to be the exact same shade of emerald as Laurent's eyes. She knew exactly the reaction she'd get by wearing it.

Once Sparrow admitted to having recurring nightmares over the past few months, Laurent went out of his way to make sure she relaxed today, even shoo-ing her from the kitchen and taking over dinner preparations to give her extra time tending and caring for all her beloved plants.

Sparrow decided tonight would be the night she'd tell him she loved him. She knew she did, and the thought didn't scare her. If Merrick didn't want to be around, she would hold no ill regard towards the gargoyle, but she refused to allow his distance to dictate how she spent her time with Laurent.

The sun had fully set on Florra by the time Sparrow and Laurent climbed the narrow staircase up to their patio, completely satiated from the delicious meal of wild caught fish and melt-in-your-mouth potatoes Laurent made. Around the flat expanse of rooftop, Laurent used his magic to set small, hovering fires in each corner to wash them in faint light as they laughed and cuddled on one of the extra wide patio chairs that had been another one of Laurent's gifts.

They were almost finished with a bottle of their favorite wine when the urge to kiss him had Sparrow climbing onto his lap. He hungrily captured her mouth as they tangled together in a fury of exploring hands and tongues. He tasted of heady wine, and Sparrow arched in his arms with a soft moan as he began slowly undoing the knot holding her robe closed.

"Laurent," she said breathlessly, peppering kisses across his mouth. The declaration of love was begging to be released, to be out in the open. Her heart fluttered in her chest as she looked deeply and lovingly into his gorgeous face.

She'd never known a love like this - never felt so incredibly adored, cherished, *wanted*. And it was all thanks to this male.

This was it – the big moment.

Her cheeks flushed with excitement.

To be mated was special, but to fall in love was exhilarating. "I want you to know how much you mean to me, and that I -"

A faint, dry cough sounded behind them, causing Sparrow to whirl around, the admittance of love dying on her lips as she rallied green battle magic to her fingertips on instinct. Laurent stiffened beneath her, the fires in the corners of the patio roaring into a bright blue hue, the deadly flames he controlled ready to fight.

"Well, this is *not* what we expected," Esmeray chuckled as she shot her gaze to Keerian. "So, ah...surprise?" Slowly, she raised her palms in mock surrender, while Keerian pointedly looked up at the sky, shoving his hands deep in his pockets.

"*Meer*! Gods above, what are you doing here?" Sparrow screeched; her voice higher pitched than normal as she hastily retied her robe. Laurent shifted and muttered a curse underneath her, his breathing uneven and she realized he was endearingly, adorably, embarrassed. And she became acutely aware of Laurent's additional minor troubles as he cleared his throat and shifted the hem of her robe further across his lap due to the remaining thickness she felt against her backside.

"We could well... ask you both the same thing," Keerian muttered, still averting his eyes, fighting a losing battle with the grin twisting its way across his face.

Laurent, getting himself under control, gently lifted Sparrow off of him, batting the green fuzz of her robe from his white sweater. "We weren't expecting such royal company," he laughed as he stood and crossed the patio to his oldest friend. "Did the Kingship already get boring?"

Letting the smirk fully take over his expression, Keerian bear hugged the fae, as Esmeray pulled a very flustered Sparrow into her arms. "What in the gods' names is going on?" Esmeray arched a bemused eyebrow to Sparrow, waiting for the female to fill her in as they broke their embrace.

Sparrow swallowed, feeling her face redden further as she took in the sight of the King and Queen with their shit eating grins on her godsdamn patio. She'd been so focused on Laurent she hadn't noticed two winged figures landing on the stone pavers five fucking feet away from them.

"We're mates, Meer," Sparrow admitted. It wasn't that she was afraid of what Esmeray would think – but she'd wanted to tell her best friend on her own terms – not caught in the act. "The soul tie bloomed four months ago at the full moon...celebration. We knew you both needed time alone, so we kept it private. We didn't want to put more on your plate -"

"On our plate?" Esmeray echoed, shaking her head, the messy bun between her horns bobbing with the movement. "Sparrow, we *always* have time for you."

Keerian wrapped Sparrow in a crushing hug before turning to Esmeray. "We need to have a celebration."

Laurent held up a hand, clearing his throat. "There's a small caveat to that," he started. Esmeray's eyes flicked from Laurent to Sparrow as she slowly pulled a bottle of wine out of her pocket of space where she stored items with her illusion magic. With a wave of her hand, the cork popped out, and she drank deep before offering the bottle to Keerian.

"What's the caveat?" Esmeray grumbled, "Don't tell me Laurent hates parties because I swear I'll mur-" Keerian threw Esmeray a pointed look. With a harsh sigh, Esmeray corrected, "I love throwing parties and I need something fun to do. These council meetings are beginning to be the bane of my existence."

"I have two soul ties," Sparrow replied quietly, looking over to Laurent who nodded with encouragement, only love and approval shining on his face. "I also have a soul tie to Merrick."

"That's not possible," Keerian said slowly, his brows knitting in confusion.

Laurent, gods bless him, filled in Esmeray and Keerian on what happened during the battle at Opal Palace, the messy aftermath of coming back to Florra – and Merrick's glaring absence.

"I'm gonna kill him," Esmeray declared at the end of the explanation, rubbing her finger over the dull grey stone on her mind speak ring that she'd commissioned prior to the battle against Adara. Each gem connected to one of their six closest friends so they could talk mind-to-mind if they were apart, or without being overheard in close quarters. "Well, first, I'm going to knock his ass in the dirt for taking his ring off –then I'm going to murder him. Properly this time." Esmeray frowned. "Wait, fuck - then you two die." She groaned, as if this was truly a debacle. "Gods, that's annoying. I actually tolerate Laurent."

Sparrow waved her hand in what she hoped was a flippant way, shooting a small smile to her friend. "It's complicated, but if Merrick doesn't want to be tied to me, it's his right to choose. I won't make that decision for him."

"We live long lives; he'll see sense," Keerian smoothed over, putting his arm around Esmeray's shoulder and lightly squeezing. "And you, my Queen – don't be nosey."

Esmeray rolled her eyes, the murderous look fading as she bared her teeth at her mate before sighing dramatically and swiping the bottle of wine, pointing it menacingly towards Sparrow. "Fine, I won't. But this doesn't get you two out of celebrating."

Sparrow allowed a true grin to appear, feeling relief roll through her at telling Esmeray what happened. Laurent was right – sharing the secret did help soothe her mind.

"So." Laurent ushered them over to the remaining chairs on the patio, pulling Sparrow down to sit next to him. Esmeray sat cross-legged in the low chair, her dark wings draping over the back and lowering. Keerian followed suit, snatching the wine bottle from his mate's hand, causing her to growl at him. "How's running the continent going?"

Esmeray groaned, pulling a second bottle out of thin air. "Ask me anything but that, Laurent, I'm taking a day off."

The four of them sat on the roof for hours, sharing wine and catching each other up on the last couple months. Sparrow nestled deeper into Laurent's side, content. She'd tell Laurent she loved him when they were alone. For now, she basked in the happiness she felt having the secret that weighed so heavily on her out in the open.

As the night deepened, Keerian and Laurent excused themselves to the kitchen to make everyone coffee, and the moment they were out of earshot, Esmeray gave Sparrow an incredulous look, causing the fae to giggle.

Sliding into Laurent's vacated seat, Esmeray hissed, "Two mates? You got not *one* hunky male...but *two*?"

"It was shocking to me as well," Sparrow confessed, "But...I don't know, Merrick isn't making it easy. He just... doesn't seem to be *as* tied to me as Laurent. In the first few days, Laurent and I couldn't get enough of each other. If Merrick had those same impulses, he didn't cave to them."

Sparrow frowned, her thoughts needling her again – that something more, something *important* was looming, some fate that was trying to come to fruition. A restless feeling flitted through her head before disappearing, leaving her uneasy. With a sigh, plastering a bright expression on her face, she shrugged. "I'm not complaining. Laurent is incredible, and I'm *thrilled* he's mine."

Glancing sidelong at Esmeray, Sparrow noted dark circles under her eyes, paler-than-normal cheeks. Heavy exhaustion was drawn all over the Queen's face.

Sparrow asked cautiously, "What's going on with Adara?"

Esmeray scowled, staring off into the distance. "I don't know, Spar. Even without the spell book she's deranged, remorseless. I can't let her go, which leaves me only one option. But it isn't a choice I want to make."

"I know before I said not to kill her, but with everything she did... it's impossible to forgive. Meer, she murdered innocent beings, killed your parents in cold blood, and framed you for it all. That's treason and murder at the *very* least." Sparrow felt anger rush through her, followed by a tendril of guilt for having pushed Esmeray away the last few months while her friend was clearly struggling.

"I killed Lord Magnamus," Esmeray said quietly. "And it scared me because after I killed him, I felt...nothing but satisfaction. What if I turn into the same monster Adara is?"

"Well, he sucked. And you want justice – not revenge," Sparrow replied, slouching back into her seat, as the ghost of a grin graced Esmeray's face.

"No, I want revenge," Esmeray clarified, though the smile continued curling its way across her lips.

Sparrow rolled her eyes and amended, "You do what is best for you – your Kingdoms. Is it hard? Absolutely. But I've *never* seen you back down from a fight."

Relief flooded the Queen's face, and Sparrow knew Esmeray had been searching for someone outside the political life she lived to tell her she wasn't in the wrong.

Sparrow only hoped she was right.

# CHAPTER FIVE
# ORLA

THE FLOWY SKIRTS OF Orla's dress did nothing to combat the unbearable heat smothering the Ruby Kingdom. Even though autumn arrived, the sweltering weather seemed to have dismissed the notion that cooler temperatures were expected.

Her anxiety rose as she walked through the palace with Marlo, flanked by two fae guards, each step taking her closer to pleading her case in front of King Eamon. The letter with beautiful and sweeping calligraphy arrived at sun up and bore a curt message that made Orla's heartrate skitter, her nerves in shambles as she read it once, twice. *"Arrive to the throne room at noon to determine the status of your stay."*

It didn't help that her own body fought against her. The incessant burning sensation that had begun the moment she awoke on the beach now engulfed her from the second her eyes opened – spreading down her arms to her fingertips, burning her face flush, and making her ears ring with a hollow screech that never let up.

After her last argument with Marlo, she hadn't changed her mind. She was going back to the Slate Kingdom where everything made sense, there was no magic, and she could start anew in a town far away from Doortan. Though she had no money, if a ship could at least take her to Bardon, she could figure it out from there - even if it meant working in a shitty tavern for a few months to get her bearings.

Marlo wouldn't change his decision either – he'd request to stay. Without even speaking to him, she could tell her companion carved out a place for himself here. His gait was longer, steady and sure, his shoulders thrown back, and his head held high. Marlo nodded and smiled as they passed servants and townsfolk while Orla watched on, sullen, as they grinned back at him or waved in acknowledgement and recognition. She envied the confidence he portrayed, the feeling of belonging that was written through every line of his body that was getting broader, healthier, and more muscular by the day. A big part of her would miss him. But she wouldn't ever admit that.

She was accustomed to his presence, his kindness and caring, and even though their conversations these days felt like they were always bickering, he was the closest thing she had to a friend.

Orla hadn't ever had a friend before.

Taking in the scenery around her, her mind whispered that this level of opulence could never be mimicked back in the Slate Kingdom. The Ruby Palace was only two stories tall – but made up for it with its sprawling size. It contained a massive market, eighteen gardens, and three white domes that could each fit a thousand beings. There was even an oasis located in the epicenter, where pools of unnaturally blue water glimmered enticingly, surrounded by tall, swinging palm trees, lush foliage with fat flowers in varying shades of red, and intricately carved marble statues depicting the gods and goddesses of Terramere.

Though she'd only seen the oasis once, when her healers begged her to leave the room for a few moments of fresh air, there was a certain allure to the natural springs that bubbled up from the golden sand the Palace was built upon. Orla hadn't seen a desert before, and though they felt mystical and brilliant, these foreign lands were too airy and bright for her.

Not to mention too godsdamned hot.

Orla asked one of her healers, a nice fae with pretty copper hair, about the Kingdom a week ago while fighting off the burning pain that hissed through her body and rendered her completely useless. The healer explained the Palace housed the King's people, with separate wings for the elite and royalty yet plenty of space for an entire town to flourish.

The healer spoke softly, while wiping Orla's feverish brow with a cool cloth, going into detail on how the Palace's town started during the Witch War a thousand years ago, and how the beings simply never left. They had children, gathered families together, and built upon the desert, turning the Palace into a hub of significant wealth. There were other cities and towns outside of the gates, but against the harsh desert, only small areas were even hospitable.

Growing up under the ever-present filth and smog of Doortan, the openness of the Ruby Palace gave Orla the feeling of being very, very small.

Now, trudging through the main hall that separated the town from the royals, Orla noted there was still a very clear separation between the common folk and the King's court. Fae guards were posted up and down the corridor, each dressed in the King's resplendent white and red armor, identical scabbards at their sides that held wicked looking curved blades.

The walls changed from grungy looking sandstone to elaborately carved panels of marble etched with designs. Orla tried to make out any of the features of the artwork but winced and avoided looking closer once her eyes landed on an image of a dragon eating fae. The lavish decorum wasn't the only thing that was different - the beings milling about were, too.

One thing was abundantly clear. There were no townsfolk here.

Orla could tell from the clothing alone that these individuals were part of the court. Flowing dresses that looked to cost more than anything Orla could ever own graced bodies of beautiful females, the twisting fabric exposing delicate skin ranging in color from lightly tanned to dark. Slits cut down their legs, showcasing jewel encrusted shoes. Males wore loose fitting silks and tunic tops, some exposing muscular, tattooed arms, others leaving their sleeves cuffed and buttoned with gems. It was a harsh contrast from the rough linen and cotton smocks she'd worn in Doortan.

She drank in every sight around her, committing it all to memory. Once she was back in the Slate Kingdom, her time here would feel like nothing more than a fever dream.

Turning down another corridor, their guards stopped abruptly in front of two towering, golden doors, signifying their arrival. The throne room loomed ominously before them, and a trickle of nerves slithered down Orla's spine, the burning sensation in her blood shooting up into her throat, making her grimace.

As the doors groaned open, Orla set her jaw in a hard line. She refused to show any weakness.

The throne room's circular shape made the already imposing space seem even larger. Marble pews with clawed feet sat in neat rows following the curve of the room, a long aisle cutting between them. Along the wall, shallow alcoves containing wide-leafed plants in vases that looked as if they were carved from hunks of gold shone and reflected the bright sun coming through circular windows set into the dome itself. At the end of the aisle, a curved dais rose, with mosaic-laid stairs leading to two thrones at the top. Orla's footsteps scuffed and echoed as she slowed. Cutting her eyes to the immaculately shining vases once more, it was a challenge to smother her disgust at the sheer amount of wealth displayed so pompously – especially now that she'd seen the clear differences between the town and court.

Marlo, on the other hand, pivoted this way and that, his mouth agape, awe shining in his eyes.

Wiping the glower off her face, Orla inhaled a steeling breath, flicking her stare forward, where her attention was stolen by the being lounging on the throne, his posture relaxed, but his eyes were hard – commanding, imposing.

Her breath hitched as she stared up at the most handsome male she'd ever seen. He looked a few years older than her, with rich, black skin. A burgundy tunic covered his broad chest, the material silky and the ties at the top loose. He tilted his head coolly towards Orla and Marlo, the movement causing his shoulder-length locs to sway, revealing sharply pointed ears decorated with studded rubies.

Though he seemed utterly bored, a muscle jumped in his square jaw. Wicked indifference simmered dangerously through his brown eyes as he appraised Marlo.

Feeling the heavy focus on him, Marlo shifted under the glare until the male's gaze swept over Orla. Orla held her ground, refusing to show even a hint of submission.

A guard stood at the bottom of the steps and boomed, "His Highness, Prince Cillian, will oversee your request for naturalization to the Ruby Kingdom. Bow."

Marlo pitched forward, bowing deeply, as Orla ripped her eyes away from the *Prince* to sink into a half-hearted curtsy. Part of her was relieved the King wasn't here, but fear coiled in her gut all the same. The Prince was probably not held to the same repose as the King. She had to tread carefully.

Prince Cillian snorted, straightening against the backing of the throne. Leaning forward, he surveyed the pair with an airy iciness. Aside from the guards, they were the only ones in the room, and Orla's nerves frayed further. There was no one here to advocate for them. If the Prince didn't approve their requests...what stopped him from murdering them and dumping their bodies in the sea?

"You need to work on the bow." Cillian's voice was scathing - aloof. Orla gritted her teeth as Marlo lowered his eyes to his feet, nodding swiftly. Although he was ridiculously attractive, she could tell the Prince was an ass – and it made her even readier to leave.

The guard cleared his throat. "Orla Grey and Marlo Asrar come forward requesting audience with his Highness. After being found on the beaches of the Kingdom, they have been sequestered in Aridden while awaiting a decision from the Crown on if citizenship to the Ruby Kingdom shall be granted."

Orla flinched as the guard read her name, the atrocious statement that she was here to become a citizen. When prompted months ago, she'd foregone her family name, choosing instead to take the surname all orphaned children received in the Slate Kingdom. And her mind was already made up.

She was leaving.

"Actually," Orla interrupted, drawing all eyes to her, "I'd like to go back to the Slate Kingdom." Prince Cillian narrowed his brows. Orla amended her words bitterly. "If your Highness...*allows*."

The painful burning intensified in her chest. With a reminder to breathe, to draw upon old manners from her days as a servant, she knitted her fingers together, holding them tightly in front of her, trying to appear meek, to appear unimportant.

Cillian frowned in disdain as he scrutinized Orla. Orla stood with bated breath as he slid his eyes to Marlo – who paled. "Is that the consensus for both of you?" The words were growly and low, causing the hairs on the nape of Orla's neck to prickle.

"No, your Highness," Marlo stammered, "I'd like to stay. I'm willing to work in whatever capacity needed to pay for housing. I'm a strong worker and served in a Lord's manor for a while now...And - and I would like to stay," he ended lamely, his voice softening and trailing off as Cillian raised a hand.

The Prince exhaled loudly, shaking his head. Orla set her face to neutral, her heartbeat pounding painfully, anticipating Cillian's next words. Waiting on another being to decide her life's course, again.

She was sick of it.

Silence thundered through the room, the tension becoming as suffocating as the heavy, hot air of the desert.

Marlo shifted uncomfortably, the movement causing Cillian to cock his head, a stony, calculating expression slowly morphing into a pretentious grin across his lips.

"Either you both stay, or you both go," Cillian declared, snapping his fingers at the guard, who, wide-eyed, began hurriedly scribbling the Prince's decision onto a scroll of parchment.

Orla inhaled a sharp hiss.

Trapped.

She would be *trapped here.*

Marlo whipped his head to Orla; a pleading look in his light eyes. "No." Her stomach churned, her pulse stumbling over itself. She swallowed painfully; the incessant burn shooting up her jawbone. "No. I'm not staying here."

Living here - against her will. Could the Prince do that? It felt illegal, but her limited knowledge of laws barely grazed the surface of the Slate Kingdom. She had no idea what the laws were here. Orla never got proper schooling, though her own tenacity and spite taught her to read and write well enough.

"There's a caveat to you staying, you know. Or going – for that matter," Cillian drawled, a spark of intrigue igniting in his dark eyes. Orla decided she hated him. "If you have fae blood, you must stay." He waved a hand flippantly, his smug sneer aimed at Orla. "Can't have fae going to the Slate Kingdom with the dome up."

That certainly seemed like a made up, bullshit law.

"We aren't fae," Orla snapped, fearing retribution for the tone, but pushing that thought down as she stared up at the Prince, her temper flaring. "We were born in the Slate Kingdom."

"Faelings can live in the Slate Kingdom," Cillian volleyed back, "they would just *look* human as long as they passed through the dome as a babe – which, in hindsight, was a loophole to the treaty signed to keep the fae *out* of the Slate Kingdom." A door on the opposite side of the room creaked open, and a tall fae with shocking red hair strolled in. Cillian flicked his eyes towards the newcomer before turning back to Orla. "Or, if a mother travelled to a different land and came back to the Slate Kingdom pregnant by a fae, the babe would be born half-fae. They would have human features in the Slate Kingdom, their *acat* stifled - until they travelled to a land of magic."

Orla barely listened. She was human. That was that.

The red-haired male, dressed in a ridiculous gold and beige robe, stopped in front of the bottom step of the dais, bowing fluidly to the Prince before striding up to Orla and Marlo.

"This is one of my personal advisors. His name is not important to you. But he was blessed with a very particular gift. He can tell how much magic is in your blood. And what your *acat* is – even if it hasn't manifested yet." Cillian jerked his chin towards the advisor. "If you both have no fae blood in you – you can decide if you both stay or go. But if either of you have fae blood, you become citizens. End of discussion." The Prince leaned back in his throne, a smirk toying at the corners of his mouth.

Orla wanted to hit him.

The red-haired fae smiled at Marlo. Unlike Cillian, there was a soft kindness reflected in his bronze eyes. A smattering of coppery freckles dotted his fair skin, accentuating his high cheekbones and full, rosy lips. "I only need to touch your hand," he murmured in a lilting accent Orla never heard before. "It won't hurt."

Marlo gingerly slid his palm into the fae's awaiting grasp. A vacant expression washed over the advisor's face. Within a few seconds, he blinked and nodded to Marlo. "Human, through and through."

Cillian clapped sarcastically from the throne.

Marlo blushed as the fae turned his attention to Orla. "Your hand, my dear." Orla glared up at Cillian, who watched the exchange with a disappointed look on his face, as if he'd expected *Marlo* of all people to surprisingly be fae.

With a resigned sigh, Orla gripped the advisor's palm.

A few seconds passed.

Then a few more.

The advisor groaned, his grip on her hand tightened, that vacant look in his eye clouding further.

And when the fae sucked in an abrupt breath, his wide-eyed, panicked expression meeting hers, Orla knees went wobbly.

"She has fae blood."

The words echoed dully through the throne room. Orla looked fearfully from Marlo to Cillian, speechless.

A steady chant began shrieking in her head.

*No, no, no.*

Orla staggered back, cutting desperate eyes to Marlo. He seemed outside himself as he took a half step away from her, leaving an icy burn raking over her bleating, blistered heart.

Prince Cillian merely grinned, extending an arm above his head in a derisively grand gesture. "Then it's decided. Welcome to the Ruby Kingdom, Marlo Asrar...and Orla *Grey*."

# CHAPTER SIX
# LENNA

T HE BAKERY BUZZED WITH activity as beings prepared for the month's full moon celebration. It was the first of the autumn season, and the excitement weaving through Florra had Lenna humming a happy tune amid the steady bustle.

She was packing up three honey cakes a gargoyle ordered when the shrill tinkering of the front door's bell made her look up to welcome the next customers to Hale's Bakery.

Wavy, golden blonde hair appeared in the doorway and Lenna grinned, heart leaping at the sight of her friend. "Sparrow!" Lenna shouted over the din of shoppers, waving her hand above her head. The fae gave her a cheery smile before gesturing dramatically behind her to the dark-haired female with night-black wings that stepped tentatively through the threshold a moment later.

Lenna squealed with glee as the Queen slid in behind her friend, ducking her head as the shop went dead silent, every customer dropping to a knee in reverence. Esmeray's cheeks grew red as she waved them all to rise.

Sparrow chuckled, rolling her eyes in a *"you know how it goes"* expression as she dragged Esmeray past the crowd, disappearing through the curtain separating the kitchens from the bustling storefront. The next few beings in line looked a tiny bit shocked as Lenna chuckled to herself, her fingers flying over the register's raised buttons as she checked out their orders. It wasn't every day the citizens of Florra saw the Queen Absolute in their quaint town.

After ringing up the next customer's purchase, Lenna passed off cashiering duties to a young human female she hired to help around the shop for the season. Lenna hastily wiped her hands against the apron protecting her mint green dress, and with one last assessing glance around the shop, she stepped through the lavender curtain.

Esmeray had a particularly delightful chocolate cookie in hand – and one already in her mouth - as she gave Lenna a beaming smile. Sparrow watched her friend with feigned disdain as Esmeray wolfed down another cookie with the same grace as the raccoons Lenna shooed out of the bakery's trash every night.

In Lenna's defense, they were three times larger and a lot smarter than any of the rodents she'd come across in Doortan.

"What brings you two heathens into my shop?" Lenna asked brightly, wrapping Esmeray in a hug. Esmeray laughed as she was squeezed tight. "It's so good to see you! How's the Queenship going?" Lenna turned to embrace Sparrow as Esmeray groaned.

"It's alright," Esmeray smiled at her enthusiasm, her nose crinkling a tad. "Just a lot of dull meetings and fancy crowns."

Lenna chuckled, her bright orange curls bouncing merrily as she whisked dirty pans to the large sink in the corner of the kitchen. It had been months since she'd seen Esmeray. The last time being the efficiently brutal visit Esmeray took her on to burn the cargo ships of Lenna's officially *ex*-husband off the coast of Doortan.

Though Keerian and Esmeray lobbied for Lenna to stay with them as they ruled Irridessen, Lenna politely declined, saying she was *always* available if they needed her to dive into the Prism, or do any Oracle duties, but would rather live a quieter life in the cozy city of Florra.

Sparrow was a common visitor, and Lenna looked forward to the nights Sparrow invited her to the house for dinner, or the visits Sparrow took to the bakery to catch up over tea and fresh pastries.

Even though both Sparrow and Esmeray were decades older than her, Lenna felt protective and motherly towards the two of them. The mind speak rings were a nice way to keep in touch, but Lenna always preferred a more "visible" visit with the Queen and King.

"What're you doing in Florra?" Lenna asked Esmeray, taking in the weariness reflected in her eyes. Her wings hung low, as if exhaustion weighed them down. "What's going on? Is there trouble?" Lenna rested her ample hip against the counter of the workspace, pushing aside a pan of cooling dough as she crossed her arms.

Sparrow sighed, giving in and plucking a cookie off the tray. "Is Hale in? Esmeray had some spell book questions for him."

Lenna shook her head. "He won't be back until later...but I know he'd love to see you both at the full moon celebration."

Perking her ears up, Sparrow gasped and shrieked, clapping her hands together so fast the bangles adorning her wrists jangled merrily. "Are you *finally* attending a soul tie gathering together?"

Lenna blushed, as Esmeray looked from one to the other, "What is going on?" the Queen sang slowly, a hint of mischief in her voice as she took in Lenna's full-on red face.

"Well," Lenna started slowly, drawing out the word until Esmeray was leaning so far off the counter in anticipation she almost fell off, "I've been seeing Hale for a couple months now, as a *bit* more than friends, and we were waiting for me to get more adjusted to life here before we-"

"Before you went to a full moon ceremony together to see if you're mates!" Sparrow squealed in delight, finishing Lenna's sentence for her.

Lenna enjoyed her budding friendship with Hale - the half-fae baker who'd helped Esmeray with translations of ancient spells before the battle at the Opal Palace. After her divorce from Leon was finalized, Lenna fell into a comfortable companionship with the male, and it quickly turned into more.

Now, feeling more adjusted to life in the magic imbued lands of Irridessen, Lenna was curious – *was* Hale her mate? With limited knowledge of the ceremonies, she wasn't sure what to expect. Hale respected her decision, but when they woke up this morning, wrapped in each other's arms, Lenna looked into Hale's deep, amber eyes and asked if they could go to the full moon ceremony together – just to check it out.

"You know, even if you are mates, it may take more than one try before the soul tie blooms," Esmeray reminded her gently. "Or it could take a stronger moon than tonight's..."

"I know." Lenna crossed the kitchen to pull a sheet of cookies out of the brick laid oven. "If we aren't mates, it doesn't change anything but... I live here, I love it here. I want to be included in your – our – traditions."

"Where are you going for the ceremony?" Esmeray inquired, hopping off the counter to snatch another cookie.

Lenna swatted Esmeray's hand with an oven mitt, earning herself a playful hiss. "Into the forest. Some of the other shopkeepers in the row are having a small get together at the base of one of the waterfalls."

"*Ooooh*, I wanna go." Esmeray jumped back onto the counter, swinging her legs and looking pitifully at Sparrow. "Can you *please* be Queen for the night so I can party?"

Lenna laughed as she scooped half the tray of cookies into a brown bag. "Most of the shop keeps either have a mate or aren't in the business of looking for one. Hale says it's the usual crowd he goes with every month." She plopped the bag into Esmeray's lap. The Queen's face lit up and she leaned over to land a smacking kiss atop Lenna's red hair, the treats disappearing into her pocket of space.

Carra, who, as legend told, hatched from the moon to bestow soul ties on the beings who worshipped her, was celebrated every full moon. The remaining eleven of the twelve most powerful lineage gods got one full moon a year where they were recognized, along with Carra, for blessing beings with their power.

Hale had filled her in on which god or goddess was celebrated when. Tonight, on top of Carra's celebration, beings rejoiced the gifts given from Alke, the God of Strength.

The full moon was the only time soul ties glimmered into existence.

And Lenna quietly desired one.

"You should come," Lenna repeated. "It would be wonderful to have you there."

Sparrow gave Lenna a tight grimace as the invitation hung in the air. It had taken time to get Sparrow to open up about what happened between her, Laurent, and Merrick, but once Sparrow admitted it, Lenna understood the underlying pain there.

Lenna woke up every morning and touched the grey stone on her ring, checking if Merrick put his back on. If she could get through to her thick-headed friend, she'd plead with him to just come *talk* to Sparrow. Merrick had been her first friend here, and she prayed the stubborn gargoyle would come to his senses.

Wrapping up another bag of cookies, she presented it to Sparrow, who hesitated a moment before accepting the gift. "Come," Lenna pleaded,

"Come have fun with Laurent and us." Sparrow met Lenna's eyes, and Lenna could see the apprehension brewing.

Lenna knew she had her own problems to face. Migraines had begun plaguing her again, even with the Prism in her possession. But she saw the stress written across Esmeray's face, the internal struggles etched on Sparrow's, and knew that, for at least a night, they could put their problems on a shelf and just soak in each other's company.

Something was coming.

But Lenna didn't know what it was.

She could feel it in the air, in the back of her mind. A sort of pregnant thrum that echoed through fate itself, whispering that they needed to enjoy days like this for as long as they had them.

# CHAPTER SEVEN
## ORLA

THERE WAS SOMEONE IN her room.

Orla could sense it as she stormed down the hall, but the screeching anger tearing through her hissed reckless fury, smothering any hesitation at the unknown stranger.

She had fae blood.

What a ridiculous notion.

Orla didn't know about her mother's past, but uptight Olivera living in a magic land and having *sex* with a *fae* was the most atrocious thing Orla ever heard.

Olivera had been exactly two things to Orla her entire life. The first being cold. And the second being the exact opposite of a motherly figure.

Orla held no love for the woman who raised her. No other family was ever introduced, though she held a hazy memory of an old man with a white beard cooing and smiling at her when she was a young child. But she didn't know who he was.

Orla's skin tone and tightly curled hair came from her father.

Whoever he was.

She decided she didn't care about that either as she glared at the closed door of her guest quarters.

It *seemed* empty, but Orla could *feel* an out-of-place aura radiating from the room. She sniffed delicately - a trick she picked up serving to quietly announce her presence before opening a door. It gave the person inside a moment to straighten up, put their pants back on, or get out of a compromising position.

Still. Silence.

It could be Marlo - prepared to recite the exciting perks that came with being forced to stay in the Ruby Kingdom. She cursed. *That* was a conversation she was keenly avoiding for as long as possible.

Before her hand could grip the doorknob, a bolt of pain shot through her temple, spotting her vision. Blinking rapidly, her sight wriggly and unfocused, she staggered back, rubbing her lids forcefully with the palm of her hand until her eyes cleared and the unsteadiness passed.

After a few seconds, the burning ache receded, settling in her lungs - a constant discomfort that ignited a fresh flare of anger.

Damning whoever *was* in her room, Orla twisted the knob and threw the door open so hard it slammed into the wall with a harsh *crack.*

She stormed across the threshold, cutting words ready to tear from her lips.

Those curses caught in her throat as the Crown Prince of the Ruby Kingdom looked up from the letter in his hands, fixing his dark eyes on Orla, a single brow raising with an air of arrogance.

"What are you afraid of?" Cillian asked gruffly, not allowing Orla time to process how he beat her back to her room.

"Excuse me?"

"This letter says, '*Orla is afraid.*' So, what are you afraid of, Orla *Grey?*" He held the crinkled parchment between two fingers, causing a small piece of the corner to flake off and drift to the floor.

Orla took a step towards Cillian, acutely aware of the piercing ring now resounding in her ears. Narrowing her eyes, she growled, "Give that to me."

She advanced closer, her blood boiling. How *dare* he throw wild, and probably untrue, assumptions around - call her fae. Just to show up here, ready to torment and ridicule her some more.

"Why?" Cillian challenged, his lips quirking as he watched her stalk across the room. He turned his back, all but dismissing her as he squinted down at the letter. "And...how was *your* life so hard? Why do you need an *easy* job?"

The hollow roar in the pit of her stomach urged her to fight back, adrenaline flooding her blood. "It's none of your business," she snapped, lurching forward to grab the letter.

Cillian easily batted her hand away as he squinted, trying to make out the words from the ruined parchment. Orla recoiled back before swiping again, missing a second time.

He snorted, the sound ultimately un-princely and pompous to her, before tossing the letter down on the desk. Orla scrambled forward to retrieve it, stuffing it into the pocket of her skirt.

But now that she had the letter back, a sinking sensation tumbled into her gut as clarity bolted into the forefront of her mind. Cillian could throw her in the dungeon to rot for the way she'd spoken to him.

Orla took a shaky step back. Should she bow? *Grovel*? Beg for forgiveness for how she'd reacted? Fuck - she should've curtsied the second she walked through the door.

The fucking Crown Prince was in her room - *his* room, his *palace* - for goddess's sake. And Orla already concluded he was arrogant, used to getting his way, and fae – which meant he had some sort of magic that he could use against her.

Before she could even spit out a half-assed apology and try to spare herself from a lifetime of imprisonment, Cillian strode towards her, crowding her back against the wall. Her breathing hitched as he invaded her space, his eyes flashing with ire.

"You want an easy job?"

Orla flinched. With a wicked grin that revealed sharp canines peeking out from his full lips he slowly lowered his mouth to the shell of her ear, causing a shiver to run down Orla's spine. "Congratulations – you just got one."

With that, Cillian disappeared down the hall, slamming the door closed on his way out.

Leaving Orla alone in her room, accompanied only by the horrifying feeling that this job wouldn't be easy at all.

# CHAPTER EIGHT
## ORLA

WITHIN AN HOUR OF Cillian's departure, leaving her seething with a healthy dose of frustration and a dash of apprehension, a quick rap of knuckles against her door made her scowl. Without waiting on a verbal acknowledgement, the knob twisted, and a head of braided, brassy blonde hair poked into the room.

"Orla Grey." The door opened wider, and a fae female stepped smoothly towards her, running a hand down her flowy, olive-green pants. She was a few inches shorter than Orla, with bronzy-hued eyes that shone with unbridled confidence, power. Her top was twisted and wrapped into a revealing halter style that exposed her toned, tan stomach and bare arms. She gave Orla a quick once-over, and thinned her lips before adding, "I'm Soren. I've been sent to move you to your new housing."

Narrowing her eyes, suspicion coiled through her - something inside her whispering that this female wasn't a regular servant of the Ruby Kingdom.

"What's wrong with this room?" Orla snapped, spreading her arms out in annoyance, knowing, somehow, Cillian had something insidious planned. The burning pain peaked at the thought, and it took all of her focus to keep the grimace from twisting across her face.

*Never show weakness.* Orla could hear Olivera's snappish words rattle through her mind, words that were snarled at her throughout her childhood.

*I am not so easily broken.* Orla reminded herself, her own mantra, one not associated with the cruel echoes of her youth. She breathed deeply through her nose and exhaled slowly, fighting to unclench her jaw.

"It's for guests." Soren's blunt tone was accompanied by a challenge glimmering in her coolly calculating stare. "You're now a citizen of the Ruby Kingdom. Which means it's time for you to move."

She'd been picking fights with people stronger than her for her entire life. But never with someone who had magic. Orla glanced down at the fae's bare arms, noticing no tattoos graced her skin, before her stare flicked up to her sharply pointed ears. Definitely fae, but with how much of her skin was revealed, the lack of *acat* confused her.

"This room is fine."

"Your room has been reassigned to a more...appropriate station befitting your lineage."

"Because I supposedly have fae blood in me? And so, Prince Cillian decided I shouldn't be squatting in his guest accommodations anymore?"

Leaning against the threshold, the fae chuckled, "If that was case, most of the beings living on this side of the Palace would've been moved."

Orla levelled a look at her. "Explain."

"I owe you no explanation. I don't answer to you." With a flip of her intricate braid, Soren turned away and began gathering Orla's meager belongings – most of which had been donations from the healers that helped her after the shipwreck.

"I'm assuming the Prince is moving me further into town? Someplace for someone with no money?" She hastily snatched away the few blouses the fae grabbed from the armoire. "Am I going to have to beg for scraps?"

Her voice pitched with emotion, and she cursed herself for allowing a sliver of weakness through. She wished the money Lenna gave her survived the shipwreck. She could really use that sock full of jewels right now. But that lifeline was currently at the bottom of the sea, reduced to shiny trinkets for the fish to bat at.

"Nope. Soren popped the "p" with a sarcastic emphasis as Orla tossed the remainder of her paltry clothes into the chest sitting open at the foot of her bed. "You're being moved into Oasees - the Palace itself. And I'll give you this piece of advice for free. The side of the Palace where the town and its beings live, love, trade, and work is Aridden. The side the royals and court resides on is Oasees."

Orla stumbled a half step at that. Leaving more questions unanswered over answered. Why would Cillian move her further into the Palace? With royalty and the assembled court?

"Why?" Orla asked, stopping dead in her tracks, half hoping this was all a sick joke. She had no idea how to navigate a royal court.

The fae shrugged, kicking the top of the chest closed. "I didn't ask," she replied bluntly. "It may have to do with your new assignment. *Everyone* works in the Ruby Palace. No matter *what* their blood deems them."

The burning feeling shot down her throat. Orla felt it tearing nimbly through her lungs. Fingers of molten fire trickled down and dripped into her core, igniting waves of pain-wracked fury. Steeling herself against the onslaught of agony, again, Orla turned, throwing open the door of the guest quarters she inhabited for the last four months.

Whatever game Cillian was playing, she knew she was nothing more than a new pawn. Something to play with and dispose of.

She thought of Marlo. Would he be happy moving to new accommodations? Was he also being sent to Oasees?

Marlo would win over the royals fast with his wit, charm, and smiles – human or not.

"Fine. Show me," she ordered, waving her hand out the door.

Soren finished locking up Orla's trunk of belongings, before snapping her fingers, the chest disappearing in a plume of white smoke.

Orla started, but before she could demand an answer, the fae held up and hand. "Your shit's fine. It's in your new room."

"But..." Orla glanced down at the fae's hands, arms, squinting as if that would somehow make a tattoo appear – something to signify this fae had magic. The healers told her *acatis* were visible, but this fae had no designs gracing her arms. "Do you have an *acat?*"

Soren raised her eyebrows, a rough snort escaping as she considered Orla with what looked like renewed interest. "Not in the traditional sense," she admitted flippantly, though a smirk curled across her lips. "But nice to know you've been paying attention."

Orla, still whirling from the ridiculous idea of possibly having fae blood, still turning over her encounter with Cillian in her mind, didn't have any desire to dig deeper into this strange female.

Finally, she decided the fae must have a tattoo on her legs.

Her brain felt too mushy to continue asking Soren questions, instead slipping back into the never-ending loop of internal confusion that wove through her mind constantly since she first stepped foot in that throne room this afternoon.

She brooded on the announcement of her fae blood, turning it around and around, inspecting it from all facets as she did with all information she gathered by being quiet and watching others.

As she recalled the way Cillian's face looked when he left her room, the fae female ushered Orla out into the hallway. Orla didn't spare her a glance as she wondered if Cillian had many friends.

She wanted to dismiss the fae blood revelation as nothing more than a political tactic to keep her here to use as free labor until she dropped to her knees, utterly spent.

Orla rolled her shoulders back, falling into step behind Soren. She'd be back here soon enough. Cillian would realize she was nothing and no one and she'd be sent right back to Aridden once it was clear her supposed fae blood did nothing.

She'd be worked to the bone and then become another nameless citizen, for however long she had to wait it out until she could escape back to the Slate Kingdom.

She just had to bide her time.

# CHAPTER NINE
# ORLA

Soren dumped Orla in front of her new accommodations and left without a word. Orla's head swum, mimicking the heat waves that fluttered just out of reach at the end of the open-air hallway. Blowing out a heavy breath, she leaned her head against the sandstone wall, closing her eyes until the roll of dizziness passed.

When she sucked in another lungful of air, she paused. The burn had dissipated from her chest for the first time in months, giving her the ability to take a steadying breath that didn't send shooting pain through her limbs.

Gingerly, she peeked open one eye, warily running her fingers down the ornate wooden door before her. Still half expecting this new room to be some elaborate prank, Orla hesitated. But before she lost her nerve, she twisted the knob and threw it open. A strangled gasp left her lips as her jaw dropped.

A huge, four-poster bed, with silky beige sheets and fluffy pillows, an elegant armoire, and a mosaic tiled nightstand sat along the right wall. The opposite side of the room sported a plush chaise and a desk with an armless chair. Covering the cool tiled floor, an ornate rug with scrolling patterns of reds and golds made the whole of the interior feel...regal.

Between the chaise and the desk, a door led to a private bathroom where a luscious looking claw footed tub immediately snagged her attention.

Her new lodging was at least double the size of her original quarters. With a hand over her heart, Orla's eyes snapped to the sheer, white drapes fluttering in the breeze against a paned glass door that opened outwards to a covered patio.

There were easily two hundred residences lining both sides of a wide hallway on the second floor of the Ruby Palace. But now her room overlooked the sprawling oasis the Palace was built around. Even from the doorway, Orla could see tall palm trees swaying, and a waft of fresh air seemed to constantly roll through the room.

She knew the original quarters she stayed in were notably temporary, though it was a small reprieve from the bunk house she shared with the other female servants in Doortan. But even staying in the guest wing of the Palace, she shared a community bathroom with ten other residents that never pumped in enough hot water for her to feel truly clean, let alone take a *bath*.

Swallowing the trepidation of what she'd have to trade to stay in this room, Orla realized it would be immensely difficult to give up this space now that it was *hers*. With trembling fingers, she dragged her belongings over to the armoire to unpack.

"You won't need those." A deep, smooth voice from the doorway startled Orla and she dropped the lid of the chest on her fingers. "But I figured you wouldn't be so inclined to move if we'd dragged you out of the guest hall with only the dress you were wearing."

Hissing against the pain, she whirled around, only to come face to face, *again*, with the Crown Prince of the Ruby Kingdom. He was leaned against the door frame, his thick arms crossed over his broad chest, watching Orla with a curious gleam in his eye.

Through gritted teeth, Orla clenched her throbbing hand, giving Cillian a lackluster half-bow. "Two visits in one day, your Highness?"

Cillian ignored her, letting himself into the room to throw open the doors of the armoire. To Orla's utter shock, dresses, tunics, pants, and other clothing greeted her. "Since you're working for me, you must look the part," he commented flatly before toeing the small chest with his boot, a wince flickering across his face.

"You're giving me clothes?" Orla asked, her brows knitting together. "Why?"

"I heard you ask that question quite a lot." Was Cillian's only reply before striding over to the plush chaise.

"Well, I went from a guest, to possibly fae, to citizen, to living in the Oasees all within a few hours so I feel like my questions are warranted. Not that your servant deigned to answer anything."

Cillian snorted as he leaned his head against the armrest and stretched out his legs. Orla frowned, hating how damn handsome he looked all relaxed and wicked. "You know, usually when I pluck damsels in distress out of the sea and gift her gorgeous clothes, she's a little more grateful."

"I'm sure," Orla replied dryly as she turned back to the closet. She gently ran her hands across multiple dresses, marveling at the soft fabric and exquisite craftsmanship. Not that she'd tell Cillian she couldn't wait to try on every single garment the second he left.

"You aren't a great conversationalist," Cillian hedged, fixing Orla with his dark eyes.

"Do you know what a conversation is?" Orla shot back, glancing over her shoulder to him, "It's when one person says something and the other answers."

"Being," Cillian corrected.

"What?"

"Being," he repeated. "We aren't *people* we are *beings*. If you live in a magic imbued land – you're a being."

Orla tried to stop her eyes from rolling. She failed. Turning back to Cillian, she crossed her arms. "Okay fine. From one *being* to another, why'd you move me here?"

Cillian grinned, showing off perfectly straight pearl white teeth. "You didn't seem to enjoy being a guest, and I figured you wouldn't want to trot all the way from Aridden every day to work. This is easier," he shrugged a shoulder, staring up at her ceiling, "plus this position means you'll need to stay where I can keep an eye on you."

Orla straightened and winced as the burning pain returned with a vengeance, roaring through her blood as if it had battered down a wall inside of her, making her breath catch. Frustration churned astride it. She'd had a few moments of sweet relief... and it made her loathe the returning pain even more.

Trying to focus her mind on something other than the agony running through her limbs, she leaned against the wall. "What exactly does this job entail?"

In response to her question, Cillian slowly rose off the chaise, his long legs stalking across the room. His expression darkened – and something that felt a lot like lust began swirling through the room.

A different sort of heat flooded her involuntarily, pushing through the painful burn. Orla tried to move away from the wall, but Cillian was faster, bracing his weight casually with an arm against the top of the armoire door, effectively cornering her.

Orla felt the air leave her lungs as he encroached into her personal space, as if even her breath itself couldn't be trusted within Cillian's delightfully devilish presence.

*He is the godsdamned Crown Prince who has been nothing but frustrating.* Orla reminded herself firmly, even as her traitorous knees suddenly felt a little weak. Cillian was brash - and frankly rude - infiltrating her room, reading her note.

She didn't trust his intentions were pure at all.

But damn, she hated that he was so good looking.

This close, she could see every angle of his face, could make out the small flecks of honey that accentuated the brown of his irises.

He towered over her, bending down until mere inches separating his lips from hers. Murmuring into her ear, as if he was telling her a secret, he growled, "I need you to be my eyes and ears in court meetings, and while staying in Oasees. I need you to tell me, and me alone, if someone seems...up to something."

Orla replayed the words in her head thrice before she could comprehend them. She fought the urge to flick her eyes down to look at his soft mouth and full, very kissable, lips. It was a lot easier to hate him when he was being a dick and not directly in her personal space. Forcing her eyes to lock on his, she cocked her head slightly, trying to regain some semblance of distance between them. "So...sit in meetings and tell you who's acting weird in a room full of beings I've never met before?"

*This was the job he wanted her to do?* His nearness made her all muddled, everything processing much slower than normal.

He smelled like cinnamon.

Orla pushed that thought deep, deep down, berating herself.

With a chuckle, a goddess-damned *dimple* appeared. "Orla Grey, you won't be *sitting* in these meetings. You're my new cup bearer." And with that proclamation, Cillian pushed off the door of the armoire, effectively breaking Orla from his thrall.

Orla blanched, "You want me to taste your wine for *poison*?"

He was already moving towards the door. "No one's going to poison *me.*" He shot Orla a flirty grin over his shoulder. "But be glad you aren't my Father's cup bearer. There's *definitely* poison in those glasses every once in a while."

Cillian gave Orla a mocking bow before departing down the hallway.

Orla stood frozen as she watched him stride away, hands deep in his pockets.

Cillian wanted her to be a spy disguised as a cupbearer.

And he smelled like godsdamned cinnamon.

The scent stayed in her room long after she closed the door and sunk against the hard-backed desk chair.

For the second time that day, Orla held the sneaking suspicion that the Crown Prince of the Ruby Kingdom didn't have many friends.

# Chapter Ten
# ESMERAY

Convincing Sparrow to go to the full moon celebration had been difficult. There were still fresh, hurt feelings surrounding mates, and no matter how much she swore to me she was unbothered by Merrick's absence, I knew there was something haunting her thoughts.

So, being her best friend, I told her either she came on her own accord, or I'd demand it as her Queen. She finally relented - though I think it had more to do with my dramatically incessant pestering than her own lukewarm enthusiasm over the event.

I slid my hands down the soft gossamer of the green dress I chose for the evening. The fabric shimmered in the light from the mosaic lamp on the dresser, casting flickering twinkles across the walls. In addition to Sparrow giving us the largest guest room in her house, she also had the "foresight" to fill the entire closet with my clothes.

I had no idea how she kept getting into my closet at the Obsidian Palace, but I held a sneaking suspicion it had something to do with the fact we were the same size in dresses – and all the ones in the closet could be worn by beings with or without wings.

Having a best friend who could wane, and break wards easily, was a real pain in the ass in the fashion department.

"Remind me to put stronger wards around our closet when we get back," I laughed, talking over my shoulder to Keerian as he appeared out of the connecting bathroom, drying his curly hair with a towel. He was shirtless, low-slung, navy pants hanging unbuttoned from his hips. I immediately forgot all about Sparrow's thievery.

"I thought that dress looked familiar," Keerian replied with a chuckle, crossing the bedroom. With a devilish smirk, he pulled me close, dipping me in his arms to lay a passion-fueled kiss against my lips. "You look delightfully radiant, and *exceptionally* edible, my Queen," he murmured, his broad hands trailing across the small of my back.

Desire flooded me from my toes to the tips of my horns. I slanted my mouth, deepening our kiss. I had half a mind to disregard the party and find our own private waterfall where we could "celebrate Alke" intertwined, but the harsh knock at the bedroom door interrupted my daydream.

It was Laurent, dressed in his regular attire – the robe of the evening being an enchanting silver color with blue trim along the edges. I subtly flared my wings so Laurent couldn't see Keerian, who took the opportunity to flop onto the bed, his gaze heating and a wicked smile playing at the corner of his lips. "Sparrow's ready. How long do you two need to finish getting dressed?"

Biting my lip, I covertly glanced over to my mate, reclining on the bed, his golden wings shining in the dim lights of our room, casting shadows against the masterpiece of his body. I suppressed a giggle as Keerian, out of Laurent's line of sight, began flexing his biceps, pretending to ignore my attention on him. I cleared my throat, turning back to Laurent who sported a bemused expression on his face.

"We'll meet you there," I croaked, throat dry, desire humming in my blood. Keerian's laugh turned into a rough purr as Laurent, realizing what he'd walked in on, made a fake gagging noise while swiftly backing away from the door.

I flicked my wrist to close and lock it before launching myself at Keerian. He caught me easily, tossing me onto our soft mattress before moving to stand at the end of the bed, his gaze never leaving mine as he began pushing the fabric of my gown up to my waist.

A moan escaped my lips as Keerian settled between my legs, his deep growl of pleasure shooting right to my core. And as his warm hands massaged my calves, as he peppered soft kisses up to the apex of my thighs, my breath caught, my eyes squeezed shut, and I knew Carra truly blessed me with the best mate I could ask for.

"GLAD YOU COULD JOIN US," Sparrow chirped, a shit-eating grin plastered on her face the moment Keerian and I waned to the base of the third largest waterfall outside Florra. Sparrow held a long-stemmed wine glass in her hand, which she daintily sipped from as she appraised me with a devilish look, her eyes sparkling. *"Was it good?"* she asked, her finger rubbing against the small golden stone embedded in our rings.

I rolled my eyes innocently, mirroring her fiendish grin, *"We only wanted to make a grand entrance."*

*"I'm sure Keerian did 'enter' in the grandest of ways."*

Sparrow's cheeky reply made me snort. *"Oh yeah, something about the full moon really gets him going."*

*"Jealous. Maybe I'll see if Laurent wants to sneak off into the woods and do some grand entering of his own."*

*"Spar, your dress is so shiny it practically glows in the dark. Not very subtle for slipping away."* Peering closer at her gown, I furrowed my brow as I realized – *"Wait – that's my dress you thief."*

Sparrow threw her head back and laughed. I joined in, earning us glares from Keerian and Laurent who realized a silent conversation was going on that was definitely about them. Gifting my most dazzling smile to Laurent, he finally chuckled, shaking his head.

I was ecstatic for my friend. Laurent was a great male, and I couldn't be more excited that my mate's best friend was my best friend's mate.

Sparrow's gown matched the silver in Laurent's robe and looked more apt for a ballroom than a small gathering in the woods. Actually, I think I did purchase it for some royal event or another, but it disappeared, and I'd never noticed.

Her golden hair was loosely curled and swept away from her face with softly twinkling blossoms. Sparrow seemed calmer, too – telling me that pushing her to come had been a good call. Laurent also seemed completely at ease being so well dressed while surrounded by brush and trees as he refilled her cup of wine with a flourish, kissing her gently on the temple before gesturing to Keerian. The males headed to go mingle with the other party attendees, leaving Sparrow and I to finish our gossip fest as we walked slowly towards the gathering, watching the rest of the guests arrive to the base of the waterfall - just out of reach from the spray of cascading water that tumbled down from high above.

The clearing was simply decorated, with a few small fires edging the trees to give faint light to the revelers. Two long, wooden tables with a smattering of mismatched chairs sat against the thick woods surrounding us, leaving most of the clearing empty for dancing and conversation. Multiple well-loved and threadbare rugs overlapped each other, creating a colorful dance floor where I spied Lenna, head thrown back with a bright smile on her face, twirling around with Hale.

A flutist and a cellist sat beside the bank of the river, playing a merry tune that I recognized from the Opal Palace. There were about thirty beings gathered, laughing, and socializing, all dressed in beautiful formal clothing in a brilliant spectrum of colors.

I stepped into the clearing, feeling the rush of anxiety flood through me for a beat as a hush rolled over the crowd immediately. Even the flutist stopped mid performance to gape at me. I was getting used to this reaction from townsfolks – especially since I doubted they were expecting the Queen Absolute to appear in the middle of their celebration – but it still made my palms sweat after being hunted for a year with a price on my head while my twin ruled from my throne.

Slowly, I raised my hand, letting magic flow through my blood, dispelling the fears that slipped through the walls in my mind. Tiny balls of light pulsed forth from my outstretched fingers, my illusion magic morphing them into playful fireflies that zipped around the clearing before settling in the branches above the musicians, cascading the party in a golden glow.

"Let's celebrate," I said simply. There was a breath of silence – and then the flutist whooped with glee, launching into a lively tune as the rest of the beings cheered, crowding around me.

The next few minutes passed in a blur as each and every guest swarmed me, introducing themselves, bowing, thanking me for blessing their humble party.

A glass of wine was pushed into my hand, a gargoyle child peeled away from her mother's skirts to flap up into the air and place a flower crown atop my head, nestling it gently between my horns as she beamed at me. I gave her a hesitant smile back, gently patting her cheek before she landed, curtsying quickly, and scurrying back to her mother. Two slim fae dressed in identical flowy blue pants and tunics embroidered with the moon phases guided me to the dance floor, spinning me around in tandem to the music. I laughed; the sound freer than I'd felt in ages. Keerian spied me quickly, and – ever the gentlemale – politely asked if he could cut in and dance with me to the sheer enthusiasm of the crowd.

The hours passed in a haze of dancing and conversating. It would be another hour until midnight, and I'd caught Hale looking up at the full moon a few times, as if gauging how much longer until soul ties would begin blooming into existence.

"Are you enjoying the celebration?" Lenna scooted into the chair next to me, sitting with Sparrow and Keerian at the long table.

I nodded, knowing the smile on my face was genuine. Lenna's cheeks were flushed from dancing with Hale, her honey brown eyes glimmering with merriment.

Hale came huffing up to Lenna's left, throwing an arm around her. "I thought I saw Laurent around here someplace, where did he sneak off to?"

Sparrow gracefully stood from her chair. "I believe he found a being that could hold a very intellectual conversation. I'm sure I bore him to tears talking about plants and birds all day."

"Nonsense," Hale chuffed, his dark mustache twitching as he crinkled his face, "he's so in love with you he'd listen to you talk about anything that bought you joy."

Laurent took that moment to appear at Sparrow's side, extending his hand and asking her for a dance. She blushed wildly as she allowed him to lead her away, the two of them commanding the dance floor with expertise and grace as the musicians played a fast-tempo song that had the party flocking towards them.

I felt a nudge of simmering annoyance emit from the spell book as it sat in my pocket of space, its presence in my mind urging me to let it out. I cleared my throat delicately. Next to me, Keerian shifted in his seat, surveying the beings dancing to make sure we weren't interrupted. "I need to talk to you about the book," I said to Hale quietly, not wanting any of the fae around us to eavesdrop, since their enhanced hearing was a factor to consider when trying to have a secret or private discussion – another reason our mind speak rings were so valuable. "There have been...issues...getting rid of it."

Hale raised his eyebrows, sparing a glance at Lenna before bowing slightly. "Come by the bakery tomorrow morning, let me take a look at it."

"Thank you, Hale." I hugged him before he bowed again, taking his leave and pulling a giggling Lenna along by the hand back to the dance floor.

"Want me to go with you tomorrow?" Keerian asked, swiping a bottle of wine to refill our glasses.

I leaned over, grasping Keerian's bearded chin in my hand before laying a gentle peck against his lips. It would be nice to spend the morning with Hale and Lenna – hopefully we'd get some answers before having to go back to the Obsidian Palace. I needed to decide on the structuring of my new advisors soon, but there were simply not enough hours in the day for me to accomplish everything. Getting rid of the infernal spell book that caused so much grief was a good place to start, though.

The spell book Adara used to warp her magic was hidden away in my pocket of space, yet I could constantly feel its otherworldly presence like a weight in my chest. It pulsed with foreign power and had been completely indestructible to any attempts at destroying it. After I used just a bit of its magic to defeat Adara, the book tried its best to get my attention. It would send pulses of *frustration* through my subconscious that I would dutifully ignore.

And then the damned thing would pout.

It was just a book. Not a sentient being.

But it felt *alive.*

Destroying a book made of paper should've been easy, but after multiple attempts, *I* couldn't blast it apart, and Laurent's flames hadn't singed a single page edge. Keerian even tried to rip it in two – also unsuccessful.

It sat there.

Pristine.

I hoped Hale had some better ideas because I was tapped out. And running out of ideas made me *very* uneasy.

I was deep in thought, mind whirring, when the screams started.

# CHAPTER ELEVEN
## SPARROW

LIKE WRAITHS IN THE night, cloaked figures slipped from the darkness blanketed trees, heavy black hoods covering their faces. Sparrow darted her eyes from one to the next, counting quickly. There were about twenty, all armed with an assortment of weapons, and none of them had wings. Which meant they were fae.

And that this was about to get bloody.

Esmeray was at her side in an instant, her nails glowing bright gold, growing into sharp, dagger-like, weapons. When it came to battle, Esmeray flourished between fighting with her fae magic and her physically enhanced gargoyle abilities.

Her friend had a gloriously fucked-up view of bloodshed - reveled in it - but in times like this, Sparrow wanted no other being backing her up. Esmeray was brutally efficient in a brawl.

With a growl, Keerian stalked to Esmeray's other side, unsheathing two short swords, the wide hilts gripped tightly in his fists. He looked every bit the part of the fearsome Golden Gargoyle that rose through the ranks of Irridessen's army quicker than any other gargoyle in history. His own delight in battling rivalled only that of his mate's.

The air thinned, thrumming with power as a luminous orb materialized behind them, courtesy of Laurent, who expertly wove smoke and magic together. As the portal grew, Lenna murmured soothing words to the townsfolk huddling together at the tree line, ushering them towards the portal that would transport them safely back to Florra.

Ever since they cemented their soul tie, Laurent's power over creating portals had grown exponentially. Portals that used to take hours to create now took only a moment. In the other sense, Sparrow's battle magic had become stronger as well, and she'd noticed her inky black *acat* that used to stop at her elbow now extended to the middle of her upper bicep.

Armed with a bow, Hale guarded Lenna's back, a blue tipped arrow nocked, as he appraised the threat with a sense that he was both deadly accurate with the weapon and adept in battle. Sparrow pursed her lips into a grim smile. The portly baker continued to surprise her.

A cloaked figure skittered forward, breaking from the shadows, its unnatural gait prompting Keerian to tense and snarl a warning. The King Consort took a step closer, his wings flaring, making his hulking size appear even larger. His hard expression promised lethal brutality as he locked in on the figure, raising one of his short swords threateningly.

"What do you want," Esmeray sneered, pulling Goldriel from her pocket of space. The long, golden staff worked as a conduit to channel her immense amount of power. The moonstone at the tip flared as she imbued battle magic into it. "We were quite enjoying our nice celebration, before you bumblefuckers crashed it."

"We came for the Oracle," the figure jeered in a hoarse voice. "But finding the Queen Absolute is an unforeseen delight."

Sparrow shot an alarmed look at Laurent, quickly touching the ring on her finger. *"Get Lenna and Hale out of here – someplace safe. There could be beings in Florra hunting her."*

Laurent flung his left palm out, making hurried slashes in the air, another portal forming out of pure white smoke. Catching eye contact with Hale, Laurent jerked his chin wordlessly towards it. Hale gave a single nod, keeping the blue tipped arrow aimed at the shadowy figure who'd spoken, while slowly backing up to Lenna. As the last being flashed through the portal to Florra, Hale released the tension on the bowstring, his thumb and forefinger keeping the arrow secured, and gripped Lenna's hand, tugging her through the second portal.

As Lenna's curly hair whipped out of view, the cloaked being closest to Sparrow let out a frustrated grunt. Laurent closed his hand into a fist, and both portals vanished with a zing that allowed air to pour back through the forest clearing. Sparrow's nostrils flared at the scent of decay wafting from the mysterious fae, her instincts screaming that something wasn't right.

"Well, I'm *so* sorry that your trip was a waste," Esmeray purred, the moonstone atop Goldriel illuminating the snarl curling her lips. "But if you still think you can take us on, feel free to test that assumption at your leisure."

The Queen was always the catalyst and *never* a peaceful negotiator.

Sparrow, Laurent, Esmeray and Keerian stood shoulder to shoulder as their foes advanced. Two closest to Esmeray began wrapping their hands in shimmering purple battle magic – a color that was highly unheard of for fae to inherit. Esmeray let out a low hiss, her battle magic throwing sharp shadows across her face. Keerian flashed his fangs.

Sparrow rallied her magic to her, her hands glowing bright green. The increased power would take some getting used to, but one glance at her *acat* reassured her. She could fight.

She would fight.

Laurent wreathed his wrists in blue flames, flexing and loosening his hands, the small fires encompassing the clearing igniting into the same unearthly hue.

A glint of metal flashed to Sparrow's right, and she whirled, whipping a vine of magic towards the source, catching one of the fae in the throat before they could raise their sword. He crumpled, silently falling into the river as death embraced him.

*"Way down do our souls go."* Esmeray's smooth voice filled Sparrow's head, filled with bitter amusement as the Queen paid homage to the lineage Goddess who blessed her - Phades, Goddess of Death. It had been a shock to all when Adara confirmed Esmeray's lineage god was none other than the most elusive, and arguably most powerful, goddess in history.

Phades had never blessed an *acat.*

Until Esmeray.

Laurent shot a burst of fire at two fae, their own battle magic paling in comparison to the sheer power radiating from Laurent.

Pandemonium ensued.

The remaining beings rushed the group at once, but Esmeray was ready. Gold magic erupted out of Goldriel, taking out two more in one shot. The others moved with unnatural speed, dodging her attack at the last second. Esmeray shrieked in rage, slashing the staff down, catching a fae across the throat with a lash of sharp sparks. Sparrow had half a heartbeat to watch the body crumple before two more jumped in to engage the Queen.

Sparrow threw her hands out, her magic snaking around the chests of two attackers, immobilizing their limbs and slithering up their throats, squeezing sharply. With a *crack* their bodies slumped, and death swept over them. Not as bloody as Esmeray but still effective.

*"Nice. "* Laurent's deep voice filled her head, and she couldn't help but snarl, flashing fangs at the next cloaked figure that bellowed a battle cry before charging her. Her rage grew with her magic, a tempest swirling inside her, and all the emotions she'd suppressed over the last four months fueled her next attack, an outlet for the wrath and pain that warred with the happiness she fought so goddess-damned hard for.

A feeling that she was exactly where she needed to be washed over her.

Keerian expertly wielded his two swords, avoiding blasts of magic while effectively disarming his opponents. Esmeray screamed in un-bridled fury as Keerian narrowly dodged a burst of purple magic that attempted to blindside the King. With a flash, Esmeray waned, her staff disappeared, and she came down on the unsuspecting attacker with a vengeance, black nails tearing out their throat before anyone could comprehend what happened.

The fight lasted minutes longer – but to Sparrow it felt like only seconds that passed in a dizzying fog. Flashes of magic and the ringing of steel filled the clearing, the cloaked beings dying silently in the chill of the night air.

Until only one figure remained.

Esmeray snapped her tattooed fingers as she stalked forward, chains sprouting out of the ground to ensnare the mysterious assailant's wrists and ankles, yanking him to his knees. Keerian was behind the captured being in a blink, his swords, dripping blood, crossed on both sides of their throat. Keerian looked up at his mate with hooded eyes filled with bloodlust, waiting for her to give the command to kill.

"Why do you want the Oracle?" Esmeray snarled, inches from the cloaked figure's face.

Silence.

With a hiss, Keerian ripped the hood off the fae's head, revealing shaggy black hair and pointed ears. The fae's pupils fully blacked out any color of an iris. His facial expression was blank, unfeeling, as those eerie eyes settled on the Queen before him.

Sparrow recoiled with a soft gasp, and Laurent moved closer to her immediately, his blue fires still churning and crackling in the background of the now too-silent clearing.

Keerian grunted from behind the trapped fae, "Answer your Queen."

The fae's mouth barely moved as he whispered in a bone scratching voice, "She is not my Queen."

"So, this is about Adara," Esmeray deadpanned, throwing her arms out in frustration before her focus narrowed back on her captive with a vendetta burning through her brilliantly green eyes. Her dress was covered with blood, but thankfully no injuries marred her pale skin. "Did Adara send you?"

The fae's expression turned blissful. "*Send* us? Queen Adara *created us*. For the purpose of glorious retribution, and we are ecstatic to accept our fate."

"Your fate is death, and no one will remember the lackey of a disgraced queen," Esmeray bit back, "So tell me, *why* does Adara want the Oracle?"

The unnerving black eyes again met Esmeray's. Keerian tightened the blades of his swords against the fae's neck. Sparrow watched as blood began seeping from underneath the steel. The fae didn't flinch.

"We are here with more power than we ever dreamed of. And for that, we will come, and continue to come, until Queen Adara is rightfully placed on the throne to bring this continent into its full power." With a gravelly voice the fae began chanting in an odd language that caused goosebumps to erupt across Sparrow's skin.

Esmeray flicked her eyes up to Keerian. The mysterious being only got three words out before his head was dispatched from his body, rolling to land at Esmeray's feet.

"Yuck." Esmeray blew out a ragged breath, kicking the head into the river. Sparrow watched the dark hair sail through the air before landing with a splash in the quick moving water. "Well, that was annoying."

The body slumped, headless, the chains holding it in place disappeared. Laurent stepped up, a disgusted leer on his lips, as he flicked a stream of fire at the body until it was nothing but ash in the wind. With a muttered prayer skyward, Laurent began weaving around the clearing with Keerian, the Ex-King's guards making quick work of beheading and burning the rest of the bodies, careful not to destroy any of the forest surrounding them.

Sparrow blew a thin breath from her nose. It was common practice to behead and burn the bodies of foes. It signaled the fight was over. But something still niggled in the back of her mind, a whisper that this was only the beginning, that something more sinister was now in motion.

"What do we do now?" Sparrow said to Esmeray, chewing unconsciously on her lip. She already guessed the answer, her blood chilling at the thought that more of these beings were out there.

Esmeray sighed, tilting her head to gaze up to the full moon now fully at its apex in the star dotted sky. "We're going to the Obsidian Palace. I need to have a chat with my sister."

# Chapter Twelve
# Lenna

Esmeray had been cool, coiled, and ready to strike before the battle at the Opal Palace. Lenna had watched Esmeray get bloody in battle and then turn around and crack a joke.

But Lenna had never seen her friend slide into the role she now wielded with utmost authority.

Queen Absolute of Irridessen.

Lenna now knew why that title was spoken in quiet, reverent whispers.

Within moments of Esmeray, Keerian, Sparrow and Laurent waning into the Obsidian Palace's throne room covered in blood, Esmeray was already shouting orders as the gold and green lights faded. The guards standing at attention rushed forward, their faces set in grim, battle-hardened expressions.

There were at least thirty warriors, both female and male, dressed in black leather armor with the Queen's golden crest on their chest plates – the silhouette of curled ram's horns with a staff in the middle. Esmeray stormed closer, battle magic still sparking between her fingers.

"I want two rotations of aerial troops over the towers. Send four elemental fae down to each bridge entrance. Put four gargoyles over the length of Pyritee Pass - I want them flying in cycles from now until dawn. Send reports directly to King Keerian every hour." Esmeray practically vibrated with wrath as Keerian stepped up next to her, gently laying a hand on her shoulder as he began barking additional commands to the Queen's Guard.

Lenna felt her hands shake as she clung to Hale. "Are we under attack?" she whispered to him, only to have Sparrow appear with a sympathetic smile on her face.

"It's just a precaution," Sparrow said to Lenna and Hale as she wove her way towards the looming dais behind them. "If those beings were under orders to take the Oracle out of play, the safest place for you both is here with us."

No one looked hurt - just royally pissed off and boiling with after-battle adrenaline. Sparrow, at least, seemed calm-*ish*, compared to the Queen thundering around the throne room in a flurry of black wings and golden sparks.

Keerian dismissed the last warriors as Esmeray continued to pace the floor in front of the dais, muttering curses, her green eyes glittering with embers of magic.

With a rough breath, Esmeray finally turned to Lenna and Hale as three new guards hurried into the room, bowing deeply before standing at attention beside Keerian. "I need you to stay here while we figure out whose orders those fuckers in the woods were under. Servants are readying the King's chambers for you to stay in. Anything you two need - please let Keerian or me know."

Esmeray cut her eyes to Sparrow, who'd ascended halfway up the dais and sat on the stairs. Lenna eyed them both as they touched their rings. Sparrow gave the Queen an almost unnoticed nod, waning in a burst of green light.

Laurent looked from Esmeray to Keerian. "Give me orders." There was an edgy temper swirling around him, as if he was holding back barely restrained frustration. Keerian pulled Laurent aside, the two males talking low and fast.

Lenna looked around the throne room and did her best to ignore the sheer drop into the caverns below. The glass floor always made her feet sweat, but knowing she was surrounded by winged beings made her feel slightly more secure. Plus, with all this talk of her importance and increased measures to keep her safe, she felt confident that at least if she did fall through the floor, someone would catch her.

Keerian and Laurent continued their hushed conversation as they made their way out of the throne room, disappearing into the now empty corridor beyond. It seemed, with the Queen's Guard activated and the Palace army on orders, the entirety of the Obsidian Palace had morphed into a warrior stronghold.

"Lenna, Hale, your room is ready." Esmeray gestured to the gargoyles standing at attention behind them. "These are three of my best fighters in the Queen's Guard. They'll personally escort you to your rooms and anywhere in the castle you need to go." Esmeray directed her attention to Hale, her commanding voice softening. "I'll be in your rooms in a bit to give you the spell book. I need you and Lenna to work on figuring out how to destroy it."

"I'm happy to serve, my Queen." Hale put a hand over his heart and bowed low.

The last thing Lenna saw as the guards ushered them out towards the hall was the glass floor rippling and Esmeray sinking down into the deep caverns below.

# Chapter Thirteen
# ESMERAY

I FLEW THROUGH THE stale air, passing the dragon lairs where Resso and his few kin lived, down past the grottos that held troves of priceless treasures and artifacts, deep into the bowels of the cavern where dirt paths wound into the depths of the mighty mountain itself.

The Obsidian Palace was foreboding, but the shadowy trail into the dungeons always shot a warning tingle through my bones.

I landed on the ledge where a carved passage veered into darkness. Tucking my wings in, I glanced over the lip of the edge to the currently empty Soul Keeper's cell - the only cage with no physical lock. The Soul Keeper's cell held prisoners by anchoring their soul to the flat rock at the bottommost part of the mountain. It was where Adara hid the previous Oracle to keep Irridessen from finding out she was our parents' murderer.

Since I mercy killed Lenna's predecessor, his soul was freed from a long existence of agony as the Soul Keeper's cell leeched his life force. The magic keeping a being trapped on the rock's narrow surface was no magic fae could recreate. Runes were etched along the rim by the Witch Queen who ruled the Obsidian Kingdom thousands of years ago.

I didn't fuck with witches. They were able to pull raw power from the earth – and could siphon a fae dry of magic. Now, the witch covens were isolated to the Jade Kingdom, hunted down and exterminated if they attempted to set foot into another Kingdom due to their actions during the Witch War.

My mood soured further as I entered the dungeons, the cacophony of cries and screams from the prisoners echoing through me. Rounding the last corner, I saw a small flicker of flames reflecting against golden hair. This deep in the mountain, even the air was wrong. Thin and cold - mimicking the air at the peak.

The one good thing the witches did during their reign was carve magic nullifying runes into every inch of the dungeons. The runes couldn't be broken like a normal ward could be, and these cells held the worst of the worst prisoners. The shitty part was, the runes nullified *all* magic down here. I felt my own power flicker out the moment I landed on the ledge, and it wouldn't return until the dirty business was done and I'd flown high enough to clear the witch runes.

The few prisoners I passed shrunk deeper into their pens. They could probably feel the rage rippling from me and didn't want to be on the receiving end of my bad fucking mood.

Smart on their parts.

I'd kill them all, eventually. These dungeons were merely holding cells while trials played out, and these prisoners all had death sentences hanging over their heads for different heinous crimes.

As I approached the last pen in the row, Sparrow crossed her arms and glared into Adara's cell, barely acknowledging me as I strode up to the bars separating us from my twin.

To my bitter satisfaction, Adara looked worse than the last time I visited her. Her ice-white hair lay limp and matted down her back, her pallor matching the grey stones against the wall. The spells she used had fed from her life force, and even though we were the same age, her face was etched with the beginnings of fine lines around her mouth and forehead.

Lands of magic bestowed lasting effects on the beings that lived upon the hallowed soil. Fae could live for easily a thousand years. Gargoyles aged similarly. Humans could reach a couple hundred years old before they began aging past their adult prime, though the last Oracle had made it to eight hundred before his untimely death. I was a few months shy of turning one hundred – though without the horns and wings I'd pass in the Slate Kingdom for a female in her early thirties according to Lenna. Adara now looked as if she'd be a couple years older than me if we lived in a land without magic.

Adara and I received our *acatis* within months of each other at twenty-three. She'd gotten hers first - lording it over me until my *acat* manifested from the tips of my fingers to the top of my upper arm. That shut up her goading, since Beyos, the God of the Ocean, only gifted her a thin wave pattern that curled around her shoulder.

*Thanks, Phades.*

I flicked my eyes across Adara's wings, a lump forming in my throat as my mind remembered my mother's white wings. Though Adara inherited my mother's coloring, her wings were now soot covered and irrevocably cracked along the boning - a nasty side effect from her spell enhanced Sentry form that wreaked havoc on the Opal Palace's throne room.

Forcing me to add *remodeling* to the already long list of shit I had to do.

I didn't know if she could fly anymore with the amount of damage along the bone structure.

I didn't care.

Adara sat ram rod straight against the small cot in the cell, a prissy frown on her face. As if she summoned *me* to *her* throne room.

"Is she talking?" I asked Sparrow, surveying the accommodations of the cell. The narrow cot was hard, the bucket in the corner was empty, and the metal plate with Adara's meal for the day lay picked over in the corner.

"Just the usual shit she spews," Sparow muttered.

"I met some of your friends," I purred, directing my attention to my twin who scowled as I fluffed the bloodied skirts of my dress. "They say '*Hi*' and hope you're doing well."

Adara took in my blood covered dress before tossing a strand of dirty hair over her shoulder. "Must have been a nice distraction from your boring duties as Queen." Adara's voice cracked, barely louder than a whisper.

I shrugged. "They seem to think *you* should be Queen, so I set them straight."

Sparrow growled, her fangs catching the light of her torch. "What'd you do to their magic, Adara?"

Adara cocked her head at me, giving me a knowing look.

"Nothing they didn't want." She let out a dry chuckle, busying herself with her nails, as if they were immaculate and clean and not cracked and dirty. "They wanted a purpose, wanted power. I gave that to them."

"Who were they?" I tried to keep my voice uninterested, as if it didn't matter to me if I knew them or not. If Adara knew how badly I needed this information, she'd refuse to answer. I had to stay civil – even though I wanted nothing more than to add her blood to the conglomeration on my ruined dress.

"No one important." Her lips tipped up into a serpentine smile, her destroyed wings tightening against her back. "I gifted them what they so *desperately* desired. You can too, sister. With the book. All dying are not yet dead."

Sparrow took a step closer to the bars. "What does that mean?"

Adara watched her carefully, her dull blue-grey eyes sparking at the question. "It means what it means. If you're dying, you aren't dead - *yet*." She jerked her head towards me, her opal horns glimmering in the flickering torchlight. With a scoff she added, "Esmeray should know *all* about that from Phades."

"I'm not having conversations with the fucking Goddess of Death, Adara," I grumbled, gritting my teeth as Adara smirked. *Fuck.* I slowly took a deep breath, forcing my face back into mild boredom.

"Not *yet*," Adara corrected pointedly, drawing out the words for emphasis, "but soon, I'm sure."

"How many friends do you have?"

Adara's smirk turned into a feral grin. She dusted off the cotton slip that covered her body. "More than you think." Adara laughed, "Turns out, I was pretty popular as Queen. And they'll come see you when the time is right."

A thought dawned on me that made my blood cool in my veins. We'd been trying to track down the missing beings that disappeared under Adara's cruel reign for months now, with no solid leads.

*Could the beings from the woods be those lost townsfolks?*

I didn't know how to broach the subject with Adara, there'd been *hundreds* that went missing - but there were only twenty in the woods. Nothing connected Adara to the disappearances besides my own paranoia and speculations.

Sparrow moved away from the cell. Down here, with magic stifled, our rings didn't work. Under her breath, Sparrow rasped, "Why do they want the Oracle?"

"Why did your friends want the Oracle?" I asked louder, echoing Sparrow's question directly to Adara.

"Why does anyone want anything? If it's not knowledge, its riches, if it's not riches, its power, if it's not power then – maybe notoriety? It's not like I can rule over anyone from down *here*." She gestured around her with a flippant wave of her hand.

"And?"

"And nothing, do what you want, Esmeray, but hear the words not being said. If the veil ripples enough, more will be revealed." With a placating sigh, as if I was irritating her, Adara rubbed her temple. "The power that could be wielded...rivals the gods themselves. It's all in the book."

*That fucking spell book.*

As if it could feel Adara's presence, the book flinched in my pocket of space, shooting a worried tremor through my mind. I clamped my teeth together, ignoring its reaction. Without breaking Adara's dead-eyed stare, I spoke to Sparrow, "Let's get out of here, we don't need to entertain this bullshit."

Not needing to be told twice, Sparrow gripped her torch and began picking her way out of the cavern, aiming for the thin air beyond the ledge where her magic would work again and she could wane.

I didn't acknowledge Adara as I turned to follow suit and get the fuck out of here. Before I turned the corner, Adara whispered coyly, "Next time, send Keerian to visit me."

"I can't *wait* to kill you," I hissed back. Adara merely laughed.

With my fingernails digging into my fists, and murderous intent hum-ming through my mind, I stormed out of the dungeons.

# CHAPTER FOURTEEN
## LENNA

ESMERAY'S LIPS CURLED WITH disgust as she dumped the spell book unceremoniously onto the mahogany desk in the King's chambers. Lenna recoiled as the weight hit the wood with a *thud*, disrupting a thin layer of dust that puffed into the air – as if even the small particles felt the wrongness vibrating off the book and sought to escape.

The Queen's abhorrence of the spell book went unnoticed to Hale as he fished a thin wire with a monocle attached to the end from his deep blue vest. Lenna couldn't help her cheeky smile as Hale's moustache twitched, his amber eyes sparkling with a curiously analytical gaze.

Hale exhaled an excited breath. "I've done a bit of research on this cover and the binding techniques. If it did come from Larimar, as the spell you showed me led me to believe, it would have been ancient even to my ancestors' standards."

"Great," Esmeray replied flatly.

With heritage ties to the Larimar Islands, Hale learned about the intricacies of spell work from his late father. Though spells were outlawed centuries ago, Hale's father came from a lineage of fae, the M'ghoen, that held a secondary power – a heritage magic - from the God of Riddles, Eek, to decode the intentions of a written spell. His father taught him how to read multiple dead languages, unravel meanings behind com-plex spell wording, and gave Hale an uncut history lesson on the forbidden magic.

Lenna wondered if Hale inherited that heritage power himself. Though he was half-fae, Hale had no *acat* nor battle magic - even though the baker could squint over a book written in a dead lan-guage, and have an alphabet deciphered in a fortnight. If he did receive a heritage gift from his bloodline, he wouldn't have an *acat* anyway, but Hale always cheerily said he'd lived as a half-fae with no magic his whole life and was at peace with the fact that there were no gifts in his blood.

Lenna called his talent magic.

Hale simply called it pattern recognition.

But she thought he was just being humble.

Esmeray was now wearing a delightful burgundy velvet gown with gold chains wrapping around her waist, thankfully changing from the bloody dress she wore prior. An unadorned, gold band occupied the space between her curled horns, a much simpler crown than Lenna was used to seeing Esmeray wear.

"We can't destroy it yet," Esmeray admitted through gritted teeth, like the proclamation physically pained her. "After speaking with Adara, whatever happened to those beings in the woods to warp their magic was a trick she learned from the spell book. I need you to switch your focus to translating it instead."

With an expert eye, Hale gingerly tapped the top of the book with his quill, visibly relaxing when nothing traumatic or earth shattering happened. Esmeray added darkly, "The book loves attention, and acts...sentient. It has its own well of magic inside it."

Hale frowned, shooting the book a disbelieving glance. He stroked a hand down his beard, a calculating look replacing the bright demeanor he'd exhibited just moments ago.

Lenna glanced warily at the spell book, as if it would spring to life and snap its heavy covers at her fingers. But it lay harmless against the desk. The black and gold cover was immaculate for being as old as Hale guessed it was, and the pages were crisp and thick. On the cover, in a language Lenna had never seen before, was an assortment of oddly shaped symbols.

Hale peered closer at the cover, his monocle glinting in the faint candlelight of their accommodations. "This language is *ancient*. And by my guess, based off the protection runes on the edges, completely forgotten. It will take some time to figure out the exact age and dialect if my assumptions of Larimar Islands is...correct." He tapped a finger against the cover, his thick brows furrowing.

Unperturbed, Esmeray shrugged, wiping the cover off from any nonexistent dust that may have clung to the book. She seemed to linger a beat before delicately clearing her throat. "The library in the Obsidian Palace is the second largest in Irridessen, with shelves of books travelling from the main library all the way down into the catacombs of the mountain. You have my permission to use the library as you see fit."

Hale bounced his head, too focused on the new challenge of interpreting the book, and not merely destroying it, to do much more than half-listen to Esmeray. Lenna could see the glint of mystery in his eye, a look she'd become accustomed to after long nights watching Hale poke through old tomes on forgotten languages and races. The victory in unravelling this book's secrets might be Hale's newest fascination.

Lenna patted his back, bringing Hale out of his churning mind and into the present, where the Queen Absolute watched him with a blank expression. "We'll start going through the library to see if we can find anything similar to this language," Lenna said. Watching Hale interpret ancient scrolls and texts for clients, and keeping him company as he translated, had some of his responses rubbing off on her.

Hale typically only deciphered crudely written family recipes, or translated an old journal to find where ancestral treasure was buried. This, in comparison, would be Hale's glorious conquest.

If the book in questions hadn't already corrupted a Princess, murdered gods knew how many beings with dark, forbidden magic, and was indirectly responsible for the deaths of the Late King and Queen.... Lenna may have even thought translating the book would be...fun.

There was definitely something wrong with her.

# CHAPTER FIFTEEN
# SPARROW

Esmeray launched through the rippling glass floor a beat behind Sparrow, a silent, seething fury etched along her face. Sparrow knew there were a hundred dismal thoughts racing through Esmeray's mind, but as she moved towards her best friend, Esmeray snapped her wings shut, free-falling for a blink, before waning from the throne room.

Sparrow sighed through her teeth as the golden light faded, her shoulders slumping forward. Turning her face to the high ceiling, she inhaled a slow, steadying breath, knowing on an intrinsic level where Esmeray was headed. It was the same place she hid when she was younger - a quiet spot away from the bustle of court. With her own mind buzzing grimly, Sparrow twisted her body, waning in a burst of green to follow the Queen to the sanctuary high up in the Palace's spires.

This late, the stars overtook the sky, dotting the darkness with twinkling light. The full moon was half obscured by rolling black clouds that slowly snaked past the tower. Crisp mountain air and the spice of straw filled Sparrow's nose as she appeared high up in the aerie where the Moon Crows lived.

Esmeray stood with her back to Sparrow against the open ledge. Her wings drooped behind her, mere inches from the hay strewn floor, as she leaned a hip against the opening.

"Talk to me, Meer," Sparrow said gently as she approached Esmeray, feeling grief and frustration roll off the Queen, tinging the air.

"What am I doing, Spar?" Esmeray asked quietly. The words were almost lost in the wind whipping past them.

"Your best. You are doing *your best* against shitty circumstances."

Esmeray shook her head, turning to face Sparrow fully. Sparrow noted the heaviness in Esmeray's eyes – sadness and angst. So typically hidden behind a mask of confidence and power. "Adara needs to die. And it needs to be me that does it. But she's my sister..." Emeray trailed off, turning again to stare blankly out to the mountain peaks. "I'm afraid the beings that went missing willingly left their homes to follow Adara, and that's dangerous. It means she still maintains allies."

Esmeray pinned her gaze, brimming with uncertainty, on Sparrow. "The council won't look into it. Trust me - I've tried allocating forces to investigate. They don't think Adara had anything to do with the disappearance of *hundreds* of citizens of Irridessen. But *something* is telling me it's her, and it might be my own biased bullshit, but I can't shake the growing dread that follows me. Like something terrible's coming."

Sparrow pursed her lips as she crossed the aerie, knowing all too well that sense of unease, that ill-boding feeling that something evil was heading their way. That presence she felt watching her seemed closer, though its intentions remained unclear. Careful to avoid stepping on the bedded down Moon Crows that served as messengers for Irridessen, she picked her way over to the ledge.

With a wingspan of more than six feet, and beaks longer than Sparrow's hand, the Moon Crows were menaces when bored - pure demons when pissed. Esmeray held a special connection with the beasties, and as children, Sparrow joined Esmeray in this very spot many nights to watch the clouds pass the open window, sitting amongst the Moon Crows in comfortable companionship. Sometimes they'd talk – about everything and nothing – sharing their dreams for the future and whispered gossip that traveled the Kingdom.

Other times, when life felt too heavy, they'd sit silently, cheeks stained with tear tracks, staring out towards the mountains hand-in-hand.

Sparrow tucked her skirt around herself, settling down in the hay, and dangling her legs off the ledge. Esmeray joined her, and the two quietly watched the clouds drift in front of the moon. It wasn't until the moon's silvery glow peeked out once more that Sparrow finally spoke, her voice raw.

"I'll tell you this story again," she started, as Esmeray leaned her head against Sparrow's shoulder, careful not to poke her horn into Sparrow's neck. "My twin, my Briar, joined Minmere on a night like this one. When the sky felt old, and the moon full."

Speaking about her own twin's death was a story Sparrow rarely shared.

Grief was a fickle thing. Some days it was manageable, curled up in the corner of her mind, an echo of a different life - a different time. Other days, it dug deep and refused to let go. When those talons sunk in, giving life and words to the pain helped soothe the knife sharp agony.

Briar and Sparrow were born a year before Esmeray and Adara, to the Duke and Duchess of Baryte who'd left the Opal Court to raise their faelings in the remote forests dotting Baryte Hills.

Sparrow wrapped her fingers through Esmeray's. "Our parents forbade us from straying into the woods, but Briar and I were young, enthralled by nature. The urge to explore overrode their warnings."

Sparrow swallowed, and Esmeray squeezed her hand. Sparrow had only told Esmeray this story twice before – and both times Esmeray listened silent and intently as Sparrow got the words out.

Grief still thrummed inside Sparrow ninety years later. A part of her soul would always yearn for Briar. Sparrow and Briar were identical, connected on such a deep level that they used to joke that they could read each other's minds. Even her parents had a difficult time telling the twins apart when sleep deprived or glancing too quickly.

"When the sun started sinking, we realized how far into the forest we'd walked. I was scared that we were lost - that no one would find us." Sparrow shifted. "We found an old trail through mangled brush, and after Briar leapt over the last patch of brambles, she turned to help me jump it. I didn't want to because I was afraid the thorns would rip my new dress. But Briar insisted she could see the smoke plume from our chimney, and that she'd help me sew my dress if it got a hole in it. Finally, I reached for her. But when Briar leaned over the top of the bush to grab my hand, she accidentally pricked her finger on a purple thorn."

Esmeray hummed quietly. In response, two beady eyes cracked open, and Sparrow's lap was taken over by a particularly fat Moon Crow. Sparrow absentmindedly stroked the soft feathers of the beastie, tracing the stark white crescent on the top of its head. "I felt it," she whispered. "When Briar was poked. It felt like the thorn stuck me as well. The spark of pain was so unexpected I cried out. Our father came running, and he found me on one side of the thorn patch, Briar on the other. The look on his face when he saw the thorns...Briar's blood...it haunts me to this day. He collected Briar in his arms and roared at me to stay where I was. I'd never seen him move so fast."

Choking up, Sparrow grew silent. It was another moment before she fought through the urge to stop speaking. "Night had fallen by the time my father came and lifted me over the brambles. I asked where Briar was, and he began weeping. I was too young to understand why. I kept thinking...*It was one tiny poke of a thorn.*"

"Martyrshade," Esmeray whispered, naming the toxic vine that grew from cursed land. In small doses, one poke could put a full grown fae in a deep sleep for one hundred years. In bigger doses, or for a faeling with no activated *acat* to counteract the poison, it was a death sentence. Due to the curse that grew Martyrshade, the only way to get rid of its effects was to have another being suck the poison out of the wound - but they'd die immediately when the tainted blood hit their tongue.

Making them a martyr.

The Moon Crow let out a throaty *harrumph* when Sparrow's hand paused, an idea slamming into her mind. "*Meer,*" Sparrow hissed, "*Martyrshade.* If the right dose was given to a being with a fully activated *acat* it wouldn't kill them – it'd just put them to sleep. If it was given to Adara, she'd sleep for a hundred years. And when she awoke...maybe the effects of the spell book would've worn off."

Esmeray blinked slowly. But Sparrow's mind churned with the notion. Adara couldn't stay locked up forever - Esmeray's advisors demanded her execution, and Esmeray couldn't stall them forever.

"It's an idea," Esmeray said carefully, her lips turning down as her eyes took on that far-away look Sparrow was becoming so used to seeing.

Recognizing that no more pets were being given out, the Moon Crow hopped off Sparrow's lap with another croak, ruffling blue-black feathers in indignation before nestling down into its straw bedding.

Esmeray tilted her head, and Sparrow could almost see the thoughts streaming through her mind at breakneck speed. "Keep telling Briar's story," the Queen murmured softly.

Sparrow lowered her chin in recognition of Esmeray changing the subject.

"There were no magically gifted healers near us. My parents were mated - if one of them sucked out the poison, they'd both die – leaving Briar and me alone. We were barely ten. We wouldn't have survived alone, and even if the poison had been sucked out, Briar succumbed to the Martyrshade quickly. She would've died anyway. My mother was a healer, but her gifts couldn't heal away a curse. She was barely gifted enough to set a broken bone," Sparrow added bitterly, glancing sidelong at Esmeray, who stared out to the mountains beyond, a tear brimming at the corner of her eye.

"My parents knew Briar wouldn't make it through the night. They bought me to her so I could say good-bye. I slid my hand into Briar's, and felt a searing, ice cold pain lance through me. I screamed and tried to pull away, but I couldn't – it felt like being struck by lightning. My father ripped my hand from hers – and then...she was gone."

"And you have no idea what happened?" Esmeray asked, as she always did, while lowering her eyes and touching her forehead. A gesture of respect for the dead.

"No, I don't know where that spark of pain came from. My mother believed I felt her pass because we were twins and shared a special connection." Sparrow never had a good relationship with her parents, and it eroded further once she received her *acat* and it didn't align with her family's gifts of healing, nor was her battle magic the same color as either parent.

"Gods," Esmeray breathed, laying back in the hay and earning a screech of outrage from one of the Moon Crows who scooted out of her way before hopping on her outstretched black wing to snuggle into her body heat. "This is so fucked up."

"Tell me about it," Sparrow grumbled before leaning back herself, so similar to how they used to sit up here as children - laid down with the Moon Crows, legs dangling off the side of the spire.

Following Briar's death, Sparrow's parents moved into the Opal Palace at the behest of Queen Elera who was close with Sparrow's mother and joined her friend in grieving.

And so, Sparrow met Esmeray and Adara, and her parents became an integral part of the Irridessen Court before Sparrow's *acat* manifested and everything went to shit.

# CHAPTER SIXTEEN
# ESMERAY

SPARROW HAD GIVEN ME a lot to think about. I wanted nothing more than to crawl into bed with my mate, but there was one thing I needed to do before I'd allow myself to sleep.

It was easy to track down Collette, since this time of night she was usually pouring over some borderline illegal concoction in the Healer's Quarters. Exactly as I figured, I strode into her office to find her peering into a vile looking jar of green liquid.

"That color immediately makes me think you're playing with poisons again, Collette," I crooned in lieu of a greeting.

The fae didn't even blink as she methodically dripped a silver-hued liquid from a thin glass dropper, screwing a cap onto the jar and giving it a shake. "This is potentially an antidote to WingRot. Or, I just created a deadlier toxin." She shrugged, as if either result was fine by her. "I'll know in a few days."

I sat on the edge of her desk, eyeing the vial with a grimace. WingRot derived from a nasty berry that grew around swamps. It paralyzed and broke down the muscle mass in a gargoyle's wing within minutes, leaving them permanently disfigured.

But if anyone could come up with an antidote, it was Collette.

After she patched me up and fixed my broken wing from my battle with Adara, I'd promoted the fae to Elite Healer of the Obsidian Kingdom. She deserved it long before I came to rule, but was content to stay in her former auxiliary position - the second most powerful rank any healer could hold - until I came to power, that is.

Unfortunately, the previous Elite Healer hadn't survived Lord Magnamus's brief reign as Regent, making the position glaringly vacant when I took my rightful Queenship.

Fortunately, I had the perfect female in mind for the job. I didn't interview anyone else, simply pulled Collette aside and asked what I needed to give her for her to accept.

An iron-clad amnesty to purchase whatever illegal poisons she wanted, and a ridiculous amount of coins later, I had an Elite Healer.

"What do you need, Esmeray?" Collette asked, barely breaking away from her putrid jar to glance at me.

"What do you know about Martyrshade?" I watched the deadly contents in the jar begin to glow. Collette snorted like the question offended her, jotting something down in a notepad.

"What do you *want* to know about Martyrshade?" Collette challenged, her short copper hair swinging as she carefully moved the jar onto a shelf behind her with other, most likely illegal, home brews sitting in an array of different sized bottles.

"Is it true if a being had an activated *acat* it wouldn't kill them — just put them in a dreamless sleep?"

Collette raised a perfectly arched brow before settling down in her chair and bracing her hands against her desk. "Are you asking in terms of delaying the inevitable with Adara? Or is someone annoying your Queenliness?"

I rolled my eyes as Collette slashed me a grin. We held an easy friendship between us because she never shied away from hard questions. Or dirty work. After Sparrow left the Opal Palace, Collette and I grew close. "Sparrow bought it up as an alternative for Adara."

"Technically, if the correct dosage of Martyrshade was given, it would be *possible* to put her into a dreamless sleep. But her utilizing that spell book...It's a risk since we don't know how the Martyrshade would react." Collette wrinkled her pert nose, muttering under her breath some sort of complex equation that made no sense to me. Clearing her throat, she said, "In my expert opinion, she'd die. The spell work ravaged her Sentry – that means those fractures run deep into her *acat*."

I let her words to sink in before I stood, giving myself a moment to mourn the brief flicker of hope I'd allowed myself to have before burying it. "Thanks, Collette."

Collette frowned, concern flickering across her face. "I'm always happy to help, my Queen."

The jar on the shelf fizzed and popped, causing us both to startle. Collette snarled a particularly filthy curse, whirling toward the shelf and snapping her fingers. Within seconds, the vivid green contents froze solid.

"Handy," I smirked as I opened the door. "Good to know you can do that."

"Good night, Esmeray," Collette drawled pointedly, flicking her hand again to shut the door in my face.

As I waned into the empty Queen's chambers, I sighed and rubbed my finger over the black onyx on my ring.

*"Are you ok?"*

*"Hi, love, yes – we're fine."* Keerian's deep voice instantly put me at ease. *"Laurent and I are going over trainings with the Queen's Guard. I'll be up soon."*

*"Okay, I love you."*

Keerian wouldn't come to bed if there was even whiff of a threat pointed towards me.

*"I love you, horns and all. Now, go to bed. Your King demands it."*

*"King Consort,"* I replied smoothly, *"Don't get a big ego, darling."*

His chuckle swam down our shared mind connection before fading, and I couldn't help the smile that tugged at the corners of my lips.

Feeling a bit of the weight disappear off my shoulders, I did just that, crawling into our bed and curling up onto my side, tucking my wings around me. Tomorrow could wait for a few more hours.

Sleep took me minutes later.

# CHAPTER SEVENTEEN
## ORLA

THE SHEER CURTAINS, WHILE beautiful and aesthetically pleasing, did absolutely nothing to combat the morning light streaming into the bedroom.

Orla groaned against the satin covered pillowcase, rolling onto her stomach to search for any small corners of darkness to lull her back to sleep for a few more minutes. Her new dwellings faced outwards and east, over the sprawling oasis, which meant all the sunrises she blissfully avoided while residing on the sea facing, west side of the Palace, were now cheerily aimed directly at her bed.

Giving up on sleep altogether as the continuous burn began simmering in her throat, Orla twisted onto her back, fisting her hands into the sheets before staring up at the ceiling. With a sigh, she sat up, swinging her legs off the side of the bed.

Her feet only *just* touched the floor when, with a soft *poof*, a silver encrusted tray appeared on the desk. Orla stilled, casting her eyes to the door with her breath held, straining to pick up any noises from the hallway. Hearing nothing, she took a tentative step towards the tray, spying a flaky biscuit, a side of jam, and a rolled-up scroll wrapped closed with a gold chain attached to a ruby necklace.

Simple and exquisite, with a single pear-shaped gem the size of her thumbnail, the necklace felt warm in her hands as she unraveled it from the parchment.

The handwritten note inside was short and unsigned, though Orla had a good idea who it was from.

*Your first day of work will begin at noon.*

*Wear the necklace.*

*Do not be late.*

With the painful burn weaving through her, Orla rubbed her chest, her fingers prickling with a needle-like sensation.

Deciding to bathe in the coldest water the Palace's innovative pipe system could muster to combat her feverish skin, Orla held the biscuit between her teeth, snatched the jam jar off the tray, and disappeared into her bathroom. All she wanted was to take a hot bath, but the damning burn that seemed to build in intensity under her skin had other ideas - so cold water would do.

As much of an annoyance it was to wake up early, Orla relished the extra time. Between choosing an outfit, and regaining control over her hair, she'd only just finished lacing her new brown leather boots when a knock on the door broke the silence. She looked up, expecting Marlo's lanky frame to be standing there.

But there was Soren standing on the threshold, with a slight frown on her face, dressed in a muted orange gown that twisted around her throat and trailed down her hips in an intricate design.

"I'm here to escort you to the council area." Soren blinked, her icy demeanor falling away as she took in Orla's outfit. "You're wearing *that?*"

Orla narrowed her eyes at what Soren was saying-not-saying.

"What's wrong with my outfit?" Orla asked with a deadly calm, sweeping a hand down the deep blue dress, the long satin sleeves swishing with the movement.

Soren rolled her eyes, gracefully stepping around Orla and through her door. She stopped dead in the middle of the room, assessing the mess Orla made that morning while trying to choose an outfit. "Gods above."

*"Excuse me?"* Orla felt that burning wrath ricochet to the surface as the fae surveyed the disaster of clothes that covered all of the bed, the chaise, and the chair by the desk.

Sure, she tried on every dress in the closet to figure out what to wear for her first day working for Cillian. Most of the gowns were in the same style she saw the court wear, with cutouts along the sides and slits in the legs, low cut, and astronomically more scandalous than anything Orla ever wore in the Slate Kingdom.

"Well, first of all, you are *excused* because I am going to take this -" Soren gestured dramatically to Orla's dress, "- as a lapse in sound judgement. This is a winter gown for winter solstice, *not* a day-to-day dress you wear on a whim."

The blue dress had long sleeves that tapered into embellished cuffs at her wrists and fanned out to her ankles. It seemed modest and professional for any meetings with the royal council. But as she peered closely...Okay, the beading *may* have been threaded and arranged to look like falling snowflakes.

Orla swallowed, the fire inside her banking as frustration welled up in her, annoyingly turning into a sheen of tears gathering at the corner of her eyes. She exhaled a shaky breath. *No weakness.* Soren's face softened a fraction, and she blew out a soft curse. "Let's start over. Can I help you find something to wear today?"

Orla wasn't sure if it was the *way* she said it, or if she was just that fucking desperate to feel like her world wasn't entirely fucked off its axis, but she felt the burn in her chest ease.

Soren gave her a small smile, showcasing the tips of her pointed canines cased in gold. With a snap of her fingers, all the disorderly clothes came to life, flying on their own accord to shuffle neatly back to the armoire.

Orla's eyes widened as she took in the now spotless bedroom. Seeing someone use their *acat* made her wary, and her mind still scrambled to come to terms with her new reality. And now, Soren's legs were on show through the slits in her gown, showing off a golden tan and lack of tattoos. No *acat* there.

Without waiting for a response, Soren cocked her head, her blonde hair woven into a single, thick braid. She glanced at the weather outside and chose a flowy burgundy dress with lace capped sleeves. It was a bit scandalous, but instead of twisting fabric exposing her middle, it ruffled around the waist before relaxing out through the skirts. "Wear this with the necklace," Soren demanded before turning on her heel and stepping out of the room, giving Orla privacy to change.

Orla pulled the dress on, before picking up the necklace and inspecting it again. "Soren?" she called, not even sure if the fae was still outside her door.

Soren reappeared, clicking her tongue in approval as she gave Orla a once over. "Much better."

"Did Prince Cillian give me this?" Orla asked, holding the ruby up to the light.

Soren raised her brow, giving her a look that screamed, *"Yes, obviously."*

"Why would Cillian give me a necklace? What does it mean?"

"Why do males ever give females jewelry?" Soren laughed, "You've caused quite a stir with your arrival, Orla Grey. Cillian's attention was merely captured first."

Orla felt herself tentatively relax, before the dam in her mind broke and all of her unanswered questions came tumbling out.

"Am I really fae? Why did Cillian want me to be his cupbearer? What am I supposed to even do for that? Is he-" Soren held up a hand, and Orla trailed off, wincing as a new wave of burning coated her throat.

"Until you get an *acat* you won't know for sure. Some half-fae never receive magic." Soren chewed her lip. "It depends on your heritage and a bunch of inherited traits that are stupidly boring to read about. But I've never seen Di-...Cillian's advisor lie about someone's lineage. Or be wrong, for that matter." As Soren talked, she steered Orla from the room, swiping her copper key off the small hook by the door as she went.

Before they made it to the hallway, Soren pulled Orla around to look at her, her tone lowering to a whisper. "Orla, no matter what happens, remember that Cillian isn't his father. There's definitely an arrogant streak there, but Cillian isn't cruel."

Orla opened her mouth to ask about the King and why he was cruel, but Soren shot her a look that said, *"do* not *ask what I know you're about to ask me."*

"*And,*" Soren nodded once, as Orla clamped her lips together. "Beings normally beg for the honor to be Cillian's cupbearer. I don't know what angle he's playing by giving the position to you. He asked me to keep an eye on you, and I owe Cillian a lot, but I'm not privy to the workings of his mind."

"Are you and Cillian..." The words were out of Orla's mouth the second the little flame of jealousy skittered into her head.

Soren threw back her head and let out a smoky laugh, her bronzy eyes sparkling. "*Goddess*, no. There's no intimacy between Cillian and I." Still chuckling, she wove her arm through Orla's, the two of them traipsing down the hall together.

Orla's mind spun to figure out Soren's angle. When she'd first met the fae, Soren gave off a cutting, hostile aura– but now they were chatting as if they were...friendly?

With an inward wince, Orla realized that Soren's original attitude may have been a direct response to Orla's own snappish defiance, and a sheen of guilt rumbled through her.

"Cillian and I grew up together," Soren explained lightly, "He's one of my best friends – even though he can be the most infuriating being at times."

They lapsed into a comfortable silence as they passed a group of fae going in the opposite direction, all wearing the matching ruby colored tunic and pants signifying their status as servants.

Orla squinted after them, a new thought floating into her mind. She wore a gown, not the typical attire of one in a serving position. "I'm not a servant here, am I?"

Soren only gave her a knowing grin.

"And neither are you," Orla finished.

"Nope," Soren said the word cheerily, her lips tipping up in a smirk as they approached a set of closed, wooden doors with ruby studded door handles, leaving Orla, once again, with more questions than answers.

# Chapter Eighteen
## ORLA

Orla could make out the sounds of multiple beings scraping chairs, loudly talking over each other, on the other side of the doors.

Soren gestured to the smaller entrance next to the council room. "This is the servant's pantry. Nonna's the Chamber Mother, and she'll fill you in on your tasks. Word of advice - don't piss her off, or your next job might be cleaning out horse troughs."

With that, Soren turned on her heel, heading down another corridor that branched off from where they'd been standing.

Orla swallowed tightly before entering the massive room. Platters of vegetables, salted meats, and flagons of wine sat on three marble countertops running the full length of the walls. A handful of beings, some in servant's attire, some not, bustled around the room. The organized chaos thrummed with life, a commonality to all the serving positions she'd held over the years.

Taking a deep breath, Orla plastered a smile on her face before spotting and approaching the Chamber Mother. She'd worked in multiple manors, under countless hand matrons and house mothers. A sense of relief settled over her. This was just another assignment.

"Orla Grey." Nonna turned to peer at Orla from behind thick glasses that made her brown eyes look twice as large. Deep wrinkles creased around her forehead, and her white-grey hair was arranged in a tight top knot at the base of her spine. Her skin was leathery, pockmarked with little brown age spots but the terse look on her face spoke to a lifetime of hard work and a no-bullshit attitude. "Glad you made it on time."

Orla bowed her head, hunkering her shoulders slightly, slipping back into the role of submission that she'd played hundreds of times. Meek, normal, servant girl here to work hard and cause no problems.

"Eyes up," Nonna snapped, causing Orla to flinch. "You aren't fooling anyone with that act. I've been on this earth for five hundred years and all you fae are the same." Nonna shoved a small, circular tray into Orla's hands before turning to snatch a golden goblet off the countertop. "Simpering fools," she huffed under her breath, "You will not go into that council room all doe-eyed and ditzy. If you can't grow a backbone, you're better off selling trinkets in the bazaar."

Taken aback by the abrupt tone, Orla instinctively stood her ground, barbed words eagerly spilling off her tongue. "I just found out I have fae blood yesterday," Orla shot back to the Chamber Mother, readjusting her one-handed grip on the tray, and extending her hand for the goblet Nonna still held. "And I hope you can forgive my *simpering foolishness*, but I was told I have a job to do, and I'm here to do it."

Nonna chuffed, handing over the goblet, as if Orla passed some sort of test. "Don't lose your head in there, fae girl. Good help is hard to find."

Orla glared at the older being, though a glimmer of respect eked through her. Nonna looked fully human, but an *otherness* swirled around her, something that Orla couldn't interpret. Nonna grunted in approval as Orla expertly balanced the goblet on the tray, before shoo-ing her towards the fae pouring wine for each advisor.

"Name," the bored sounding servant asked as she approached.

"Orla Grey."

The fae huffed, "Not *your* name. The name of the advisor you're serving."

"Oh," Orla replied, "Prince Cillian."

The fae almost knocked a bottle of wine off the counter as he hastily wiped his hands on his linen apron. "Ah, the Prince's new cupbearer. You don't wait for me to pour his Highness's wine. You do that yourself. Over there."

He pointed to a small alcove tucked into the corner where a sheen of what Orla assumed to be magic separated a few shelves of wine from the rest of the collection on the countertops. "As long as the Prince already keyed your essence into his magic, you can go through the barrier and pour the wine. The Prince put that barrier up himself to separate his wine from the King's."

Orla assessed the barrier with disdain as she approached. Yet another separation those with power lorded over those without. Magically protected wine bottles. Orla sighed through her nose and popped out her hip, a scowl marring her face as her eyes fell onto a familiar piece of parchment folded in front of the center bottle. It was too far away to read, especially with the shimmering magic billowing in front of her.

Realizing she had no clue how Cillian's magic would know to let her through, Orla adjusted her grip on the tray. If she slammed into the barrier, at least the tray wouldn't go clattering to the ground, and she'd just pour Cillian some of the regular wine that had been checked for poison and hope he didn't notice.

Taking a tentative step, she toed the barrier with her boot, relaxing as her foot passed through with ease. Letting out a hiss, she stepped through fully. The magic was warm, like being submerged in a nice bath.

She hoped the burning that finally disappeared from her ribs would stay away long enough for her to test out the glorious bathtub in her room with something other than ice water after this meeting. With a wistful sigh, Orla placed the tray on the small counter and ripped the note off the bottle.

*Glad you wore the necklace.*

Orla read the note twice before flipping it over, finding no other words on the back. Confused, she rubbed her fingers over the ruby pendant. Not knowing what type of weird power move Cillian was playing, she folded the thin parchment up into quarters before stuffing it in her pocket and grabbed the wine bottle the note had been resting against.

After crossing back through the barrier, Orla followed the other servants lining up at the entrance to the council room where Nonna surveyed each being before permitting them to enter the meeting.

Orla held the tray at chest level like she'd been taught as Nonna stomped down the line, stopping to scowl at a servant holding a tray of some sort of thin bread. "Stand up straight or I'll have you scooping pig shit for a month." The fae servant paled and fixed his posture. Nonna eyed him for another second before giving a curt nod, allowing the servant to enter the council meeting.

As Orla shuffled forward in line, Nonna gave her a cursory glance over, her withering stare steeling Orla's resolve to be such a good godsdamned cupbearer that the old hag would weep with wonder at her feet.

The Chamber Mother finally nodded, and Orla entered the council room.

# CHAPTER NINETEEN
## LENNA

LENNA WRAPPED THE THICK, woven blanket tighter around herself as another bluster of mountain chilled wind ruffled her hair. The Obsidian Palace was hauntingly beautiful, but Lenna knew her heart and soul yearned to be in Florra. Sitting against a plush chaise on the balcony that jutted from the King's chambers, she gazed out to the Zircon mountains, breathing in a lungful of fresh air.

The Prism of the Oracle had been down in the treasure troves beneath the Palace, and her first visit here was with the late Regent to request the artifact – ending with Esmeray barging into the throne room, learning dragons were very real, and securing the heavy stone used to look into the web of the past. She glanced over at the dull crystal cluster with a smile. The Prism was currently being used as a paperweight for the parchments Lenna and Hale wrote their notes on.

Sparrow waned to Florra to retrieve it the morning after the fight at the waterfall, and Lenna was relieved to have the Prism back in her hands. It was a part of her, a comforting weight that seemed to settle her soul.

Looking out to the mountains eye-level with herself, Lenna marveled at how high up she was. She wondered if the late Fae King ever felt uneasy being up here, even if his mate had wings. At least the floors were thick black stone - no unnerving glass in sight.

The silvery mist rolling through the peaks was mesmerizing to behold. It looked as if the mountains themselves were breathing deeply, expelling that shimmering fog from within their rocky lungs and pushing it down the scraggy terrain like fallen clouds. Lenna snuggled deeper into the chaise, feeling her eyelids grow heavy as the warm blanket and tranquil silence lured her to close her eyes. Hale had gone down to the library, and Lenna opted to stay in here, neither of them wanting to leave the spell book alone on the off chance someone tried to steal it.

Realizing a nap wasn't the best way to keep an eye out for thieves, she cleared her throat, shaking off the lure of drowsiness to get up and go check on the infernal book again.

Hale stuck it in a nightstand dresser, since there weren't too many places they could hide it in the already secure bedroom protected by the Queen's Guard. Lenna peeked into the drawer, confirmed the book hadn't sprouted legs and ran off, and decided to take up her post again on the balcony.

Her solitude was interrupted within minutes of her return to the outdoor chaise. Hale's booming voice carried down the halls as he chatted away merrily with the guard that escorted him to and from the expansive library in the Palace. A beat later, Lenna heard the doorknob to the King's chamber creak open and Hale's labored breathing as he lugged what sounded like half the library's collection into the room.

Hale dumped a stack of dusty books on the desk before laying a smacking kiss on top of Lenna's head. "I found some real ancient tomes we can go through," he said excitedly as he tugged Lenna up, carefully keeping her bundled in the warm blanket. Lenna smiled at the male, and Hale's eyes crinkled as he beamed back at her. His long locs were pulled back into a bun that displayed the slight points of his ears, one of the few fae traits Hale inherited from his father. Lenna thought he was utterly handsome. Every time he entered the room, she felt herself drawn to him, and wondered if Carra would ever bless them with a soul tie of their own.

This longing was a different type of ache that filled and numbed her chest. No longer were the pangs related to feeling alone, fueling a sense of desperation and recklessness that would coat her tongue like oil.

No. Now it was more of a...wildness that heated throughout her being, as if she was riding her horse at breakneck speed through a field, feeding that fire that spread and radiated through her bones and made her stomach drop. It made her giddy and lightheaded, a force of reckoning to compare to all of her new life's experiences. Around Hale, even the worry over her recurring headaches abated, the sense that something loomed in her mind an afterthought every time he stole her lips in a kiss.

"What did you find?" Lenna asked surveying the musty books on the desk. They were all thick, covered in dust, and smelled faintly like dirt. She wondered how old they were.

"I spoke to the scholars in the library, and was told they searched through the past thousand years to find mention of the spell book under the direction of Queen Elera but didn't find anything mentioning *this* book in particular. I decided to start *my* search much further back." Hale pulled out his monocle from the small pocket on his deep green vest. "Ten thousand years to be particular."

Lenna widened her eyes, staring at four books displayed on the top of the desk. "These books are ten thousand years old?"

Hale shrugged, pushing the cover open on the first. A spider skittered across the yellowed parchment. Lenna recoiled as Hale simply brushed the bug off the page and peered closer to the odd symbols stamped in the corners. "See these markings? They're similar to the ones on the spell book – only slight differences. It could be a sigil of protection magic that wore off over time."

The symbols were very similar, as Hale noted. Lenna absentmindedly traced one on the library book as Hale retrieved the spell book. She hadn't touched the spell book except to shove it back into the nightstand last night before they went to bed. It seemed oily in her hands. *Wrong.*

With a small notepad and quill, the two of them spent the next few hours scouring the library books for any similarities to the particular book radiating a threatening aura against the desk.

Lenna shuddered as the spell book gave off a pulse of irritation, jarring her teeth. She swallowed as her head began aching. "I'm going to put this back in the nightstand. I can't concentrate when it gets in this sort of hissy fit."

Hale looked up quizzically. "What?"

Glancing at the spell book laying on the desk, Hale squeezed his brows together, worry flitting into his expression. "What are you feeling?"

Dark spots wobbled into her vision, and she rubbed her sore temples, blinking the haze out of her eyes until her sight cleared. The book pulsed again, in time with the thudding in her head. Growling out a curse, Lenna stood to move the book into the nightstand. "Do you not feel that?" Her fingers closed around the cover. "It's like - "

The moment she touched the book, a high-pitched ringing slammed into her ears, and she stumbled, pain barreling through her head. Lenna took one single, wheezing breath and blacked out.

# CHAPTER TWENTY
# ORLA

THE COUNCIL ROOM QUICKLY grew boring as the meeting dragged on into the evening. Orla stood at her designated post behind Cillian, earning more than one scowl from the other fae in the room. She made sure to glare right back.

She didn't know what she expected from a magical council meeting, but this, in comparison, was ridiculously dull. Listening to advisors drone on and on about garden yields and trade figures made her practically fall asleep standing up. Cillian barely fared better, his eyes half lidded, lounging at the head of an oval table, in a chair that was more similar to a plush throne. Another stark divide from the narrow-backed wooden chairs the council sat upon.

It took an exorbitant amount of effort to stay alert and still, to keep an eye out for anyone who held ulterior motives without drawing unnecessary attention. She fought the smile off her face at the idea that she was earning her own money for the first time in her life – money Olivera couldn't steal under the guise of keeping it safe.

*I am not so easily broken.*

She kept that thought playing through her mind as she drew herself up taller. Though the clear divide between the rich and the poor irked her, she wanted to stay in a room that didn't face the water – the sea still held too many difficult memories of beasts and shipwrecks. The bathtub and the super comfortable bed were a huge bonus, too.

A mean-looking mountain of gargoyle, the Ruby Palace's Advisor of War, was currently rumbling about a disturbance in Irridessen, where a powerful Queen had taken over the entirety of the continent. Orla gathered from the bits of information that this was another magical land - but not one allied with the Ruby Kingdom.

"It is a *travesty*, your Highness," Lord Batair spat, his grey wings rustling as he slammed his hands against the birchwood tabletop. Cillian appraised the male with an impassive expression, his chin leaned in his hand, covering his mouth. "Irridessen's line of succession *clearly* stated one Princess would rule the Opal Kingdom, and the other, the Obsidian Kingdom. Our spies report Queen Esmeray has taken *both* and Queen Adara is locked in the dungeons under the Obsidian Palace."

"Did your *unsanctioned* spies tell you Queen Esmeray took over both thrones because her sister murdered King Scottrell and Queen Elera, and attempted to stage a coup to take Irridessen for *herself*?" Cillian cocked his head slightly, a few of his locs falling in front of his face, utterly unfazed by the Lord's temper. A smug smile twitched behind his fist. "Seems like Queen Absolute Esmeray completed what Adara failed to do."

"Spies?" The wiry blonde fae seated next to Lord Batair shot out of his seat, yellow magic simmering at his fingertips. "We *trade* with Irridessen you fucking oaf! Having spies in Irridessen negates *all* our trade deals for the coming winter!"

Orla gritted her teeth as Cillian nodded his head slightly, his gaze catching hers. The signal that he needed a refill of wine. Orla'd been relieved to learn the common, unspoken, mannerisms of serving translated easily between the Slate Kingdom and the Ruby Kingdom.

The fae and Lord Batair were in each other's face now, yellow magic zinging up the fae's arms. "Get your spies out of Irridessen immediately. If Queen Esmeray finds them, she'll *delight* in delivering them back to us piece by piece. Adara cut off our access to trade for the summer, and Queen Esmeray *just* reopened Irridessen's borders. Do *you* want to go another season without being able to pass a ship safely through Irridessen waters? The Larimar Islands give us our main supply of seeds and grain for the winter."

"We could go around the Slate Kingdom to Larimar-"

"Good luck with that," Cillian interrupted dryly, "That route takes twice as long, and your ships would be in the perfect position for the beasts on Dragon's Peak to intercept."

Orla silently slipped out of the council room, the commotion fading to a muffled din as the massive doors were shut by two guards. In the pantry, Cillian's magic barrier gave Orla the creeps as it caressed her face gently while she passed through. She didn't know if she'd ever feel comfortable around this much magic. Her palms prickled, leaving an ache in her fingers. She cracked her knuckles, trying to relieve the uncomfortable sensation.

Before she could grab the wine, a puff of smoke and a rolled up note appeared on the shelf in front of her. She grabbed it quickly, unrolling it before the smoke dissipated.

*Having fun yet? You look ravishing in that dress.*

Orla read the note twice, feeling heat rush into her face. Whatever Cillian was playing at, she wasn't going to be a simpering female in his game. He hired her to do a job, and she was determined to do a good one.

He wouldn't ever want her, truly fall for her, because she was only Orla Grey. The flirty note, the necklace, Cillian's random visits - it wasn't real attraction. It couldn't be.

He was the Crown Prince for an empire. He had an entire Kingdom of beautiful females to keep him company.

She refused to wind up in his bed as something to keep his mind off his duties.

She refused to be used and discarded by a male in power ever again.

But as she slid back through Cillian's barrier, she stuffed the note in her pocket.

"Unprecedented dragon activity has been reported north of Dragon's Peak. And there is confirmation of a new nest near Glimmer Lakes."

As Orla stepped back into the council room, a squat male with brilliantly red eyes and small grey horns was standing up at the far side of the table, a stack of parchment on the table in front of him. Orla's hands trembled at the mention of dragons, causing Cillian's goblet to shake slightly as she sat it on the tabletop. He shot her a questioning look, but she averted her eyes, shrinking back to the wall behind him, clasping her hands tightly behind her back.

Cillian shot her one more concerned look before turning his full attention back to the advisor. The Lord stuttered to a stop when Cillian cleared his throat; his panicked stare fixed on the Prince. "Do you know what species is moving north? Wyverns? Or plain, four legs, two wings, dragons? Are there eggs in the nest? Hatchlings? Was a mare spotted with it?"

The advisor hunched forward, swiping hastily through a few pieces of parchment, his red eyes darting across the pages before he swallowed and slumped back in his chair, taking a quick sip from his own wine glass. "The reports do not specify, your Highness."

Deafening silence fell across the council table. Orla took a calming breath, trying and failing to fight the shaking in her fingers, the ache in her palms intensifying into a sharp sting. She prayed she'd never see another beast like the dragon that shipwrecked her boat and killed Dollin and the ship's crew ever again.

The dragon's roar... the fire that ravaged their poor, wayward boat... the sheer size and aggression of the beast still haunted Orla's dreams.

Orla glanced at Lord Batair; his expression unreadable aside from a slight frown on his ruddy face. She turned her attention to the fae with the yellow magic. He sat back in his chair with his arms crossed, regarding the entire council room with unfiltered dislike. As if he felt the weight of her stare, he flicked his eyes up to her. Orla quickly looked away, focusing on the advisor who held Cillian's attention instead. He was sweating profusely, dabbing at his thick neck with the back of his sleeve.

She thought back to the questions she wanted to ask Cillian about each advisor, hoping that would help her get acquainted with who each one was. One meeting wasn't enough to decide who acted suspicious.

Cillian stood suddenly, the rest of the council scrambling up simultaneously before bowing low. He inclined his chin toward the end of the table. "Lord Anomar, be grateful my father wasn't here for your lackluster report. Next time, make sure you have all the information prior to bringing it to my attention."

The advisors stayed silent as Cillian picked up his goblet, languidly swirling his wine around as he met each of their eyes before stating, "Your King will be at the next council meeting. I suggest you all get your shit together prior to that. Dismissed."

A couple of the advisors paled at the announcement; Lord Anomar seemed to sweat even more. Only Lord Batair seemed unruffled as he shoved through the doors.

The council room emptied quickly, but when Orla moved away from the wall to begin clearing the table, Cillian placed his hand on her wrist. "Walk with me."

Before she could question it, he strode into the servant's pantry, weaving through the beings working, nodding acknowledgements to a few as they passed. He even winked at Nonna as the Chamber Mother noticed the Prince in the midst of the room. To Orla's shock, Nonna blushed, batting her hand at Cillian before turning back to bark at the beings washing dishes. Cillian slashed Orla a grin as they headed to the back wall of the pantry, where tall rows of shelves stacked with wine, jarred food, and linens stood tall.

Cillian turned, walking confidently down the aisle between the last two rows of shelves. Curious and a tad apprehensive, Orla hesitantly poked her head around the corner, finding Cillian standing in front of an old door at the end of the aisle, the threshold and part of the wall covered in the red sheen of his barricade magic.

Before Orla could ask where this led to, Cillian opened the door and gestured for Orla to pass through the magic. Curiosity won out, and Orla felt the warmth of Cillian's magic caress her gently as she stepped through and into a dark, empty hallway.

"Where are we?" Orla asked, as Cillian closed the door behind them, throwing them in darkness for a heartbeat before an orb of red light flared to life in his palm, bathing the bare, sandstone walls in an eerie glow.

"These are the old servant's corridors. But they haven't been used in centuries," Cillian explained, reaching back to grab her hand as they wound through the dusty hall. "The tunnel travels to the main entrance of Aridden and branches off back to the Royal Wing." Orla couldn't see his face, but the pressing shadows around them made her scalp tingle with nerves.

"I use them to avoid the inevitable mass of Lords in the hallway who are milling around to request a private word with me, trying to gain favor before having to deal with my Father." He let out a bitter scoff. "They think my words hold sway with King Eamon."

Orla craned her neck towards Cillian. "I thought being the very fancy royal Prince of the Ruby Kingdom was supposed to be illustriously wondrous."

Well, it's not," Cillian bit out, causing Orla to stiffen. He sighed, squeezing her hand gently before muttering, "I'm the Prince of a Kingdom ruled by a tyrant, with no power to enact real change."

They walked in silence. Cillian seemed lost in thought, and Orla became distinctly aware that if Cillian murdered her right here, no one would ever find her. Throw in the ominous light swathing the walls of the narrow corridor, Orla felt her stomach roil with a pang of fear, replaced quickly with the familiar burning sensation that spread up her throat and down her fingertips.

Cillian stopped abruptly, and Orla almost collided with his back. "Why don't you like dragons?" He turned to her, his handsome face distorted by the light he held. "Every time one of the advisors mentioned them, you looked as if you'd faint with fear."

Orla opened her mouth, before closing it again, feeling the sinking feeling of shame and loss ice down the fire in her veins. She didn't know those emotions passed over her face, nor that the Prince was paying such close attention to her. Cillian waited, neither of them moving, though their bodies stood mere inches from each other.

"A dragon attacked my ship," she admitted quietly, "I was on my way to a better life in a new city, and a dragon appeared in the middle of a storm. It destroyed our boat, and I got washed up on the shore of the Ruby Kingdom, badly injured. Marlo and I were the only two left alive from the attack."

Cillian leaned against the wall, crossing his arms as he asked, "Did you know any of the deceased?"

Orla shut out the memory of Dollin.

She hadn't seen him since they were young adults, when he begged her to leave Olivera and come live with him and his family. Gods, he had a younger sister. *Did his family know what happened? Did they think he was lost at sea? Did his sister wait for his return?* Orla swallowed against the lump in her throat. He'd helped her escape Doortan and ended up dead.

"My cousin, Dollin, was on that ship," she croaked, as tears began to cluster, threatening to fall. She cleared her throat delicately, trying to get the rush pinpricking her eyes to recede.

A single drop slipped down her cheek, only for Cillian to gently brush it away, the touch sending little zaps of lighting down her spine.

"I am truly sorry for your loss," Cillian responded, nodding once, and placing a fist over his heart.

Orla didn't know how to respond, so she bowed her head, turning away from his emotion packed gaze.

Cillian seemed to consider his next words carefully. "I want to show you something."

He guided her further down the hall, still gripping her hand in his.

They finally approached another narrow door, and Orla's heart beat faster as the sheen of red magic covering the threshold came into view. Whatever was behind this door was a carefully hidden secret held by the Prince.

Nerves kicking in, her teeth ached from how hard she clenched her jaw together. A sense of awareness prickled across her fingers, across her cheeks, the aching burn travelling from her lungs to her legs.

Cillian looked at her once more, something like guilt flashing across his face before he opened the door, tugging Orla through the barricade with him.

# CHAPTER TWENTY-ONE
## SPARROW

"Explain it to me like I wasn't there."

Sparrow paced across the King's Chamber, only halting briefly to straighten out the pot of a prickly leafed plant sitting on the desk. She hadn't stopped moving since throwing open the doors to find Hale trying desperately to wake an unconscious Lenna, surrounded by the Queen's Guards.

"You *weren't* there," Esmeray interjected pointedly, leaning against the desk at her side, her nails rapidly shrinking from the battle-ready daggers she waned in with. One of her Queen's Guards alerted her that something happened to Lenna. Esmeray appeared next to the bed ready for bloodletting against an invisible threat a split second later.

Sparrow shot the Queen a withering glare. "Humor me."

Hale tore his gaze from the sleeping form of Lenna tucked in bed. "She was telling me that the spell book was emitting some sort of negative energy, and that she was putting it back in the nightstand." Hale sniffed through his nose, loosening a weary sigh. "Lenna picked up the spell book and... fell to the ground...began seizing."

Sparrow shook her head, grimly looking over to the book still on the floor. "Then Lenna had a – a premonition?"

Hale slowly bobbed his head, thick moustache twitching. Apart from being the solely activated Oracle, Lenna was also blessed by the God of Sight, Moirai, with seer abilities. The Prism of the Oracle allowed her an unobstructed view of the past, but being a seer allowed her glimpses into the future, usually in the form of a confusing riddle.

Loud voices appeared on the other side of the door a moment before Laurent and Keerian burst into the room, the latter rushing over to the prone Lenna with a gruff curse.

"She's alright," Esmeray murmured to her mate. "Just sleeping now."

Sparrow was sure the first thing Esmeray did after waning in and assessing the situation was to notify Keerian that Lenna was fine, but she knew the legendary warrior loved Lenna fiercely and needed a bit more reassurance than a rushed, mind-spoken conversation.

"Was the healer here?" Keerian asked, ripping off his leather gloves to brush a massive, yet gentle, hand across Lenna's forehead, checking for any sign of fever.

Esmeray crossed the room to her mate, tugging him away from Lenna and rubbing his arm. "Collette just left. She confirmed Lenna is fine, and gave her a potion to have her sleep for a few hours so her mind and body can recover."

Keerian nodded, the always-assessing warrior mind calculating all the factors. "What was our favorite seer saying before she fainted?"

Laurent stepped towards the bed and dipped his head to Hale, both males stony faced and quiet. Sparrow finally stopped pacing to stand next to her mate, his large frame immediately easing her mind as he absentmindedly ran a hand down her arm.

It was Hale that spoke up, the half-fae adjusted his seating position on the edge of the bed, his voice still a bit wobbly. "*The dead rest, the living are restless. All answers you seek lie through the veil. When the Queens meet, the lands divide, and a new Queen will begin her ascent to power."*

Esmeray sighed with exasperation, her midnight wings drooping slightly behind her as she scrubbed her hands across her face. "What the fuck is that supposed to mean?"

Sparrow rolled her eyes at her friend's theatrics, but the heaviness of the words rang across the room.

"Whatever it means," Keerian replied quietly, "It has to do with that damn book."

It was Esmeray's turn to grimace, and with a half-hearted wave of her hand, the spell book levitated and floated over to her. "I'm not touching you," Esmeray snapped at the book before using her illusion magic to conjure up an iron box. The book landed in the box with an indignant *thud*, and Sparrow shuddered as a wave of frustration rolled off of it and through the room. Esmeray clenched her hand into a fist, the lid flipping over and snapping shut. A moment later, both book and box disappeared.

"Do you think it's wise to put it there?" Laurent prodded Esmeray, noting the disruption in the air where Esmeray's pocket of space rippled.

Esmeray sighed, "No, but it seems like the book's trying to tell us something. That dread Lenna and I both feel radiating off the book is intensifying, meaning whatever's about to happen is going to happen soon. It's escalating – like a warning. Why only the two of us can feel it...I don't know." She rubbed a hand down her spiraled horn, a frown pulling at her lips.

"I can feel it, too," Sparrow whispered, drawing everyone's eyes to her. "It feels odd, like, it sucks the warmth out of the air and leaves every-thing...hollow. And since Esmeray took possession of the spell book, I've felt this...presence following me, watching me, for months now."

She shuddered, feeling that disembodied presence hover close again. "Whatever is out there...it knows we have the spell book."

Esmeray knitted her brows together. "Keerian, Laurent, Hale – do any of you feel anything particularly foul emitting from the spell book?"

"No," Laurent muttered, gripping Sparrow's hand as she felt a sinking pit of dread fill her stomach. Keerian and Hale echoed Laurent's statement.

"Are spell books normally so volatile?" Keerian asked Hale.

Hale grunted, "My father had a few spell books he used to learn new languages, but they never reacted to anyone." With a wince, realizing he just admitted to owning illegal spell books in front of the Queen Absolute, Hale bowed his head to Esmeray. "He knew they were forbidden and the spells in those pages stayed uncast, but as one of the last descendants of the M'ghoen, my father's curiosity usually won out against fears of persecution. He kept them purely for research purposes. My family personally burned them upon his death."

Esmeray ruffled her wings, giving Hale a droll look. "I'm not here to condemn you for any parts of your past, Hale. I'm here as Lenna's friend, not as Queen. Gods know I've had my fair share of partaking in illegal activities, but you're family. Anything you tell us, anything you know, stays between this group."

"Consider yourself exempt from any formal interrogations," Keerian added with a wan chuckle, clasping Hale's shoulder. Hale's expression relaxed as he shot the King and Queen a relieved smile.

"But you said it yourself, those other spell books were burnt. This one is immune to any damage," Esmeray sighed.

"If you, Sparrow and Lenna are feeling a sentience to the book, we should consider what the three of you have in common," Hale started,

"If we narrow down some factors, it will give us some ideas as to why the book is so...aware."

Sparrow watched the exchange, fighting a wave of weariness that threatened to tug her down. She leaned her head against Laurent's chest, her mate absentmindedly caressing her back.

Esmeray caught her eye and the two exchanged a dismal glance between them. The year-long battle against Adara almost broke Esmeray. Her best friend continued to toe the line between right and wrong but ultimately always chose the correct path – even though the path was a little more morally greyish than anything else.

The only thing that kept Esmeray going, kept the Queen razor sharp and focused, was saving her mate. Sparrow looked up at Laurent's determined expression and thought to herself... what *wouldn't* she do to save *her* mate?

# Chapter Twenty-Two
# ESMERAY

Lenna's prophecy rattled the lot of us.

As we sat around the atrociously long dining room table, the five of us converged to the head, unconsciously scooting our chairs as close as possible to each other. With the remaining seats in the dining hall empty, the significance of what we faced lay before us. It really was lonely being Queen. But I was still not used to going into a turbulent situation with... this much support backing me.

We didn't know for sure who Lenna's newest prophecy concerned, but Moirai used Lenna to give us this information, in his own stupid, coded, not-straightforward way. And, not to be dramatic, but I was the only one fully convinced it was directly about me.

Sparrow argued that Adara's cronies wanted Lenna, not me, at the full moon ceremony, and that the book reacted to Lenna as well as herself. Laurent and Keerian wisely stayed quiet as Sparrow and I had one of our all-out spats in the hallway outside the King's chambers before coming down to the cavernous dining hall to eat and mull over the prophecy and the spell book.

But now, sitting next to me, Sparrow seemed lost in thought. She barely looked in my direction as she plopped into her chair, taking the head of the table, with Laurent on the other side of her. It was the silent symbol that she forgave me for our stupid argument. Though neither of us would ever outright apologize to the other. It was part of the reason our friendship lasted so long. We would yell, fight, and then decide it wasn't worth risking ninety years of friendship over and we'd go get a drink or some shit instead.

I watched Sparrow adjust her skirts around the carved arm of her seat. Keerian and I hated sitting at the head whenever we ate and usually avoided the dining hall for meals. After long days of ruling, the last thing we wanted was to mingle with the assembled court at dinner. But tonight, my Queen's Guard was split between redirecting anyone from interrupting our dinner and guarding the door to the King's chambers where Lenna was still resting.

Hale had been convinced to join our awkward dinner, though I knew he was counting down the bites of food between him being here and resuming his vigil of the sleeping Oracle. I hoped Carra gave them a soul tie sooner rather than later.

We made it to the end of dinner, and servants were busy clearing away our half-picked over food, when the interruption I'd been subconsciously waiting for finally came.

I didn't know what I truly expected, but there was an air of inevitability that *something* greater was fast approaching as the door swung open. My magic coiled through me, braced against the threat of an invisible danger and an inevitable fate that seemed determined to push me into a corner and watch me claw my way out. Whatever prophecy Lenna had, whatever the spell book's aura meant...those bleating warnings of something coming morphed into terrifying uncertainty.

It was no longer a question of *when*.

The frenetic energy in the air told me it had arrived.

The female gargoyle that appeared was short and muscular, with light grey horns and textured black hair pulled into a tight, low bun. Sharp, ruby eyes shone with calculated intelligence, but her furrowed brow told me whatever message she was here to deliver wouldn't be good news. Her battle suit was black with gold pauldrons, signifying she was part of the Obsidian Palace's standing army, but the patch on her forearm showed the outline of golden taloned wings – the sigil for the aerial ranks.

She strode directly to Keerian, bowing to the both of us before engaging my mate in a quiet conversation. Keerian's face gave nothing away, always the level-headed Commander, but he grunted in acknowledgement as the female spoke quickly and quietly. Even with fae hearing, I couldn't decipher the conversation. I had a feeling that was due to how utterly exhausted I was.

Keerian raised his hand to the female, and she bowed again before stepping back and standing at attention. "Captain Imala, please inform the Queen and our friends about what you know."

*Ah, Ballah.* Merrick promoted the red-eyed gargoyle from servant to an all-female aerial unit he created before fucking off to the Opal Palace. It was one of the more respectable things he did since the Obsidian Palace's aerial ranks had followed a strict "no female" rule for gargoyles. Which I always argued was bullshit. With a more slender wing structure, and less body mass to contend with, every female gargoyle I knew could outfly her male counterparts easily when given the proper training.

That was one of the first rules I threw out the window when I became Queen Absolute. And the early days after my coronation was such a turbulent time that not a single advisor challenged me on it. Especially after Resso took care of Lord Magnamus. None of those stuffy fuckers dared to piss me off.

Ballah's eyes glowed in the torchlight, her hands clasping the short, curved sword at her waist. "We received reports from our aerial surveillance team in the Opal Kingdom. There has been radical movement on the outskirts of Calcity. More than fifty fae reported with purple magic are converging on the city. Our unit was informed of the attack on your Majesties and the Oracle. I took the liberty to bring this news straight here."

My stomach twisted. Calcity was a farming town fifty miles away from the Opal Palace. The population was small and definitely didn't have powerful beings milling about its cottages.

Adara was making her move at last.

It would be outright decimation.

For Calcity to be attacked in the early beginnings of my reign…it set a dangerous precedent, showing the world that all was not united in Irridessen. That bred the possibility of more problems cropping up - within our borders and outside it.

"Captain Imala, I want twenty Elite Warriors posted in and around Lenna and Hale at all times. Send in the Queen's Guard from the hall."

The gargoyle bowed again before hustling out of the room, my Queen's Guard filing in with her departure. Thankfully, it was late enough that the few royals that were housed here were asleep, and we could hopefully take care of this situation before involving any unwelcome opinions.

What was the point of being Queen if I had to ask permission to do shit anyway?

I glanced over at Sparrow, her hands clasped tightly in her lap as she fiddled with the ring on her finger. The vacant look in her eye disappeared, leaving a raw ruthlessness that I rarely saw in her. If she tried to contact Merrick, I wouldn't have been surprised. The fact that her demeanor currently looked like she could spit venom convinced me that that bastard still hadn't put his ring back on.

I knew what I was about to say would gut her, but I needed to make sure I had an ally on the throne in case something happened to Keerian or myself. The one drawback of the soul tie - if Keerian or I perished, the other would die as well.

As gently as I could, I broke the news. "Sparrow, please wane Hale to the King's chambers. Then, take one of the gargoyle Queen's Guards and go wake up the cranky lizard in the caverns. I've named you Heir Absolute to the Kingdoms of Irridessen in case of my death. Have a gargoyle translate to Resso. He'll make sure any grabs at succession from yourself and Laurent are...unsuccessful."

My best friend shot up so quickly it knocked her chair backward. "*No*," Sparrow hissed, her golden hair whipping around to stare at me incredulously. She pointed a finger at my chest, green sparks flickering against her palms. "I'm fighting with you."

"No. You're not," I said quietly, holding her challenging stare before turning to Laurent.

The anger simmering in her aquamarine eyes was expected. The relief shining in Laurent's solidified my decision.

I pushed my chair back slowly, stretching my wings out as I addressed both of them. "Keerian and I talked this through at great length when we were crowned. We have no heirs. We're surrounded by enemies on our continent, as well as Ingotheria, and I refuse to see my parents' empire crumble under a weak ruler."

Nodding to Sparrow, my heart cracked at the wrath and defeat etched on her face. "You grew up in the Opal Palace, Sparrow, and have *always* been destined to do great things. You understand the laws, care about the beings living here, have a soft heart and strong *acat*."

She opened her mouth to argue, but I rushed on. "You're my Heir. It's already done. Though I wish I could've bought this up in a different way..." The muscles in her jaw flexed, most likely holding back every damn curse word she knew.

"I wish I could've announced this over a party with enough wine to drown in but shit's tough. Welcome to ruling - it's a bitch." I hated this conversation, though a small part of me settled now that it was out in the open. Relief that Irridessen would be safe even if I was gone. "Laurent, we need a portal made to the outskirts of Calcity, and then you *and* Sparrow are to stay here."

I took a deep breath, my gaze sliding to Keerian. He stood with me, arms crossed, a determined look in his eye. Keerian's horns glinted in the torchlight as he gave me a single nod of approval. Steeling myself, I said, my voice strong even with the quiver in my throat, "If that is my last order as Queen, you damn well better respect it."

Laurent bowed, and I saw how easily he could slip into the role of King Consort. He'd been formidable during his days as Spy Master for my Father, and I couldn't be more grateful at how gracefully he took this news now. "The portal will be ready."

I felt Sparrow's bristling irritation, though I did my best to ignore it. She could be mad at me all she wanted. Sparrow never reveled in fighting and bloodshed. She did it for me against Adara when no one else had my back.

And I needed her to do this for me as well.

Sparrow had been trained in court negotiations from a young age and hated the fact that she was naturally gifted at it. With her quick wit and brilliant mind, she could look at a diplomatic issue, ask the right questions, speak to the right beings, and enact true change. She was not a killer. Her battlegrounds should be courtrooms, council meetings, gods – even a throne.

Deep down, the gnawing thought that occasionally resurfaced in my mind, dug in again. I knew she would make a much better Queen than me.

WITHIN A HALF HOUR, the portal was ready, along with Captain Imala's aerial unit, the fae half of my Queen's Guard, and two dozen soldiers - both gargoyle and fae, handpicked by Laurent for this mission.

Keerian stood tall at the mouth of the portal, dressed in his shining golden armor, in that self-assured and confident way that always made the energy between us ignite. Keerian caught my eye, shooting me a smirk that brightened his moss green eyes as my King waited for the signal.

I moved to his side in my new full black battle armor custom designed to allow flexibility for both gargoyle and fae battle tactics. It covered the base of my throat to my wrists, imbued with magic that reinforced the material against swords, arrows, and most battle magic. But the best part was that it gave Keerian some semblance of peace that I was at least slightly defended in case we got separated.

Goldriel pulsed faintly in my hands as I imbued the hallowed staff with my battle magic, my nails already razor sharp and ready for the physical side of the bloodletting.

No crowns adorned our heads. We were King and Queen, but tonight we were death swift and merciless.

Every warrior in the room snapped to attention as I strode down from the dais I'd waned onto. My staff clicked against the glass floor as I held my chin high, refusing to let a sliver of doubt slither into my mind.

"I want aerial overhead with archers at the ready. Fae units - cast wards and protection magic barricading as much of the city as possible. This needs to be dealt with efficiently and quietly. We go in, we exterminate, we come home." I held their full focus as my words rang out. It was an almost dizzying high to go from the Princess who was considered a volatile risk and commanded little respect to the Queen Absolute who was both feared and admired.

Keerian rolled his shoulders back, raising his voice as he added, "These enemies have magic that we don't know the full extent of. All fae, utilize your *acatis* over physical attacks. Gargoyles - if you prefer to shift into Sentry, do so now." Keerian paused, sweeping his surveying eyes across the soldiers, allowing the orders to sink in before thrusting his long sword above his head, bellowing, "For your Queen! For Irridessen!"

The warriors shouted the words back, gloved hands banging sword hilts against breastplates. Ballah's unit roared as half shifted into Sentries, maws howling, the booming of wings stretching and flexing, preparing to take flight, echoing through the throne room. Gargoyle archers whooped, knocking arrow shafts against horns. For the legendary Golden Gargoyle, their King, to speak before battle – this was their moment to seize glory.

Keerian turned to the side of the portal, commanding each unit to line up and pass through. My mate kissed me swiftly as the last of the Queen's Guards dove into the blinding white light.

"Don't do anything self-sacrificing or I'll tie you to our bed and never let you near a battle again," Keerian murmured as his teeth nipped my bottom lip in warning.

"Let's get through this fight, and then you can tie me to our bed anyway." I kissed him fiercely, feeling his soft groan as he devoured me, sinking my hand into the scratchiness of his beard. All too soon, he pulled away, releasing me gently, his fingers tipping my chin up to meet his eyes.

"It's a deal, my Queen," Keerian growled, saluting me with a wicked grin, the heat of his gaze making me all too eager to get through the bloodshed as quickly as possible. He moved fluidly, vaulting through the swirling smoke with a battle cry, his golden wings glinting before disappearing, the portal transporting him towards the fray.

I gripped Goldriel tightly as I turned to face my next battle. Alone in the throne room, the only sound was the soft humming from the portal and the solid beating of my heart. I took a deep breath, centering my mind to prepare for the inevitable loosening of magic, pushing myself into that place where I could do what needed to be done while damning the consequences.

Keerian knew I needed these few seconds alone to get into the right mindset to fight, and as I stood there, watching the light pulse, I let out a long breath, drawing myself up straight and flexing out my wings.

Laurent built the massive portal before heading into the depths of the caverns below with Sparrow and a gargoyle guard to forewarn Resso and his cave-mates of the forthcoming battle and my potentially last decree as Queen Absolute.

Death didn't scare me. But the weight of responsibility bestowed onto me from the aftermath of my parents' murder gave me pause. I had to do right by Irridessen, by my subjects. Naming Sparrow as Heir assuaged some weight off my shoulders and helped me focus on the fight ahead. I wouldn't let Adara win - her allies were about to come to a bloody end. I'd deal with Adara later - once I spoke with my advisors.

I centered myself, a slow grin spreading onto my face as I bared my teeth. I would always protect my Kingdoms. I would always protect my mate, and I would always protect those who couldn't protect themselves. I sent up my own battle cry and dove into the portal.

But the moment I launched into the smoke, I knew something was very wrong.

Suspended amongst the nothingness, the portal warped and changed around me, the pressure building unbearably against my body, a high-pitched shriek filling my ears. I couldn't move, couldn't even thrash against invisible bands of power that kept me rooted firmly in place.

My magic went dead silent inside of me – frozen - unable to rally to my aid. I felt the air thin in my lungs, and I couldn't inhale.

Pinpricks of black hazed my vision and there wasn't a single thing I could do.

For the first time in a century, I felt vulnerable.

Fear was a lump in my throat, and sheer panic set in. *Keerian.* He'd be out of the portal by now...right? He was okay...*right*?

Deep, blood red smoke began undulating around me, twisting, and writhing, faster and faster, building in momentum until I was ensconced in disorienting light.

With a snap, I felt those bands of power release me, the roaring in my ears making me grit my teeth until it was painful.

As I was torn from the dining hall, I had a split second to scream before the portal enveloped me, ripping me from the Obsidian Palace and into the unknown.

# CHAPTER TWENTY-THREE
# ORLA

THE ROOM WAS CRAMPED and circular. Carved into the walls were small cubbies, filled to bursting with thick scrolls and dusty books. A single, hackneyed chair backed up to the shelves, the cushion lumpy and loved as if someone spent many long hours nestled amongst these tomes. With a flick of Cillian's wrist, the orb of glowing magic flew from his hand and separated into three, each darting out to settle into an iron lamp. The red light flared upon contact with the metal, turning into soft white lighting that illuminated the space with a cozy aura.

Orla's sight adjusted, as she turned, taking in each wall and its contents, a low whistle of admiration escaping her lips. "Where are we?"

"This is my private reading collection. My father has a knack for destroying any history that doesn't fit into his storied reign. I've saved as many as I could and hid them in here behind every single ward and barricade I know how to create. Over the years, I've amassed quite a collection." He surveyed the room, a flicker of pride flashing across his face. "I don't believe in hiding away the truth, and one day, when I rule, these documents will go back to their rightful homes in the Ruby Palace's royal library."

"These books are all banned?" Orla questioned, her eyes darting across each shelf. There must have been hundreds, if not thousands, of books and scrolls, all crammed into the alcoves. The majority were so tattered they seemed as if they were on the brink of disintegrating. Only a few were still in mint condition, shining, unblemished, against their worried counterparts.

Nodding slowly, Cillian gestured to the sole chair, "Sit, please."

Orla sat, her gaze following Cillian as he paced the room, avoiding her as if he was summoning the courage to begin a conversation Orla wouldn't want any part of. The way Cillian said *please* put her on edge. Whatever he was about to tell her he wanted her sitting down for. Orla's nerves crawled, skittering under her skin.

Suddenly, the coziness of the secret library and the valiant nobility of Cillian saving books soured in her mouth, the comfortable space now claustrophobic.

"Do you know how fae powers typically cross through a family's lineage?"

Orla, surprised at the conversation starter, nodded warily. "A bit, the healers who helped me when I first arrived explained it."

"When I had my advisor read your lineage, he confirmed that you have fae blood." Cillian went on, tracing his fingers down the spine of a book that seemed to startle at his touch. "My advisor is loyal to me. But after you left the throne room, he admitted he glimpsed your blood's heritage, and the strength of your *acat*."

Orla stayed silent. If she had magic, she wouldn't be able to return to the Slate Kingdom.

The aching burn in her lungs flared, her fingers tingled.

"I believe you're the last living descendant of an extremely powerful line of fae called the *Vitraro*. Dragonmind Fae. The same beings my father spent a good bit of his life extinguishing," Cillian sighed, his dark eyes pained as he finally surveyed Orla. "My council noted dragons were seen moving north from their typical grounds in Dragon's Peak. Dragon activity *was* quiet – until you and Marlo came here. Dragons sighted this far north, dragons patrolling the seas, they sensed *you*. They sensed your blood's heritage the moment you passed through the dome protecting the Slate Kingdom."

Orla's ears hollowed out. The familiar fire piercing through her body seemed to pulse and writhe within her. She stared at Cillian; her mind completely blank.

Rejecting this idea as ludicrous was the first thought she half-formed, but it dwindled away as she tried and failed to come up with any sort of argument.

Dragons.

Dragons that sensed her and crept closer, beasts of death that loomed over her like the shadow of an executioner's axe. She barely escaped the first brush with the monsters that she went her entire twenty-four years of life believing to be fictional - she wasn't fooling herself into thinking she'd outrun multiple.

"What does that mean?" Orla asked deadly quiet, as Cillian watched her with a wariness she knew was directly related to the expression on her face.

Cillian cleared his throat. "There were three tribes of *Vitraro* who used to live at the base of Dragon's Peak. My father spent decades wiping them from existence. The last *Vitraro* died by his hand about twenty-ish years ago."

Orla stood up quickly, suddenly done with this conversation and its absurdity. "This is nonsense."

"It most certainly is not," Cillian countered, closing the gap between them to slam his hands on either side of the chair, forcing her back to sitting. "The *Vitrato*, the Dragonmind fae, were powerful. They could speak to dragons mind-to-mind, they bonded with dragons and rode them into battle. After my mother died, my father turned his focus to the *Vitraro* and decided they were a threat to his rule. He decimated nests of wyverns and dragons, and when the *Vitraro* came out to defend them, he had an army waiting with one order – to not let a single Dragonmind leave the battlefield alive."

"Only gargoyles can mind speak with dragons," Orla challenged leaning forward in the chair, her anger rising in time with the pain that travelled along her jaw. It grew painful to speak.

"Gargoyles can mind speak to dragons *only* if the dragon begins that conversation, *only* if a dragon deems them worthy, and *only* between a short distance. Anyone from the *Vitraro* heritage can communicate with the entirety of the species - dragons, wyverns, and drakes. The Dragonmind are the only fae line that can ride as well, connecting with their bonded dragon on such a deep level that their dragon can sense their emotions and speak mind-to-mind regardless of the distance separating them. Before their fall at my Father's hands, once a Dragonmind fae earned their *acat,* they were taken to the base of Dragon's Peak to find their *kindered* - their soul bonded dragon."

Orla heard enough. She never wanted to *see* a dragon again – let alone ride one. She shot to her feet, shoving past Cillian and crossing the room to the door. "I'm leaving," she snarled, shooting one last venomous glare at Cillian. Guilt flashed all over his face as he approached her, palms raised. It did nothing but stroke her temper further.

Speaking hurriedly, Cillian said, "My advisor sensed your blood, your lineage and your heritage, and told me you are not half-fae, Orla. You're *fully* fae, nothing human is in your blood. Your true self was stifled, living in the Slate Kingdom under the magic-nullifying dome. But now that you're here, your *acat* will manifest, and you'll become the being you were meant to be."

"No." Orla threw the door open, her heartbeat pounding blood into her ringing ears as she felt the fire inside her lick up her throat, boiling, her rage growing red-hot. She whirled back to Cillian, suddenly wanting nothing more than to release all her fury onto him. "I don't believe you. I *am not* fae. And I'm *definitely* not a Dragonmind fae."

How dare he. How dare another male in her life lie and tell her stories of how special she was.

She was nothing special.

She was just Orla Grey.

Another nameless female falling victim to the cutthroat games of powerful males.

Why, why did they all have to do this? *Why* did she play pawn in everyone's games?

Memories of rough hands, whispered lies, acid coated words of men murmuring love only to use her for the night and dump her the next morning, laughter as dark figures circled her, held her down... It all flashed through her mind at a dizzying pace, building to a crescendo.

She roared out her pain, frustration enveloping her as she realized how utterly useless it was to ever believe she could have a normal life.

She wanted to go *home*.

She wanted to get the fuck out of this fever dream of a life before another being took advantage of her. Preyed on her.

"Fuck you," she sneered, the word ending in a choking sound as tears boiled over, dripping down her flushed cheeks. She shoved her hands into his chest, but it didn't do anything.

Cillian stood before her, hands in his pocket as he watched her quietly.

"*Fuck you*, fight *back*," Orla yelled, rounding on Cillian, hating him, needing him. Needing him to leave her alone, or to laugh and tell her it's all a joke, hating that she needed him to wrap his arms around her as she fell apart.

Cillian gently grasped the sides of her arms, pinning them to her sides. She tried to rip herself out of his grasp, but her vision swum, another wave of tears spilling forth. "You're fully fae, Orla, and I believe our paths crossed for a reason. The moment you stepped into the throne room...I haven't been able to get you out of my head."

"I don't want an *acat*," she hissed, "I don't want to be a part of this Kingdom, I want to go *home*. Fuck you, *fuck* you."

"I'm so sorry I have to be the one to tell you this," Cillian whispered, his eyes glistening as she uttered every curse she knew at him. She'd worked in manors and kitchens for over a decade. The barrage of curses that spewed forth was long.

He lowered his head, his own breathing labored, mirroring hers. She stuttered out another sob, her shoulders stiffening as he pulled her closer, wrapped her in his arms, holding tight. Cillian turned his head slightly, his dark eyes filled with pain and remorse, his words ragged and gravelly. "Orla, you have a very powerful *acat* that's going to manifest soon. The *Vitraro* is your heritage, but your *acat*, your god gifts, will be stronger than these lands have seen in years. My advisor felt your *acatis* strength. I need you to help me save my Kingdom, my people, from my father. Gods, *please*, Orla. Above everything fucking else, please don't hate me."

Her ears began ringing, an eerie screech that made her grit her teeth so hard she thought they would crumble from her lips. With her vision blacking at the edges, silver tipped spots blurred Orla's vision further.

She wobbled in Cillian's arms, her knees numb, the fire inside of her devouring every last drop of blood in her body.

Orla had the distinct awareness that Cillian yelled out her name as her legs gave out from under her.

But then she whited out, and there was nothing but unending agony within her mind. Tunnels of fire ignited through her, blazing hotter than any forge.

She was the tinder on a pyre, burning alive, and she screamed into her unconsciousness, completely lost to the brutal pain. White-hot knives dug into her, mercilessly ripping and tearing through her skin, her muscles, her very soul.

Making her anew.

# Part Two

---

## The EMBERS

# Chapter Twenty-Four
## ESMERAY

As I came back to consciousness, the ringing in my ears subsided. I groaned, my entire body stiff and aching, sprawled against a cold, hard floor. Blinking back tears that ripped free from the portal's vicious winds, I rose onto my hands and knees, not entirely trusting my legs to hold me up. I gingerly stretched out each wing, relieved to feel no pain besides a little bit of tenderness.

*Where was Goldriel?*

I squeezed my eyes shut, my breathing shaky, trying to get reoriented in my body. I patted the ground around me for the cool hilt of the staff, feeling only confusingly smooth stone.

*Where the fuck was I?*

Wiping my watering eyes with the backs of my hands, my mind began slowly piecing together my jumbled thoughts. I slugged through each thought, trying to click my last memories back together.

My nails skimmed over the stones below me. *"Think,* Esmeray," I mumbled to myself, my throat raw. My eyes burned, and I growled as I strained to lift my head up, my horns feeling heavier than normal, to take in my surroundings.

Squinting, I blinked furiously, trying to clear the watery film that refused to dissipate. I was in a dark room, entirely made up of black rock. The portal was gone, leaving me stranded with not a clue to where it deposited me.

*Did Laurent's portal accidentally transport me underneath the Obsidian Palace?*

Like a tsunami, everything came flooding back. Adara's cronies were converging on Calcity, Keerian's kiss, the portal, the red smoke. I jumped to my feet, my heart hammering in my chest. I rallied my magic to me but –

"I apologize in advance, but you will not be able to use magic here." A voice both ancient and new, wickedly cruel and achingly kind, blooming and withering, spoke softly from behind me.

I whirled around, searching for the source of the words, and froze.

I needed no introduction.

I dropped to my knees as I stared into the face of death herself.

Phades, the Goddess of Death, the goddess who bestowed her *acat* unto me, sat upon a throne of bones. While her body was wraith-thin, female - her face was nowhere near humanoid. A ram's skull, with thick, black, curled horns, appraised me, cocked to the side as her sightless sockets stayed trained on me.

And in her moon pale hands, clasped ever-so-gently, was Goldriel.

The Goddess of Death, the Goddess so feared that she was only mentioned by name from those who reverently whispered it beside deathbeds and on moonless nights when the lands of the living felt too still to be alive, tapped Goldriel against the ground. "Queen Esmeray, I must apologize for the interruption, but it was pertinent that we spoke before you went any further down your current path."

"Am I dead?" I whispered, my palms slick with sweat, panic roaring through my head. *Keerian – was Keerian dead already?*

"No," Phades answered plainly, her jawbone clicking with the word.

I wasn't dead but was somehow talking directly to death. The relief of still being alive was overshadowed by the overwhelming confusion of my current situation. "Where am I?" I heard myself ask.

"Behind the veil," Phades drummed her fingers against Goldriel's handle. "In Minmere."

Minmere. The final resting place for all souls. The Kingdom of the Dead. I shook my head. "How?"

Phades clacked her jaw together again, annoyed. Well, that made two of us. I tried a different approach. Reasoning with a death goddess hadn't been on my list of things to do today.

I held my hands up, dully noticing how Phades focused on my blacked-out palm. "My mate, Keerian, is waiting for me on the outskirts of Calcity to fight against Adara's followers. I need to go back; I need to fight to protect my people from an awful magic."

The Goddess of Death was silent for a moment, Goldriel still in her hand. Thin, black robes hung off her bony frame as she leaned back against her throne. "Time works differently behind the veil, because time is well...*dead*. You could be here for a minute, or a year, and be back to the land of the living with not a second of your time lost."

*What?*

"I need to get back to Terramere. Adara warped fae magic somehow, and I need to save a town from her followers." I took a step forward, shortening the distance between us. I spoke calmly and firmly, still all too aware that I had zero magic on my side, and no escape route in sight.

Phades chuckled softly. "Your problems are larger than Adara."

With a flick of her fingers, a ripple in the air next to her appeared, an iron box clattering noisily from of its depths.

My heart sank.

I dropped my hands to my side.

"I am going to tell you a story," Phades said nonchalantly, "About two sisters who loved each other very much."

She crooked her finger towards the iron box, its lid flying open. I swallowed as the spell book tumbled out of it, sliding a few feet across the floor before settling. My mind went wholly blank.

I tore my eyes from the spell book that had been stored securely in my pocket of space to level them to the Goddess of Death, who, apparently, knew exactly what it was. It made sense my lineage god would know about the book, but it still felt like a violation.

It made me hesitate, wondering if I needed to prepare to fight a god.

"Long ago, my sister and I fell from the realm of gods, Aurramere, landing in your realm of the living, Terramere, with the dangerous knowledge that we were immortal, all powerful, and utterly free from the complexities of our home realm. We did everything together, exploring lush forests and giant caves, walking beneath the waves and surveying mountain ranges. It was only us, and all the time in the world, something with which I was completely content. But Faune was not. She wanted more for us – for the beautiful land we found ourselves living on."

My eyes widened in surprise.

My mother used to tell Adara and I stories of the gods when we were children, and our favorites had always been about Phades and Faune. To hear the true story, from the goddess herself, made it feel as if my mother was still here, tucking me into bed, softly weaving tales about epic adventures of the gods into those last moments before sleep overtook me.

Phades continued, her pitiless eyes fixated on the spell book. "So, Faune began creating. She created the first human ever – a sniveling thing really – and I watched my sister's love for me begin to be shared with this *otherness*. I hated it." Phades reached out, the spell book flying through the air, landing in her outstretched hand.

"Faune loved that little being, and, over time, it grew old and wrinkly. Which, with our lifespan, was seemingly quick. I was relieved when her creation died. That is, until I realized how gutted my sister was. She was heartbroken, taking her pain and rage out on the same lands we loved so dearly. Well, while she'd been nurturing and growing her creation, I continued to travel - alone. I finally grew so bored with these lands that I began exploring my power, finding a quiet, peaceful place where I didn't have to listen to Faune cooing over her human, or going through one of her emotional rampages. It was hidden, eternal, and empty."

"Minmere," I murmured quietly.

Phades clicked her jaw in confirmation. "My power took me behind the veil, into an empty god realm, long forgotten. But Faune didn't have my power and couldn't enter. I offered to bring her creation here, thinking that it was nothing more than a quiet burial place where we could honor Faune's magic. I carried the human through the veil, and it woke up. I thought maybe the human hadn't been truly dead, until I brought it out of Minmere and it immediately died again in my arms. I realized then that the human could only be '*alive*' on the other side of the veil, so I deposited it in Minmere and went to tell Faune."

The spell book began humming, the symbols etched along its spine glowing with a faint golden light. Phades ignored it. "I showed Faune what happened, expecting her to be overjoyed, but she was still distraught. So now, I had this odd being wandering around an abandoned god realm by itself, unable to leave. But it seemed happy – or at least at peace." Phades's fingers tapped against the book cover, the sounds jarring my own nerves. A chill went down my spine, sinking into the marrow of my bones.

"After some time passed, Faune made another, and then another. And they would grow old and die, and I would carry them to Minmere, letting them rest behind the veil after a full life with Faune. But Faune wasn't content, and she began creating different types of creatures, until we realized we weren't as omnipotent and isolated as we thought."

I thought back to the story my mother had told me, and the differences between the two - where Phades had always been cast as the shadow, the dark power, the true neutral – neither good nor bad. Faune had always been shown as the beautiful, smart, blessed goddess. To hear that she ravaged the land, that Phades had been the voice of reason, left my mind whirring.

With a croak, Phades cocked her skull to the spell book. "Other gods became interested in Faune's creations but couldn't figure out how to get into Terramere, still stuck above, in our home realm. Faune's humans began reproducing, and the tens turned into hundreds, and hundreds into thousands. Those other gods began bestowing gifts onto Faune's creations, some giving strength and wings, others slivers of magic, learning that even though they were in Aurramere, they could get small pieces of themselves earthside to show off their power."

"Faune was thrilled with the attention, but I did not trust these other gods, especially since they could not see her creations were beginning to rebel, fighting amongst themselves with their newfound gifts. We also learned that gifts could travel through bloodlines. If a god imbued one being, its offspring would sometimes inherit that same power."

I shifted, my eyes darting between the book now fully glowing, and Phades.

I knew this story ended with a bloody war between gods – especially once the gods found out they could kill each other.

It was an old saying, usually muttered between rivalling royals, *"Only a god can kill another god."*

"Well," Phades sighed, "another goddess found out how to travel earthside, right around the time Faune grew reckless, imbuing beings with her direct god power, usually to the point where the creations would just...combust. Faune and this other goddess began trying to outdo each other, seeing how much magic a being could hold, taking it right to that threshold of life and death, until the other goddess created a being so powerful that it decimated an entire forest in one burst of wrath. Of course, this frustrated Faune, as well as every other god in Aurramere who yearned to come earthside. Everyone wanted their power to be the strongest in Terramere. We found out only those of us earthside could imbue our raw, direct god power into a being, opposed to the gods above who could only bestow what you call your gifts – your *acat*. We were selfish, jaded with immortality, and stupid, young, gods. But this realization became the catalyst of the God War."

I hadn't heard this part and wondered who this other goddess was. My mother never mentioned any other gods walking our lands. I wondered if this part of history had been erased.

"Another goddess figured it out soon after and came earthside to negotiate a stop to the war. Of course, because we are gods, not a single one of us wanted to relent. We came up with a compromise, instead."

Phades laughed, the sound flat. It did not echo through the still air. "There was a much smaller number of gods left after the war - we delighted in killing each other and then bestowing our gifts on the dead gods' lineages, which ended up having...odd effects on the beings once the magic began to mix. But we decided that, since Faune's creations were now wholly self-sufficient, gods could continue giving gifts, but only to the lineages of the beings they already bestowed upon."

"To make sure this rule was followed, myself, Faune and the other two goddesses, made our own side agreement. Since we had lived amongst the beings, seen the chaos they could impose on themselves, seen the decimation that wreaked havoc on Terramere during the God War, we could choose one sole being to bestow an exorbitant amount of our god power unto – to keep the scales of fate balanced if powerful enemies arose from any angry gods."

"These beings would be able to manage and control the other creations that held less power, but also keep the gods in check, as well as ourselves. We could not bestow our raw power onto another until that first being died. The four goddesses that lived earthside could imbue a Vessel, a being with so much of a god's power that the being in question would undoubtedly find themselves in a ruling class. The caveat of that - we could also disrupt a lineage line, taking it away from another god."

Something inside me hollowed out and I felt like I was staring back in on my younger self, sobbing outside of a closed door, my parents arguing in the other room, the newly minted tattoo covering my arm burning like wildfire. Its origins unknown.

I knew then, truly, in my soul, why I had always been different, always been stronger, more powerful, more feared than loved. I knew then why my mother's stories stuck with me decades later. Why her soft-spoken voice held so much of my attention as a faeling.

"Am I a Vessel?" I asked, facing Death.

Phades inclined her head, those curled ram's horns, identical to my own, all but damning me to her answer.

"Of course."

# CHAPTER TWENTY-FIVE
## LAURENT

THE ICY ROT OF the dungeons engulfed Laurent like an old friend. It seemed a lifetime ago that he was the Spy Master for King Scottrell, walking these dungeons to interrogate and break the Kingdom's enemies. The prisoners who remembered him backed away from the bars of their cells as he passed.

That had been a different time. A different path.

Aella, the Goddess of Destruction, blessed Laurent with gifts to manipulate and control fire. It came in handy when the interrogations drew too long, when lives depended on answers being obtained quickly.

King Scottrell had been a just and virtuous ruler for the citizens of Irridessen. But a ruler often found himself battling against his own morals. Laurent understood that balance, how Esmeray now found herself inundated between doing what was honorable and doing what was needed.

And now there was a chance that vestige would fall upon his mate, currently striding alongside him, an expression of vengeance carved against the angles of her beautiful face.

They had taken one of the Queen's gargoyle guards down to the dragon lair, where Resso dutifully ignored them until they admitted

Queen Esmeray may be in danger. After that, the ancient beast huffed out steam and allowed the gargoyle to speak with him. Dragons were a peculiar species - especially the cave dragons that lived underneath the Obsidian Palace. There were only about six left, all male, and rarely left the caverns unless they needed to hunt. Resso, the oldest and crankiest, kept the other five in line, and apparently still held a soft spot for the Queen Absolute who used to smuggle cow carcasses down to the lair for him in exchange for unbridled access to the treasure troves the dragons guarded.

Now, Sparrow strode in front of him, her soft pink gown exchanged for chestnut brown leathers, the material so creamy Laurent could barely restrain himself from running a hand down her legs, her back, any inch of her he could reach. The dress had been gorgeous, but those tight pants were lethal, and Laurent had a difficult time focusing on the task at hand as his eyes drifted over his mate appreciatively.

As if she could feel his stare on her, she sashayed her hips - just a bit. Fucking gods.

She threw him a grin over her shoulder as they traversed deeper into the dungeon. Laurent let out a pointed exhale, mentally calculating how long this would take, and what the shortest path was from here to Sparrow moaning and grinding beneath him.

Sparrow stopped suddenly, jerking Laurent's attention to the present. With a smoky laugh, she slipped into an empty cell, tugging Laurent in behind her.

He was on her in an instant, kissing her buttery soft skin, fisting that lush hair in his hands. She kissed him back, their lips only breaking apart momentarily to deepen their angle. She let out a breathy moan that had him sliding his hand down her thigh, pressing her flush to his body so she could feel exactly what those godsdamned pants were doing to him.

He backed her up to the stone wall, his hands finding the laces to her breeches. He could have her now – quickly.

A wet-sounding cough from a prisoner in a cell nearby rattled through their small cloud of privacy, reminding Laurent of exactly where he was and what they needed to accomplish.

With a groan, Laurent pulled back first, every molecule inside him begging him to stop being so task-driven and to enjoy the little detour.

"We need to focus," his traitorous mouth said as his body hated him for it.

With a sad frown, Sparrow sighed, "I didn't know Esmeray was going to name me Heir. I don't know what she's thinking."

"You're beautiful and brilliant; *I* would follow you to the ends of the earth and beyond." Laurent's brows knitted together as he took in the pained expression on his mate's face. "Esmeray doesn't do anything without a solid reason, and she knows you have the skill to lead Irridessen in the worst case that something happens to Keerian and herself."

Laurent watched the mask slip. Sparrow was as bad as the Queen when it came to hiding her true emotions, and Laurent saw it happening more and more recently. With this reveal that Esmeray and Keerian decided Sparrow would be their successor, Laurent understood the mounting pressure building on Sparrow's shoulders.

The flirting, the kissing - all a distraction from the tidal waves of emotions Sparrow was not ready to face. He understood it and it didn't scare him.

With tender hands, he cupped her face. "I'm here to empower your decisions, support you in any way that I can. I know this is a big ask, and that you feel blindsided by it, but *you are not alone.*"

"What if I'm not good at this? What if I screw up?"

"You were raised in court politics, lived in the Opal Palace for years, and have the backing of a big fucking dragon, an ex-Spy Master, and the Queen's word. You won't fail."

Sparrow blessed him with a smile, a genuine smile, that made his heart lurch at the sight. "You know, if I have to be Queen, that makes you King Consort."

Laurent chuckled, leaning down to press his lips to hers. "Well, lucky for you, I bet I look damned handsome as sin in a crown."

With a giggle, she leaned into his chest, returning the kiss with one dripping with passion and promise. "I think you look handsome in everything, and doubly handsome in nothing."

"How about this - let's get the dirty business done, and then retire to our chambers until Esmeray and Keerian return?"

"Deal."

With one last kiss, they departed the empty cell, weaving their way down the last few rows of the dungeon to the dark end of the hall.

Adara was waiting for them, leaning against the cell door with her hands wrapped around the bars. A wicked gleam filled her dull blue eyes as Sparrow came into sight. Laurent stayed a few steps behind her.

"I see congratulations are in order, Sparrow. Which of your *two* mates is this one?" Adara's voice was rough with unuse, though poison barbed disdain still managed to lace every word.

Baring his fangs, Laurent appraised the dishonored Princess. "Hello Adara, it has been quite a while."

"Ah, the Spy Master. Why, I always took you more for a *'listening not talking'* male." Adara smirked, "Though I heard that your other mate doesn't want the competition. How *is* Merrick these days? Seems like he hasn't been available to follow you around like a lovesick dumbfuck, Sparrow."

Sparrow glared at her. "Tell us about the spell book."

"What spell book?" Adara asked, running her fingers up and down the thick, magic nullifying bars of the door. She peeked up at Sparrow through her lashes, a saccharine smile playing against the corners of her mouth.

"Don't play coy, it doesn't suit you in the slightest," Sparrow sniffed. Laurent had to work to keep his face neutral, bored. Watching Sparrow speak in that cutting, charming tone was wildly enthralling.

Adara's ruined wings rustled with irritation. "For someone who continuously groaned about court life, you seem to be right back in the middle of it once more."

Sparrow kept quiet.

The silence ticked on. Laurent didn't move as Sparrow stayed locked on Adara, the two females silently shooting daggers at each other with their eyes.

Finally, Sparrow huffed dramatically, turning away from Adara, and stepping up to Laurent. "Well, this was a waste of time, let's go back upstairs."

As they turned to leave, Adara's impatience ran out.

"It isn't *really* a spell book, you know," Adara spoke up, following them down to the corner of her cell, her face pressed against the corner. "It's a book that can *show* you spells - if you know where to look."

Sparrow shot Laurent a glance that conveyed a triumphant *'got her'*.

Slowly, Adara pushed off the bars, pacing up and down the cramped cell. Laurent counted the steps. Five to one side, five to the other.

They waited.

"I could only translate a couple parts of it. The book wouldn't let me read the rest."

"What do you mean?" Sparrow prodded. Laurent positioned himself casually against the wall to the side of the cell door.

"I forced the book to show me. It didn't want to. But the book has its own power, its own well of magic," Adara bragged, "I siphoned out a little of its power, and then I held onto that kernel of magic for a few days. I came back, pushed down my own magic deep inside of myself, and that kernel floated to the top. The book recognized its magic in me. But it thought I was someone else, the being that was keyed to unlock its knowledge."

"So, you used the book's magic against it." Laurent murmured, "That is *very* smart."

Adara preened at the compliment, addressing Laurent directly. "I found out I could ask it to show me spells. Then, I wrote them down. I couldn't translate them on my own, and the book wouldn't translate them either, but thankfully, I had willing helpers."

With an air of curiosity Laurent leaned forward. "How did you find the spell that would transfer Esmeray's soul tie?"

At that, Adara stopped pacing, her head whipping from Sparrow to Laurent, as if she just realized what was missing...*who* was missing.

"Where's Esmeray?" she demanded.

Sparrow chuckled, inspecting her own nails, something Laurent had watched Esmeray do time and time again to unnerve her adversaries. "You know, I've known you for a century, Adara, and I *never* knew you were a dirty, parasitic, siphon. It makes sense since your water magic is so...lackluster."

"If you want to talk about keeping powers a *secret*, Sparrow, have *you* told your mate about *your* secrets?" Adara hissed.

"I know everything there is to know about my mate's powers, but we're here to talk about *you*, Adara," Laurent interjected smoothly, though the words rang through him. He couldn't look at Sparrow, couldn't give away to Adara that he had no idea what the fuck she was talking about.

*What was Sparrow hiding?*

The thought worried him. If she hadn't told him, was it because it was a power that she was ashamed of? Or something that she kept in the dark to reveal at a time that suited her - like Adara did with the siphoning?

Sparrow stilled beside him.

Adara looked from Sparrow to Laurent for a long moment. "I took the book's magic, touched the cover, and asked it to show me a spell to transfer a soul tie. It opened to a blank page and then the words appeared in that same, ancient language. I bought the paper with the spell to the Opal Palace's master scholars and asked them to translate it. I told them it was a code we recovered from Esmeray."

"Which scholars?" Sparrow nudged.

Adara frowned, and Laurent noted her attention on this conversation was wearing thin. "It doesn't matter. I killed them after I got what I wanted."

Laurent nodded again, and that Spy Master role he knew so well took over. He sidestepped from Sparrow's side, the movement leaving him cold without her calming scent of honeysuckle and lily enveloping him. He slipped closer to Adara, as if to tell her a secret. In a low voice he questioned, "Did the book show you how to warp fae magic?"

Adara wanted Keerian because Esmeray had him first. If that same play worked again, if he could keep Adara focused, they could hopefully get something out of her that would be useful to their friends defending Calcity. It was the least he could do here – away from the fighting.

Adara shot Sparrow a glare of utter loathing before turning to Laurent, her white wings flaring out, intentionally blocking Sparrow's view of them.

"It did," Adara breathed, her attention solely focused on Laurent now. "But it was the last thing the book showed me before it realized I was siphoning its magic to trick it. After that, all it would do is scrawl very ostentatious notes to me if I asked for anything else. Imagine my embarrassment asking a master scholar to translate a note that said I was a *thief* and a *fool*."

"What's their new power?"

Laurent felt Sparrow shift uncomfortably as Adara reached out and stroked his knuckles. He had to push down the wave of disgust as her cold fingers made contact. "It's death. Pure and simple. The book showed me how to harness chaos magic. My followers exchanged their souls and *acatis* for greater power. I was able to summon chaos magic from the God of Chaos himself to overtake them, break them apart, and remake them into something *new* - something better."

A pit of dread hollowed out inside Laurent. The God of Chaos, Massis, had fallen into disfavor with the fae centuries ago. He'd once bestowed gifts of siphoning, but he'd gone mad in his thirst for power, creating his new gift, chaos magic, that was said to turn even the most docile fae into a murderous beast. The tiny bits of lore still swirling around in covert whispers said Massis found a new horde of devout followers after the fae turned their backs on him - the Witch Covens in the Jade Kingdom.

The purple hue of Massis's chaos magic became a beacon for frenzied fae to hunt down and exterminate, causing the unique color to fade out of existence swiftly. Other gods stopped gifting purple battle magic, not wanting their power to be mistaken for the depraved *acat* of a fallen god. With the damnation of Massis and chaos magic came a wary fear of siphons, causing any fae with siphoning gifts to typically keep their power a secret to avoid retribution.

But for some sinister reason, the witches embraced the gifts of siphoning, honoring the tyrant god with blood sacrifices to Massis every full moon. A complete affront to Carra herself.

"I named them the Unmarked," Adara murmured, her eyes turning to stare into Laurent's own. "Since embracing their new chaos magic burned their *acatis* from their skin."

Laurent grinned, feeling his own mask slip on as he pushed down the fear that they were getting entangled with Massis. He ripped his hand from Adara's grasp. "Thanks," he replied cheerfully, shoving from the wall, moving back to Sparrow, and wrapping his arm around her slender shoulders to lay a kiss against her hair.

It was as much a reassurance to himself as it was part of their play against Adara as Sparrow shot Adara a simpering look. "Thanks for the help. Sit tight, Adara."

The two of them strode away. Adara's screech as she realized she'd been played enticed the rest of the prisoners to begin shouting, the cacophony following Sparrow and Laurent as they headed to the dungeon's ledge and waned out of the caverns in a flash of green light.

# Chapter Twenty-Six
# ESMERAY

"Which brings us to the purpose of this visit." Phades hefted the spell book up to her bony chest, her fingers tapping the cover expectantly.

My hands trembled as I tried, again, to unlock my power. There was no response – not even a flicker of magic to access.

I was a Vessel.

And there were potentially three other extremely powerful beings out there that could match me in strength.

The creation of Vessels was a closely kept god-secret. Which made me dread why it was coming out now.

Phades held up the book, facing the cover to me. It emitted a hum in her hands. "One piece of the compromise after the God War was that all gods were forced to return to a god realm, and to never return to Terramere. Any god found to breach that compromise would be sealed into a desolate and magic-barren realm – unable to gift their *acat* to a being ever again. The four of us that were currently earthside agreed – if only to solidify the sanctity of keeping the power to create a Vessel to ourselves. But Faune was devastated to leave her creations behind in Minmere and Terramere. I knew for fact if she tried to sneak back to

Terramere, to return to your lands, it would mean her death. So, I made the difficult decision for her."

I realized with a start where this story was heading. "The compromise said you had to return to *a* god realm – not necessarily Aurramere."

Phades cocked her head, the movement eerie and wicked. "Precisely. I stepped through the veil to stay in Minmere with the souls of my sister's beloved creations, guarding their eternal peace here. I learned how to summon souls to Minmere as they passed, and after a while, souls began slipping into the afterlife without my guidance – as if they knew where to go as death took them."

"And Faune went back to Aurramere," I stated. This part of the story I knew but had always been told it was due to an argument amongst the sisters – not because of Phades' love and sacrifice for Faune.

Phades let out a chattering sound that made me wince. "Faune went back to Aurramere with the other two goddesses, unaware of my decision to return to Minmere. Before we separated, each of the four goddesses earthside created a book and imbued it with our own well of direct god power, to one day be utilized by our Vessels when necessity dictated."

Phades looked down at me, her raspy voice hardening.

"This is not a spell book. It is the Book of Phades - a collection of stories about Faune and I, how I grew my magic, and details of the God War. But while it holds my power, the book can show you answers to whatever you ask. Your sister, Adara, directed the book give her the spells she required to steal your soul tie."

Phades chuckled roughly. "At first, the Book of Phades thought it was *you* - my Vessel - taking its power. You and your twin share so many similarities that the well of magic within the book was confused. But after a while, the book realized what Adara was doing, and it refused to show her anything else. So, Adara began siphoning tiny morsels of power, anything the book couldn't protect, to simply to bolster her own fae magic. And the book damned her by draining her life force every time she took for herself."

I inhaled abruptly, my mind racing. Adara stumbled upon what we thought was a spell book that could recreate *my* magic. I had it all wrong. Adara hadn't translated a forbidden and long forgotten fae spell book...She stole god power from the Book of Phades.

Ether coated my tongue at the realization Adara was a siphon. It was a gift that my father's line inherited rarely, yet a strong heritage magic that dated back to a time when fae received the gift of siphoning regularly - before it became a gift solely given to the witches. It made fucking sense when I thought about it. Adara's water magic was weak. I always thought that was all she got.

But all along, she hid her true gift, a heritage power that showed no *acat.*

The Book of Phades could do nothing against Adara's powers as a siphon, but it could take from her. Adara essentially bargained years of her life for small bits of stolen god magic.

Phades stood suddenly, Goldriel in one hand, the Book of Phades glowing in the other. Her black robes billowed behind her as she stepped away from her throne. "You hear it calling to you, and yet you shove it in a box, afraid of what would happen." I didn't respond. "Imagine my surprise when I found my life's story, trapped and rattling around Minmere. I decided then and there that we needed to speak more...personally."

"I didn't put your book in Minmere. I put it in..." My voice trailed off as the pieces clicked into place. "My pockets of space...It isn't a pocket, is it? It's a way through the veil...into Minmere."

"Ah," Phades crooned gliding over the floor towards me, "I believe you are understanding now. *You are my Vessel.* You have *every* power that I do, and from what I've seen, what has been whispered throughout Minmere, you are quite fearsome."

Only a few feet separated us now, and I fought to calm my breathing as Phades towered over me.

"I leave you with these last words, Queen Esmeray. It is of utmost importance that you take my book back with you and *learn*. There is no trick, no gimmick, no wayward power grab. The Book of Phades cannot corrupt, cannot manipulate you into anything." Phades pushed the book, and Goldriel, into my hands, before trailing a death-cold finger down my cheek. I stared up into the bottomless abyss of her eyes.

"Find the Book of Faune. It will lead you to Faune's Vessel that is currently earthside," Phades murmured, the bleached bones of her face half shrouded in shadow. "Together, the Vessel Books can keep the gods where they belong. There are disturbances in the realms. I can feel the tremors even here, beyond the veil."

I nodded numbly, not entirely sure what exactly I was agreeing to.

Phades huffed a cold burst of air against my face before turning back towards her throne. "Oh, and Esmeray? Master my power. Remember, you are the Vessel of Phades, you do not bow, you do not acquiesce to anyone. You are more powerful than you know."

A humming filled the air around me, jarring my very bones until my teeth chattered. Phades waved her hand, blood red smoke swirling up from the floor, engulfing me completely. I felt the smoke wrap tighter around me, and with a flash of bright light, I disappeared from the hallowed halls of the afterlife.

# CHAPTER TWENTY-SEVEN
## ESMERAY

PHADES WAS RIGHT - no one noticed I slipped through the veil. I didn't know how long I stayed in Minmere, but nothing in Irridessen changed on account of my travels.

Keerian flew over to me, his golden wings half extended, ready to launch into battle at the slightest hint of trouble. "Adara's cronies are picking their way through the woods. We got here just in time and may still hold the element of surprise. I sent Captain Imala's aerial unit into the city with two fae that can wane large groups of beings. They're evacuating now to the Opal Palace."

I nodded, my mind still reeling at the fact that I just left fucking *Minmere* and Keerian had no idea. "Did you feel anything weird after you went through the portal?" I asked hesitantly.

Keerian paused and furrowed his brows. "No? Why?"

I shook my head, waving away his concerned expression. "I'll tell you later," I muttered as a fae signaled there was movement in the tree line. The sounds of swords being drawn kissed the night air, and I pulled Goldriel out of my pocket of space – *fuck* – out of Minmere.

I snuck a peek through the veil, dread rising up my throat. But it looked the same as it had since I was a young fae – just rock walls. I had half a thought that I'd see Phades lounging on her throne of bones, but thankfully the only things in the rip were two empty bottles of wine, and the Book of Phades - still glowing around its edges. After my wayward trip, I almost felt as if I should tidy the space up. I frowned at the empty bottles, feeling like I was desecrating hallowed ground.

"I thought we put that thing in a box," Keerian commented, looking over my horns at the book discarded in the corner.

"It didn't *like* the box," I grumbled back, hastily swiping my hand to close the veil. The book sent a pulse of irritation at me, but I ignored it as I turned to Keerian, Goldriel tapping the ground as I mustered up a dazzlingly innocent smile that only seemed to add to his suspicions that something was up with me.

My mate shot me another puzzled look before kissing me swiftly. "Don't forget our deal," he growled before unsheathing the sword from his back.

I pushed down all thoughts of Phades, giving Keerian my usual smirk.

The Goddess of Death was going to have to wait until after Keerian and I got done banging each other's brains out once this fight was wrapped up.

An unnaturally cold breeze blew across the clearing as figures silently appeared through the shadows, wisps of purple magic weaving on its own accord through the forest.

Around me, battle magic began flaring from the fae on offense, preparing to be unleashed. I imbued more magic into Goldriel, my golden light flaring through the moonstone atop the staff.

"Hold," Keerian grunted, his sword raised as more black robed beings skittered out of the trees. "*Hold,*" he snapped as a fae near the back flared their battle magic further, bathing the tree line in pale blue light.

We stood atop the curtain wall surrounding Calcity. The gates below us were shut and warded against intruders lest we were forced to retreat. Sentries, wings tight and tails thrashing, dotted the tops of the battlements, claws digging grooves in the stones, positioned to take flight and attack on Keerian's command. I loved fighting in Sentry form, but my *acat* was harder to control. Transforming into a beast was my last resort during fights once the well of my magic burned out.

Ahead of us was a cleared expanse of dirt road, giving us an unobscured view of the forest where we could glimpse purple magic flaring, illuminating the shadows stalking between the trees.

Our warriors stood shoulder to shoulder in front of the gates at high ground atop a gentle slope. The enemy would need to cross the dirt road *and* begin to climb the small incline to reach us – we could pick them off one by one if needed.

I felt my ring heat, and Sparrow's voice filled my head. *"Adara warped those fae from the woods with a spell from Massis. The beings gave up their* acatis *for chaos magic. Adara called them the Unmarked."*

*"Thanks for letting us know."* I heard Keerian's voice reply, as we exchanged a grim glance.

Fuck. Massis was not who I wanted to tangle with.

He was too close in connection with witches and his chaos magic was the power of legend. Massis used to gift his power of siphoning to the fae, but once he began experimenting with chaos magic, the fae turned their backs on him, seeing the god for what he truly was – a monster.

Fae with chaos magic were exterminated centuries ago, the lore that they'd be possessed by Massis's demons when they burnt out their magic making them too dangerous to keep alive. That was centuries before my parents' time, but even so, I glanced towards the tree line with newfound fear rising in my chest.

*"Don't die."* Sparrow's voice filled my head again, and I realized she was speaking only to me. *"I've realized I can't wear most of your crowns because I don't have horns and honestly it makes me not want to be Queen anymore."*

I smiled, despite the battle ahead of us. *"I've been gone less than an hour. Are you already in my closet?"*

*"Yes,"* Sparrow admitted, as her slight laugh filled my head, *"I'm having much better luck with your dresses. I don't need wings to pull most of them off."*

*"I'll see you soon, don't even* think *about going through my jewelry box."* I shot back to Sparrow; my mood slightly improved. Sparrow screeched with glee as my ring cooled. The thought of going into battle while there was so much left unsaid between us nagged at my focus, but knowing my best friend was exacting her "revenge" by raiding my closet made my heart soften and my concentration able to hone in on the foe before us.

Now to just get through this battle, and maybe I could have a few hours of peace with my mate before I pondered the visit with Phades.

"Chaos magic?" Keerian directed to me softly, worry shining in his eyes as he surveyed the shadowy figures skittering out of the trees. "I didn't think Massis was gifting that to fae anymore."

"He isn't. The only way beings can inherit of Massis's gifts these days is through heritage magic if they have a bloodline dating back far enough." *Like my father's line.* I thought to myself bitterly.

"Fucking Massis," Keerian cursed. "What the fuck even *is* chaos magic?"

"I have a feeling we're about to find out." I jerked my chin towards the trees, narrowing my eyes, lips tipping up in a snarl as my golden battle magic flickered through my fingers.

Purple smoke poured from the Unmarked, creeping just above the grass, inching its way to the dirt road. My eyes darted through the mass of beings now leaving the ambiguity of darkness and stepping into sight.

*Fuck.*

Fifty was a low estimate.

"Get ready," Keerian called, "When they hit the dirt road, take your marks."

The sound of bows being drawn from the wall behind us signified this battle was mere seconds away from starting.

The purple haze swept over a patch of wildflowers growing tall on the side of the path.

And I realized immediately what chaos magic could do as those wildflowers shriveled up and died the moment the smoke touched them.

My stomach plummeted.

Keerian sucked in a breath, having seen the same thing I had.

"FAE, *RETREAT!*" I bellowed, as Keerian and I launched off the wall, beating our wings hard towards the enemy. "GARGOYLES – GET IN THE AIR!"

Gargoyles and Sentries leapt to action, filling the night sky and taking defensive positions around Keerian and I. The mist lashed out like a many-headed snake as the front line fae began waning, reappearing atop the wall.

But one fae didn't move fast enough. The smoke touched his boot, burning it, before slithering up his body. There was nothing we could do except watch in horror as the fae screamed, thrashing, while the smoke covered him completely.

We hovered in midair. A whimper sounded from the walls as we all stared, helpless. Within seconds, the shrieks of pain gave way to unnerving silence, and the dead fae slumped against the ground, his skin desiccated.

The Unmarked crept closer.

I flapped my wings, staying close to Keerian as I called upon my battle magic, my eyes trained on the invisible line in the sand – the signal to release my wrath down onto the enemy. Archers drew their bows back, arrows nocked. Fae, safely atop the walls, rallied battle magic that could span the distance. We waited as the shuffling lines of Unmarked advanced closer.

I held my breath.

The first of the Unmarked stepped onto the dirt road, and mayhem ensued.

# CHAPTER TWENTY-EIGHT
# LENNA

LENNA STOOD IN THE store front of Hale's Bakery, though instead of pastries packing every erratically painted shelf, books and candles filled the spaces. A calm anticipation settled over her as she peered around the room, her mind unconsciously looking for something.

The curtains leading into the kitchen fluttered open, causing Lenna to turn. A warmth filled her heart at the sight of the crone, his withered hands gripping a gnarled wood cane. His white hair was long and immaculate, and his bright blue eyes crinkled into a grin as he beheld Lenna.

"I know you," Lenna whispered, her steps making no sound against the wood floor as she approached. "I watched you die."

The Oracle smiled sadly as he extended his hand to her, the light color of his skin spotted with age. "Come, Oracle, I must show you something."

Lenna took his hand, his skin cool against hers, though a pink tinge colored his cheeks. She allowed herself to be led through the curtains, but instead of stepping into the sweltering kitchen, her bare feet met the rocky ground of a cliff overlooking a stormy, churning sea. A mellow breeze ruffled her curls.

The Oracle looked out beyond the water, illuminated only by a waxing moon and stars that dotted the cloudless night sky. Lenna closed her eyes, *the sound of the waves crashing against the rocks far below rhythmic and soothing.*

*"Do not worry for me, dear Oracle," The crone spoke. His voice was peaceful. "I'm thankful every day that Queen Esmeray bestowed a fortunate death upon me."*

*"How are you speaking to me right now?" Lenna asked, taking in the simple dove grey robes of her predecessor, the wind whipping by having no effect on him. He was still. So still. Yet an aura of power and grace radiated from him.*

*"The veil between Terramere and Minmere is thin this night. As an Oracle, our souls are connected through Moirai's power. I am able to visit you here, in your subconscious, when that ripple between realms allows. I am not sure as to why it is so slight tonight, but I didn't want to miss the opportunity to speak with you before the coming war."*

*The words jarred through her, and Lenna swallowed against the lump in her throat. Suddenly, the rough seas below sounded more like the clash of swords, the galloping hooves of lethal war horses, the cries of the wounded and dying. "War?"*

*Nodding slowly, the Oracle shuffled towards the face of the cliff, his head tilted to peer up to the sky. "A time will come where what is right is not what was written by fate. You have the Prism. It's the key to unlocking the history that was long concealed."*

*"What am I looking for?" Lenna questioned.*

*The Oracle answered simply, "The beginning."*

*In the distance, the first rays of the morning sun began breaking over the horizon. Lenna felt the breeze die down, and even the waters below seemed to lull. The Oracle began fading before Lenna's eyes as the light streamed through him. "Remember, Oracle, the sun will always rise to a new day."*

*With a last smile to Lenna, the Oracle disappeared.*

LENNA STIRRED, A WEIGHT against her side bringing her slowly to consciousness.

"I tried to move them, but Sparrow said if I did, they would steal my rings while we slept." Hale's gruff voice held a hint of laughter, and Lenna cracked opened an eye to see four chunky juvenile moon crows happily nestled against her back, stealing the warmth radiating off her body.

Slightly smaller than their adult counterparts, the juveniles had pure white feathers and were immensely crankier.

Hale sat next to the bed in an ornate rocking chair, a large tome balanced on his lap. From the tired look lining his face and under eyes, Lenna figured he stayed awake all night watching her sleep.

Giving Hale a sleepy smile, Lenna reached for him. "I heard moon crows sneak into the bedrooms around the aerie if the opportunity presents itself."

Hale stood and stretched with a groan. "I left the balcony doors open. I thought the fresh air would be nice." He chuckled softly, worry easing off his face as his eyes darted around Lenna, as if he had to assure himself that she was okay. "I only nodded off for a few minutes, and when I woke up, there they were, the little beasties."

Moving to sit on the side of the bed, Hale grasped Lenna's hands in his. Concern flickered through his dark eyes as he gently rubbed his thumbs over the backs of her hands. "How are you feeling, dear? You gave me – us – quite the scare."

Lenna carefully sat up, doing her best not to disturb the birds still curled up and snoozing on the soft duvet.

"I feel... well rested for sure," she admitted, wriggling her toes. "I had a conversation with the previous Oracle in my dreams. Somehow, he was able to cross into my subconscious and give me a warning for what's coming." Lenna sighed heavily, nestling deeper into Hale's side. "With the latest prophecy, I fear it's all connected."

She recanted every detail of the dream, wanting Hale to hear while it was still at the forefront of her mind, unmuddied.

He listened patiently, stroking her curls as she settled her head on his shoulder.

"We need to tell the others," Hale said when she'd finished. "Can you use your ring to call Sparrow and Laurent up here?

The vision of the previous Oracle's death had long been burned behind her eyelids, even after Esmeray's grief filled declaration that it had been an act of mercy to release him from the Soul Keeper's cell. Now, knowing he was in Minmere, at peace, was comforting.

Hale filled her in on the night's activity, a tremor of uncertainty in his voice when he told her Esmeray announced Sparrow as her Heir, and that Esmeray and Keerian hadn't returned to the Palace yet. Lenna sent a prayer skyward that her friends were okay, not wanting to send a message through the rings and interrupt them if the fighting waged on.

"Seems I missed out on a lot," she muttered, shooing Hale off the bed so she could slide out without jostling the feathery demons that wasted no time burrowing into the vacated space.

"I can find Sparrow and Laurent and ask them to come up here. You need to rest," Hale protested as she hurried over to their shared armoire, hastily throwing on a dark green slip dress and overcoat.

Lenna passed Hale, pressing a kiss to his jaw. "I feel very well rested, remember?" Stuffing her feet into her boots, she struggled to tie them in her hurry towards the door. "We need to be with Sparrow or Laurent. Find out what's going on in Calcity."

"I trust you, but if you feel like you need a healer, tell me – okay?" Hale grabbed his cloak, tying it quickly around his shoulders before bending to help Lenna finish lacing up her boot.

"Nope." Lenna patted his cheek as she threw open the door to their bedroom, their Queen's Guards snapping to attention the moment she breezed through the threshold. "But the endearing recommendation is so sweet."

# Chapter Twenty-Nine
# ORLA

Everything was too damn loud.

Servants in the hallway outside of her room rolled carts with too-squeaky wheels, doors along the corridor echoed as they slammed shut, voices laughed raucously. Even the fucking wind was too noisy, whooshing through the room, disrupting the light curtains and the tinkering windchimes hanging on her balcony.

Orla growled low in her throat, as she tossed and turned in the bed. *Did no one in this godsdamned palace ever sleep?*

"Hey, Orla I – holy *shit.*" Orla sat bolt upright, her pulse quickening, as Marlo stood at the end of the bed, gawking at her, a tray of tea and pastries in his hands.

Orla felt her cheeks heat up with embarrassment. Was her hair a mess? She awkwardly tried patting it down. "What's wrong?" she asked, swiping the wayward strands out of her face. Her fingers, usually deftly quick at twisting back her curls, stumbled against her ear.

Her *pointed* ear.

With a gasp and a colorful string of curses, the conversation with Cillian, the memories of fainting from earth-shattering pain, tumbled over her. She lunged past Marlo and into her private bathroom, slamming the door behind her, and engaging the iron deadbolt.

Chest heaving, she stared at her reflection in the small mirror. Her rounded ears were gone, replaced with arched fae ears.

She bared her teeth. Her human, slightly crooked teeth were gone, and perfectly white, straight teeth with sharp canines reflected back at her.

"No, no, no, *no,*" Orla whimpered, ripping off the long-sleeved dress she still wore with utter horror. The thick material tore with ease, as if it was nothing more than thin parchment. Orla's eyes widened. From her fingertips to her elbows, covering both forearms, lay brilliantly red, thick swirls tattooed against her brown skin. "*Fuck.*"

"Orla, are you alright?" Marlo called, concern in his voice as he knocked, the sound so violent and booming that Orla flinched. She couldn't even answer him, the strange reflection in the mirror keeping her full attention.

Orla stood there, mouth agape. Though the difference was slight, she could *see it.* From the slimmer bone structure of her face to the slightly longer, lean limbs, even her hair, usually frizzy and knotted in the mornings, was less tangled, the tight curls perfectly fluffed around her head like a halo.

Cillian was correct.

She was *fae.* Not half fae, with the less pointed ears and more human-like softness, but *fully* fae. It sundered through her being as she tried and failed to wrap her head around the information, everything it meant. Manifesting an *acat* had broken open her very soul, unlocking her true blood, her true self in one fell swoop.

Orla sunk to her knees, leaned against the bathroom door, and cried.

# Chapter Thirty
# KEERIAN

The night's shadows lengthened with the breaking dawn, as if even the darkness wanted to hide the destruction and slaughter from the new day. Atop Calcity's border wall, Keerian sullenly regarded the sun rising up from the horizon, swathing the raging battlefield below in fiery hues of orange, as he grimly nocked an arrow and chose his next target.

After one hundred and fourteen years on this earth, ninety of those spent in service fighting for Irridessen, analyzing battlefields was second nature.

But it didn't take an esteemed eye to notice they were losing.

Brutally.

It was reflected in the weary gargoyles beside him, soaked in sweat and gore, pulling their bowstrings taught with shaking arms, in the feeble battle magic of the fae along the wall. The colorful blazes of power that held the line overnight were now reduced to short bursts, and even those were burning out at an alarming rate. The gargoyles were exhausted, the fae were lagging.

Keerian loosened his arrow, and it buried deep into the throat of an Unmarked below. The Unmarked snapped the shaft in two, and continued to fight without faltering, even with gushing red blood weeping from their neck.

Calcity had been a trap – one they completely and utterly fell for.

Adara hadn't sent fifty Unmarked to ransack the small town and terrorize the residents in an attention-grabbing tantrum to undermine Esmeray's rule.

She sent five hundred.

The Unmarked must have been gathering for weeks – *months* - camouflaged by the dense forest outside of Calcity, only moving under the obscure cover of darkness until they released that deadly smoke now permeating a half mile wide. He personally flew its radius to see if there was any way they could switch strategies, attack from behind, gain some sort of advantage back after being taken so royally by surprise.

But the thick woods revealed no weak spots. The Unmarked had thoroughly covered their tracks, staying deep in the tree growth to hide their true numbers from any of the Opal Palace's roving patrols. And when the Unmarked began their march, that smog undulated around them, carving a sheer path of death through the groves from their abandoned camp to the outskirts of Calcity.

The billowing fog still clung to listless grass and the bodies of Irridessen's fallen, their souls resting in Minmere's depths. Neither the smoke nor the enemy themselves slowed during the long hours to sunrise. So, Keerian fought, and killed, and fought and killed, killed, killed as many Unmarked as he could.

They didn't know much about the God of Chaos, and that left them all feeling off-balanced and paranoid. Massis had fucked off and stayed out of Irridessen until Adara went poking around in that godsdamned spell book.

Per a rushed mind-spoken conversation with Laurent, Keerian asked the fae to grab Hale and go to the library to see if they could find something, *anything,* on chaos magic that may turn the tides of the fight to their favor. His ring had been silent since.

That, in itself, was not a good sign.

Next to him, Esmeray picked up a fist-sized chunk of the crumbling city wall from a dwindling pile, glaring at the combat below as she imbued the rock with her illusion magic, fashioning it into a golden tipped arrow. With a mumbled curse, she strung it against a bow she crafted from another piece of rubble. At full power, Esmeray could create items out of thin air. Now, resorting to illusioned debris...

It meant even her deep well of magic was running dry.

She chose a mark – and drew the bowstring back with a hiss, her arms trembling with the effort.

Keerian watched the arrow fly with a twang, burying itself into the eye of an Unmarked fighting against the gargoyle soldiers still airborne. He continued to be awe-struck at how adept at fighting his mate was without any proper training. If they lived through this, he'd tell her that.

*If* they lived through this.

The smoke covered the ground about a foot deep, forcing gargoyles to expend more energy soaring above it. Keerian's years as a Commander told him they lost a majority of soldiers as the night gave way to morning. It was difficult to look at the bodies lying on the ground, and he pushed down the nauseating wave of guilt that threatened to crush him.

For now, he'd shove that emotion deep into his own steel box to unpack at a later date.

*If* he lived that long.

Or, he'd be seeing the soldiers of his fallen army in Minmere, so he guessed he could apologize to them then. But he'd rather deal with remorse instead of the finality of death.

He watched a female gargoyle bellow in rage as she dove from the sky, her dagger flashing silver in the morning sun before slicing across the throat of an unsuspecting Unmarked, bathing the blade in a gush of red. The gargoyles that continued to fight on the front lines couldn't afford to swing a heavy sword and risk losing their balance in the air. Daggers were his decision because if even the tip of a wing touched the desiccating smoke, they'd die. It crippled them further that the smog forced their own fae warriors to fight from the top of the wall - those who relied on strength in their swords and weapons having to resort to firing battle magic from a distance - without hitting one of their own in the air.

All along the wall, the beings surrounding them looked as bad as he felt. Sweat-soaked, drained, dredging up whatever they could afford for one more arrow to fly, one more flash of battle magic to hit an Unmarked.

Aligning an arrow against his bow, Keerian glanced towards his mate. Her dark hair was pulled back, highlighting the dribble of blood that trickled down from her scalp. She swayed, just a little, as she gripped another rock in her hand, the stone warping into an arrow that she mindlessly nocked again.

He fired.

She fired.

The target they both silently chose died.

Their supply of arrows was grossly inadequate compared to the number of remaining enemies. Especially since it took multiple well-placed bolts to stop a single Unmarked. Hence why Esmeray was using rocks and her already waning magic to try and bolster their arsenal.

She imbued another rock, the illusion flashing and wobbling - but holding. Keerian loosened another arrow with a grunt, taking down the fae he previously hit in the neck. The Unmarked slumped to the ground and didn't rise again.

The gargoyle fighting the fae threw the King a curt nod before launching higher in the sky, searching for their next opponent.

"I'm about to Sentry," Esmeray croaked, her dark wings fanning out behind her. They'd been in the melee for hours before alighting to the wall to rest their wings. Blood covered her armor, and he knew his own fared no better. Just thinking about it made his skin feel stickier and his body more weary. Between the two of them, they must've killed close to seventy Unmarked, and that was *with* Esmeray using her battle magic.

Keerian watched her wing twitch, a small tremble, and knew there was no way her Sentry would hold her above the smog. But he knew Esmeray would fly purely out of spite - injured wing or not. He had to ask though, since that tremor could be the difference between life and death for the both of them if her wing gave out. "Do your wings feel strong enough to carry you?"

She frowned, her left wing drooping. It was the one that gave her recurring issues after the fight with Adara. As much as she flew to strengthen it over the last four months, that wing would become unbalanced during long flights. And they'd been flying for hours over the smoke, hovering, diving.

Keerian begrudgingly had to hand it to Merrick. His aerial unit was the only one still flying, stopping only for short breaks before launching back into the fray. But even then, there were only fifteen left. The fae threw another synchronized barrage of magic at the approaching masses, but where one Unmarked fell, another took its place.

Esmeray had sent out an urgent message to the Opal Palace to send all of their top flyers but only a handful were flown out with flippant reassurances that more were on the way.

That had been hours ago.

Keerian gritted his teeth, mentally recounting which advisors were currently residing in the Opal Palace, and who may pause sending reinforcements. He held a growing suspicion there was at least one council member waiting to see if the King and Queen truly survived this attack. With no blood related heirs, the Opal Palace could simply reject Sparrow's succession, giving the throne instead to whichever power-hungry Lord claimed it first.

That thought alone had him growling and nocking two arrows simultaneously, the pair whizzing across the dirt road and dropping another Unmarked.

Sparrow sent the remaining seventy-five gargoyle warriors and twenty-five fae through a portal from the Obsidian Palace, leaving only a couple Queen's Guards behind to protect the Oracle, but at the rate they were felled, the fresh warriors barely made a dent in the Unmarked below.

"We've killed at least half," Keerian noted quietly, as an Unmarked rammed into a hovering gargoyle, causing them to drop into the smoke with an agonizing shriek.

"I'll be fine," Esmeray rasped as Keerian watched her push to shift, rallying his only magic to Sentry right beside her. If she was determined to go back down there, he would too. He slipped his mind down the shimmering magic that connected him to his golden Sentry. But before he could sink into it, Esmeray let out a small gasp, her green eyes widening.

And then Esmeray froze, with that perfect fae stillness, a determined look darkening the planes of her face as she breathed, more to herself than to him, "It cannot corrupt, it cannot manipulate."

"What?"

Esmeray looked out to the fray beyond, and he could practically see a reckless fucking plan forming between those curled horns.

"Clear the battlefield," Esmeray ordered softly, avoiding his incredulous look as she reached into her pocket of space, pulling out the spell book.

His eyes narrowed swiftly, skepticism of her command replaced immediately with apprehension as the black and gold cover gleamed in the morning light. "What the fuck, Esmeray."

"Trust me." Was all she said.

Keerian grappled with his thoughts for a moment but ultimately relented. Esmeray had an idea that would hopefully save the warriors below fighting for their life, their Kingdoms. They were burnt out.

And there was no way Esmeray would debase her magic with spell work.

He told himself that last bit confidently, though a flutter of doubt drifted through his mind as his mate averted his gaze, her blood-stained hands tightening against the spell book as she surveyed the destruction, the fighting below, the Unmarked still standing at the edge of the tree line, silently waiting for their turn to fight, to wear down and kill their warriors. Her face screwed up in concentration, her breathing rapid and shallow.

A weight settled in his gut, yet Keerian knew the next word he spoke could come at the cost of very heavy consequences. His eyes trained on the Queen beside him, taking in her bolstered stance, the determined glint in her eye, the night-black wings that slowly unfurled as she straightened her back.

Queen Absolute Esmeray took a single step towards the edge of the wall.

# Chapter Thirty-One
# Esmeray

*"RETREAT!"* Keerian bellowed to the gargoyles beyond the wall. I chewed my lip as the word spun the Unmarked into a frenzy, a handful disengaging from the dense forest, their magic lashing out, attempting to ground the aerial warriors before they could peel away.

Four went down shrieking, the poisonous smoke pouncing as they fought the entire way to Minmere. The line of Unmarked, sensing victory, edged closer.

I kept my face impassive, though I counted every figure, marked every shadow lurking in the trees beyond. The Book of Phades thrummed in my hand, in rhythm with my own heartbeat.

I had taken its magic once before, on a snowy mountaintop high above the Obsidian Palace, in a final, desperate attempt to defeat Adara. But I severed that connection, refusing to allow my *acat* to fully intertwine with the book's, from fear of my magic being irrevocably warped by what I thought were deadly spells.

Though I held a healthy dose of doubt this would work, I approached the book now with the reverence I showed the death goddess herself, and the book's sentience seemed to respond in kind.

"C'mon," Keerian murmured, his eyes straining towards the gargoyles weaving between the renewed bursts of chaos magic, fighting for every inch closer to the safety of the warded city.

The first gargoyles shot beyond the wall, landing heavily into the courtyard below, and healers quickly attended to their injuries.

I took another step towards the broken and crumbling ledge.

The Unmarked scuttled further out of the woods.

Phades wanted me to use the power in her book?

What better way to test out her request than against enemies of my Kingdoms.

As if it could read my innermost desire, the Book of Phades hummed with glee in my hands.

When the last of our warriors cleared the wall, I felt Keerian turn to me, slowly, warily, his gaze darting between the book, and my face.

Opposed to my own rapid breathing, he held his breath.

I felt the book's power shimmering with anticipation. Like it knew what I was about to do.

Around me, the wind seemed to die down, and even the morning sun on the horizon paused its ascent into the day. Time itself stopped.

Watching. Waiting.

"Way down do our souls go," I breathed as I slammed the drained thread of my *acat* into the well of god power emitting from the Book of Phades.

Blinding light filled my vision, and I gasped as intense, ice-cold magic thundered into me.

The Book of Phades blazed in my grip, bright as a star.

*The power of nothing and everything, infallible, intangible, omnipotent.*

The words jarred through me, and I gritted my teeth against the onslaught of raw magic tearing through my veins.

*Glorious, vicious Queen, will you accept my gift this time? If you want the power of a god, all you have to say is 'yes.'*

It could have been the sentience of the book, it could have been Phades herself, but I flicked my eyes out to the hulking mass of Unmarked.

Cold, sharp anger sliced into my heart, butchering all doubt.

I would never hear my father's deep, booming laugh fill the halls of the Opal Palace again.

I would never again hear my mother's bedtime stories, feel her comforting presence next to me as I learned to fly.

I would never get back that first year with Keerian, when we were separated by a Kingdom with a price on my head.

I would never get back the innocence of sharing a bedroom with my twin, dreaming about what we would do once we received our *acatis,* our whispers and giggles hidden in the stillness of night.

My breath caught as the rage for all I lost burst from my soul.

I thought of my weary, bloodied mate now, our friends waiting anxiously for word of our survival, Adara sitting in her dirty cell with that smug look on her face.

I thought of Irridessen.

Irridessen needed a Queen that could protect them.

They needed a Vessel.

*Yes.* I replied to the Book of Phades, no longer second-guessing my decision.

The book's magic lunged as the word rang through my mind, digging into my feeble string of power, coiling and weaving through it, binding tightly around the waning strands of my *acat.*

There was no bottom, no limit, my magic bolstered and grew at a rapid rate. I threw my head back, fighting to get a breath down as Phades's direct god power careened into me.

That golden magic coated my skin and then I was glowing, swathed in effervescent light. The Book of Phades dimmed as I took, and took, and took its magic.

A searing burn travelled down the back of my neck so swift and unexpected that I screamed.

Keerian bellowed my name - but it sounded like he was miles away.

And as my magic amplified, unchecked, unlocked - as Phades alluded to - I felt a shift roll through the realm.

I had a distinct awareness that the wall shuddered, spiderwebbing and cracking beneath my feet.

Then, with a deafening howl, a pillar of golden light ruptured from me, shooting high into the sky above at such a ferocity that the fae archers scrambled away with a cry.

Distantly, I heard the book clatter to the ground.

As the last of its iridescence faded, I heard the voice again - soft, and satiated, marking me.

*Vessel.*

With that, the remaining magic, that pillar of golden light, changed its direction with a roar, crashing into my soul.

I withstood the force, absorbing every drop of direct god magic Phades bestowed upon me. In addition to the gifts from my *acat,* the realization of her words slithered over me. *The Book of Phades cannot corrupt, it cannot manipulate.*

The book *itself* could not corrupt, but with this level of power...what *couldn't* I do?

I narrowed my focus onto the figures beyond the wall, where almost two hundred Unmarked remained, their black, blown pupils trained on me. In synchronization, they rallied their battle magic into a wave to hit me with a collective blow.

But they had all come out of the trees.

I smiled.

Their chaos magic now seemed...*unremarkable.*

The victory that felt so close they could taste it, lured every Unmarked from the thick foliage and onto the dirt road, blood-lust overriding any other sense.

I could feel my pulse pumping in my ears, my heartbeat thudding strong against the rush of adrenaline, my new, feral, god magic thrashing inside of me, ready to be unleashed.

Gold magic shimmered against my tattooed palm. I raised my hands and released Phades's gift directly at the wall of chaos magic barreling towards me, at the Unmarked who were now standing squarely in *my* trap.

An arch of brilliant gold slammed into ink purple, so dark it was almost black, with a deafening *boom.*

"Only a god can kill another god," I growled, shoving against the chaos magic wielded by beings who were now no match for me. Against god power, that purple wave faltered and shattered, smothered thoroughly by my light.

On and on, a full breath passed as I unleashed myself against the horde.

And as my omnipotent power winked out, cut off, as I clenched my palm into a fist, it seemed as if the entire world hung on a precipice while my glittering magic faded and the dirt road came back into view.

Below, the Unmarked were reduced to no more than charred bones and ash. Their desiccating smoke dissipated listlessly as the universe seemed to let out a breath of its own and began moving around me once more.

A reverent hush rolled over the wall as our warriors, and Keerian beside me, peered out to where the remains of the formidable enemy lay.

Scorch marks gouged through the earth - all that remained of Adara's army. My eruption of power had wrecked the outskirts of the forest in front of us, the once lush foliage of the tree line now pushed back a couple hundred feet, leaving twisted branches stripped of leaves and uprooted stumps in its wake.

Not a single Unmarked survived my new power.

"The Queen of Decimation." A being whispered behind me, ripping my mind back to the reality of what I'd done. The fae nearest to me fell to their knee, reverence shining in their eyes as I turned stiffly towards the rest of my soldiers, feeling as if I was locked in an alternate reality, an out of body experience that shocked me to my very core. One by one, they all dropped low, knee bent, head bowed.

For a heartbeat, it was silent.

And then the cheers began.

I didn't allow myself to mourn the loss of who I was before.

# CHAPTER THIRTY-TWO
# ORLA

A SOFTER RAP AGAINST the bathroom door came hours later. Orla hadn't moved, sullenly watching the light blues of the sky turn darker and purplish through the small window above the tub.

Olivera was not her mother. The woman who raised her was fully human, now a stranger, to everything Orla's reflection showed. The magic that activated her *acat* and revealed her true being tore open her entire history, flipping it on its head and showing Orla her entire life had been a lie.

*But what was the truth?*

Orla didn't know. It was a sick relief that the woman was not her mother, but it left an ugly stain behind, a stain that made her realize with Cillian's words about her heritage, that not only did she not know who her parents were, the King killed them along with the rest of the *Vitraro*.

She leaned against the hard wooden door, her mind unable to comprehend that she truly manifested an *acat*. The small sliver of hope that Cillian and his advisor made a mistake about her heritage and fae blood was gone. Replaced with the scrolling ink that sunk deep into her skin.

"Orla?" Soren's smoky voice slipped under the door. "Are you wallowing?"

Orla groaned, knowing that Marlo would give her space to sort out her shit on her own terms, but Soren absolutely would not. Even though she only just met the fae, she had the distinct impression that Soren would stand there all evening until she came out.

"Look, I know you're probably all cranky and doing some sort of fucked up *'woe is me'* shit in there, but listen, okay?" Orla heard a chair scrape across the bedroom floor, and figured Soren dragged it over to sit outside the bathroom.

"I remember when I got my *acat*. It's what faelings look forward to from the moment we're old enough to understand that we'll one day have magic. Our families would only ever tell us about the thrill, the euphoria, of our *acat,* and conveniently leave out the part that it fucking hurts." Soren laughed, and the sound was sweet, laced with a dry humor. Orla couldn't help but curl closer to the door, a small smile tugging at the corner of her lips, imagining a young Soren with wild blonde hair and striking bronze eyes angry at the world.

"Well, my *acat* appeared when I was twenty-one. At the most inopportune time, I might add. And it sucked. Yeah, it's a blessing from the gods. Whatever. It was the worst pain I could imagine, and then when I thought I was about to pass out, the pain doubled. It's agony."

Something soft clicked into her soul. She could never return to the Slate Kingdom now, not with the dome that kept all fae out, but that left her with a semblance of permanence. No longer was she working towards escaping these lands of magic. Now, she needed to figure out what to do for a long life. Fae lived for centuries.

She didn't have to figure it all out now. She had time.

Standing on unsteady legs, she steeled herself, whispering the words she always chanted during every pitfall in her life. *I am not so easily broken.*

Orla opened the door.

Soren was lounging on the chair as she expected, her eyebrows rising as Orla stepped, naked, into the bedroom. Hopping up, Soren quickly snatched her robe off the armoire and tossed it over to her.

"Thanks." Orla caught the robe, quickly tying it shut and sat down on the chaise. "What's your *acat*? Also, this has been driving me crazy, where is your tattoo?"

Soren smirked, crossing back over to her chair. "I'm a mimic. It's a gift from the God of Riddles, Eek. I can absorb another fae's battle magic and then wield the same power they have for a while – until I run through it all at least."

Orla blinked in surprise. Stretching cat-like, Soren continued, "When I absorb another fae's power, my gift creates a mimicry of their *acat* onto my skin. I've been helping Cillian, and you, unknowingly, by absorbing that burning pain you've been feeling whenever I can to give you some relief. But you didn't have an *acat* yet, so no tattoos for me." Soren eyed the deep red tattoos on Orla's hands. "Though I'm very excited to see what your *acat* looks like on me now. I love the color."

"Oh," Orla said softly, thinking back to all the times she'd been around Soren – how the aches and pains in her lungs had disappeared for a few hours after. She was suddenly embarrassed by how abrasive she'd been to Soren the first time they met – the fae had been helping her the entire time.

Soren cupped her palm, a glowing ball of pure white light materializing and bobbing in her hand. "I still have battle magic even if I'm not mimicking someone else's gifts. But the white light changes if I take another's power."

"Thank you," Orla locked eyes with Soren, hoping that the fae understood the reasons behind the words.

With a small smile, Soren squeezed her hand into a fist, the white orb disappearing. "That's what friends are for, Orla. I'm sorry I didn't admit it sooner, but Cillian wanted to be the one to tell you."

"Do you know what my *acat* is?"

"No, I don't. Until you use it for the first time, I won't be able to mimic it, either. And I can only mimic lineage gifts." Soren gave Orla a pointed look. "So if you have a super rare heritage gift, don't tell me what it is. I don't want to be jealous, *okay*?"

Orla squeezed her lips together. Soren's knowing look had her thinking that Cillian may have filled her in on Orla's *Vitraro* heritage, and that Soren was telling Orla in a round-about way, that her secret was safe. Soren nodded once. "A forewarning for you - prepare for questions from the other residents of Oasees. Fae are fickle beings. If you have a powerful *acat* you become...interesting."

Orla swallowed, Cillian's words about her long-exterminated heritage bubbling to the forefront of her mind. She turned, sitting down at the edge of her bed, examining her new tattoos.

"Cillian said I can help you learn how to use your *acat*." Soren followed Orla, sitting down next to her and reaching out her hand for Orla to take. "Get you ready to pass the Culling."

"Culling?" Orla asked, wracking her mind, trying to think if she'd heard that term used before.

"Fucking asshole," Soren mumbled, her nostrils flaring, "*He* was supposed to tell you about the Culling."

Orla shook her head. "I was...yelling at him after he admitted I was fully fae. And then I erm...passed out."

Soren hesitated, obviously uncomfortable with the turn of conversation. "The Ruby Kingdom and the Topaz Kingdom are the only two lands that still enact it. It's inherently...barbaric."

"Tell me," Orla demanded, the usual burning pain that accompanied any spike of fear was gone. Her shoulders relaxed automatically as no twinges of agony dug in. It made her acutely aware of just how much tension she'd kept in her body since arriving to the Ruby Kingdom. When was the last time she breathed deeply?

"Well, there's a list that gets populated a few days before the Autumnal Equinox from the Crown. It details a list of what powers are acceptable for the beings in the Ruby Kingdom to possess and which are...not." Soren sucked in a breath. "Before the Equinox Ball, every being who manifested an *acat* in the last year is bought before the King. They must prove to the King their *acat* is not on the Culling list. King Eamon has made it into his own personal spectacle, having beings present their gifts before the Ball. And in his mind, you're guilty until proven innocent."

Panic rose up, and as grateful as she was that the fiery pain she dealt with for months was now gone, apparently thanks to her manifested *acat*, she once again heard the haunted words Cillian mentioned in that infernal conversation. His father made sure anyone with *Vitraro* blood was exterminated. She was certain *that* was on this Culling list.

"What happens if you have a power mentioned on the King's list?" she questioned, her mind already tripping over itself trying to figure out how she was going to flee, a whiplash from her *just* thinking she could have a life here.

Soren's plush lips thinned, an expression of disgust coloring her expression. "You die. The King doesn't fuck around with that. If a fae is found with one of those powers, its immediate execution – no trial, no imprisonment."

King Eamon would kill her if he discovered her heritage, and now she couldn't go back to the Slate Kingdom due to the dome that kept fae out. Orla looked down at her tattoos. A gift from a god that was going to land her on a kill list didn't seem like such a gift after all.

Cillian had a fuckton more explaining to do if he was so interested in protecting her.

With a shrug, Soren clicked her tongue. "You'll be fine. Cillian wouldn't let anything happen to you, and I'm an excellent teacher. We'll figure out your lineage gift and go from there. You won't be in danger of the Culling."

"I hope so," Orla muttered, staring at the coiled red swirls that covered her arms. "I sure fucking hope so."

# CHAPTER THIRTY-THREE
# ESMERAY

KEERIAN TRUDGED THROUGH THE doors of our quarters in the Opal Palace, his boots squelching against the pristine tile, leaving footprints of muck and gore in their wake. But I fared no better, blood and mud patterned against the floor behind me. The sun had risen, arched, and began its descent in the sky over the long hours after battle, and this was the first moment Keerian and I could be alone.

Over the course of the day, I could tell he was stewing - that confusion over my actions rolled into fear, into anger. His thoughts were carefully hidden, facial expressions blank. We tended to the wounded, reassured the townsfolk that their city was safe, and Keerian stuck forcefully to the bare facts whenever questioned.

Yes, the Unmarked were following Adara.

No, we didn't know who the Unmarked were before they turned to chaos magic.

Yes, we are all *so* thankful for Queen Absolute Esmeray.

Calcity's inhabitants returned while we cleaned up rubble, though word traveled rapidly that I obliterated over half of the enemies in one fell swoop. Crying citizens had thrown themselves at my feet, weeping in thanks, wanting to touch my hand, begging me to accept tokens of gratitude, asking me to bless them, their children, their town.

I smiled as much as I could, accepted their small gifts and baubles, though their keening wails of newfound devotion left my mouth tasting like ash. For the citizens of Calcity, I was their savior, which definitely improved my reputation from the once feared Traitor Queen, but Keerian barely *looked* at me, and I couldn't blame him.

Now, standing face to face in the soft evening glow coming through the pearlescent windows, the weight of what I'd done sunk in. My hands shook on their own accord. Keerian deserved an explanation.

I wasn't ready to face everyone back at the Obsidian Palace, and I needed time to process the dizzying power settling into my bones. Power that was seemingly here to stay. So, before waning here, I shot down Keerian's ring that I was going to clean up before heading back to the Obsidian Palace, and he told me he wasn't letting me out of his sight.

The normally romantic and kind gesture felt vaguely threatening, causing my already fraying nerves to unravel further, making me second guess everyone in a paranoia that I'd felt plenty – but never from Keerian.

I pushed that feeling down, assuring myself that his intentions were pure.

I thought the Book of Phades would give me a short-lived boost to my existing magic that would naturally ebb away as I wielded it. But when I peered inward, to the thread of magic deep inside of me, a thick, braided cord of rolling gold met my mind's eye. Something was now unlocked within my soul, and my power responded in kind.

I didn't just *use* the magic from the Vessel Book, I *took* it.

Now, standing in the foyer of our chambers, I felt too big, too turbulent. I stared at the last bit of sunset through the glass doors, inhaling the sweet aroma of flowers wafting from the gardens beyond. It all seemed so…delicate. Fragile.

My sensitive ears still rung with the cries of the dying, the sharp crackles of magic, and the zinging of arrows released from taught bowstrings. The metallic scent of blood still filled my nose, dried and flaking against every inch of skin not covered by armor. In comparison, the whispered sighs of the weeping willow outside made me skittish, its peaceful song so at odds with the cacophony of death echoing in my head.

Unlike the Obsidian Palace, neither Keerian nor I wanted anything to do with my late parent's room. That entire wing of the Opal Palace stayed locked. The Prism's replay of their death continued to haunt my nightmares. Multiple advisors offered to begin renovating the wing to suit Keerian and me, but new furniture and a coat of paint wouldn't wash away the images of Adara slashing my father's throat, my mother thrashing in their bed as their soul tie claimed her life as well.

Thankfully, my old bedroom survived Adara's short rule, and it remained one of the only places in the Opal Palace that didn't dredge up horrors.

I took a deep breath through my nose, closing my eyes for a beat before whirling to face Keerian. This edgy feeling of not knowing my mate's thoughts made my heart squeeze painfully in my chest. I opened my eyes slowly, taking in his stiff posture and guarded expression as he stood just out of reach.

"Are you going to be rational?" I asked, my voice hard, ignoring the hurt that flashed through his stare. His jaw flexed, his own glacial resolve slipping over his rugged features. My breathing became labored.

I felt as if I was seconds away from losing my fucking mind. Sucking in a shaky gulp of air, I continued hoarsely, "Because I don't know if I can be right now, and I need to know if you're with me or against me." My traitorous voice cracked, and I turned away from him.

Fuck. Keerian and I never fought. But the way he looked at me after the battle, after he saw what I'd done...I couldn't read the expression. And it scared the shit out of me to even have this conversation.

Keerian let out a rough hiss, the fire that swam through his eyes illuminating the purely predator gaze fixed on my every move. "When have I *ever* been against you, Meer?"

I threw my arms out wide, a manic laugh escaping between pants. "You're looking at me like..." I shook my head rapidly, my hands dropping heavily, throat tightening. "Like I'm..." I couldn't finish the thought aloud. I touched the black gem on my finger.

*"A monster."*

Keerian lowered his chin in my direction, the brimming anger diffusing into pain, making my heart plummet. We regarded each other silently.

My magic swirled through me, but our soul tie burned brighter.

"Do you know what it was like for me to sit in that room, in *this palace* for a year while Adara held me captive?" he croaked, his voice achingly raw, the shiny luster of his golden armor lost under caked layers of grime, exposing a vulnerable side of him that I rarely saw.

My eyes widened as he stepped closer, his broad hands tentative, gripping my forearms gently and pulling me into his arms. I relaxed into his touch. Keerian reached up to cradle my cheek.

"It was terrifying. I'd never felt powerless, never felt trapped and helpless before. But I was. I couldn't fight, couldn't *risk* getting killed because it would mean your death as well."

Keerian's fingers shook as he tiled my head up, his lips inches away from mine. The wild look in his eyes searched my face. Our rage abated, leaving a primal angst that overflowed with emotion.

"I did what I could to lay low and gather information because *that* was the only way I could be useful to you. I've trained as an elite warrior for almost one hundred years and my power was stripped completely by Adara and that spell book within *seconds*. I don't have fae magic. I can only trust my training, my Sentry, and my instincts. And those were all ripped away by the spell book you just used."

Oh, *oh*.

"Keerian," I whispered, my heart aching. He refused to speak about his time as Adara's captive, and I didn't want to push him to divulge until he was ready. For him to tell me this, to admit to feeling helpless because of the book I just wielded in front of him...

I was a fucking dumbass.

"I didn't use a spell," I confessed, gripping him to me tighter.

And then I told him everything.

About the portal turning red and transporting me to Minmere, about Phades and her throne of bones, about the Book of Phades written after the God War, about her sacrifice to stay in Minmere for her sister.

About Vessels.

About me.

He listened for what felt like an hour, his hand in mine as we sat on the floor of our chambers, wings wrapped around us, silently deciding together that we didn't want to get gore on the furniture.

I told him about Phades alluding to the power in the Vessel Book, how she told me her god magic would not corrupt.

I cried and he held me.

And then he teared up, and I held him, although he vehemently denied that counted as crying. He told me about the terror he felt trapped in the tower, how Adara used wards to keep him contained, how he had no idea what was going on outside that small room. He admitted he tried to lure Adara past the wards so he could kill her, how his heart hammered with trepidation as she danced against that threshold and never crossed it. The fear that one wrong move on his part and we would both be ended.

Hearing that Adara tormented him, the guards stationed outside his door mocked and goaded him, that he felt so alone and lost, made me see red.

My strong, loving mate, trapped in that little, circular room atop the highest spire of the Opal Palace...

I wanted to reduce the entire Palace around us into rubble. With the new god magic coursing through my veins, I bet I could.

But as he spoke, his voice became clearer, surer. As if getting the words out, giving them life, brightened that dark stain on his soul. I felt lighter after confiding in my mate about the visit to Minmere, and the new power that rumbled through my blood. From the way his moss green eyes seemed to sparkle, I could tell our conversation was healing for him, too.

"So, do you think there's any direct god magic left in her book?" Keerian asked quietly, stretching out his wings before standing, pulling me up with him.

"I don't think so," I admitted solemnly, "Before I took its magic, I could feel its presence, and now I can't. I wonder if Lenna or Sparrow will feel anything from it or if now it's just...an old book that we need to translate and read. But I wonder if something other than this new power was unlocked within me...if I somehow damned the very beings I swore to protect."

"I'm sure we'll find out soon enough," Keerian said dryly. He shrugged off the sheath that was strapped between his wings before unbuckling the various pieces of armor protecting his thighs and shins. "But in the meantime, get that battle suit off."

I tracked his movements, stilling as he began wrestling his under shirt off. "What are you doing?" I breathed, the air between us immediately growing taught again. But in a much different way.

"Well, we won a huge battle, found out you have the power of a god, and talked about our feelings. So, now, I'm going to fuck you senseless. Then we're going to clean up, throw on a crown, and go do the King and Queen shit." Keerian smirked proudly as my jaw dropped. With a smug smile and a darkening gaze, he slowly undid the laces on his breeches, until they hung loosely against his waist. I flicked my eyes down hungrily, taking in the length of him visibly straining against the material.

"We're covered in blood," I murmured, my desire for Keerian a hypnotizing allure. Even my Sentry perked up in my soul, howling to be let free to love the male in front of me.

"And my most intrinsic desire, my Queen, is to take you as you are - fearlessly, wickedly, and completely. Give me your worst, your quietest wishes and your cruelest monster, because my beast loves yours so wholly. Covered in blood or crowned in diamonds...there isnt a single thing about you that I would ever dream of changing."

My chest heaved, the air in the room pulsing with desire as I pulled free the ties on the front of my leather suit, the first layer quickly sliding to the floor. Keerian stepped behind me, expertly undoing the clasps along my spine, before moving to the buckles on my lower back, freeing the top from my wings and exposing my skin to the cool air. He bent down, pressing a soft kiss against the side of my throat.

A slight pause, and I felt Keerian straighten before his fingers trailed softly down the back of my neck. "That's new."

"What?"

"A tattoo…You have a new tattoo right here."

My fingers darted out to where he traced the patch of skin, his tender touch giving me goosebumps. Aside from first receiving my *acat,* when Keerian and I locked in our soul tie, my tattoo spread slightly, deep black ink filling in my shoulder and travelling up to the base of my throat, and Keerian's increased from seven thick bands around his right forearm to ten – which spoke loudly to his prowess as a gargoyle.

I'd never heard of a being receiving a tattoo from a god any other way.

"What is it?" I asked, but before he answered, I already crafted two mirrors out of thin air, holding them at an angle to where I could peer at it myself.

It was still red around the edges, and I thought over the moment when I first accepted the magic from the Book of Phades.

I'd felt a *burn*…

And there, on the back of my neck, lay an odd symbol – a four-pointed star with a black crescent moon in the middle.

My heart started pounding. I felt a rising wave of panic twist my gut at the unknown, at what this tattoo symbolized, what it would mean for our future –

Keerian let out a low whistle, his eyes on my new tattoo and a single brow quirked. He must have read the pure fear that flitted across my face because he let out a growl. His broad hand wrapped around the base of my throat, igniting every single piece of my soul, tugging me towards him. His fingers slipped into my hair, his lips hovering so close to my own that I could feel the ghost of a kiss. "Get out of your head, my love. Stay here, with me."

That panic ebbed away as quickly as it came on.

I chucked the mirrors onto the rug, and they disappeared in a zip of gold light.

Keerian let out an appreciative rumble, gripping the base of my skull tightly and tilting my head up to meet his lips. The duality of his hard grip, coarse beard, and his whisper of a kiss made a shiver of anticipation roll through my core.

"I need you, now," I moaned, panting out the words as I rolled my hips against him.

He captured my throat in his other hand, crashing his lips to mine, our mouths battling for dominance as our kisses turned from sweet to frenzied. He pulled back swiftly, leaving my chest heaving, my body thrumming with need. Our eyes locked, a million questions and answers flowing between us.

Keerian dropped to his knees before me, his palms slowly trailing down my back, massaging down my thighs, before he slid off my boots and tossed them by the door to the bathroom. I threaded my fingers through his hair, my nails scraping against his scalp, wanting him closer, wanting him everywhere.

His hands wrapped around my waist, and he peppered kisses across my bare stomach before working my tight leather pants down, patiently waiting as I stepped out of them. I grasped his shoulders for stability, and he leaned his head back, his long hair swinging away from his face, revealing a wickedly feral gleam in his eyes.

I tugged him up, and he was on me in seconds, his lips taking searing kisses with a snarl, causing a moan to escape from my throat. I buried my hands in the thick curls around his horns as he backed us towards the massive bed, his mouth never leaving mine, our breathing heavy and labored.

Keerian hoisted me up, and I wrapped my legs around his waist as he lowered us onto the duvet, my wings spreading wide as he laid me on my back. "I swore I would tie you to this bed," he murmured, sliding his hand up to pin my wrists above my head. "But, sadly, we don't have the time for that." He pressed my captured wrists deeper into the mattress with one hand, the other starting a slow sweep down my body.

I arched into his touch as his rough palms slid up my breasts, replaced quickly with his teeth and tongue. I gasped as his hand continued lower, brushing past my navel.

"I love you," Keerian whispered gruffly, raising his head to lock eyes with me. "And if loving you meant our fall from grace, then it would be my highest honor to follow you into damnation."

I opened my mouth, letting out a small whimper as I took in the sincerity in his expression. "Keerian, if I damned us all..."

He shrugged, slashing me that damning grin. "Then it'll be an insane party in the afterlife." Keerian kissed away my worry as he spread my thighs, and I wriggled him closer to me, using my legs to hold him in place.

He gently slid a single finger inside me, and I gasped, clenching around him. Keerian chuckled hungrily as my body bucked, aching for more. His thumb brushed my clit as he worked me agonizingly closer to that wave of euphoria. He knew exactly what I needed, starting off slowly before increasing the tempo, one finger becoming two, moving faster, harder, until I was a writhing mess underneath him.

I could feel my orgasm building swiftly, and all I could do was grasp the ring on my finger, rub the onyx gem on the band. *"Please."* Keerian eyes shone with molten desire, that ruthless grin on his face all but baring his teeth at me, before pulling out and licking my arousal from his fingers with a guttural growl.

*"You taste like paradise,"* Keerian crooned. *"Be my undoing."*

He knocked my legs wider, his wings spreading behind him. As he sheathed himself inside me in one strong thrust, the thickness of him stretching me so deliciously, I let out a blissful moan, my back arching off the bed. He slammed into me again, wings flaring, before leaning over me, our lips melding as our soul tie brightened inside of us, overshadowing our other gifts.

My hips rocked, and I met his rhythm, rolling up as he hit that deep place within me, my body locked around his. He pressed his forehead to mine, one hand holding my wrists, the other braced on the side of my head, careful to avoid the sharp tips of my splayed wing and horn. We moved in perfect tandem, pulling us closer and closer to that brilliant release.

And there was only us, only this room, only our souls.

I shattered with a cry, Keerian following close behind with a roar.

And in that moment, I understood exactly what type of monster I'd become to protect this love.

And it didn't scare me the slightest.

# CHAPTER THIRTY-FOUR
## SPARROW

SPARROW GAPED AT THE Queen atop the dais, her mind spinning. She'd always known, deep down, that Esmeray's magic was different – but to have it confirmed...

Esmeray truly was the only being in existence with an *acat* from Phades. And now she was also blessed with the god's direct magic.

The Vessel of Death.

When the massive flare of gold illuminated the entirety of the Obsidian Palace's throne room, and Esmeray and Keerian landed upon the raised dais, Lenna and Sparrow shielded their eyes. It had been the first sign to Sparrow that Esmeray's magic was now...*enhanced*.

And when Esmeray casually extended a hand, and a blanket of shimmering magic shot up the throne room walls, creating impenetrable wards glittering with power, Sparrow *knew* something big happened during the defense of Calcity. The wards hummed with power, protecting the room from any outside ears, as Esmeray launched into the events from the night before.

Now, clacking the tip of Goldriel against the dais, Esmeray paced, shooting increasingly odd looks at Sparrow. Sparrow pursed her lips.

The Book of Phades had been handed off to Hale at the end of Esmeray's testimony, after Lenna ruffled through its pages and announced she didn't feel any weird sentience from it. Sparrow checked too, and true to Esmeray's word, the Book of Phades was now indeed...just a book.

But the feeling that someone or some*thing* was still watching Sparrow remained. It made her uneasy, defensive, her instincts squirming nervously as she tracked each of Esmeray's movements, desperately trying to remind herself that this was her best friend – that no matter how much power Esmeray now held, it was still Esmeray – not an enemy, and that Esmeray would never use magic for nefarious purposes.

Esmeray took the god power and obliterated the Unmarked in a single blast.

Sparrow thought back to her visit with Adara, a sliver of reassurance easing through her tight chest.

Adara stole that magic and corrupted it.

Esmeray accepted it to save an entire town of people.

Hale practically vibrated with excitement as he was handed the Vessel Book. With a quick bow to the King and Queen, Hale promptly scurried out of the throne room to begin – in his words – the thrillingly glorious work of interpreting a god language. Lenna trotted behind him, chuckling as Hale blindly grabbed her hand and shoved nose deep into the book's pages.

Laurent sat on the first row of the stone pews facing the dais. His robe draped around him, in hues of orange and soft peach, complimenting the color of Sparrow's forest green gown. Esmeray and Keerian had changed before returning to the Obsidian Palace, though their attire was much more casual - dark cotton pants and heavy sweaters.

Keerian looked as if he was falling asleep in his throne, his chin in his hand and his glazed, half-lidded attention on Esmeray who continued to pace the circumference of the dais.

"There's three more of these books just...waiting for their Vessel to claim the magic in them?" Laurent asked, breaking his contemplative silence.

"At least the Book of Faune is waiting for its Vessel to claim the power. Phades didn't give me the names of the other two gods that could create a Vessel." Esmeray stopped pacing, cocking her head to stare at Sparrow, her brows knitting for a moment before she sighed and slumped onto the throne next to her mate.

Sparrow's magic surged inside her at that look, as if it were responding to a threat.

Ignoring her *acat*, Sparrow fisted the fabric of her dress, shooting a glance at Laurent before turning to the Queen. "Did you not think to ask?" Sparrow asked with a sniff, earning a hiss in return.

"Sorry, no, I didn't. I was a little shocked to be in *Minmere* so excuse me for not thinking clearly," Esmeray snapped, Goldriel's moonstone flashing. Keerian threw Esmeray a look that relayed an order to *calm down*. His mate grumbled a curse before shoving Goldriel back through the...veil. Sparrow inhaled a long, slow breath.

Her magic bubbled to the surface as she shoved it down further, taking a step towards the dais. Squinting at Esmeray, Sparrow retorted, "So, you have god level power, and you aren't even sure what you're supposed to *do* with it?"

Esmeray reared her head back, baring her fangs at Sparrow. "Do *you* want to go ask Phades - since I did such a shit poor job?"

"Did I *say* you did a shit poor job?" Sparrow countered, her magic weaving through her in answer to her rising temper. Usually, her power slumbered peacefully inside of her, stirring awake only when she rallied it forth.

But now, her soul felt like a churning sea, crashing against the walls she so tediously erected to control it.

"Adara *told us* that book gave her spells, gave her something from Massis's arsenal to create the Unmarked."

"Phades never even *mentioned* Massis-"

Laurent coughed pointedly, the sound breaking through the tension. "Arguing between us will not solve anything," he said, glancing from Sparrow to Esmeray, "Phades said the Book of Faune is needed - so we should focus on finding it."

Esmeray blew out a loud exhale before raising her hands. "You're right."

"I may regret asking this, but does anyone have a plan?" Laurent crossed and uncrossed his legs, and though his words felt light, Sparrow noted the undercurrent of wariness in his tone.

Keerian and Esmeray had enough going on. Lenna and Hale held no powers that would keep them safe. No one else could be trusted. The advisors in the Opal Palace dragged their feet to help defend Calcity - one of the reasons why Esmeray sequestered them in the throne room, wards surrounding the doors to keep prying ears from overhearing.

Sparrow knew the next council meeting would be...bloody.

Before she could think it all the way through, Sparrow stepped forward, feeling her magic twine around her and settle in response. "I'll go look for it."

"Are you sure?" Esmeray's face softened as Sparrow climbed the dais and sat on the top level, fanning her skirts around herself, and leaning back on her elbows against the cool obsidian stone.

Sparrow turned her head to Laurent, who inclined his own in approval. "Well, you have a continent to run, and I've already tried on all of your dresses. There's really nothing more to court life that I'm interested in at this time. Laurent and I can look for the Book of Faune while Lenna and Hale focus on decoding the Book of Phades."

Esmeray grinned, and Sparrow felt something ease further in her soul. "You know, you're brilliant." Esmeray moved off the throne to sit next to Sparrow on the steps, squeezing Sparrow's hands with her own.

"I know," Sparrow let out a light laugh, "Though I have no idea how we're supposed to find where the Book of Faune is. We might need to spend some time in the libraries to see if there's any mention of it."

"Wait." Keerian sat up straighter. "If Lenna uses the Prism...if Lenna touches Esmeray and the Prism, now that Esmeray has power directly from Phades-"

"Then she could look through the past with Esmeray anchoring, follow the thread of Esmeray's god magic, and see if Phades was with Faune when they hid the books," Laurent finished nodding slowly, before glancing sideways at Sparrow. She could feel his warring emotions battling between wanting to keep her safe and wanting to help Esmeray and Keerian. "And if we run into an all-powerful Faune Vessel while we search for the book?"

Keerian sat forward on the throne, like he'd only just thought about that, too. "What *if* the other Vessels aren't as warm and fuzzy as you?"

Esmeray shrugged, angling her head backwards to smile innocently at her mate. "Then it's a good thing I have the power of a fucking death god and can wane far."

"Well then, at least it'll be interesting," Sparrow huffed sarcastically. "It *was* starting to get a little dull around here."

# CHAPTER THIRTY-FIVE
## ORLA

THE KING WOULD BE at the council meeting today.

While it seemed, in itself, like a major deal, the additional significance was explained to Orla by one of the gargoyle servants as they spent hours buffing the driftwood tabletop until the wood gleamed and their arms ached.

King Eamon attended every meeting and royal event last year, but hadn't gone to a single one this year. Instead, he'd secluded himself in his private wing of the Palace, only meeting with advisors in his study with no Oasees servants present.

And of course, stuck in the doldrums of menial labor, the nine other servants Nonna chose to prepare for the King's return began spreading rumors as to the *real* reason King Eamon was finally breaking his isolation.

One servant was confident the King had come down with a nasty sickness and hid his affliction until he was healed. Another countered that it was *actually* because King Eamon seduced two new mistresses and stayed cloistered up with them in his bedchambers. A third said it was because he'd been in the Topaz Kingdom having an affair with their

Queen. The gossip spread, gaining speed, and descending rapidly into utter nonsense.

The last account Orla heard was that King Eamon spent all his time gambling the Ruby Kingdom's wealth on the outcome of Fire Chicken races, and was ashamed to stand in front of his council and admit the Kingdom was flat broke.

Neither partaking in the rumors, nor giving the other servants any inclination that she cared, Orla kept her head down and focused on the work at hand.

And there was a ton of it to complete before the King's return.

First, the entire council room needed to be scrubbed, the table polished, the chairs wiped until they shone. It had taken an entire day before Nonna finally gave her single nod of approval and dismissed the ten of them to bed with the warning that if they were late in the morning, they'd be reallocated to cleaning codpieces for the Palace Guards.

On the second day, cleaning commenced in the servant's pantry. Every surface had to be pristine, every nook and cranny dusted. It took Orla and the others another full day before the hawk-eyed Chamber Mother muttered her concession and let them go.

Orla had been so exhausted that she trudged back to her room and collapsed onto her bed, not even bothering to take off her boots or headscarf before letting sleep take her.

The goddess-damned sun rose three hours later.

Finally, the dreaded day arrived. Since Orla was Cillian's cupbearer, she didn't have to report to Nonna until noon. She spent the morning soaking in the tub, the water as hot as the innovative plumbing system would allow, and then sat at her desk and did her hair. Two days of demanding work had her curls puffy and irritated. It took a solid hour to soothe them into twin braids that started at the crown of her head and ended at the nape of her neck in perfectly symmetrical fluffy clouds that settled around her shoulders.

Getting dressed was easy, since Soren swept into her room on the way to her own duties to choose her outfit. Saving her, as Soren always did, from the vicious cycle of trying on, overthinking, and changing into something else.

Soren's choice was pale yellow gown, with silky sleeves that cinched at her wrists, covering the *acat* on her arms, leaving only the red swirls on her hands visible. It put Orla at ease to know the King who killed the entirety of her ancestral line wouldn't be able to see the *acat* in full. Even though Cillian explained the differences between her lineage and heritage gifts, she didn't want any of the King's attention to fall on her, or any questions on the powers she'd yet to manifest.

Cillian's words still hung ominously in the back of her mind, the plea to help him save his Kingdom from his father's cruelty, the reveal that the increase in dragon activity was on her account. She hadn't seen Cillian since their fight in his secret library, but her mind grappled between disappointment and relief every evening when she stepped into her room and he wasn't there.

There'd been a note left on her pillow the night before, only two words written in Cillian's swoopy calligraphy, and Orla glanced at it only once, too tired to process it until morning.

*Forgive me.*

Orla had woken up with a scowl before stuffing the note in her desk drawer with the others.

She wanted to hate him, but when she pushed deeper into that thought, she couldn't find anything concrete to hate him *for*. Sure, Cillian was cocky and arrogant, but he'd told her more about herself, hadn't kept her heritage a secret so she could prepare for whatever came of it.

She couldn't even dredge up more than half-bit, lackluster annoyance that Olivera wasn't her blood.

That thought only gave her relief.

But she could hate Cillian a little, secretly, for asking her to risk
herself for him – for his Kingdom. She held onto that idea, letting
it ignite the fire inside of her that no longer burned painfully, only
warmed the blood in her veins and spilled energy through her.

The knowledge her true parents were dead brought with it a tinge
of sadness since she couldn't recall a single thing about them. She
wished she could remember *something,* but all her earliest memories
stayed locked in her inner mind, and no amount of wracking her
brain for answers did anything except leave her with a headache.

She looked down at her dress again with a growl. To think Cillian
picked this gown especially for her made her cheeks flush, and it took
all of her might to not ruin the outfit with the glower on her face
as she thought of the insolent ass and his requests to use her for his
personal gain.

The dress's neckline plunged lower than anything Orla ever wore
before, and she was a bit self-conscious at the amount of skin revealed. Silk dipped between her breasts in two separate panels, before
twisting and wrapping around her waist, pooling to her ankles. Soft
pleats in the skirting made the material swish with every step.

But her modest approach to clothing, drilled into her by Olivera,
was irrevocably changed at the sight of herself in the mirror. With
a stifled gasp, she stepped closer, running a finger down the glass,
drinking in her reflection.

The dress was gorgeous.

She *felt* gorgeous in it.

Orla spun in front of the mirror, marveling at the agile movement of her fae body and the complimenting dress that fanned and fluttered around her.

A rising tide of self-actualization smothered out the sour remarks brandished against her in the past from Olivera. Suddenly, the other scandalous clothes hanging in her closet became more interesting, her curiosity piquing at how she'd look in them, how she would feel striding through the halls of the Palace in something that made her confident and proud.

But right now, she didn't have time to survey the armoire's contents with a new viewpoint. She had to get to work before Nonna ordered her to muck stalls until winter.

As she hurried down the hall to the Servant's pantry, arriving exactly two minutes before noon, food preparations were already underway, the servants hustling around in a synchronized flurry of movement. The meeting would start soon, and every single one of the dishes had to be perfect. Orla got assigned to plate a nauseatingly rare cut of meat, and she took extra care to avoid splashing the red juices onto her clothes.

"Hurry up and finish that before I send you to Aridden to catch rats in the bazaar for a month." Nonna appeared at her side, surprisingly stealthy for a human her age.

"Yes, Nonna," Orla chirped as she placed the last few slices of meat on the plate. All she needed to do now was get Cillian his wine and line up for Nonna's final inspection.

"Remember," Nonna boomed over the din of servants all groomed and dressed in their own finery. "Bow low when the King enters the council room, *do not* make eye contact with His Majesty, and *always* stay against the walls unless you are expressly asked to collect something."

A chorus of "Heard, Nonna," and "Yes, Nonna," filled the room. Orla passed off the heavy platter to another servant, hastily wiping her fingers on a discarded towel.

Wine.

She snatched a gold chalice off the counter, rubbing the rim with her sleeve to make sure it was impeccably polished - and slammed right into the Prince's barrier so hard her teeth snapped together.

*What the fuck?*

Orla shoved against the barrier, finding it completely solid, as if it were made of stone.

Her pulse quickened. Why, *why*, on today of all days, why couldn't she get through? Was it because her *acat* manifested? Or because Cillian was pissed at her for refusing to help him stage a fucking coup against his father?

She shook her head, trying to clear the confusion and the embarrassment of colliding full force into the barricade while surrounded by the other servants.

Swallowing against the knowledge that she very well may be resigned to rat-catching duties for a month, she turned and sought out Nonna.

"What do you mean, the Prince's magic will not allow you to pass through his barrier?" Nonna snapped as Orla tried to explain what happened. "Didn't his Highness give you a key to allow you to move through his protection magic easily?"

Orla started to say no but stopped. "The necklace," she whispered, touching her throat. After her fight with Cillian, she'd taken off the ruby pendant and thrown it into a drawer in her desk, not wanting anything of Cillian's on her body after their argument. She had no idea the gift was her key through the barrier. Nonna looked ready to spew venom at her, but Orla cut her off, already bolting towards the door.

"I'll be right back," she swore over her shoulder to the fuming Chamber Mother. Her new fae body was incredibly fast, and she took a moment to marvel at her power before coming to a skidding halt in front of her door.

Running the distance from the pantry to her bedroom would've taken her human body at least fifteen minutes, but her fae body completed the run in less than five.

She lurched over to her desk, yanking the necklace out from underneath a pile of quills and Cillian's notes before she paused, the chain clasped loosely in her hand. For a moment she stood there, staring at the gem strung on the thin chain.

And then Orla stuffed the necklace in her pocket with a smug smirk.

She gambled it didn't have to be *worn* to let her pass through the barricade. Just on her person. She could still continue her silent protest against Cillian while fulfilling her duties and not irking Nonna further.

She made it back to the servant's pantry in four minutes, her chest barely heaving although she full out sprinted across Oasees. Slightly awe-struck at her newfound agility, Orla approached the barrier a second time, tentatively extending a hand to touch the magic.

The red shimmering magic parted, curling invitingly around her fingers. With a deep breath, she stepped into it. Easing the rest of her body past the warm magic, Orla couldn't help the wide smile working across her face.

It worked. The necklace in her pocket was the key to the Prince's barrier.

Just in time, too, as Nonna's raised voice called for all servants to assemble for final inspection.

# CHAPTER THIRTY-SIX
## ORLA

AN AIR OF TREPIDATION hung throughout the packed council room. Orla's eyes darted between advisors, taking in their body language, who they spoke to in hushed tones, who pulled out a seat for another to sit.

Orla refused to *help* Cillian in his still-secret bid for the throne but having the ear of King Eamon's Heir – whether through a coup or through succession– *would* be beneficial for her overall.

Unlike the previous meeting, where Cillian had already been seated as the servants entered, his chair was empty and moved from the head of the table. A larger chair – an *actual* throne, with intricately carved arms and a high back - had taken over the head.

A reminder that when the King was present, the Crown Prince of the Ruby Kingdom would be pushed to the side.

Not a single advisor looked her way as she swept around the table to the far corner of the room where she was to be stationed as Cillian's cupbearer. She adjusted her skirts with a hand, using the motion to covertly glance at the papers scattered across the tabletop. Nothing caught her eye that could be important.

As she straightened, Cillian's red-haired advisor walked briskly towards the seat to the left of the Prince, her movement catching his attention. Their stares clashed.

Orla's stomach clenched as his eyes widened slightly. The red-haired advisor glanced from her now pointed ears to her tattooed hand gripping Cillian's wine. A flicker of fear crossed his face before he winced and schooled his expression into one of neutrality.

Panic lanced through her. He knew her *acat,* her heritage. Had admitted it to Cillian. And she still didn't even know his name, or the extent of her magic.

*Would he tell King Eamon she was the last descendant of the fae line the King personally hunted down and exterminated?*

Orla cursed herself for forgetting to ask Soren who he was. She hadn't expected to see Cillian's advisor *here.* The swirling secrecy around him made Orla believe Cillian kept him out of sight. But the red-haired advisor *was* loyal to Cillian. It took her racing mind a few breaths to wrap around that, as she set her face into what she hoped was a look of innocence - or at least subservience. And if Cillian trusted him, did that mean he was backing Cillian's attempt for the throne?

If so, she had just as much dirt on him as he had on her.

Beyond the hall, a trumpet wailed, causing the few council members still milling about the room to rush over and stand behind their chairs. Those already sitting rose rapidly, all focus shifting to the door. The tension in the room spiked, the silence growing heavy and uncomfortable. Orla's throat tightened.

King Eamon had arrived.

Two hulking fae entered first, long spears in hand, dressed in what Orla presumed was the uniform of the King's personal guard.

With the same short brown hair, formidable builds, and lightly tanned skin, Orla guessed they were twins. Without speaking a word, the pair filled the rest of the already cramped space, their bulky, bronze armor a glaring distinction from the light, flexible armor of the Oasees guards. The King's personal crest shone against their breastplates - a half-risen sun with a small flame atop the rays.

With a menacing survey of the council chambers, their message was clear.

*We protect the King. Not the Kingdom.*

Orla bowed her head as the Crown Prince entered next, to show respect, yes - but mostly to ignore the feel of his gaze that swiftly sought her out. As the rest of the room murmured their chorused greetings, Orla flicked her eyes up, regretting it immediately as they locked with Cillian's.

Dressed in his usual black, with his locs pulled back into a bun, accentuating the hard planes of his face, Orla hated the heat that flooded over her. Not the fire of pain that plagued her prior to receiving an *acat,* but a burn all the same, a *pull* to him that gripped her mercilessly.

A thin gold circlet lay atop his head, and that was enough to rip Orla from the confusing thrall of attraction. He was the Crown Prince, had confessed to her that he was a usurper to his father's rule, and was *severely* off-limits. So ridiculously off-limits that Orla thinned her lips and broke their eye contact first.

Somehow, even in this extremely crowded room, Cillian was able to meet the storm in her expression easily. Too easily. But at least he could now see she had her *acat.* And once Soren began training her, she would never be a powerless pawn again.

The thought emboldened her as she straightened, a caveat she hadn't given much thought to before. Orla prayed whatever her *acat* was...that it was lethal.

But not deadly enough to end up Culled.

Cillian stopped next to the head of the table, his focus turning from Orla to level a nonchalant stare at the door with the tip of his chin.

A ripple of power swirled around the room as the King of the Ruby Kingdom appeared. The advisors and servants alike tensed, all but Cillian, who surveyed the rest of the room with the same callous air Orla saw him wield like a weapon in the past meeting.

King Eamon strode in, gloved hands clasped behind his back. He dressed more casually than Orla expected for a King, with a simple, pleated, ruby colored tunic and dark pants. No weapons adorned his waist, and the only reminder of his royal blood lay in the hammered gold crown atop closely cropped grey hair.

Orla and the rest of the room bowed low as the King stormed to the head of the table, Cillian stepping to the side for his father to move past him.

The King's deep brown skin contrasted handsomely with his silvery beard and hair. Orla risked a glance from father to son, noting the same high cheekbones, full lips, and dark irises. But there was something colder, harsher, in the King's eyes, something that sent a quiver down her bones.

Orla swallowed thickly, causing the servant stationed next to her to drive an elbow into her upper arm. Fucking fae hearing.

Her gulp must have been too loud or obnoxious. *Gods.* She turned her head slightly to take in the petite, half-fae female next to her, subtly flashing the servant a sharp canine. The female pursed her lips, but faced front again, taking a half step away from Orla. Orla gritted her teeth together to keep the smirk of satisfaction off of her face.

But her smugness dropped fast as Soren stepped into the room holding a jeweled chalice. Her blonde hair was pulled back into an intricately braided topknot, and she was dressed in a sultry black gown that crossed between her breasts with sheer panels stitched into the sides. Soren strode across the room, gently placing the chalice in front of the King, before lowering her eyes and backing up until her back hit the wall beside Orla.

Orla blinked rapidly. *Soren was King Eamon's cupbearer?* Her mind scrambled, and as if Soren could hear her racing thoughts, the fae snuck Orla a hard look and discreetly shook her head, before her eyes settled back on the King in front of them.

"Be seated," King Eamon rumbled. Chairs scraped against the tiled floor as the advisors hastily followed his order.

Whatever trance the King held the room under with his entrance was quickly broken. There was work to be done. Orla moved forward, placing Cillian's wine in front of him, avoiding a look at him directly. The rest of the servants placed cups and platters on the table before sliding back to the outskirts of the wall, a few slipping quietly from the room after depositing their goods.

King Eamon leaned back against his chair, raised his wine to his lips and took a long swig before slamming the golden chalice against the tabletop, bellowing, "Tell me *who* decided to pull our spies out of Irridessen?"

The unease threading the room did not lift, and Orla steeled herself for what would no doubt be an exceedingly nerve-wracking meeting.

TWO TENSE HOURS PASSED as Orla stayed on high alert. Her muscles ached from standing so still, so rigid, believing the King would detect her *Vitraro* heritage and attack if she loosened her posture in the slightest. With the achingly slow passing of time, the number of advisors dwindled as the King dismissed them. Each one bowed low and scuttled from the council room in haste. With Orla's enhanced fae senses, she heard more than one loosen a heavy sigh as they made it safely to the hall beyond. She took a mental note of those beings for Cillian.

As more council members left, so did the servants assisting them, until only Orla, Soren, and two male servants remained.

Over the course of the meeting, Orla stepped out of the room only twice to refill Cillian's glass.

The first time was during an intense argument between Lord Batair and the representative for the residents of Aridden, about a fight that broke out between guards and townsfolk over a stolen family heirloom. Orla watched the volley of insults get tossed back and forth before King Eamon hammered his fist against the table for silence.

Cillian had tapped his finger against the side of his empty cup, and Orla slipped out of the room, grateful for the break.

His cup was also conveniently empty when the trade advisor, Lord Oswine, noted that dragon activity was moving further north *again*, with the added confirmation that it appeared to be either dragons or wyverns but his source was too terrified to get close enough to the beasts to confirm if they had two legs or four.

Dragon activity was a point the livestock advisor, Lord Barrett, tried and failed to bring up earlier in the meeting before being abruptly dismissed from the room.

But whichever species, it was now having a negative effect on trading as the newest nest was mere miles away from a port town. Captains were refusing to utilize that harbor, citing concerns of dragon attacks, instead sailing past their destination and up the coast to dock further north. Their demands for wages were increasing as well as the price of the goods that now had to be moved from the northern tip of the Kingdom back down to the southern cities over land.

Orla had been more than happy to hurry out of the room during that conversation, staying a few beats longer in the servant's pantry to make sure her breathing was under control.

The last thing she wanted was to look weak in front of King Eamon – she was doing her best to keep her *acat* out of the King's line of vision - praying she could draw upon the notion of servants staying completely invisible to the beings they served.

All of the lower-class advisors had been dismissed by the time she reentered the room, leaving only Lord Batair, Cillian's red-haired advisor, who had stayed silent the entire meeting, Lord Oswine, two cruel looking gargoyles that seemed to have something to do with the War Advisor, and two haughty looking fae that Orla assumed were soul tied, judging from the way they finished the other's sentence.

Orla placed Cillian's cup back on the table, keeping her eyes low before backing up until her hands touched the wall.

Safe.

Invisible.

Soren took that moment to covertly touch Orla's fist with her pinky, a reassuring gesture that had Orla's shoulders relaxing an inch.

"Lord Oswine," King Eamon snapped, causing the wiry fae to flinch, "Dragon activity is not a concern of mine. What is this I hear about you classifying reports on Irridessen as low priority?"

"Your Majesty, there is nothing to report in Irridessen that we do not already know." Lord Oswine started, straightening in his chair, "Queen Absolute Esmeray seems content with staying in her own lands, which is why I don't understand why Lord Batair is *continuing* to infiltrate the Opal Palace."

"No, *no,*" Lord Batair cut in with a snarl, his steel grey wings rustling with indignation, "*You* seem to forget Queen Esmeray has an immensely powerful *acat.* I don't put it past the bitch to have an ulterior motive. She took over the Opal Kingdom and the Obsidian Kingdom. I wouldn't be surprised if she claims the Larimar Islands first before setting her sights on Ingotheria."

Lord Oswine narrowed his eyes, his yellow battle magic crackling between his fingertips, before he countered, "Queen Esmeray's parents ruled the Opal and Obsidian Kingdoms *before* her succession. How is it different now that she's ruling with her mate, King Keerian?"

"The Golden Gargoyle is one of the greatest fighters Terramere have ever seen. And my *low priority reports* confirm she *also* has the Oracle in her council." Lord Batair leaned forward, spit flying off his lips towards the trade advisor. "We have a huge imbalance of power here, and where there is an imbalance, there is only one path forward. Queen Esmeray and King Keerian *will* either attempt to take over the Larimar Islands before setting their conquering sights on Ingotheria, *or* they will start spitting out heirs and do you *want* that bloodline to get stronger? The rumor is the Queen's *acat* is from Phades herself, making her the first and only being to be blessed by the Goddess of Death. I would sleep better in my bed at night knowing Queen Esmeray has been taken off the chessboard."

The War Advisor drew himself up to his full height and addressed King Eamon directly. "I request an increase to the number of spies in Irridessen, placing some in the Obsidian Palace as well, and I request we begin working on an action plan to attack King Keerian. His death means hers, and he'd be easier to get to."

King Eamon snorted, causing Lord Batair to plop back in his chair, a look of utter bloodlust curling his lips as he appraised Lord Oswine, who held his hands in his lap, the sparks of yellow battle magic dispersing. "Lord Batair," the King replied, "I approve the motion of increasing our spies to the Obsidian Palace, though I want no harm to befall the Golden Gargoyle – yet."

Orla shifted nervously, trying to keep the fear from showing on her face. The King commanded power. She was told he brandished it with an iron fist. He had to only *sigh* and both of his short-tempered advisors fell silent while he toyed with the idea of assassinating a King Consort.

"Lord Oswine," King Eamon continued, slowly removing his gloves and placing them delicately against the tabletop, "I have decided that Irridessen should be seen as what it is. A threat. And it is not going to be overlooked, especially since the Queen is in control of the Oracle."

"But, *but*," Lord Oswine stuttered, his eyes jumping from the gloves on the table to the King's cruel face. Lord Batair exchanged a triumphant glance with the two gargoyles seated next to him.

King Eamon cut off the trade advisor with a single raised hand.

A hand covered in intricate red swirls.

Orla's breath caught in her throat.

"Your services are no longer needed." King Eamon finished quietly, clenching his hand into a fist.

Lord Oswine yelped in pain, shooting from his chair, yellow battle magic sparking up his arms as he clawed at his neck. A ragged choking noise filled the room.

Orla looked on, horrified, as the advisor thrashed against the King's magic, fighting, wheezing, before his struggles grew limp.

With a heavy *bump,* Lord Oswine crumpled against the tabletop, dead.

"Meeting adjourned," King Eamon noted dryly as he stood, his King's Guard stepping up and taking their imposing positions at his side. Cillian slowly got to his feet, his eyes sweeping over the remaining council members, pausing to give a discreet nod to his red-haired advisor who had risen, along with the rest, to bow as the King tugged on his gloves.

As he headed for the door, King Eamon turned, addressing the two soul tied fae directly, "We are hosting the Topaz Kingdom in one month for the Autumnal Equinox. I expect the visit to be...remarkable."

With that, the King stalked from the council room, completely disregarding the dead fae slowly sliding off the side of the table. Soren shot Orla a look that conveyed *'do nothing,'* before she fell in line behind Cillian, exiting the room with her head bowed.

It was only when the King and the Prince were out of sight that gravity finally claimed the body, a dull *thud* jarring through the room, making Orla jump.

She was *so* fucked.

# CHAPTER THIRTY-SEVEN
## LENNA

"*Stop* jostling me."

"I'm *not*. Your wings are taking up the entire chaise!"

"Then go sit *on the bed.*"

They'd been at this for an hour, and Lenna was no closer to unravelling the complex web of the past then when she first threw herself into the Prism, even with Esmeray anchoring her and holding the Book of Phades. Collette had refused to clear Lenna for any Oracle-related duties until now, stating Lenna needed to recoup and rest before attempting to find the Book of Faune. But now that the healer had approved her journey into the past, Lenna found herself with little solitude as her family constantly hovered, concerned that she would succumb to the strain and faint again.

Lenna focused on the slightly brighter thread that seemed to weave through every other piece of the past, the beginnings of a migraine thudding in her temples. She refused to tell anyone that the headache was worsening, because she hated being on bedrest for the past few days, and knew her limits would be tested on this task, but was fairly certain she could discern when to stop and take a breather.

Now and then, she'd unravel enough to mentally pounce on the thread of history linked to the Vessel Books, only to be rewarded with a flash of vision that quickly flitted from her subconscious mind before disappearing back into the tangled shrouds.

At some point, Sparrow and Laurent entered the King's chamber, though Laurent listened to two seconds of Sparrow and Esmeray bickering and hastily found someplace else to be.

"Dearests, I adore you both, but you're making it hard to concentrate," Lenna grumbled, keeping her eyes squeezed shut to hold her fading connection to the Prism. Her headache could potentially be linked to the two females squeezed next to her on the chaise lounge, who both seemed fidgety and bored as they sat on the balcony in utter silence.

"Sorry," Esmeray and Sparrow sheepishly muttered in unison.

Slowly creeping through the Prism, further into the past than she ever dared travel, Lenna pushed her mind into the glowing strands, making sure to keep a firm grip on the thin thread connecting her to Esmeray's anchor. There was so much to dig through it felt like trying to find a single needle in a mountain-sized pile of needles.

If she could just get an image to appear for longer than a split second, she could project it into Esmeray's mind so the Queen could help decipher where the Book of Phades came from – or hopefully glean some insight on where the Book of Faune could be.

Lenna saw a flash of rock, a scrawling of ancient runes carved into the surface, with a thick layer of moss covering half the inscription. Her heart leapt as she forced the image into Esmeray's mind, but as soon as it appeared, it was gone again, disappearing into the interwoven motley.

"Shit," Lenna cursed, screwing her eyes shut to grasp at the memory. "I saw an image of...of runes carved on the wall behind some moss. But it disappeared before I could project it."

Gritting her teeth against the mental strain, the thread from Esmeray and the Book of Phades slipped and squirmed out of her clutches, as if Lenna could only look at it indirectly, and when she tried gripping onto it, it would slide away again, just out of reach down another braid of the past.

It was very frustrating.

Laurent had admitted, before he fled the room, that the further in the past Lenna dove, the harder it would be to project a memory, and he was damned correct.

"Well, there's only cave systems throughout the entire lower half of the continent," Sparrow confirmed cheerfully, "Besides the mountain range surrounding the Obsidian Palace."

Lenna and Esmeray groaned.

"And Florra has caverns behind the waterfalls," Sparrow added, fluffing her hair over her shoulder, and stretching her legs out to lean against the chunky pillow Esmeray had begrudgingly created out of thin air after Sparrow complained about not having a head rest.

Lenna pursed her lips, gently easing out of the Prism. Once her consciousness was again firmly planted into her body, the migraine gleefully sunk in its claws. Slumping back into the chaise, Lenna felt disappointment roll through her.

"I'm sorry," she whispered, feeling a tear slide free.

Esmeray shook her head rapidly, pulling Lenna into a hug as Sparrow hopped off the chaise to squirm against Lenna's other side. "You have nothing to be sorry for," Esmeray replied firmly.

"We'll get to the bottom of it." Sparrow leaned her head against Lenna's shoulder, the three females silently holding each other. Lenna smiled through the pangs of her migraine.

They had each other, and together, they'd figure it out.

# Chapter Thirty-Eight
## ORLA

Attempting to keep her footsteps unhurried, while pure panic bleated through her mind, Orla made her way back to her room, hands trembling.

Beings wandered about the corridor, talking and laughing, with no clue the King just murdered an advisor in front of the council.

The scent of spices mingled with the salty air of the distant sea. Shouts rang out from the oasis, though after tensing, Orla realized it was just beings playing in the springs, calling out for friends to join them, and no danger lurked nearby.

The constant din of overlapping voices put Orla on edge as she squeezed past two gargoyles whose wings took up the width of the hall.

Orla usually left her quarters for work before any of her neighbors awoke, and didn't return until well after dinner, when most of the others inhabiting the rooms around hers were either at one of the taverns in Aridden, or already in bed. To have so much *vibrancy* spilling forth– it was too overwhelming after everything Orla witnessed in the council meeting.

Those red, swirling tattoos covering the King's hands...they were identical to her own. It rolled her stomach as she thought back to how King Eamon wielded his *acat*. She wanted power. But she was not a killer.

The King murdered an advisor – a *Lord*. In front of her. Lord Oswine's death sentence was carried out while his only crime was that he *disagreed* with the King. King Eamon would kill Orla without a second thought if he even *suspected* she had a forbidden heritage. She had to run, had to get as far away as possible and –

She paused as she took in the cracked, open door to her room.

Her nostrils flared delicately, but with the multitude of beings in the hall, she couldn't scent *who* was in her room. But there was only one being that enjoyed strolling into her space at his pleasure at the absolute worst times.

She shook her head. There was a battle of wits to be had with the Crown Prince.

Orla stormed into her room. "I am not fight-....*oh*," she stopped in her tracks as she took in her visitor.

Cillian's red-haired advisor smiled wide. "Not who you expected?"

Orla's mind rapidly scrambled from preparing for an argument with Cillian to having a civil conversation with the weirdly secretive fae. When faced with uncertainty, she'd learned to read between the lines of what someone wanted.

And how to get them to confess to their own motives.

"I don't know your name," Orla started.

"I never gave it to you," the advisor replied, standing casually near the door to her balcony. "I tend to avoid newcomers since they rarely end up in Oasees. But you, Orla Grey, seemed to have exceeded all expectations. And I'd very much like to learn more about you. So, I will tell you my *name* if you tell me a *fact*."

Orla crossed the room slowly, cooly assessing the male before her. His skin was pale with pinkish undertones, yet bright coppery freckles dotted his nose. Long sleeves covered his arms, but his hands were free of any trace of an *acat*.

From a lifetime of being a servant, she'd nailed down the intricate art of observation. It was one of her best talents - learning who someone was just by watching them, by breaking down the small tells presented to give her an idea of who they truly were.

With a smirk, Orla stated, "Your accent tells me you aren't from the Ruby Kingdom, yet you know Cillian very well. Your skin is very light, but the freckles on your face tell me you used to spend long hours in the sun. Maybe from a job you held before becoming so important to his ass-holi-ness?"

She prowled closer, keeping her eyes locked on his.

"I know your *acat,* yet I don't know your name. I'll hazard a guess that you and Cillian grew close only *after* your power was revealed. And *that's* when you became important to Cillian, and he elevated your lowly station. There's your fact."

"My name is Dimas Citro, and I did mean a fact about yourself," Dimas admitted ruefully, though a pleased smile dragged at the corners of his lips. With a dramatic sigh, Dimas crossed his arms, leaning against the desk.

"You should've been more specific," Orla mused, pleased with herself as she turned from the fae to kick her boots off and busying herself undoing her braids, sectioning a small piece of her hair in front of the mirror propped against her nightstand, waiting for Dimas to announce why he was standing in her room.

Dimas watched her in the mirror's reflection for a moment. "Your *acat* is not the same as the King."

Oh, he was getting straight to the point then.

"How do you know?" Orla shot back, halfway annoyed at the coursing relief that statement shot through her blood. Abandoning the braid, she pulled her sleeves up, revealing more of the red scrollwork wrapping up to her elbow on each arm. "It looks pretty fucking identical to me, and if that's the case, does that mean I'll have the same gifts as him, too?"

"No." Dimas crossed the room to sit on her bed, the casualness making Orla grumble under her breath as she turned back to focus on her hair. "The King's *acat* comes from the God of the Sky, Akash. That magic lets him manipulate air, which, unfortunately, means he primarily uses it to suffocate beings that piss him off."

"And mine?" Orla hedged, twisting off the end of one braid to begin another, wincing at the small tangle that pulled her scalp.

"If I am correct - and I usually am." Dimas inspected his own hair over Orla's shoulder, crinkling his nose while patting down a wayward strand. "Your *acat* comes from Akash's sister, Aella, the Goddess of Destruction. Aella enjoys gifting flames. Or some form of it."

Orla looked at her hands, mulling over the idea that she could create and wield fire. The thought of being able to blast fire at someone sent an uneasy thrill through her. It seemed dangerous - a gift of pain. But it would also make her lethal, able to protect herself.

"And you told Cillian you knew my heritage gift."

"Of course," Dimas replied.

"So, I'm a descendant of the Dragonmind fae, and Aella blessed me with her *acat*." She peered closer to Dimas. "And you *only* told this to Cillian?"

Dimas nodded slowly. "I warned the Prince about your heritage gift, because when an unknown threat shows up shipwrecked on our shore, it piques my curiosity. But I'd never be so cruel as to notify the King of that knowledge."

"Because of the Culling? Or because of something...else?" Orla hedged, wondering if Dimas knew of Cillian's plans to usurp his father.

With a nonchalant shrug, Dimas stuffed his hands in the pockets of his linen pants. "If your power manifests for you to control fire, you won't find yourself on the wrong side of the Culling list. Fire magic has never been outlawed."

"And no one will suspect that I'm *Vitraro* since its my heritage gift."

Dimas grinned knowingly, turning to leave.

"Wait." Orla jumped up, taking two steps towards the fae that just provided her an immense amount of peace, though he stayed mum on the topic of a potential coup. "Why are you telling me this?"

Dimas gave her a bland smile. "Cillian figured you wouldn't listen to him and sent me instead. He figured I'd get a warmer reception. Which – by the way you stormed in here looking like you wanted to smite me – was a good call. Cillian didn't want you bolting at the first whiff of danger, so he sent me to alleviate your...concerns."

"Well, he was right about that," Orla surmised, throwing Dimas that same, expressionless smile, as she crossed the room and tugged the door open. "But now that I know you only came because Cillian was too cowardly to fight with me, you can tell him next time he sends a lackey, instead of showing up himself, I'll seek him out and set him on fire."

Dimas bowed, chuckling as he crossed the threshold back into the corridor. "I shall relay the message."

"Good."

And with that, Orla slammed the door in his face, though it didn't grant her the satisfaction she'd hoped for.

# Chapter Thirty-Nine
## Sparrow

THE SURGES OF POWER radiating off Esmeray meant the Queen was about one moment away from fracturing.

They left Lenna in the King's chambers, curled up in bed, assuring the Oracle she needed sleep to get rid of the headache Lenna finally admitted to having after diving so deep into the Prism. Esmeray felt distant to Sparrow as they tucked Lenna into the sheets and agreed to leave the doors to the balcony open for any sneaky Moon Crows to come visit. Her calm felt forced – as if she kept the farce up for Lenna's benefit only.

That cool mask Sparrow knew too well lay hard and unyielding against the icy angles of Esmeray's beautiful face. Between the gentle reassurances and tight smiles, Sparrow concluded the Queen Absolute had a plan.

One she wasn't keen on sharing with the Oracle.

Sparrow waited until Esmeray softly clicked shut the door to Lenna's room before rounding on her – only for her friend to easily sidestep her approach and briskly stride down the hallway.

"Where are you going?" Sparrow sped up to grip Esmeray's arm. Esmeray whipped around; sharp teeth bared into a snarl. The pure undulating power rippling around them seemed to pause, the air itself shimmering golden. Esmeray, with the power of a god, and a very short fuse, made Sparrow's palms sweat.

"I'm getting to the bottom of this. One way or another."

Sparrow swallowed as Esmeray ripped her arm free, stalking down the hall. Even the skeletal hands gripping the candles lining the walls seemed to flicker and dim as Esmeray passed, her wings tucked tight, her sheet of blue-black hair draped around her like a cape.

Sparrow was three paces behind, her gauzy skirts crumpled in her white knuckled hand. A pulse of magic extinguished the lights behind them. Without breaking her pace, Esmeray raised her fingers and snapped, the buttery soft navy dress the Queen wore fading away with a golden shimmer, slowly revealing Esmeray dressed in her black battle leathers, a hooded cloak concealing her prominent horns from view.

"Fuck," Sparrow barked, lunging to grab Esmeray before a flare of gold filled the hall, waning them away.

Ice-cold mountain air rushed around her as she plummeted closer to the unforgiving floor of the caverns below the Obsidian Palace. Sparrow felt her magic disappear in a heart lurching blink. Before she could even collect the breath to scream, she was yanked up, up, as Esmeray flared out her wings with a screech, soaring them both to the narrow ledge that led into the dungeons.

"What the *fuck, Sparrow?*" Esmeray yelled, her eyes filled with wild fear, "I could've dropped you."

"I didn't know you were waning down *here.*" Sparrow stood on shaky legs, brushing the dust off of her pale pink dress, acutely aware of the death she just narrowly avoided.

With her magic nullified thanks to the witch runes carved in the stones, she wouldn't have been able to save herself, and would've died from impact with the rocky ground. Or fallen straight into the Soul

Keeper's Cell - the ominous stone plateau jutting slightly above the floor, the slab open and foreboding.

Sparrow shivered. Esmeray let out a ragged breath, driving her hands through the strands of her hair. "Gods, Sparrow," she laughed, the sound hollow and flat. "thank the gods my wings were healed enough to carry you."

Sparrow threw her friend an appreciative grin that felt too faked as she wrapped her arms around herself. "Me too," she admitted before steeling herself, pushing down the screaming instinct inside of her to wane the fuck out of here now that she could feel the tiniest bit of magic reawakening inside of her. "Why are we down here?"

Esmeray's lips thinned, a spark of wrath glinting through her eyes. "To talk to Adara."

"I'm coming with you."

"Fine. But don't get in the middle."

Sparrow held her breath as the pair ventured deeper into the tunnels, Esmeray's black cloak billowing ominously around her. She felt out of place in her too-cheery dress, the edges of the gown now soot covered and ragged as they made their way past the cells of other incarcerated beings awaiting judgement for their crimes.

The howling and racket that normally filled the space was absent, a pregnant pause permeating the air. The silence dug against the frayed edges of Sparrow's nerves. The prisoners were never this quiet aside for one sole reason.

They knew Death walked amongst them today.

Sparrow's heart thundered as a thought so bone cold that she hoped it wasn't true whispered in her mind. One glance at the tautness of Esmeray's wings confirmed for Sparrow why they were here - and why Esmeray wanted to come alone.

Esmeray wasn't simply visiting her twin.

The Queen was here to pass judgement without telling her court, or even her mate. This was between sisters, and Sparrow suddenly felt too involved.

"Hello, Sister," Esmeray crooned from under her hood as they approached Adara's cell.

Adara had the good sense to back up as Esmeray wrapped her tattooed hand slowly around the bars of the cell door, her nails growing into deadly, jagged points.

"You spoke to Phades," Adara whispered, her eyes widening with a fleck of fear.

"I did."

Dressed in her dirty slip, her snow-white hair matted and frizzed, those once beautiful wings cracked along the boning, Adara looked so small, so breakable, in front of the Vessel of Death.

Sparrow hovered behind Esmeray, keeping her mouth shut.

With a soft chuckle Adara's body shivered, and she seemed to remember herself, her eyes deadening as she slowly stepped towards her twin with her chin held high. "You killed the Unmarked."

"Every last one of them that you sent to Calcity," Esmeray purred back, her eyes locked with Adara's, though her face showed nothing of her motives. Only the curled lip, bared teeth of disgust showed through the mask. "Why Calcity?"

Adara shrugged, crossing her arms and appraising Esmeray with the exact same level of disgust, their expressions identical in every way besides their coloring. The same features, with starkly opposite ideals.

Sparrow's soul ached as her mind drifted to her own twin, Briar. If she'd lived, would they have been close? Or would they be each other's biggest threat, locked in a never-ending power struggle, like Esmeray and Adara?

"Calcity wasn't the target." Adara laughed, her sharp fangs flashing back to her twin. "The goal was for *you* to kill them all. Excellent job on that."

Sparrow's mind raced as she touched her ring. *"Why would Adara sacrifice the beings that were undyingly loyal to her? That wanted her back on the throne?"*

Her hands reflexively closed into fists as she realized, without magic, their mind speak rings didn't work down here. Although Esmeray seemed to be on the same line of thought.

"So, you wanted me to kill the only allies you had?" Esmeray cocked her head to the side. "That's the dumbest shit I've ever heard, Adara."

Adara clicked her tongue, running her fingers through the ends of her knotted hair. "It was a necessary sacrifice. A means to an end. Living in the shadows of their ancestors' selfish decisions…Who wouldn't want to make their own name for themselves?"

Adara began pacing slowly under Esmeray's stare, a beast trapped in a cage. "To take over the Kingdoms – all of them – is the quietest dream of every ruler. To hold absolute power. Everybody wants to rule the world."

Esmeray scoffed, "No, they don't."

"Then you are a fool," Adara shot back. "*I* found the Book of Phades. *I* siphoned its power. *And I asked it.* The Vessel Book gave me the key to rule *everything.*"

"And how do you rule everything?" Esmeray murmured, a wicked gleam darkening her eyes.

"War," Adara breathed.

"We aren't at war with the other Kingdoms," Sparrow said, glancing to Esmeray.

With a pointed nod at Sparrow, a smirk worked its way across Adara's face. "But you will be."

Adara stretched out her wings, the right one trembling as she extended it, causing her to snap it shut with a hiss that could've been from pain or embarrassment. Sparrow felt that keen presence over her shoulder, watching her. But she brushed it off, focusing on the way Adara slinked closer to Esmeray.

"The Slate Kingdom is the key to it all. The beginning and the end. And it's been out of the power struggle for too long." Jutting her chin to Esmeray, her opal horns gleaming, Adara whispered, "Thanks to the Book of Phades, and Massis himself, I put it back in."

Sparrow knitted her brows together, something inside her twisting. "The Slate Kingdom is full of humans. With a magic nullifying dome surrounding it. It's no more a power player right now than you are in this dingy cell."

Adara's smile turned feral. "What dome?"

Esmeray froze. "What did you do, Adara?"

"The question *should* be...What did *you* do Esmeray?" Adara tutted, approaching the door of her cell, careful to avoid the razor-edged nails Esmeray crafted.

Sparrow glanced from the Queen to Adara, jolting at the impact of the nails being on display as she realized Esmeray could now use magic down here, even with the witch runes. And Esmeray was showing Adara exactly how powerful she'd become.

"The Unmarked came from the ancestral lines of the original one hundred fae that created the dome of protection, keeping those worthless humans eating, breeding, and fucking on the lands of the seventh Kingdom. Lands ruled by a weak ruler. The dome was the only reason he was never challenged. Content to sit on his island."

With a soft, broken chuckle, Adara leaned closer to her twin, her horns resting on the iron bars of the cell door. Esmeray didn't move. "One hundred fae created the dome. The key was bloodlines. You *kill* one hundred fae whose ancestors can be linked back to the dome's creation, and the dome...disappears."

Adara crooned through the bars, "You killed the one hundred, sister. And the Slate Kingdom is ripe for the taking. The rest...well you've been asking me for months now where those missing beings were. I figured I'd bring them out, show you what exactly chaos magic could do."

"But one hundred Unmarked with chaos magic wouldn't have been enough for you to accept your god power. Oh yes – the book told me *all* about Vessels when it thought I was you." Adara leaned closer, her voice lowering. "I needed you desperate, I needed you to feel helpless, and I needed you to take that killing blow against an enormous enemy."

She shrugged. "So, the other four hundred Unmarked were really just for show."

"No." A tremor wobbled Esmeray's word, the first inkling to Sparrow that Esmeray was completely out of her element for how this visit was going. "If the dome falls, it nullifies the entire agreement from the Witch War. The Ruby Kingdom and the Topaz Kingdom will lay claim to the Slate Kingdom again. And we're allied with the Slate Kingdom...we'd have to fight to defend it."

Adara hummed, her chapped and peeling lips inches away from Esmeray. "You started a war by killing the Unmarked, causing the dome to fall. And you took the god magic, making you too dangerous for other rulers to let you stay alive. They *will* ultimately kill you, and I will rule. I will rule every single one of the Seven Kingdoms of Terramere. And I will *decimate* every *single* being that does not bow before me. Who will follow you now, sister? When you've dragged Terramere into another unnecessary and long, bloody war? Who will be left to bow to you?" Adara laughed a crow's laugh. "I'll be here, in this cell, patiently waiting. And when the victor comes to lay claim on the Obsidian Palace, I'll have them release me. And then I will take *every Kingdom* ravaged and broken from the war and *no one* will see me coming."

To Sparrow's shock, Esmeray staggered back a step, her breathing unsteady, rubbing her hands before clenching them into fists. Sparrow felt queasy as the dizzying information sunk in.

Esmeray was right.

They knew the Ruby Kingdom and the Topaz Kingdom held a lot of hate for Irridessen. If the Slate Kingdom was unprotected...Ingotheria would lay claim to their lost lands, and Irridessen would have to intervene.

The bloodshed would be exorbitant.

On a continent solely comprised of defenseless humans.

"You," Esmeray snarled low and quiet, trembling with barely leashed anger as she bared her teeth at Adara, gold sparks flaring and dying out at her fingertips as the magic touched the dead air of the dungeon. Sparrow reached out a comforting hand, though the words of consolation died on her lips as Esmeray slapped her palm against the handle of Adara's cell.

The lock sprung free.

With a groan, the hinges gave way and Esmeray burst into the cell with her twin, shooting a hand out to wrap around Adara's throat. Adara sputtered in panic, gasping, as Esmeray slammed her against the wall, her black wings flaring, cutting off Sparrow from intervening. Adara grunted with pain as her head collided with the stones, a trickle of blood seeping down her tangled strands.

Adara clawed at Esmeray's arms and the Queen retaliated with a sharp slap across her face, Adara's shocked yelp echoing through the dungeon's tunnels. Struggling, Adara bowed her head, managing to knock Esmeray to the dirt with a well-placed headbutt, her horns sinking into the soft flesh of the Queen's shoulder. Blood rushed forth. Adara withdrew, red sliding down the length of opal slowly, dripping onto her brow before she wiped it away with a satisfied sneer, her eyes darting up to the now-open cell door. But before she could make a run for freedom, Esmeray rolled to her side, tucked in her wings, and lunged.

"Esmeray!" Sparrow yelled, as the sisters tumbled to the ground, wings, teeth, and nails flying. But Adara was clearly no match for the Vessel of Death. Within moments, Esmeray staggered upright, her clawed, tattooed hand holding Adara firmly in place, fisted in her mangy hair. Blood pooled onto the dirt floor from Esmeray's shoulder, though she didn't seem to notice as she dragged Adara out of the cell, past Sparrow, still rooted to the ground in pure shock, and down the hall.

Adara tried to break free, twisting, screaming, lashing out at Esmeray. Esmeray didn't even acknowledge it as she ruthlessly yanked her twin along. Adara shrieked curses as her bare feet tried and failed to find purchase against the soft ground.

Sparrow's heart hammered in her chest as Esmeray and Adara disappeared around the bend in the tunnel, heading for the caverns beyond. Quickly, her fingers shaking, Sparrow bundled her flowy skirts back in her hands, racing to catch up with the twins.

She stopped dead in her tracks as she laid eyes on the scene before her. At the edge of the rocky ledge, right outside the thin air that held a trickle of magic, Esmeray released Adara's hair. Adara collapsed to her knees, but Esmeray merely reached down, gripped her throat and pulled her up to stand.

They faced each other - one light, one dark. Sparrow watched with terror as Esmeray cocked her head slowly to her twin, whispering something to Adara, making her blanch.

"Can you fly?" Esmeray asked louder, her tone icy, as she ran her tattooed finger along the cracks on Adara's wing. Esmeray's question jolted through Sparrow, those three words coated in a venom laced promise.

Adara's eyes widened. She backed away a step, whimpering as she chanced a look down, down to the bottom of the caverns, before turning pleading eyes to Sparrow.

Esmeray let out a breathy laugh, and whispered, "I don't think you can."

Faster than Sparrow could react, Esmeray shoved Adara over the cliff's edge, straight into the yawning maw of the Soul Keeper's Cell below.

# CHAPTER FORTY
# ORLA

ORLA DOUBLED OVER, HER body pouring sweat, sticking to the deep green shirt and matching pants she'd donned for her first training lesson. It was nearing midnight, and she decided having an *acat* may be more trouble than it was worth.

Her hair was slick with beads of perspiration, the salty rivulets dripping down her parted and panting lips, drying out her already parched throat.

"That was almost better," Soren noted with an annoyingly deadpan air as she sat atop the half wall circling one of the outdoor training rings in Oasees. The cool night breeze sweeping through the columns did little to reprieve Orla from the grueling training Soren dragged her to three hours ago.

Between exercises to strengthen her legs and core, and sprints of the ring's circumference, Orla was acutely aware of every aching muscle in her body. After each set of exercises, Soren would have her stand in the middle of the arena and meditate - working to create that oh-so-important first connection with her *acat* that would bring it to the surface of her soul to access whenever she needed.

As she took up the meditative positioning Soren showed her, Orla fought to even her breathing, trying to focus on the task at hand, and not on why Soren hadn't mentioned anything about the council meeting, or about her role as the King's cupbearer. If Soren knew Orla's mind drifted elsewhere, she didn't bring it up.

"Grasp that thread inside yourself. Plant your feet. Remember, you are *immovable* and *rooted*. Find the path in your mind where your power sleeps and imagine hooking it through your fingers. Good - now push it out of your body." Soren imitated the movement, bringing her palms up and rotating her wrists, sweeping her hands away in a circular motion.

It seemed so easy that it annoyed Orla immensely.

Her lungs quivered through a side stitch that she was convinced was actually a phantom knife between her ribs. Orla closed her eyes - again seeing nothing but the darkness behind her lids. Fighting to take a steady breath through her nose, she dug into her mind, as if she was wracking her brain for a memory.

She was about to open her eyes and tell Soren this was stupid.

*Wait -*

A glint of red appeared in the depths of her consciousness.

Orla lurched towards it, imagining her fist snatching the thick cord, and shoved it out, her hands replicating what Soren showed her.

Soren yelped.

Orla's eyes flew open, just in time to see the tail end of a trail of fire smolder out, and Soren's hand raised in front of her, a gleaming shimmer of Orla's *acat* weaving against Soren's palm.

Orla's mouth popped into an "O" as Soren gave her a bright grin, pulling her palm closer to inspect the design inked on her palm. "That was perfect, and also why I'm training you *here* and not on one of the grassy rings."

Soren's mimicking gift absorbed the flare, leaving the fae with a small, few inch long swirl of a tattoo. As Orla watched, Soren cupped her hand, a small flame appearing in her palm. With a grin, Soren pushed the flame higher and higher, until it sputtered out, the temporary *acat* disappearing from her skin. "You were right, you can wield fire."

With a sheepish smile, and her heart doing somersaults in her chest, renewed joy surged through her. She created *fire*. No more would she be powerless, vulnerable. No more would she be subjected to the whims of lesser beings or the ulterior motives of a certain Prince.

She was Orla.

Powerful, strong, fucking *fire wielder*.

Between the Culling and her own fears of dragons, she hoped her heritage gift stayed slumbering inside of her. If she kept to the Palace, where the King who hated dragons lived, maybe the beasts would steer clear. Orla just had to stay *inside* the confines of the Palace and *not* step foot outside.

But her interest in her *acat*, in her lineage gift, invigorated her spirit. Fire magic had never been outlawed, so if she could conjure a flame for the King during the Culling, she'd be in the clear to live a good life here.

Her thoughts staggered at that – such a contrasting idea to how she'd felt when she first arrived. But she had a job, had friends, and gods above, the Ruby Kingdom felt a little bit like it could be her *home*.

Three more attempts had her magic surging closer to the surface each time, though no more bursts of flame appeared from her hands, only embarrassingly pathetic plumes of black smoke. Sweat continued to roll down her face, but the grin plastered on her flushed cheeks was as immovable as the stone columns surrounding her.

"Okay." Soren hopped off the wall with a clap, bouncing on the balls of her feet. "I want you to try something else." She jogged closer, her fingers expertly tying her hair up into a ponytail.

Before Orla could react, Soren whipped her hand out, a ball of white light hitting her square in the shoulder and causing her to stumble back. The small sting disappeared quickly, and she laughed, rubbing the small hurt, "What was that for?"

"Use your gift to hit me back," Soren replied, shortening the distance between them, creating another small orb of magic that bobbed in the air between them. "Try to control how much of the thread you pull. Create a fireball the size of your fist, and throw it at me."

Orla nodded, squaring her shoulders, and diving headfirst into her thread of magic, the ease of accessing her *acat* feeling like a huge accomplishment in the short time she'd trained. A couple hours? And she already produced fire?

Her small moment of confidence cost her when Soren's magic smacked her thigh.

Soren laughed as Orla cursed colorfully. Holding onto her *acat* while her eyes were open and she was actively avoiding Soren's attacks was difficult, and it took another half hour before Orla was able to grasp her *acat* while avoiding the balls of stinging light Soren kept chucking at her with ruthless precision.

With a haphazard swipe, Orla rocked back and loosened her mental grip, trying to ease the flame from her mind outward and through her hands. This time, she felt the fire roil through her blood, warming her. In the span between seconds, the thrill turned to terror as a sheer wall of red-hot flames roared from her palm, engulfing Soren completely.

Orla gasped, squeezing her fist shut on instinct, the magic mercifully winking out. Stumbling forward, Orla screamed Soren's name. *Not*

*Soren, please not Soren*. They'd grown close so quickly. If she killed her...If her magic burnt Soren...Orla would never forgive herself.

A pressurized hum filled Orla's bones as the ball of fire enveloping Soren dissolved with a *woosh*, revealing a wild-eyed Soren panting, a huge smile on her face, as the mirror of Orla's *acat* grew and wove around Soren's left arm.

"Well, fuck," Soren said, a bit breathlessly, "I think you won."

Orla choked on a sob-laugh as she gripped the faé into a fierce hug, the apologies pouring forth as tears streamed down her face. "I thought I killed you; I couldn't control it."

Soren chuckled, hugging Orla back fiercely. "I'm a mimic, Orla. Don't apologize, I should thank you – that's some of the strongest magic I've had the pleasure of absorbing." Soren pulled out of the embrace, cupping Orla's tear-streaked cheeks. "I'll have fire magic for a fucking *month* from that one hit."

The two females grinned at each other, Orla's relief that Soren was alright making her a little jittery. "It'll be much easier to train you if we both have the same gift, anyway." Soren threw her arm around Orla, steering them both to the half wall to sit down and catch their breath.

A slow clap sounded from the edge of the training ring, and Orla stiffened as Soren's ears perked up, the pair twisting around towards the source of the noise.

Dimas, dressed in all black, crossed his arms, an amused smile on his face as his eyes dragged down Soren's mimicked *acat*. Orla focused on the cloaked figure leaned against the column, still mockingly clapping, a smirk tugging at the corners of her lips as Cillian shoved off the pillar and swaggered closer. He shoved a hand into the pocket of his black pants.

"That was impressive." Cillian nodded to Orla before he turned to Soren. "Are you being nice?"

Soren growled, flashing the Prince her gold-capped fangs. "I'm always nice."

Dimas snorted, and Orla pushed her lips together to keep the smile off her face when Soren scowled and flipped Dimas off.

Cillian looked from Soren to Orla, before pinning Soren with a loaded look. "And?"

"She'll be fine." Soren glanced quickly at Orla before scuffing her boot against the stone floor.

Orla kept her mouth shut, though the words not being said made her uneasy. It seemed like Cillian and Soren were agreeing upon some earlier planned conversation, some secret, that Orla wasn't privy to. The clipped tone the two of them spoke in, curt and low, made her feel on edge and defensive.

But before she could gauge any more of Cillian's reaction, Dimas whistled low, and Cillian threw the hood of his cloak back over his head. "Great. Soren, it's in motion already. What we expected. We're meeting tomorrow night. Orla – I'll come collect you from your room, Soren – you know where to go."

Soren nodded briskly. Cillian turned away, keeping to the shadows as Dimas met him at the rim of the arena. Within seconds, the two males slunk back into the night.

"What was that about?" Orla whispered, rubbing her palms together as she cut her eyes to Soren.

Soren sighed, flipping the top of the water off and taking a long sip before muttering, "That...that was the confirmation we needed. We're going to save our Kingdom."

# CHAPTER FORTY-ONE
# MERRICK

MERRICK HATED THE HOURS between the end of dinner service and sleep. During the day, his routine was structured, busy, making it easy to focus on the tasks at hand.

But after the nightly mayhem of supper in the Opal Palace's barracks, the constant din of loud laughter, plates clinking, and mugs of ale slamming against the tabletops made Merrick too wired to immediately collapse into bed for the blissful nothingness of rest.

That quiet time was when he brooded, alone in his room, desperately trying to find something to fill the yawning pit of depression that sliced open his soul.

He needed to keep his thoughts occupied. Merrick told Esmeray he would oversee the renovations of the throne room – but thankfully, all he'd needed to do so far was sit in on a few meetings and approve or veto the recommended changes.

He died in that throne room.

Until Sparrow pulled his soul back into his body.

And when he woke up, his hand in hers, their eyes locked – and their soul tie bloomed.

It should have thrilled him. But it felt...hollow.

His moodiness had nothing to do with the fact that Sparrow was also mated to his best friend.

Merrick thought having a soul tie would awaken some emotional, primal, overpowering sense of love in his soul. Not just this...base level feeling of attraction he held for Sparrow. Which he had anyway since the moment he first laid eyes on her.

But after the battle against Adara, he saw the way Sparrow and Laurent looked at each other and *knew*.

Laurent was Sparrow's true mate.

Not him.

There was no jealousy in his heart for his oldest and closest friend. Sparrow tried talking to Merrick, but he knew even *she* felt the difference between the soul ties inside her. Her connection with Laurent was incandescent, blazing, their *acatis* growing before Merrick's eyes. Her soul tie to Merrick was just...dim.

His *acat* hadn't changed in the slightest.

His sleep was filled with recurring nightmares of floating weightless against never-ending blackness, nightmares of waking up in a rocky cavern, the air thin and cold, with a massive white beast lurking through the shadows.

In an attempt to actually *do* something productive – and to stay away from sinking into the closest bottle of liquor - Merrick put together an all-female aerial unit for the Obsidian Kingdom. He personally oversaw their training for a month, until the darkness festering at the corners of his mind found him again.

Merrick begged Esmeray to move him to the Opal Palace. She tried to promote him to Commander.

He refused.

*I just want my old position back.* He'd told her. *No bells and whistles –let me work with new recruits, train them, mold them into fighters.*

So, she relented, and Merrick was given a new unit of gargoyles to train. It was what he did best – pouring out his knowledge and expertise, teaching them so they wouldn't make the same mistakes he had.

The only caveat what that Esmeray gave him his own quarters. *I'm putting you in your own housing. You need space, Merrick, to sort your shit out.*

It had taken all of the three months since his arrival for the higher-ranked Commanders to stop sneering at him, to begin to earn respect on his own – respect not tied to being the Queen's friend, not tied to the actions in the Opal Palace's throne room.

But it was a start.

He trudged heavily down the corridor to his room. It was quiet, the stark white walls unadorned aside from the orb-like sconces that bathed the hall in a warm glow.

Merrick felt a ripple of exhaustion weigh down his wings. It had been a rough day – he'd broken up two fights between recruits, poured over battle reports from Calcity, and drafted-and-crumpled-up four letters to Captain Ballah, trying to put into words that he was sorry for not being at Calcity, that he commended her bravery, that he would grieve with her for the females that fought all the way down to Minmere.

But the words didn't capture his grief correctly, felt too little too late.

A week had passed since the Battle of Calcity. A week since he raged and swore at the advisors and Commanders who gave the order to stand down. Merrick threatened to fly out to Calcity himself to help, to fight, to do something, *anything* to support his King and Queen in battle.

When his yelling finally attracted enough negative attention, his supervisor sat him down in the barrack's cramped meeting room and told him if he flew to Calcity, he would be labeled a deserter, and wouldn't be welcome back – no matter *what* Queen Esmeray decreed.

Two Commanders flanked him for the rest of the day, just to make sure he obeyed orders.

He still didn't understand why.

The pure helplessness was enough for him to put his ring back on. He'd stared at it for a long moment, wondering who he should reach out to, who would know what was going on in Calcity, when word finally arrived, shouted through the halls and ringing out in the courtyard.

*The Queen of Decimation razed Adara's supporters in a single blow.*

Merrick promptly slipped the ring off and shoved it back into his drawer before mentally adding "*Coward*" to the long list of shit he was.

Frustration dogged him as he slipped into the cool darkness of his quarters. The room was quiet. As his eyes slowly adjusted, Merrick groaned out a curse, shuffling further into the room and loosening the buckles on the sheath at his waist.

A rustle of leathery wings from the shadowy corner of his room had Merrick drawing his sword with a snarl, pointing the blade towards the intruder.

"That is *no* way to greet your Queen," Esmeray said lightly, amusement lacing her words as she clicked his lamp on.

Esmeray leaned against the back of his reading chair; her wings tucked in tight to her sides. She was dressed in black leathers, looking the part of someone absolutely up to no good. With casual curiosity, her eyes flicked down to the point of Merrick's sword, mere inches from her throat.

"Carra's tits, Esmeray," Merrick hissed, tossing his weapon on the bed.

"What language," Esmeray crooned as she crossed her legs, regarding him with a half-smirk filled with mirth. "Is that how these soldiers talk when I'm not around?"

"Why are you here?"

Esmeray raised an eyebrow.

"Who *knows* you're here?" he tried again, pointedly.

Esmeray rolled her eyes. "No one. And I'd like to keep it that way."

"Keerian?"

She shrugged. "I told him I'd be back in an hour." With a coy smile, she winked at Merrick. "He's currently taking a bath."

Merrick growled, wishing with all of his might that the damned Queen would keep some things to herself. Not that she'd ever shied away from being vulgar. His wings rustled as he leaned against the side of his bed, folding his arms across his chest as he surveyed the newly minted Queen of Decimation. Rumors swirled around the Palace that Esmeray held god-level power now. That she was the Vessel of Death, giving truth to what had been merely fantasy.

Merrick didn't listen to gossip, and yet, as Esmeray settled against the back of the chair, Merrick noted the strained look in her eyes, a look he knew she was trying to downplay with humor and indifference.

"What happened in Calcity?" Merrick asked quietly. Esmeray grimaced and made a casual sweep of her hand towards the door. Shimmering gold slid up the walls, glowing faintly with intricate symbols. Wards. To protect this conversation from eavesdroppers passing in the halls.

With a deep breath, she told him everything.

Merrick uttered a filthy curse once Esmeray finished.

Phades, Massis, Adara, Esmeray – the power players churned through his mind as he gave Esmeray another glance.

Esmeray frowned, surveying *him* for a beat, as if she was assessing Merrick's mental state. She folded her hands tightly in her lap, finally nodding to herself before stating. "Anyway, I'm here because I need your help. I have reason to believe my council is entertaining spies from the Ruby Kingdom."

Merrick knitted his brows together, searching her face. "How do you know?"

"I sent word for aid during the battle in Calcity. The Opal Palace ignored my request. When I really sat down and thought about it – there's only two options as to why." Esmeray held up two fingers, ticking them off as she continued, "One – some fuckers decided to see if I'd die in battle so they could grab the throne for themselves, or two – someone on my council is working with another Kingdom to isolate and divide Irridessen from within."

"And you think King Eamon would be bold enough to send spies here?" Merrick rubbed his palm down his horn, thinking back to how swiftly his requests to send help to Calcity were shut down.

"I had the suspicion –now I have confirmation," Esmeray said simply.

"How?"

"Because *my* spies in the Ruby Kingdom told me." Esmeray stifled a smile as Merrick gaped at her – utterly shocked at the revelation. This was the part of politics that he'd never understand. The seedy shit that slithered through every tiny loophole in the Treaty of Terramere.

If a spy was rooted out, they were killed. And their bodies were usually shipped back to the Kingdom they hailed from. In creatively brutal pieces.

It made him thankful every day that Sparrow's soul tie to Laurent meant his best friend was no longer the Opal Kingdom's Spy Master.

Merrick sighed deeply, "What do you need me to do?"

"I need you to figure out who is entertaining this list of names." A small roll of parchment appeared in the Queen's hand, and she tossed it over to Merrick. "And I need the spies to die. Then I need you to put your *fucking* ring back on, and tell me which council member betrayed me."

The last part seemed more like a personal attack than a demand. Merrick flicked his eyes up and suddenly, Queen Esmeray was gone, replaced by Esmeray his friend – the friend that taught him waterfall jumping, that defended him in the throne room – that almost died *herself* to spare him, Sparrow, Laurent, and Lenna from a painful death by her twin's hands.

"Why don't you want to be around us?" Esmeray asked softly, a shade of hurt shadowing her features.

Merrick opened his mouth, closed it, a lump in his throat constricting his words. "I...Fuck, Meer. It's hard. I-" He shook his head. "What did it feel like when you received your soul tie?"

Esmeray stood slowly, her black wings extending as she gave him a tight smile. "It felt like pure euphoria," she admitted, "like being truly awake for the first time in my life."

The lump formed thicker in his throat. Merrick lowered his eyes, praying that Esmeray wouldn't see the silver-edged tears threatening to fall. Needing something to do, Merrick broke the seal on the rolled piece of parchment, quickly reading the names the Queen received from her own spy network.

Five names.

Five Ruby Kingdom spies in the Opal Palace.

Five swift and merciless deaths.

"Put your ring back on," Esmeray murmured as she crossed the room, "and come home."

Merrick waited until she waned away in a flare of gold before allowing the first tear to fall.

# Chapter Forty-Two
## Lenna

Evening fell softly over the Obsidian Kingdom, carrying with it a decadent breeze that fluttered through the curtains of the glass paned doors. Autumn had officially taken over the last days of summer, announcing its arrival through a cacophony of color and deep, earthy, scents.

Leaves swathed in hues of gold, red, and bright orange overtook the trees dotting the mountainside below snowcapped peaks.

It was all so surreal to Lenna, the distant views so perfect and picturesque, yet a part of her longed to see what the waterfalls and forests surrounding Florra looked like now.

She'd yet to return to the city since the battle at the base of the waterfall. And as she looked over the balcony, a wave of homesickness crashed through her, bringing with it fond memories of the bustling town, the cozy apartment above Hale's Bakery, the soft crackle of a fire as she read a new book aloud while Hale rubbed her feet, the two of them laughing and sharing a bottle of wine before tumbling into bed.

Taking a small sip of her tea, Lenna's mind drifted back to Doortan, dredging up a mental image of the weather in those first few days of autumn. It always seemed so...soggy. The leaves rarely changed – opting instead to fall from the trees in rain-soaked clumps, coating the land-scape with the damp musk of rot. Doortan would be cold and wet for weeks, until the first sprinkles of snow turned the ground into slush, souring the crops and moods of everyone living in the gloomy manor.

It was fitting, she decided, that her new home held so much vibran-cy, electrifying the very air, and quickly dismissed any other thoughts of Doortan from her head.

Hale, sitting next to her on a new, larger chaise lounge – courtesy of Esmeray – murmured a few unintelligible words as he scrawled an-other line of notes onto the parchment resting next to his knee. The Book of Phades sat open in his lap, the sinking sun gilding the pages as he continued talking quietly to himself, lost in thought. Since Esmeray gave the book to Hale, he'd bought it with him everywhere.

" – doesn't make sense. Pronoun, conjunction…And conjunction again?" Hale grumbled, flipping a page back and forth, a crease be-tween his brows deepening in concentration. His locs were pulled back, held out of his face with one of her headscarves, the ends of the light beige fabric wrapped tight and tucked back into themselves.

She watched Hale continue to argue with himself a moment more, before deciding to meddle.

"What are you tittering about over there?"

Hale looked up from the book, a fevered glint in his eye visible through his thick monocle. "I translated enough of the smaller words – pronouns and conjunctions mostly – to understand the beat of sentence structure, but the tones and patterns don't add up."

Tapping his thick fingers against the page in question, Hale huffed, "Here, the sentence reads, '*her and,*' and then -" He flipped the page, gesturing wildly at a small runic symbol at the top of the next page. "*For.*"

Lenna peered over his shoulder, resting her chin against his soft wool sweater to see the rune. It was a small circle with a line through the middle. The symbol – like the rest of the book – written in red ink so dark it was almost black. Hale's eyebrows shot up to his hairline as he tapped the character again for emphasis.

Lenna stared at it for three seconds before shooting Hale a silent reminder that she was waiting to be shocked by the odd little circle with a line through it. "What am I looking at, Hale?"

"Ah, right. Well, the next symbol on the top of the next page *should* be a word that I do not know, continuing the sentence *'her, and.'* But I know this rune. And it says *'for.'*"

Lenna squinted at the page, flipping it back and forth as her brain jumbled the weirdly shaped runes together.

"Her. And. For." Lenna's brows shot up as she caught the meaning of Hale's ramblings. The sentence made no sense. Because –

"Words are missing."

Hale nodded enthusiastically, shifting through the book. "It's a pattern that is prominent throughout the pages. A sentence starts off, and when you flip the page, it has nothing to do with the sentence before." Hale took a deep breath, blowing out his conclusion. "I believe Phades telling Esmeray the Book of Faune is needed is *because the books cannot be read separately.*"

Lenna gawked at Hale, her eyes darting through the runes at face value.

"If the Book of Faune is needed to even complete a translation of the Book of Phades...Then we need that second book quickly."

Lenna unraveled herself from the assortment of blankets on the chaise. Hurrying into their chambers, she quickly slid on a thick cardigan, before stuffing her feet into the first slippers she could find. The grey faceted stone was in her hand before Hale even crossed the threshold.

Hale tucked his monocle into the small pocket of his trousers, the two of them falling into sync as they rattled off ideas to each other.

"It could've been a safety mechanism. Making sure whoever got their hands on only one book wouldn't be able to understand the volatile information," Hale said as he gathered up his parchments filled with notes.

Lenna snorted, fishing out additional blank pieces of paper and a magically-filled quill from the desk, organizing them in the leather bag Hale kept his supplies in. "Before Esmeray took its power, I would not call that book *safe.*"

Waving his hands in a motion that conveyed a gesture of "*you-know-what-I-mean*," Hale chuckled, the light in his eyes twinkling. "Fine, fine. I digress. But from a purely academic perspective, if Phades and Faune swapped pages, the story would most likely jump from one page from Phades, one page from Faune, and so forth. Now, knowing that, I can try and translate *this* book based purely off of runic symbols so when we get the Book of Faune, it'll be easier to read through it."

"And you're sure the pages in the Book of Phades aren't just...out of their correct order?"

"Pretty sure."

"But not positive?"

Hale sighed dramatically, clutching his heart. "If these pages are only out of order, and not some sort of divinely separated story spanning at least two Vessel Books from the most powerful goddesses in history, I am going to eat my vest and have words with Phades when my soul transcends to Minmere."

Lenna froze.

The thought of Hale's death sundered through her like a tossed stone disrupting the shallow end of a peaceful pond. He'd only been in her life for half a year, and yet, in that moment, and in memory of a hundred little moments before, she finally understood what it meant to be in love.

Without a second thought, she whirled towards him, her lips meeting his in a passionate kiss. A surprised grunt from Hale had her rising up on her toes, slanting her mouth over his. A soft thump told Lenna the Book of Phades was tossed onto the bed, and Hale wrapped his arms around her, deepening the kiss as he ran a hand through her hair.

"You cannot go to Minmere anytime soon," she said breathlessly, pulling away an inch and running her fingers through Hale's coarse beard. "Because I love you." A choked sob punctuated her words.

"I love you, too, dear," Hale whispered, the emotion swirling over his face more beautiful than the changing leaves and the mountainscape surrounding them.

A blush crept over Lenna as she kissed him again. It was the first time she'd allowed herself to utter those words while truly meaning them. During a bleak few days after the battle at the Opal Palace, Lenna had shown up to Hale's home with a half-drank bottle of wine and a tear-stained face, just to barge into his living room and share the sad tale of her previous marriage.

She'd wanted to get it off her chest, the warring emotions of attraction she felt for him against the guilt that she was still – at the time – technically married.

Hale had quietly listened to her guilt-wracked rant, her fears, and when she'd run out of words, when a headache began thrumming against the side of her temples, he gently took the wine from her hands, bought her a glass of water, and tucked her into his bed before taking up a spot on his couch to sleep. She'd woken the next morning, crusty eyed and embarrassed, but Hale greeted her with a delicious homemade breakfast in bed, a dozen wildflowers, and an offer.

To live there, with him, in his apartment, when she felt ready. Lenna never regretted the recklessness that encouraged her decision. And she moved her meager belongings into his home above the bakery the day the ink dried on her divorce papers.

Once, Lenna worried that without a soul tie, she was fighting against time itself until Hale left. But after months with this male, after friendship turned into attraction, and that attraction deepened into *this*, she knew.

With or without the god's approval, Hale was hers, and she was his.

It was that love she chased in her youth, that adoration and respect she dreamt of. Here, in the kind eyes of a half-fae baker that had seen her – truly seen her – and accepted her for who she was.

They stood like that, staring into each other's souls for a long moment, the Prism and the Book of Phades forgotten. It was only when the sound of rustling wings and the muffled voices of the Queen's Guard floated in from outside their room did they break apart. Lenna's chest burst with happiness, and it took all of her willpower to slip out of Hale's arms, hopping over to the bed to retrieve the book and hand it back to Hale, a dazzling smile plastered on his face as he kissed her forehead. "You love me."

"I love you," Lenna agreed, "And you love me right back." Hale nodded, his deep chuckle causing her to steal one more kiss before she turned to the door. Lenna reached out her hand, and Hale slipped his fingers through hers. "Ready to start another adventure?"

"I'd follow you anywhere." Hale replied.

# Chapter Forty-Three
# ESMERAY

"Your Majesty, the Oracle is requesting an audience." A Queen's Guard posted out front of my late mother's study poked his head in, the first interruption in hours.

"See her in, please." I rubbed my face with my hand, glad for the break from the monotonously boring reports of the Slate Kingdom's ruling class. My spies were succinct and detailed – typically to the point of boredom. None of my elite warriors could ever be considered poets, that's for sure.

So far, all reports were dry, nothing of interest or concern, and there was only so much I could read about the Slate Kingdom's grain stores and cargo surplus for the coming winter before my eyes blurred and stuck, my lids heavy with fatigue. In the comforting ambience of the study, it was difficult to not lay my head against the desk and close my tired eyes for a minute.

The Queen's study was cozy, with a crackling fire sputtering away merrily in the corner. Densely packed shelves of books took up wall space from the floor to ceiling, save for a black obsidian frame above the desk that held the royal portrait of my mother and father right after their soul tie bloomed, their faces painted in a way that beautifully captured the pure love in their eyes.

Everything in the room was painted or stained dark - black walls, deep, burgundy staining on the wooden desk, even dusk-purple curtains, heavy and velvet, embroidered with small scrolling vines that crept up from the floor.

The small group I sent to the Slate Palace doubled as fighters, with orders to protect King Dalen and his family from the whims of Ingotheria. King Eamon knew the dome was down, my spies confirmed it, and my team of fae had a note from me explaining that, while the dome had fallen, Irridessen stood with the Slate Kingdom as they always had. I couldn't bring myself to explain the reason *why* the dome was gone.

I hoped Ingotheria hadn't caught wind of that either.

Merrick tracking down the spies posted in the Opal Palace was imperative – and he was empowered with full backing of the throne to take whatever actions deemed necessary.

Lenna's bright curls bounced through the door. Hale followed, the Book of Phades clutched in his arms. As the door shut behind them, they bowed low, before Lenna popped up, crossing the room to throw her arms around me in a hug.

I hugged the Oracle back fiercely, feeling the tension in my shoulders melt a fraction as her warmth embraced me.

Fumbling in her pocket, Lenna pulled out the Prism with a flourish, setting it on my desk, looking like she was about to burst with information. Hale, still behind her, was flushed, almost vibrating with enthusiasm.

Raising my brow, I glanced from Lenna to Hale. Their auras flooded the room with tangy excitement. "Do either of you want to explain *why* you're in my study with all of this wild energy?"

"Lenna said she loved me."

"Hale had a revelation about the Vessel Books."

These two sentences were said in sync, and I wasn't sure which one I wanted to dive into first. My eyes darted between them, as Lenna took in Hale's words and blushed a violent pink. The baker gave her a sheepish grin, before the two launched into further explanation about the Book of Phades.

I paused their enthusiastic chatter briefly, calling Keerian, Sparrow, and Laurent to meet in the study. Hale took over explaining his findings as the six of us crammed into the space, listening with varying degrees of attention. Keerian and Laurent wore matching expressions of rapt focus, Sparrow picked at her nails while perched on the edge of my desk, and Lenna slowly circled my bookshelf, head tilted, mouthing title names and pulling down the ones she was going to steal.

"If the Book of Faune is needed, my theory is the two Vessel Books are a tandem read to avoid an easy translation of whatever story is in here. Without Phades explicitly telling Esmeray to find the Book of Faune, we wouldn't have known *why* the basic translations are inconclusive." Hale finished off, holding court in his own way, his chest puffed out and his astute eyes eager.

Lenna dumped a stack of books onto the corner of my desk and plucked up the Prism, cupping it gently in her palm and extending it for all of us to see. "I'm going into the Prism," she announced firmly. "Alone."

Sparrow began to argue but Lenna cut her off with a wave. "I need to clearly see where I'm going. The past gets tangled around the history of the book, and having an anchor adds additional memories."

I spoke up, Sparrow worrying her lip while fiddling with her ring, obviously speaking with Laurent. "Lenna, I'm fine with that. *But*, since you're going *really* far into the past by yourself, Collette will be present to make sure you're alright."

"Can't have you falling over and knocking the sense out of your sweet head in case this triggers any fainting spells," Keerian added.

Lenna nodded, a fierce glint in her honey tinted eyes. "We do this now."

I called my Queen's Guard to collect Collette. Sparrow and Laurent had a hushed conversation with Hale as Keerian wrapped Lenna in a tight embrace, taking low and quickly to her while she nodded along, determination set on her features.

Sometimes I forgot that Lenna – brilliant, headstrong Lenna – was only human.

In all actuality, she was the strongest of us all.

"Stop hovering," Keerian muttered in my ear an hour later.

I hissed back, "Sparrow's closer."

Sparrow, sitting to my left at the end of the bed, shot me a coy smile, our bickering on the balcony during the first bout to try finding the Vessel Books fresh in our minds.

Lenna lay propped against the pillows in her bed, both hands gripping the Prism as it glowed incandescent and radiant. Hale was as close to her as he could get without touching her. Laurent hovered by the desk with his features schooled and his arms crossed, and Collette was sitting next to the bed on a wooden stool, straightening the vials of swirling smoke and acrid liquids littering the nightstand in case Lenna needed a healer once resurfacing from the past.

The Prism pulsed with pure light, and I wondered what Lenna could see - if there were memories flying past her mind of the first fae civilizations, the first tribes of gargoyles, wondered if she could see my ancestors as they grew and built a world of magic.

Laurent glanced at the thick hourglass against the desktop, the trickling sand noting forty-nine minutes had passed since Lenna dove into the Prism. It was inherently dangerous to be in the folds of the past, that deep, for too long, and we agreed once an hour was up, Hale would touch Lenna, his anchor line would flare at the contact, and that would alert Lenna to resurface into reality whether she found the book or not.

The minutes slipped by slowly, my mind drifting to the Ruby Kingdom spies on my land, the fallen dome, my twin in the Soul Keeper's Cell, and a certain gargoyle Captain who'd be providing me an update this evening on where he was at in his hunt.

I hadn't told anyone about my visit to Merrick, not even Keerian, just in case nothing came of my search. The intel and the five names could be a dead end, and those spies could already be long gone, safely back in the Ruby Kingdom.

"That's an hour," Laurent said. Hale took a deep breath, his large hand sliding over Lenna's, his eyelids fluttering closed as his mind shot through the Prism.

I held my breath as ten seconds ticked by. Hale gasped, his eyes flying open, readjusting to the dimness of the King's Chambers.

"I found her," he wheezed, panic flaring across his face, "But - "

Lenna's eyes shot open, but it was not her familiar, bright honey-brown that stared back at us.

Her gaze was dulled, flat, the little streaks of gold that were normally sparkling and lively now muted and murky.

Sparrow and I shot up, a shout escaping my lips as Lenna snarled. She spoke, and my magic swelled inside my soul, telling me that, though her voice sounded the same, the words themselves belonged to Moirai, the God of Sight.

*"Twelve voices babble over each other, all louder than the next. But it is the silent one that speaks the loudest - says the most by saying nothing at all."*

Lenna's eyes narrowed, her head cocked to the side. Slowly, she turned to stare at me. "You seek the Book of Faune, Vessel?"

"Yes," I retorted to Moirai.

"The Book of Faune has not seen the light of day since Faune herself hid it. Going down that path will reveal the truths you so desperately seek, as will it confirm the questions in your heart."

"Where is it?" Laurent stepped closer; his hands balled into fists at his side. Keerian lurked behind him, his grim expression assessing the situation.

With a rattling gasp, Lenna pitched backwards, spasms rattling her body against the soft pillows.

Collette immediately sprang into action, uncorking a vial with her teeth and dumping its contents down Lenna's throat. Lenna's muscles relaxed a heartbeat later, a small sigh from her lips breaking the thrumming silence of the room, her lids fluttering closed.

"She'll be fine," Collette murmured to Hale, who had tears in his eyes, face pinched, as he gripped Lenna's hands in his own. "She's sleeping. I gave her a tonic to minimize the seizures and let her rest until her mind catches back up with her body." With a pointed look at the Prism, now back to its grey coloring, Collette noted flatly, "I recommend putting *that* someplace far away until we confirm Moirai is no longer channeling her."

Hale blanched, before snatching the Prism and tossing it over to Keerian, who shoved it haphazardly into a desk drawer.

"Seizures?" Sparrow asked, concern lacing her soft question as she smoothed a hand over Lenna's duvet. "Is that a side effect of being so deep in the past? Or because she's also a seer?"

"It could be," Collette noted somberly, "though I'm not well versed in seer magic. But with the amount of power Moirai just shot through the Prism, into her, to deliver a prophecy, we won't know until she wakes up."

"I'm sorry," Keerian interrupted, "Are you saying fucking *Moirai* just slipped from Aurramere into Lenna's mind, through the Prism, to talk to us?"

"I think so," I replied, "Lenna's a seer and an Oracle, both gifts from Moirai himself. Her being both...means she has a stronger connection to him. If she's poking around god history, it was only a matter of time until the gods noticed."

"Fuck," Keerian blew out a breath, running his hands through his beard.

Collette seemed the least fazed of us, swiftly capping and uncapping her potions, smelling some with a grimace, and sorting them into two piles. "It's not as uncommon as you think," she said, "I've heard of gods channeling before - though not Moirai." She nodded to me, her short copper hair swinging. "King Scottrell once was channeled by Beyos before his soul tie to Queen Elera, during a mighty storm that almost capsized his boat. When Beyos slipped from Aurramere into his mind, King Scottrell was able to calm the entire *sea* to keep his ship and its inhabitants safe."

"I never knew that." I frowned.

Collette shrugged, "We are beings with magical gifts from gods - sometimes the gods show off when the veil between realms is thin enough to do so."

A soft groan startled us as Lenna stirred. Hale was there in a blink as she cracked open an eye.

"My mouth feels like sand," she grumbled. Relief shot through me at the sight of her normal eyes. Collette wordlessly handed her a glass of water, instructing her to sit up slowly and take small sips.

As Lenna drained the cup, she leaned her head back, adjusting the pillows behind her neck to keep upright. "Okay," she started slowly.

"Lenna, you just had a fucking god use you as a mouthpiece and popped off another prophecy." Keerian crossed the room to sit on the bed, tucking his wings behind him. "You take a nap, and we'll talk about this later."

Lenna gave him a sleepy smile before turning her head to Hale, the baker gently pressing a kiss to her forehead.

"You're all so smothering," she admonished weakly, a slow grin spreading across her plump lips as she let out a breathy chuckle. "But I found it. I found the Book of Faune."

# CHAPTER FORTY-FOUR
# ORLA

MARLO RUBBED HIS STOMACH leisurely as a soft breeze blew through the balcony doors. Orla, laying on the chaise, swallowed the last bite of sugary tart Marlo bought to her room as an apology and a tentative truce.

It had been a couple weeks since she'd seen him last, and Orla realized a lot of the resentment and anger she held against Marlo had to do with her own fears and limitations - not Marlo himself.

He'd shown up to her door, apologies spewing forth, and a tray of treats in his hands. Orla had thrown her arms around him in a hug, all forgiven between them. After seeing the cruel side of these lands, after seeing the dark side of the crown, Orla learned the type of easy friendship she had with Marlo was worth holding on to - cherishing.

"Did we finish off the entire tray?" Orla asked as she leaned her head back into her pillows.

Marlo grunted an answer.

"Good, if I eat another, I might explode."

With a groan, Marlo sat up, scrubbing the stubble of blonde on his cheeks with his nails. "So, the Prince really demanded your help tonight but wouldn't tell you what he needed?"

Orla shrugged a shoulder, checking the time against the visible sky through her balcony doors. Night had fallen a few hours ago, and now, bright stars dotted the darkness, the inky hue counting down to Cillian's arrival.

"I didn't know *'super-secret midnight trips'* was part of your job description."

"I didn't either," Orla admitted.

The two sat in quiet silence for a moment, before Marlo straightened. "How are you doing with your...fae-ness?"

Orla scrunched her nose. "I'm still processing that. But it's quite a relief to find out Olivera isn't my mother. She never seemed to care what happened to me, as long as it didn't tarnish her reputation." Orla let herself sink further into that mindset, testing if any sort of grief would flutter to the surface.

None did.

"The other part is just a shitty amount of unanswered questions."

Pushing away thoughts of her life in Doortan was easier when she stayed busy, but now, talking to Marlo, those chasms in her heart seemed to split open wider, begging her to be introspective, to look further. A breath later, Orla reconsidered with a wide smile. "The fire wielding is super cool though."

Marlo chuckled.

It was almost second nature now, after training with Soren until the sun crested the horizon and spending the morning calling to the flames leaping through her in response. Now, with only a little concentration, she could coax a small ball of fire to appear in her hand, the curling reds and oranges harmlessly licking her fingers.

She demonstrated for Marlo, his laugh wild with awe, as she poured the flames between her palms, the tendrils coiling around her wrist like a fiery serpent.

"How are you feeling? Being here?" Orla fisted her hand closed, her magic fizzing out as she squinted at Marlo.

Marlo sighed dreamily, his sky-blue eyes blinking slowly. "I love it. I ended up taking a position with a shop owner in the bazaar – he's half-fae and sells trinkets charmed with a bit of magic. He even allowed me to live in the small room above the shop. His mate and him just adopted a faeling, so they moved to a larger residential area in Aridden."

Orla grinned, sensing the ease and happiness that rolled through the room. "I'll have to come visit you and the shop."

"You should," Marlo agreed with a nod. "I'll make you buy something – I've got weekly goals to meet."

The two laughed, all tension eased between them. Orla glanced fondly at Marlo, his bright eyes so full of life as he recanted stories of the odd beings he met, the unique goods that he sold.

It was crazy, she thought to herself, how much changed between them in a month, how much *they* changed since becoming citizens of the Ruby Kingdom.

"What do you think happened to Lady Lenna?"

The question sobered Orla with quickness. "I don't know," she whispered quietly. "But she was kind, and she helped us. I hope she found some good in life."

"Me too," Marlo agreed, looking out to night beyond. "Me too."

THE KNOCK CAME TWO hours later. Marlo had already bid her goodbye, and Orla swore up and down she'd come visit his shop in the next few days.

Another rap against her door had her steeling herself, her breathing already jumpy and erratic against Cillian's unknown request. Orla threw the book she'd tried distracting herself with on the desk, crossing the room and unlocking the deadbolt on her door.

Cillian breezed past her without a word, dumping a lumpy package on her bed.

"Hello to you, too," Orla muttered as he closed her balcony doors, sealing them with a burst of red magic that shimmered against the glass.

"Put those on," he said as his magic knitted itself slowly across the walls.

With apprehension, she approached the bed, finding the package was actually a tightly rolled up cloak, black leather pants, and a matte black long sleeve top that seemed to contain some sort of flexible armor. "Why am I putting this on? And what're you doing?"

"This barrier will keep people from looking into your room too closely. From the outside, it'll seem as if you merely went to bed, but it will alert me if anyone tries to get in here while we're gone."

"Someone would try to break into my room?"

"This will tell me if they do."

"Who is this elusive '*they*?'"

"You're asking a lot of questions, and not doing a lot of changing. We need to go before the gates close."

Orla was halfway to the bathroom before she stopped, her spine stiffening as Cillian's words sunk in. "The gates?"

Cillian appraised her silently from the corner of his eye, his hands steadily weaving thick red magic across her walls.

"We're going outside the Palace?"

"Obviously."

She turned towards him, throwing her arm out wide. "I can't go outside the Palace gates." Her *whole* plan to avoid her heritage gift hinged on staying *inside* the palace – away from dragons.

"Says who?" Cillian demanded, dismissing the red magic and looking over his shoulder at her, a scowl marring his handsome face.

"Says me," she hissed back, ignoring the darkening look in his eyes. "You said there's dragons out there, and I have no desire to see one."

"Go get dressed, Orla." Cillian let out an exasperated sigh through his teeth, waving his hands in frustration before returning to his magic, as if *she* was being unreasonable for not wanting to trot outside the safety of the Palace.

"No."

"Why?" He whirled towards her, red sparks flitting across his palms. A challenging look flashed across his face, as he stormed closer, stabbing a finger in her direction. "Are you *afraid*?"

*Orla is afraid.*

*Orla is afraid.*

The words from Lenna's letter came roaring back into her brain, burning her carefully laid plans to cinders as her temper flared hot and fast.

She was no longer afraid.

She was Orla Grey, fucking fire wielder.

Orla threw down the bundle of clothes, flames churning against her knuckles as she let his question sink in. "Fuck you," she spat, teeth bared. Though she was more irritated with the way her pulse quickened and her breathing hitched whenever he was near her – not so much his needling comment.

Cillian cursed, storming towards her. Orla stood her ground, glaring at him from underneath her lashes, but from her position near the bathroom door, Cillian easily crowded her against the wall, careful to not touch her, yet his mere presence had her desperate to feel his body pressed against her own. "Fuck me yourself," he growled.

The words hung heavy between them.

Realizing how close they ended up to each other, Cillian's nostrils flared, his eyes widening, searching her own. Orla's breath hitched, her lips parting slightly as a ripple of anticipation passed between them.

Her temper rapidly morphed into a churning wave of desire. Cillian, dressed head to toe in black leather, with carefully twisted locs pulled back to showcase his strong jawline, his dark skin shadowing sharp cheekbones, did nothing to help spark her fury again.

She crossed her arms, trying to maintain the space between them.

He crossed his right back.

"You want to use me," she snarled, albeit halfheartedly. "You want me to do something for *you* to further *your* cause. A cause you won't fully tell me about because you see me as disposable."

There it was, that anger, her rage, simmering beneath the serrated sheen of lust.

Anger was good.

But rage...Rage was way fucking better.

Her breathing came in pants as she ripped her gaze from his, shoving him back a step. He staggered, swallowing hard as she pushed him further. Cillian took two steps backwards, but Orla stalked towards him, her voice rough and her heart hard. "I am not here for your use; I will not allow you to fuck me over. So, no. I'm *not* interested in whatever the *fuck* your secret trip is."

With her fangs bared, she jabbed a finger into his muscular chest. "And I have absolutely *no* interest in fucking you."

As the words left her mouth, Cillian's back hit the wall by her bed, and she realized again just how close they were.

They stared at each other, chests heaving. The smell of cinnamon washed through her as she slowly craned her neck up to meet his deep eyes. Tentatively, Cillian lifted a hand, cupping her cheek, his thumb trailing softly over her bottom lip.

With a soft gasp she leaned into his touch. His other arm wrapped around her waist, tugging her flush to him. Between the thin lining of her dress, she felt every inch of his body, molded perfectly against hers.

"You have it all wrong," Cillian said huskily, every thought and spark of anger eddying out of her mind, everything honing in on just him – just his touch, just his body against hers. "I don't want to use you. I want *you* to use *me.*"

And then he crashed his lips against hers.

# CHAPTER FORTY-FIVE
## MERRICK

IF ARDRICK HADN'T SKIPPED dinner service in the mess hall, he would've evaded Merrick's trap. But the spy, the first name on the list Esmeray gave Merrick, stepped right into a carefully laid snare.

According to a bundle of forged documents, the fae hailed from Shar, a large city at the base of the Zircon mountain rage.

But after carefully digging through the Palace's archives, Ardrick didn't *exist* six months ago. Yet his documents were filed accurately, all signed and stamped "*Official*" by Lady Belinde, the Trade Advisor for the Opal Kingdom.

That was the first red flag. Typically, recruitment paperwork was filed and signed by one of the Commanders, or the Lord of War. But it was another piece of the puzzle Merrick threw himself into the moment the sun rose after Esmeray's visit.

The second red flag was that Ardrick was assigned to tenth rank, but when Merrick asked tenth rank's Captain if a fae named Ardrick was on his squad, the confused look on the Captain's face confirmed that no, there was not.

And now this.

Merrick crept through the Great Hall; wings tucked tight at his sides as he slipped behind a pillar. He watched Ardrick laugh boisterously with a group of beings. He wore the official armor of the Opal Kingdom's army, but no recruit with half their salt would *ever* skip such a special dinner service.

All of the other warriors were currently gorging themselves on a special meal of the cook's finest cuts of meat, enough wine to drown a dragon, and heaps of imported cheeses and fruit - a dinner Merrick personally paid for to "raise morale."

While it did raise morale as a whole, it also flushed out the rat that used the dinner service as an excuse to slip out of the barrack's dining hall uninterrupted. Merrick tailed him, sticking to the shadows.

The spy stopped in the middle of the Great Hall, saying something indecipherable to two fae females before they traipsed away, giggling.

Merrick held his breath as Ardrick stood silently, alone, watching the females leave the hall. The spy looked around suspiciously, before slipping through the unguarded doors of the throne room.

With a short breath, Merrick palmed his dagger, counting the beats of his racing heart before sliding from his hiding place, crossing the hall in two long strides.

Merrick braced himself against the slightly cracked door, thanking the gods that the hinges were well oiled. He held his breath, peering through the small crevice that gave him a decent view into the throne room.

"No, no one suspects me. Tell our King that my efforts were not in vain. The dome is down, and I have suspicions that Queen Esmeray herself...Yes, I'm looking for it. No, there's no leads on the book."

*Who was Ardrick reporting to?*

Merrick watched as the fae paced at the foot of the dais, a small golden trinket gripped in his hand.

It was some sort of magic object for communicating long distances, but more rudimentary than the mind-speak rings Esmeray commissioned. To use it, the communicator needed to speak aloud.

Which meant Merrick heard enough damning evidence.

Pulling a piece of parchment from his jacket, Merrick hid his dagger between the folds. He allowed himself one deep breath before flinging open the door and striding into the throne room.

Pretending to read off the blank parchment, Merrick looked up, coaxing a look of confusion across his face as Ardrick froze.

"Recruit," Merrick snapped, praying his performance sold. "This room is off limits, what're you doing here?"

"Sorry, Captain," Ardrick muttered, his eyes downcast, as he hurried towards the doors to exit.

"Woah, apologies aren't going to cut it." Merrick shuffled to the side, holding out his hand. "Why aren't you in the dining hall?"

Ardrick stood slightly shorter than Merrick, a closely cropped head of straw blonde hair hiding shady eyes. Merrick noted the short sword at the fae's side stayed sheathed.

"I was – oh, this is embarrassing," Ardrick stuttered, raising his hands in feigned innocence as the lies spilled out. "I was supposed to meet a Lady here. She told me the throne room would be empty."

Before Merrick had time to reply, Ardrick struck. Merrick's sword quivered in the sheath across his back, the metal tearing free, flying across the room, landing in Ardrick's grip, twisting and melting until it was nothing more than a molten tendril of iron, twining around the spy's arm.

With a hiss, Ardrick swung the whip of metal.

Merrick tucked and rolled out of the way, growling as the tail end lashed against his wing, leaving behind the sharp tang of magic and blood.

"I was wondering if you'd wisen up, *Captain Merrick,*" Ardrick chuckled, unsheathing the sword at his side, twirling the blade in his hand while the liquified remnants of Merrick's sword continued to writhe around the spy's upper arm. "It's pretty pathetic it took you this long to realize I was right under your nose."

Ardrick shrugged his shoulders. "But that's the thing with Ir-ridessen," he goaded, "you all live in this false sense of security. Ill intentions slide right by you."

Merrick waited until the toe of Ardrick's boot came into view as he curled up against the cool marble tile, the flickering image of him in this position, during the battle against Adara, threatening to consume him. He could faintly hear Sparrow's screams, feel his soul being tugged from Minmere, feel the echo of warm blood trickling out of him.

*Too much blood. He was losing too much –*

Clarity snapped back into focus.

This wasn't Adara, and Sparrow wasn't here.

And Merrick was very much alive.

With a roar that shook the half-restored pillars, Merrick swung up, scattering the sheets of parchment at Ardrick's face, causing the fae to flinch. It gave Merrick the split-second opening he needed as he buried the dagger – the entirety created out of thick blown glass – into the spy's exposed neck.

Ardrick's watery pupils blew wide as Merrick gripped the fae's breast plate, sinking the blade in another inch.

"You underestimate Irridessen," Merrick spat, feeling the fae's blood coat his hands. "We see your intentions, and will hunt you down like the prey you are."

Merrick yanked the blade out, the spy taking one last rattling gasp, his eyes bulging as blood poured out of his slashed throat, bathing the white armor. Ardrick staggered a single step backwards before collapsing, the molten iron splattering against the ground.

The pool of blood spread against the pristine white tiles. Merrick sunk to his knees, throwing the dagger away from him. It clattered loudly against the floor, specks of blood flying from its glass blade. Calming his roaring heart, Merrick breathed deep, filling his nose with the scent of death.

Merrick had done his research on Ardrick - enough to know the fae could summon metal to him, could melt down steel blades, and could unarm Merrick with a flick of his wrist.

And that was why, after a quick trip to the Palace's armory, Merrick came equipped with a glass dagger – something completely immune to the metallurgy magic the spy wielded. A sick sense of pride bloomed through his chest as he glanced down at the dead fae crumpled against the floor.

His mind flashed between the *now* and the *then* at a whirling pace.

Then, against Adara, the blood seeping onto the tiles had been from innocent lives sacrificed for nothing.

And now, as the spy's blood trickled from the gash in his throat, Merrick slid the small scrap of parchment from of his pocket, dipped his finger into the cooling blood, and drew a line through the first name on his list.

One down.

Four to go.

# CHAPTER FORTY-SIX
# ORLA

NUMBLY TRAILING AFTER CILLIAN, Orla unconsciously touched her fingers to her swollen lips. She'd been kissed plenty of times before but *nothing* like that.

The kiss completely knocked the rage out of her, consuming her until she was nothing but a smoldering mess of ash. When Cillian's lips took hers, she melted into his arms before throwing her hands around his neck, slanting her mouth to deepen the kiss. The moan that slipped out of Cillian's throat was enough to undo her, completely restructuring her entire perspective on life.

*Fuck. Fuck.*

She was so utterly fucked. They were a frenzy of clashing teeth and tongue, only broken up once Cillian pulled away, desire, dark and edged, flooding through his expression. It gave Orla a sick sense of satisfaction that he seemed just as off-kilter and ruffled as she did.

"Please, put the clothes on," he'd croaked, his tongue running against his bottom lip, as if he wanted to taste every last trace of her.

Orla's feet automatically turned towards the bathroom, picking up the bundle of clothes from the floor on the way.

Neither spoke when she reappeared, her hair slicked back with water and cinched with a thick leather band to lay against the base of her neck. The cool water had been a relief from the churning chasm of heat thrumming through her.

Now, piecing her brain back together bit by bit, the pair crept through the outskirts of the training rings, their black cloaks softly billowing against their ankles.

Cillian stopped abruptly, wrapping his arm behind him to pull Orla flush against his back. "Guards," he murmured.

Orla's throat dried out as they stood, frozen in the shadows, the muffled voices of the guards gaining volume until Orla could've sworn they were right in front of them. But then the voices softened and disappeared.

After what felt like an hour, Cillian's arm relaxed and they swept through the white sandstone arch, her boots feeling the transition from gravel floor to soft sand immediately.

"This way," Cillian jerked his head, a single loc swaying against his forehead. Orla stayed close, no argument on her lips, his words ringing through her ears.

*I want* you *to use* me.

Gods above, she was so fucked.

Cillian led her around the outskirts of the Palace walls, reality settling around her shoulders. There were dragons out here.

"We aren't going to see any dragons...right?" she breathed, her voice no more than a whisper.

"We shouldn't."

"That's enlightening," Orla huffed, darting her eyes towards the night sky.

They trudged through the sand silently. As Orla chanced a look behind her to where the Palace squatted, she swallowed her unease. In front of them, darkness loomed, the moon gilding the sand in soft silvery light.

"C'mere," Cillian whispered, as the sound of *something* shuffling in the sand startled Orla.

"What the fuck are those?" Orla yelped, jumping back as the creatures came into view.

They were *almost* horses, but where there should've been soft muzzles were maws filled with fanged teeth. Their coats were matte black, leathery, and rippling with muscle. The beast closest to her snorted a plume of mist, fixing its hauntingly red eyes on her.

"Desert kelpies," Cillian said. "Obviously."

"Oh, right. *Obviously.*"

Orla took a step backwards, and the kelpies' feet came into view. Instead of hooves, their legs ended in talons. "I shouldn't have looked at their feet," she announced dryly, doing her best to keep her tone neutral, as the kelpies pawed at the ground, their claws kicking up sand with the movement.

Cillian chuckled as he reached into his pocket, producing two strips of dried meat. He handed one to Orla who took it hesitantly, though her brain told her to turn tail and book it back to the palace.

"I've raised them since they were pups. Just think of it like riding a horse. You'll be fine." Cillian said breezily, holding up the treat.

"I've ridden one horse in my entire fucking life," Orla growled, cursing the damned Prince and that perfect, stupid kiss for dulling her common sense. She followed Cillian's lead, extending her hand out flat, palm up, presenting the desert kelpie with the meat.

Their solid red eyes scanned her. The larger of the two took a step forward, nostrils flaring, before gently bowing its head, taking the offering from her. Orla winced as warm breath tickled her palm, but she didn't move, staying rooted to the spot as the kelpie grunted, crushing the meat in its sharp teeth.

Cillian grunted, "Figures."

"What?"

As the larger kelpie swallowed the dried jerky, it bobbed its head, huffing Orla rapidly. She felt its muzzle bump against her cloak, the fabric fluttering with the beastie's breath. With tentative fingers, Orla stroked the kelpie's nose, marveling at the odd texture.

"That's Basilisk. He's *typically* very rude and only allows me to ride him. But seems he likes you more tonight," Cillian smirked, patting the beast's cheek. "You can ride him."

"Who's the other one?" Orla asked nervously, keeping her eyes on the desert kelpie now very interested in sniffing her entire outfit, pawing the sand with those lethal talons, looking for more treats while completely disregarding Cillian.

"This is Banshee." Affection laced his words as he patted the neck of the smaller kelpie. "She's fiery and can be a bit temperamental." Cillian jerked his chin to Orla with a sly grin, "Reminds me of you, actually."

Orla flipped him off.

Cillian only chuckled, before leaping onto the beast's back in one fluid movement, Banshee shifting beneath him.

She evaluated Basilisk with a wary eye. "Is he going to buck me off?"

"No," Cillian rubbed his face with one hand, wrapping Banshee's reins in the other.

"Try and bite me?"

"Nope."

"Can I walk instead?"

Cillian raised a single brow, "Do you want to walk twenty miles into the desert?"

"Not particularly," Orla confessed, squinting her eyes.

Cillian gestured wordlessly to Basilisk, the silent, yet sarcastic, response of *'well, hop up then,'* causing Orla to grit her teeth, uttering a short curse and a little prayer as she jumped onto the kelpie's back.

Orla whooshed out a breath of thanks as the beast stayed solid and unyielding beneath her. With the talons, the kelpie seemed much more stable than the horse she'd ridden in Doortan, where with every hoof clop, she felt as if the beast's leg would slip right out from under her and make her tumble off its back.

With an approving grunt, Cillian steered Banshee towards the horizon, gave a short whistle, and they were off, Orla having all of one second to feel secure before Basilisk exploded into a run, keeping up with Cillian.

They flew over the sand, the kelpie's feet adept at grappling the soft desert terrain. Orla's heart slammed into her throat as she white knuckled the reins, the kelpie running so fast tears ripped free from her eyes.

Basilisk ate up the miles with ease, and it wasn't until Cillian slowed Banshee to a walk that Basilisk balked his speed, falling in line a few strides behind.

"It's right up here," Cillian said quietly.

"What is?" Orla asked, as the reminder that there was actually a reason Cillian invited her out tonight caught up with her from the Palace – twenty miles away.

"The meeting of the minds." Soren's voice floated over to them from the other side of a small sand dune, a laughing tone lighting up the words.

Cillian led Orla and the kelpies over the dune's crest. Soren held a flickering flame in the palm of her hand, winking at Orla as she approached. The small amount of illumination lit up the area - just enough for Orla's eyes to adjust. Dimas stood next to Soren with his hands on his hips, and a pair of fae that Orla recognized as the soul tied advisors from the council meeting nodded in greeting.

"Soren," Cillian inclined his head to the group, pulling Banshee gently to a stop. "Dimas, Ghilori, Ose. Thanks for coming." Soren curtsied sardonically, keeping her little spurt of fire close to her chest.

Cillian dismounted Banshee, the kelpie immediately coming up to Basilisk and nudging his flank. Basilisk shuffled under Orla, an unspoken request for her to get off. She swung a leg over, awkwardly sliding from the beast's back before the pair prowled away, swallowed up by the night.

"Where are they going?" Orla whispered as Cillian led her over to the group.

"To hunt," Cillian replied simply, slashing her a boyish smile.

Orla crinkled her nose, causing Cillian to snort out a laugh and Soren to flick her attention rapidly between the two of them before pursing her lips suggestively. Orla waved her away, feeling a blush tinge her cheeks.

"I know it's been difficult to meet with my father's renewed interest in ruling, but I appreciate you all." Looking around, Cillian addressed the male Orla learned was named Ghilori, "Any issues getting here?"

Ghilori shook his head, "Ose waned me."

"Dimas?" Cillian asked.

Dimas gestured to Soren who was twisting tendrils of fire through her fingers with a manic grin on her face. "Soren waned me."

Cillian looked from Orla to Soren, "Can you teach Orla to wane? She has enough of an *acat* to do so, and it would help tremendously if more of us could."

Soren shrugged, nodding to Ose, Ghilori's mate, who ducked her head bashfully when Soren purred, "Of course. Us females always have to make up for the utterly *lacking* abilities of the males in this group."

"I have great abilities," Dimas retorted, rearing his head back to stare at Soren incredulously.

"Of course you do." Soren crooned placatingly, rolling her eyes.

Cillian threw Soren a scathing look before sweeping his palm out, a shimmering red dome converging around them.

"So sorry," Orla interrupted, pinning Cillian with a look, "What *exactly* is this?"

Soren perked up, a wicked grin plastered on her face. "This is the beginning of the end for King Eamon's reign."

# Chapter Forty-Seven
## ESMERAY

My eyes were so fucking dry it was driving me crazy. Based on the moon, it was after midnight, and the burn from the grey stone on my finger jolted me out of sleep. Not that I was sleeping very deeply, anyway.

Lenna tracked the Book of Faune to an underground grotto somewhere close to Florra. Sparrow and Laurent waned back to their home an hour later, preparing to search for the Vessel Book in the intricate cave systems that wound west towards the Zircon mountains, and in the caverns behind the waterfalls closer to the city.

I hoped they found the Book of Faune quickly, but with the amount of tunnels leading to Florra, we all quietly realized that if the book *wanted* to be found, it would have been already.

The prophecy was still up for assessment, but we were all too fucking tired to do much more than repeat the lines back to each other, the silence between words punctuated with Lenna's soft snores. She'd been awake long enough the reveal the location, and then – per Collette's advisement – took another vial of tonic and passed out. We all retired to our own rooms pretty soon after.

"Keerian," I whispered, stroking my fingers through my mate's hair, the tight ringlet curls fanned around his face against his pillow.

A grunt let me know he was just as worn out as I was.

"Merrick's here."

"Get out, Merrick," Keerian slurred, his lips barely moving as his closed eyes scrunched up in sleepy annoyance.

I fought the eye roll as I shook him again. *"Merrick is here."*

My words registered as Keerian's eyes flew open, and he sat up with a start. "Where?"

"Staircase by the dragon lair. I told him to stay there."

One of the perks of being a rebellious youth was that my knack for uncovering trouble led me to find a permanent portal in the Opal Place that connected to the dragon lair beneath the Obsidian Palace. My parents tried to hide it from me for years, instantly regretting its existence when I came home for dinner on more than one occasion smelling like dragons.

In my defense, the dragons liked me, and they had cool shit in their caves from thousands of years of hording treasures.

"Let's go," Keerian grunted, tossing off the sheets and stretching out his wings. I got a good glimpse of his bare ass before he chucked a pillow at my head. "Get your head out of the dirty thoughts, Queen."

I rolled out of bed, quickly donning a pair of black leggings, a deep burgundy sweater, and boots.

As soon as Keerian finished strapping an assortment of weapons to him, I held out my hand, the two of us waning into the throne room of the Obsidian Palace and slipping through the glass floor, diving deep into the caverns below.

The dragon lair lay opposite the dungeons, and I felt a small sense of relief as we soared left, away from the Soul Keeper's Cell.

At this time of night, the few dragons here were either out hunting or fast asleep in their dens. We only caught a glimpse of silvery scales once before flying around the bend, aiming for the small ledge that connected to the staircase trailing up to the portal leading to the Opal Palace's Great Hall.

Merrick sat on the edge, his legs swinging over the side. Even as we closed the distance, I smelled it – blood.

The narrow ledge was too small for us to all stand, so Keerian and I hovered in place, his golden wings reflecting the firelight from the lantern Merrick sat next to him.

"Why are you covered in blood?" Keerian asked as we approached, his senses to the scent just as honed as mine.

Merrick said nothing, holding up a scrap of parchment with five names on it. The top name on the list crossed out with blood.

"That's dramatic," I muttered. "Did you not have a pen on you?" I ignored his curse and flapped closer to read the name. *Ardrick.*

I filled Keerian in on Merrick's mission after we left Lenna and Hale's room, and I think my mate may have been a tad jealous.

Keerian's exact words had been, "Damn, Merrick gets to have all the fun." That statement had been uttered in a gloomy tone.

I was surrounded by theatrical males.

I already missed Sparrow.

"How'd it go?" Keerian asked.

Merrick sighed, "The spy had some sort of magical object that let him funnel information to someone - but I don't know who." He held out his hand, revealing a small golden bauble shaped like a teardrop. "They know the dome is down, and they already suspect you had something to do with it, Meer."

I thinned my lips.

Merrick held the gold bauble out to me, but I shook my head. "Hold onto it. You can throw it in your dresser with your mind speak ring that you never wear."

"Who's being dramatic now?" Merrick growled, flicking his middle finger up to show me the ring he now wore, the gems shimmering in the torchlight.

"Still you," I smirked, shooting him a dazzling smile that had Keerian chuckling and Merrick huffing in thinly-veiled irritation.

"Anyway, four are left?" Keerian asked.

Merrick nodded tightly. "The second name on the list is a half-gargoyle, half-human named Jargo. I'm going to pay him a visit and see if I can keep him alive long enough to get some confirmed answers."

"I'm going with you," Keerian announced, cracking his knuckles.

"Me too," I said.

Keerian shot me a look. "You need to get some sleep. Don't tell me you've gotten more than an hour here and there over the last few days."

I sighed, exhaustion *was* making my wings heavy. "Fine. But I want it documented that I'm going to bed because *I* want to – *not* because you told me to."

"Duly noted, my Queen." Keerian bowed his head in a move that seemed pious, though the smug look on his face said otherwise.

Merrick rolled his shoulders, a dribble of blood seeping from his wing catching my eye.

"You're hurt," I admonished, flapping closer to touch down next to Merrick and peer at the cut along the outside of his wing near his talon.

"It's fine. Ardrick got one good hit on me before I killed him."

Keerian stayed hovering past the ledge. "Well then you definitely need my help. Poor Merrick," Keerian gave me a wide-eyed look, speaking in a loud whisper, "One little spy and he's all beat up."

"Play nice, or else *I* will hunt down all the spies by myself," I crooned, slashing my mate a saccharine smile.

"Where's Sparrow and Laurent?" Merrick asked, causing the two of us to grimace.

We debated what to tell Merrick about their mission to search for the Book of Faune, ultimately deciding we wouldn't bring it up – but would tell him if he asked. *Dammit.*

I waved my hand, a golden sheen slithering against the entrance of the staircase and enveloping the three of us in a sound ward. "They just left a few hours ago – Lenna narrowed down the location of the Book of Faune. According to Hale's research, we need both books to translate whatever god story Phades aimed us to."

"Where."

"Florra," Keerian said quietly, "The Book of Faune is somewhere in the cave systems running either behind the waterfalls, or up between Florra and the Zircon mountains."

"There's twelve fucking waterfalls and hundreds of miles of caves between Florra and the base of the Zircon mountains," Merrick said, scrambling stiffly to his feet. "Did Lenna tell you *anything* more specific?"

*Twelve voices babble over each other, all louder than the next. But it is the silent one that speaks the loudest, says the most by saying nothing at all.*

"Carra's tits," I hissed, the prophecy spoken mere hours ago clicking through my tired brain. "The prophecy *was* about the Book of Faune. There are twelve *active* waterfalls, '*twelve voices babbling*,' – and one that dried up a thousand years ago. It's nothing but a rocky precipice now."

"*The silent one speaks the loudest*," Keerian recanted, his moss green eyes sparking with recognition. "The book could be in the caverns behind the dried-up waterfall."

"Sometimes, you geniuses terrify me," I said, addressing both males, my smile widening, the tips of my fangs resting against my bottom lip.

Keerian laughed deeply, landing next to me, the three of us shuffling to squeeze onto the tiny ledge. He bent his head, kissing my forehead, my horns, the tip of my nose, before settling his lips against mine. "Fly on up to bed, tell Sparrow and Laurent on the way."

I nodded.

"Then, go to sleep, I'll be back by tomorrow afternoon. This little trip gives me a chance to see the Opal Palace's standing force, and I want to check their progress after the attack on Calcity, since they were too *untrained* to help."

With a snort, I kissed him back. After my last correspondence to the advisors in the Opal Kingdom, condemning them for not sending the necessary warriors to reinforce our unit against the Unmarked, their reply was that their housed army was mostly recruits, and they couldn't, in good faith, dispatch untrained soldiers as back up.

If Keerian, the famed Golden Gargoyle, assessed the ranks, no one would again dare to tell us '*no.*'

I almost felt bad for the new recruits – and the fully trained soldiers – as I knew Keerian was about to lay down a ruthless, Obsidian Palace worthy, training regiment.

"Have fun rooting out spies and bullying the Opal Palace's army," I said with a flutter of my fingers as I hopped off the ledge, my wings sweeping out with my ascent back up through the caverns to the glass floor. "I'm going back to bed. Send me a message through the rings if things get too interesting."

Merrick waved, Keerian blew me a kiss, and I was off, soaring up through the dragon's lair, the allure of my soft bed calling my name as I shot a message to Sparrow's ring to have her and Laurent check the caves burrowed behind the dry waterfall.

Her sleepy voice filled my head as I landed against the now-solid glass of the throne room, telling me to go to sleep and to stop bothering her so late.

I laughed tiredly and waned, landing against my mattress. I was asleep in mere seconds, boots on and all.

# CHAPTER FORTY-EIGHT
# ORLA

THE SAND STILL HELD an echo of the sun's warmth, while the temperature in the desert continued rapidly dropping. Orla focused on the dancing flames spitting from the small bonfire she'd created, feeding it another morsel of her magic.

Sitting in a tight circle, she felt Cillian's knee brush her own, her heartrate skittering with the contact. She glanced at his chiseled profile from the corner of her eye, the strong angles of his square jaw, the stubble of beard shadowing his chin, full lips holding a reddish hue from their kiss, heating her better than any fire could.

"We need to prepare for the Culling list," Soren said from her right. Dimas, Ghilori, and Ose were seated on the other side of the circle with matching somber expressions.

"Has King Eamon given you any insight into what magics may be banned?" Ose asked, her voice low.

Soren shook her head. "He's having meetings about it, but I haven't been summoned for them."

"Do you think he suspects you?" Cillian's harsh tone was punctuated by a quiet growl from Dimas.

But Soren only shrugged a shoulder. "He isn't allowing any servants in those meetings. The only advisor I can confirm with him is Lord Batair."

Dimas leaned forward, his voice hard. "You feel even a *whiff* that something isn't right, and you get the fuck out of there, Soren. You wane to the safe house. Don't be a martyr."

Orla was shocked to learn Soren's position as cupbearer for the King was for her to spy. The female was in danger every day to further Cillian's revolution, to provide information to those determined to place Cillian on the throne.

And she'd been doing it for years.

Quietly. *Successfully.*

It sent a tempest of guilt through Orla that she'd been so closed-minded and quick to dismiss Cillian's plea for help. Orla wished *she* could mimic Soren, wished she had that same steel in her spine.

"If you get confirmation on any gifts...Ose and I have a list of beings in Aridden who manifested unique *acatis* since last year. If you get any foresight-"

"-we can begin sneaking beings with cullable magics to one of our secured locations." Ose finished Ghilori's sentence, her mate nodding as they swapped grim looks.

Ghilori and Ose were in charge of smuggling those with banned *acatis* from the Palace, under the cover of Ghilori's work with the King as an advisor on dust and sand storms. He left the Palace for weeks at a time to track weather patterns, and Ose could wane multiple beings with her over far distances by what Orla gathered. The pair of them were able to save almost all the beings with illegal gifts last year, though two fae that refused to go were beheaded by King Eamon when they were found to have gifts noted on the Culling list.

Orla swallowed, her throat scratchy and aching in the desert's dry wind. Gods. These beings risked their lives daily to make the Ruby Kingdom safe for everyone. And what was Orla doing?

*Nothing.*

"Soren, keep an ear out, but don't do anything self-sacrificing to get information. With the Topaz Kingdom coming, we need to lay low and wait for their visit to blow over before we take further action." Cillian turned to Dimas. "Have you heard which royals are arriving?"

"Rumors are swirling, but nothing is set. King Wei-Li is the most likely, with Queen Yan and Princess Yin staying behind for the Topaz Kingdom's Culling, but until I know more, we need to be prepared for the...worst case scenario." Dimas slid his eyes to Cillian. A muscle jumped in Cillian's jaw before he grunted his agreement.

A rumble started in the depths of Orla's mind as the group lapsed into silence, each lost to their own mulled thoughts. Ose sighed tiredly, leaning her head on her mate's shoulder. Ghilori gently swept a strand of her silky, dark hair out of her face, tucking it behind her pointed ear lovingly.

Cillian's face tilted up to the sky, brows furrowing, his gaze bouncing between the clouds. Watching him from under her lashes, she knew Cillian was shouldering an enormous amount of stress. But he'd willingly taken the responsibility for a chance to better his Kingdom. Daring to launch a coup against King Eamon...he could be labeled a traitor, killed on the spot, if anyone caught a whisper of treason.

"Was there a reason you wanted us to meet out here instead of at the normal spot?" Ghilori asked Cillian. "Did someone catch on?"

A wave of nausea pitched through Orla's stomach, causing her to sway and plant both palms firmly against the warm sand, anchoring against the dizzy sensation sweeping through her. She swallowed thickly, screwing her eyes shut as she breathed deep, willing her mind to calm.

Her magic bubbled up inside her, pressing hard against her soul, an urgent *tug* deep inside her sense of self. Orla felt for that twining thread of her *acat,* running her mind's finger down the red strands, trying to get her power to settle.

"Are you alright?"

Orla sucked in another inhale through her teeth, feeling her stomach flip and squirm. She nodded in answer to Soren's whispered question as her fire zipped through her, chasing away the queasiness.

A slow drumbeat started in her temples, low and rhythmic. Not quite a headache - more like...pressure. She blinked her gaze open, coming face to face with Soren crowding her air and staring at her with a concerned frown.

"I'm fine, really." Orla waved Soren away, needing room to righten herself. As the words left her mouth, a thundering rumble rattled her head, louder this time, causing her to wince and spit out a curse.

"What's wrong?" Soren scooted closer, tone clipped, her bronze-hued stare darting across Orla's face. "Do you want me to wane you back to the palace? We can get you a healer?"

"No," Orla and Dimas said at the same time.

Orla reared her head back, shooting Dimas a confused look, though Dimas, looking guilty, only cut his eyes towards Cillian.

But it was Soren who snapped, rounding on the Prince, *"What the fuck,* Cillian?"

Cillian averted his gaze as he stood slowly, addressing Ose and Ghilori, "Go back to the Palace. Further instruction will be sent in the next few days." Dimas slowly unsheathed his dagger from his waist, nodding curtly at Ghilori.

Ose thinned her lips, her expression one of suspicion, but did as her Prince bid, wrapping her slim hand around her mate's forearm, the two of them waning in a flash of blue.

The moment the light faded; a shrieking scream shot through the quiet night. Soren scrambled to her feet, pulling Orla up with her, her finger pointed threateningly at Cillian. "Whatever you think you're doing, stop it. We're going back to the Palace, *right now."*

"What're you talking about?" Orla slurred, her teeth chattering together as that booming drumbeat got louder, louder, in her ears. A haze of smoke poured off her *acat,* filling her lungs, her magic heaving in response, growing and twisting through her bones.

Even Dimas looked paler than normal as he stepped closer to the Prince. "Your theory was right, but now's not the time to push it further. The kelpies are heading this way, we need to leave."

Her magic flared dangerously, acting on its own accord. Orla shoved her *acat* down hard, trying to keep her attention on the argument going on around her, wondering why Dimas had a weapon out, attempting to shake the nauseous rumble from her brain.

Cillian gritted his teeth and let out a shrill whistle, the kelpie's hoarse scream in response getting closer. "Go, with Soren, Dimas," he snarled. "I'll take Orla back."

The red thread of her *acat* began thrashing wildly, though she fought to smother it, to contain it. Her mind spun between her attempts to calm her power with the drum beat pounding in her head. She felt as if she'd burst into flame if she lost her focus now, panic whining through her as her magic fought back, begging to flow freely.

She yanked against the thread, and the bonfire sputtered into ash, though the coursing power inside her refused to bank. If anything, it built higher, heavier, weighing down her limbs until she shook.

Dimas shook his head fiercely. "We leave together. Soren, can you wane the four of us to the Palace?"

Cillian sighed harshly, throwing Dimas a look of utter frustration. "*Kindered.*"

Orla scrubbed the heels of her hands into her temples, her vision swimming as a rough voice seemed speak right to her soul. *What was happening to her?*

She was too hot, shaky and lightheaded, her *acat* broke her hold – flooding her blood from her feet to the tips of her fingers with power in a rushing *woosh* that left her panting, her vision edging and blurred as she fought to get air down. She opened her mouth to call for Soren, but the words died on her lips, her lungs soot stained.

Soren drew herself up taller, her wide-eyed stare meeting the Prince's resigned, blank, expression. Orla caught him ever-so-slightly shake his head, flicking his eyes to Dimas's back. Soren blinked, the fear in her face replaced with determination as she took a quiet step closer to the red-haired fae.

Soren balled her fists, flipping her hair back, the blond tresses almost glowing in the darkness. Cillian, beside her, took a step backwards, closer to Orla, and she saw his mouth move, though she couldn't make out what he said as a thunderclap in her mind had her *acat* flaring brighter, wilder, immobilizing her.

"*Kindered!*"

The voice bellowed through Orla, causing her to reel backwards with a sharp cry. She stumbled when her *acat* slammed into her again in response. Axis tilted, the sand rushed up as she dropped to her knees hard, her breathing coming in rapid gasps, her body breaking out in icy sweat.

The air around her hollowed out - or maybe it was the mounting pressure in her ears as her magic bashed into every corner of her mind, filling it with dancing flames.

*Thump, thump, thump.*

The drumbeat was louder now, but still slower, more languid, than the sheer racing of her own pattering heart, spurred on by the careening magic zipping through her.

Orla blinked furiously, off balanced in the sand, struggling to stand up. Broad hands gripped her, but she relaxed into them, knowing, distantly, it was Cillian.

She tried focusing on him, but there was too much power flooding through her, her vision doubling and wavering. Orla watched his lips move in a daze - but couldn't make out the words as that deep, heavy thudding jarred through her bones, vibrating her to her very core.

It was a steady tempo, though every few beats it got louder.

She crinkled her nose, dark spots popping and fading away, leaving her eyes dilated and blurred. It was too much; she was going to *overheat* -

But as if she'd been on fire and dunked in the ocean, the flames of her *acat* extinguished in a mighty gust.

Orla gasped down a lungful of cool desert air, her eyes flying open as her magic paused wreaking havoc on her soul, instead slowly seeping through her in a simmering familiarity, filling her, humming with glee, throwing her into sharp, terrifying clarity.

She knew exactly what made that drumming sound.

Knew it because it haunted her nightmares.

*Wings.*

Soren screamed as a massive dragon dropped from the sky with a roar.

Covered from snout to tail tip in shining red scales, with twin horns jutting from its head, the dragon banked, sail-like wings with talons at the tips flaring out as it landed heavily before them, sand spraying in all directions from the force.

The dragon lifted its maw to the night and bellowed, a jet of black-edged fire ripping through the clouds. Orla's breath hitched.

*"Now, Soren!"* Dimas shouted as he whirled towards Cillian, attempting to grab his arm. But Cillian jerked out of the way as Soren pounced on Dimas, the flash of white light waning the two of them back to the safety of the castle.

The massive beast lashed out a forked tail, sweeping up a torrent of sand as time itself froze. The dragon snaked its head, its lips peeling back to reveal a row of fangs. Finally, its gaze settled on Orla. She stiffened, her feet rooted to the ground.

Every thought eddied out of her mind.

*"Kindered."* The voice in her head rumbled again, softer this time, ending almost in a question, a silent request.

The dragon dipped lower, pinning a single, slitted eye on Orla as every molecule inside of her pushed at her to approach – not to bolt. As if in a trance, Orla took a single step forward right as the kelpies rounded the dune, skidding to a halt as they beheld the predator before them. Banshee screeched, frothing from her mouth as she stood in front of Basilisk.

The trance broke as the dragon whipped towards the two kelpies, a hungry hiss accompanying smoke pouring from the beast's nostrils.

*"NO!"* Orla screamed, drawing the dragon's eyes back to her. The beast almost looked...apologetic, as it let out a disappointing grumble, settling back onto thickly muscled haunches.

She had a distant awareness of Cillian throwing a wave of red magic over the kelpies – a protection barrier between them and the beast before her.

"Orla," Cillian said quietly from a few yards behind her, "That's the only one. The only dragon here. You have a choice to make. Your soul knows what to do, it's in your *blood*."

Everything in Orla's soul, in her entire sense of *self* shifted so abruptly she let out a rattling breath. Without looking at Cillian, she whispered, "I am not so easily broken."

And Orla stepped into the role of her ancestors before her, unafraid. "Kindered," she replied, her voice aching, the word slipping past the lump of emotion in her throat.

A victorious scream broke from the dragon, and to Orla, the sound was that of triumph, of defiance, the type of cry she felt ricochet through her bones, the sound she wished she could recreate as she looked back on her life of shattered promises, a past filled with rage and frustration.

The dragon huffed out more steam, as Orla felt her footsteps quicken, as if everything was *here*. The answers to her past, the questions of her future, the clarity she so desperately craved.

Every step closer to the beast brought upon a renewed sense of balance, of righting a wrong she'd been too young to understand as a child.

But for once, she knew *exactly* who she was.

She was Orla Grey, the last of the *Vitraro*.

Orla drank in the shimmer of every single scale. This close, she could see the way the beast's horns faded from black to bone-white, could see the thin membranes stretched between each spike trailing down the dragon's neck, and how they shimmered, ruby-hued, in the soft darkness. This close up, the beast towered over her, easily ten, fifteen, feet tall.

The dragon cocked its head, tail lashing in a way that seemed feline and curious.

The voice in her mind, gruff and deep, was the voice of the dragon itself.

Orla reached inside her own *self*, finding the red thread of her *acat*. And there, tightly wound between it, so slight she'd missed it when first searching her *acat,* was a softly glowing golden thread, nestled between the coiling red. Orla touched it and whispered back.

*"Kindered."*

And Orla was not afraid.

# CHAPTER FORTY-NINE
# KEERIAN

JARGO WAS AN EASY target and completely blindsided by Keerian and Merrick. They found the spy passed out in a private room, a flagon of ale tipping precariously from his grubby hand as he sprawled out on his mattress in the barracks.

It seemed not only Esmeray held the power to grant certain soldiers their own lodgings.

Keerian pursed his lips as he motioned Merrick forward, the gargoyles careful to not startle the spy on the bed, though it probably didn't matter if they'd knocked over a lamp, barged in half delirious with drink, tripping over their own wings and singing jaunty shanties - judging from the stench of sour hops wafting from Jargo, he wouldn't wake up anytime soon.

"Wish we had a fancy fae with us to ward this room from sound," Merrick groused as he slipped through the door, disgust coloring his features as he took in the second name on his list. Two daggers appeared in Merrick's hands, and it took one well aimed flick of his wrist for both blades to embed themselves in Jargo's wing.

The spy lurched up as pain splintered through him, but Keerian didn't allow the male a moment to scream before he clapped a hand over his mouth, gripping one of the spy's thick brown horns in the other to hold him steady.

"None of that," Keerian simpered darkly, pulling Jargo's head up as Merrick stalked towards the bed, drawing the spy's attention to him. "We just want to have a quick chat."

Jargo's gaze darted between Merrick and Keerian, his pupils blowing wide as he took in the infamous Golden Gargoyle before him. Kerrian smiled, showing off his sharp teeth, the canines now fully capped in gold – a side effect of Esmeray and him getting hammered one night in Baubble. That female could talk him into anything.

But it definitely was a nice touch as Jargo gave a muffled scream, spit splattering against Keerian's palm. The scent in the air spiked with alcohol and sweat, and to Keerian's dismay – the fucker pissed himself.

"I will remove one dagger for every question you answer correctly – got it?" Merrick snarled, shoving a finger into Jargo's face.

"And don't think you can lie," Keerian added blithely, "We already know everything about you."

Jargo whimpered, his throat bobbing as he tried and failed to nod with Keerian's firm grip holding him in place.

"Question number one," Merrick threatened, pulling another dagger from his belt. "Are you relaying information to King Eamon?"

Jargo shook his head as quickly as he could against Keerian's grip.

"Wrong answer," Merrick said smoothly, as the dagger flew from his fist, burying into the curvature of Jargo's wing. The spy's eyes rolled back as he wailed, though the sound deadened as Keerian held on.

With a groan, the spy flapped his hands, trying to speak.

"I will move my hand, but if you scream, we'll kill you," Keerian warned, tugging the spy's horn roughly.

The spy nodded rapidly as Keerian relaxed his grip.

"That's a good chap," Keerian crooned, lightly smacking Jargo's cheek twice as he removed his hand and stepped back. Jargo panted, his brown eyes shadowed with agony, his wings twitching and spasming. Merrick must've nicked a ligament because the spy's left wing was completely flaccid, drooping beneath him on the bed. "Now, we asked if you report to King Eamon and you said no. Did you want to try again?"

"I don't," Jargo said through his teeth.

Keerian and Merrick waited.

Jargo straightened as much as he could with the blades in his wings. "I'm here to *find* King Eamon's spies."

Merrick outright laughed, "Why should we believe you?"

"I'm here under the direction of Prince Cillian, Crown Prince of the Ruby Kingdom."

"Is that not the same thing?" Merrick scoffed, pulling a fourth dagger out of his boot. Keerian wondered how many damned daggers Merrick even had on him. "Father and son?"

Jargo narrowed his eyes. "The Ruby Kingdom is not as united as it appears. King Eamon's days on the throne are limited in favor of Prince Cillian."

"A coup?" Keerian asked, his eyes darting over to Merrick.

Jargo inclined his chin an inch, speaking through panting breaths. "A *revolution.* I was dispatched here for the same thing you two seem to be hunting. To find the spies King Eamon smuggled over here and..." he thinned his lips, nodding to Keerian, the ending clear.

"Again, why should we believe you?" Keerian asked, crossing his arms.

Jargo bristled, a grimace twisting his features. "I'm half-gargoyle, half-human, and spend a considerable amount of time finding myself discriminated against for my blood." With a hollow grunt, the spy continued, "Prince Cillian is different, ruthless, but fair to *all* of his citizens -

regardless of blood. To have him on the throne would be a blessing. The Prince wants to do away with the Culling, wants to sever all ties from the Topaz Kingdom in favor of a stronger alliance with Irridessen and Larimar. I wanted to help, so I offered myself to the Prince a few months ago after my partner was killed."

Keerian felt his heart thud heavily and shot down the mind-speak ring to Merrick. *"I want to believe him."*

Merrick huffed but stepped forward. *"You've gotten soft under that crown, Goldie."* Jargo shrank back. With a second, more irritated growl, Merrick sheathed the dagger in his hand and gestured to Jargo's wings. "I'll take those out, and we'll get you to a healer on one condition. You speak to Queen Esmeray, tell her everything you know about the Ruby Kingdom's plans, and help us with this - " Merrick unrolled the piece of parchment with the five names and tossed it to the spy. "Do any of these names mean anything to you?"

Jargo tentatively reached for the scroll, holding it open with trembling fingers, his eyes darting across the page. "You killed Ardrick?" he asked, deadpanned.

Merrick nodded as he rounded the bed.

"Good. He was a dick."

Keerian chuckled darkly as he read Merrick's body language. Without alerting Jargo, they both lurched forward and gripped the hilts of the daggers in Jargo's wings, pulling them out simultaneously.

Jargo yelped, clapping a hand over his own mouth to muffle the noise.

"It's better if you don't see it coming," Keerian said apologetically, wiping the dagger against his pants before handing it back to Merrick. "Trust me." Dribbles of blood seeped from the three incisions.

With a hiss that smelled of ale, Jargo shuddered as he reread the list. "Smoth and Hamm are nasty – way worse than Ardrick. But Rinci..."

He tapped his thumb against the parchment. "...is the worst. Brutal, merciless. She'd kill a being just for looking at her too long. Rinci's half-fae - elemental magic, she can wield sand - and half-gargoyle, like your Queen. "

"Great," Merrick grumbled, exasperation cutting his words, "Another bloodthirsty female. Is it a genetics thing? Are all half-fae, half-gargoyle females just - "

Keerian coughed pointedly, sweeping a hard scowl towards one of his oldest friends as a bubble of protectiveness welled through him. "Careful how you speak about my mate, Merrick."

Merrick rolled his eyes but wisely shut his mouth. Addressing Jargo, Merrick asked, "Are they still in the Opal Palace?"

Jargo shook his head, "I was trying to head Ardrick off before he relayed information of the fallen dome back to King Eamon, but I ah..." He looked guiltily from Merrick down to his lap. "It was a special dinner service, and I didn't think he'd miss it, and then I had a drink or two and...yeah."

Merrick gave the spy a droll look. "Do you know where they could be? Our intel told us they were in the Opal Palace."

"They *were* all here - until a couple days ago. They were invited to stay to renegotiate trade deals with Lady Belinde, but after Calcity, they began getting suspicious of me. Left a note for the servants to find thanking Belinde for her hospitality and saying they were headed back home with their King's terms."

*"That's one of the council members Esmeray has suspicions on."* Keerian relayed down the ring to Merrick. *"She's been a thorn in Esmeray's side since her coronation. We believe she supported Adara silently."*

*"Lovely,"* Merrick replied flatly.

"So, you stayed to keep an eye on Ardrick. Did your Prince have you act as double agent? Our intel told us you support King Eamon."

"Of course," Jargo paled as he tried to move his collapsed wing and nothing happened. "Prince Cillian has my loyalties, and I knew the risks. But Rinci, Hamm and Smoth...they are looking for something. The King thought it was in the palace, but they never trusted me – not enough to let me in on their mission. They thought I was only here to learn Irridessen's army movements."

Merrick started, as if remembering something.

Keerian, sensing the spike of anxiety rushing off his friend, clapped Jargo on the shoulder, the spy wincing. "Apologies for the rude wake up, but you're coming with us. My Queen will have some questions for you. But the good news is...we have a pretty badass healer in the Obsidian Palace that has an affinity for fixing gargoyle wings."

# CHAPTER FIFTY
# SPARROW

*The blonde faeling stood with her back to Sparrow.*

*Her long hair blew softly in a phantom breeze that seemed to roll and dance around her small body, delicate purple flowers circling her head like a crown. The faeling didn't turn as Sparrow moved closer.*

*Sparrow felt a lump form in her throat. The air hollowed out, pressure building in Sparrow's head, her ears, her chest tightening with guilt, loss, love, and sadness. The heaviness became unbearable, and Sparrow staggered back as a sharp jolt pierced through her heart. The soft grass laying between her and the faeling seemed to shorten, the distance between them shrinking.*

*Sparrow fell to her knees as Briar turned to face her. "It was supposed to be me," Briar said sadly, her voice still filled with childlike song - a song brutally cut short by a bramble of Martyrshade. The faeling touched Sparrow's shoulder, her hand cold. "It would have been my burden to bear."*

*Tears flooded her eyes as Sparrow stared at her twin, dressed in the soft black, velvet gown she'd been buried in under a beautiful flower patch in Baryte Hills over a hundred years ago.*

Briar reached out and wiped away the single tear that escaped and tracked down Sparrow's cheek. "Don't cry," Briar whispered, "I'm sorry."

The air swirling around Briar suddenly stopped, and Sparrow was yanked back into her own body, a realm away in a cozy townhouse in Florra.

# CHAPTER FIFTY-ONE
# ORLA

ORLA'S HEART HAMMERED. *"You waited for me?"* She asked the mighty red dragon, as the beast crouched, settling down against the desert sand.

*"Is that the question you want to ask me?"* The dragon cocked his head. *"But yes. Your birth was celebrated throughout Dragon's Peak. I knew, from the moment I laid a single eye on you, that I'd be yours."*

The dragon gently pushed a memory in her mind, and Orla saw the rough ledge of Dragon's Peak, where at least ten dragons and wyverns howled their approval and excitement to the sky as an old man, his skin wrinkled and spotted with age, white beard blowing gently in the breeze, held a tiny infant out for the beasts to see. Orla saw her pudgy baby hands clapping with glee as the beasts took to the air in a flurry of colorful scales, circling around her, scenting her. Until the only red dragon dove closer, roaring out his excitement.

*"I am Seysei,"* the dragon chuffed, pleased, as the memory faded from her mind, *"And you are Orla of the* Vitraro."

Banshee screeched a warning. Orla's ears perked up, her enhanced fae hearing honing in on the clink of metal armor, the low voices of warriors drifting over to them from the other side of a tall dune.

Seysei's head curled around Orla protectively, sensing the same thing she had, before nudging her gently with his snout towards Cillian and the kelpies.

"*The King does not take kindly to our kind. His patrol is coming.*" Seysei growled as he pushed off the sand. "*Go with the Prince, I will come for you when it is safe.*"

Orla grappled with the golden thread in her mind, wanting to know more, wanting Seysei to give her another memory desperately, but the dragon was already turning, his massive wings spreading, as he launched into the sky. Cillian and the kelpies were beside her in an instant, and Orla numbly climbed onto Basilisk's back. Without prompting, Basilisk lurched under her, the kelpie racing over the sand.

They thundered back towards the Palace grounds, and once the lights off the oasis came into view, Orla felt a piece of her soul tug with longing, back to the beast in the desert. *Her kindered.*

Slowing to a walk, the kelpies heaved hot breath that curled through the cool desert air, Banshee striding to stay on pace with Basilisk. "Tell me literally anything about you," Orla demanded quietly as Cillian opened his mouth, "I need to process this entire night, and I'd prefer to do that with a bottle of wine in my bathtub and *not* right here."

With a frown, Cillian asked, "What would you like to know?"

Orla flailed her hands, her palms slick with sweat as a hundred emotions warred through her. Panic, excitement, fear, anxiety, thrill – overwhelming emotions that she'd sift through and inspect when she could, though now she promptly shoved them nice and neatly into a dark, empty part of her. "Something easy, fuck. How old are you?"

"How old am I?" Cillian grumbled, "I just turned thirty."

That helped soothe every screaming feeling in Orla as she gave him a surprised glance. "Wow, that isn't what I expected."

"What do you mean?"

"Well, I'm living in a land where beings can age to be a thousand years old. And you are *only thirty*." A panicked laugh escaped her lips, before it overtook her, hunching her shoulders as she howled, half laughing, half sobbing, as Cillian rolled his eyes, crossing his arms defensively over his broad chest, his hips rolling on instinct as he matched the kelpie's pace.

"Would you prefer me to be two hundred years *older* than you?"

Orla's hysterics took over fully, tears breaking from the corners of her eyes to trail down her cheek, bolstering her courage to dip into something that veered closer to dangerous-feelings territory. "Gods no. Okay I want to ask another question. Tell me about the different types of dragons."

"That isn't a question."

"Fine, will you *please* dazzle me with the knowledge you have on dragons?"

Cillian smiled sweetly, sarcasm dripping from his lips. "Of course. What would you like to know?"

Orla wracked her brain but realized she couldn't even come up with a question since she literally knew nothing about the species to even form a foundation of a thought.

As if he could read her minds, he snorted, though without further prompting, Cillian started, "There are two core species. Dragons are the largest – four legs, two wings set on their back, breathe fire. Wyverns have two hind legs, and their wings are forward facing with claws and talons at the end that act as both wings and forelegs. Wyverns are smaller than dragons, but much faster since they're less bulky."

Cillian faced forward, his gaze pinned on the Palace in the distance, though his soothing tone kept Orla from fracturing. "Drakes are a sub-species. Four legs, but they don't have wings, and can breathe fire. They typically don't grow as large as a dragon or wyvern, and they can be a little finicky about well...everything. There's also the legendary species - hydras. They would've looked like a dragon – just *much* larger and with multiple heads. Legends say that the goddess, Aella, rode a hydra during the God War - a great beast with five heads that breathed golden fire. And when the war was won, she brought her beast to Aurramere with her. But scholars argue if the species truly existed, or if it's just lore from god stories."

Orla committed the information to memory. "Can Wyverns breathe fire?"

Shaking his head, Cillian said, "No. But they make up for it with their agility and the fact they typically travel in packs, whereas dragons and drakes are more apt to hunt and live on their own – aside from when they gather at Dragon's Peak."

With a sideways glance, Cillian added, "I have a book on the different species. I'll give it to you. My father tried to burn it, but I was able to smuggle it out before it was destroyed."

Orla caught his fierce gaze, his determined expression that caressed and soothed her frantic thoughts. "Thank you," she replied softly, hoping Cillian knew the gratitude far extended from his offer to loan her a book.

Banshee and Basilisk slowed further, sensing their journey was almost up. One last thought wove around her mind, and Orla blurted out, "Why'd you kiss me?"

Cillian groaned, his head tilting back. "I thought you were asking me easy questions."

Orla scowled, even though another manic giggle threatened to spill out. She felt drunk, completely out of her mind, as she looked at Cillian. His black hood was pulled back, and their fast ride through the desert allowed more of his locs to escape their holding, falling around his shoulders. She wanted to kiss him again.

As they rounded the last sand dune, the royal stables came into view. And with it, two figures shadowed against the soft light of the gate. Cillian cleared his throat. "Dimas and Soren are waiting on us. Soren will take you back to your room. I need to talk to Dimas."

"You didn't answer my question," Orla said, trying to keep her tone light, though nerves and anxiety warred within her. *What if Cillian regretted kissing her?*

"How about this?" Cillian said in a low voice as they neared their friends. "I'll tell you next time I kiss you." Orla's blood spiked with desire as Cillian shot her a wink, the kelpies coming to a stop twenty feet from the stable entrance.

Orla and Cillian dismounted, Cillian approaching Dimas first. "Anyone see us?"

Dimas shook his head. "No. And the stables are clear if you want me to help you get the kelpies settled."

Cillian agreed, shooting Orla and Soren a single glance before disappearing into the warm stables. Basilisk and Banshee followed their master without needing to be led. Orla hoped the beasties got extra jerky for a treat tonight.

As the males faded from view, Soren turned to her. "Ready?"

"For what?" Orla asked.

Soren laughed lightly, offering Orla her hand. "I'll take you to your room."

As Orla took it, Soren spun, the two of them waning away in a flash of white light.

Orla steadied herself as her bedroom door burst into view. The red barricade, sensing her arrival, faded to nothing, winking out as she pulled her key out of her pocket. "Thank you," she said to Soren.

Soren stayed next to her, chewing on her lip. "Do you want to invite me in so we can gossip about males and talk about our feelings?"

Orla groaned inwardly at the offer. All she wanted was a hot bath and time to brood and figure out what the actual fuck happened from Cillian's kiss to the meeting of rebels, to her *kindered* dragon. Soren seemed to catch her flinch as she unearthed a second room key, taking two strides to the door next to Orla's, and unlocking it with a flourish. "Maybe next time, sound good?" A glimmer of hurt in Soren's voice registered too late as the fae slipped into her room, shutting the door softly behind her.

"Neighbors," Orla uttered aloud as she entered her own room. "She's my goddess-damned neighbor."

Ten minutes later, as she lay in the heat of the bathtub, soaking her freezing limbs, she wondered if Cillian had given her this room *because* Soren was next door. The thought that Cillian orchestrated it settled in her gut with a pang of regret. All this time, she'd wondered if Cillian needed a friend, and it seemed the Prince thought the same about her.

With a sigh, Orla stood, the bath not as enticing as her thoughts turned complex, Seysei's arrival rattling in her mind. And Soren seemed upset Orla turned her offer down. Orla grappled with her emotions, the mental image of the flash of hurt crossing Soren's face making Orla feel...guilty.

"*The blonde fae would be a good friend to have.*" The voice rumbled through her, startling Orla.

She said cautiously, "*Seysei?*"

"*Do you have many other dragons chattering around in your head?*"

Orla blinked. "*No...But I didn't know you could pop in my head and read my thoughts whenever you felt like it.*"

Seysei's grumble rolled down the connection, and Orla realized the sound was a laugh. She continued, "*Can you always read my mind?*"

"*If you keep hold of that thread in your* acat *I can,*" Seysei confirmed. "*But if you let go, the* kindered *connection is still there, but we cannot communicate.*"

"*Oh.*" Orla didn't know what else to say so she asked, "*Do you think I should go talk to Soren?*"

"*I do. I'm going to hunt since you wouldn't let me eat the kelpie. Loosen your connection until morning. Gossip is only interesting to me once I have a full belly.*"

Orla couldn't help the grin tugging against the corners of her mouth. "*Okay, Seysei.*"

Gently, she released the golden thread of her *acat*, before coaxing the red strands apart until the gold stood out on its own. As she climbed from the water, quickly drying her body, she untangled the thread of her heritage magic completely, until it glimmered separately from her lineage magic. That way, she could access Seysei quickly or connect solely with her fire wielding without the dragon in her head as well.

Orla hurried to get dressed, choosing a blue sleep set and a chunky robe, slipping her feet into matching slippers. She snatched a bottle of wine she'd taken from the servant's pantry, before padding next door, knocking quietly.

Soren opened the door a beat later, a bright smile cracking across her face as she beheld Orla. Suddenly awkward, Orla extended the bottle of wine. "I'd love to gossip with you."

Soren laughed, ushering Orla into the room. "I thought you'd never ask."

# Chapter Fifty-Two
## CILLIAN

Cillian kept his pace unhurried down the empty hall of the royal wing. Dimas, beside him, tugged at the cuffs of his white tunic, loosening the button on the stiff fabric before rolling the sleeve to his elbow.

They changed in the stables. Sulking around Oasees in a black cloak was one thing, but in this wing, Cillian played his part - of the Prince devoted to his King. The bright, gaudy clothes felt more and more like a noose around his neck as the days wore on, the embellished robe buttoned up to his throat more like a costume for a fake role than an actual outfit.

Felt more like a collar, leashing him to his royal status.

Clothing was a weapon. His mother taught him that. What one wore was as much a political statement as belting on a sword or donning a crown.

The thick hem of the robe snapped around the tops of his boots as Cillian and Dimas wove their way through the quiet royal wing. This time of night, the court was asleep in their rooms, none the wiser their Price had left the Palace grounds.

As they should be, with dawn only a few hours away. He felt Orla's presence coil against his barricade an hour ago, and it had been a relief to know she was back in her room, safely tucked in bed. The invisible wards he erected around her and Soren's rooms made it so he'd be alerted if anyone crossed their thresholds with ill intentions, and though it was a strain on his magic, the wards were erected every evening, keeping him sane and able to rest without having to sleep in the damn hall between their doors nightly.

He knew the hard conversations with Orla were coming, but the sparkle that lit up her gorgeous, dove grey eyes, the feel of her soft lips against his...Cillian would pay any price to keep her safe, keep her happy.

Even if it cost him his own damned soul.

Dimas finished rolling up his other sleeve as they came to the corner leading to Cillian's private hallway. "I'll see you in the morning," Cillian muttered, averting his eyes from his advisor. Dimas nodded once, turning on his heel to depart.

"There you are." A snide voice gave Dimas and Cillian pause as Lord Batair rounded the corner, his strolling gait at odds with the stupid look on his face. "King Eamon was asking for you."

Cillian straightened, shooting Dimas a warning glance. "I'll go see him now. Good night, Lord Dimas."

Batair tutted, holding up a hand, sweeping beady eyes from Cillian to Dimas. Cillian tensed. "The King requires *both* of you. I was just coming to fetch the Prince from his golden sheets."

Fighting to keep his body language smooth, unruffled, Cillian leveled a flat, snarky expression at the Lord of War. He'd always hated Batair, and now, with Orla in the Palace, Cillian pondered how best to kill the male without anyone noticing. His words cutting, Cillian crossed his arms. "Lord Dimas is currently working on assignment for the Topaz Kingdom's visit. I'll go to my father now. If his Majesty needs to relay information to my advisor, he can tell me."

Lord Batair shrugged, though the shit-eating grin on his face was almost gleeful. "Apologies *Prince,* but the King called us for an emergency meeting."

Cillian rolled his eyes, knowing that pushing any further for Dimas to skip this meeting would bring too many questions. "Lead the way, Batair." With a dismissive gesture, Cillian fell into step behind the gargoyle, exchanging a wary look with Dimas as they headed towards the King's private chamber.

Dimas hastily unrolled his sleeves and rebuttoned the cuffs.

"I found them, your Majesty," Lord Batair crowed as they entered King Eamon's private study. Cillian bowed as his father glared at him from behind wire rimmed spectacles. Dimas mirrored the formal greeting.

"Where were you?" King Eamon snapped, "I sent Lord Batair to fetch you a half hour ago."

"Apologies, your Majesty." Cillian regarded his father with a cool expression. "I couldn't sleep, and asked Lord Dimas to walk with me. The new guards chosen for overnight patrol started this evening, and though their skills came highly recommended, I wanted to evaluate them, personally, during their shift – to make sure there are no weak points in our defenses."

*Lie, lie, lie.*

The new rotation of guards was shit, chosen personally by Dimas to allow them to slip out of the Palace without interruption.

King Eamon shuffled parchment around his desk, already bored with Cillian's presence. It had always been this way, only made worse when his mother passed.

But boredom was better than suffocation - a punishment Cillian caught when he bucked too hard against the image King Eamon expected him to live and breathe. With the taste of revolution on his tongue, Cillian pressed his lips together, glancing around the room.

The last time he'd been here, months ago, everything had been tidy, neat. Books organized, parchments filed and stacked properly, quills nicely laid out against small wooden stands.

Now, it looked as if a windstorm had blown through – which, with his father's air wielding and temper, one probably had. Books were thrown off the shelves, loose pages scattered across the floor. The desk was covered in askew piles of parchment, glass shards from shattered inkpots, and rivulets of ink that had dried against the dark wood.

His father's personal guards, the twins, Droward and Droll, stood at attention behind the desk, identical jeers on their faces. Cillian merely swept his eyes over them, not acknowledging their presence in the slightest.

King Eamon gestured to the two chairs in front of his desk pointedly. "I've received news from Sir Ardrick in Irridessen, our speculations are confirmed." King Eamon settled back in his chair, carefully watching Cillian. Cillian waited, keeping his features smooth as his heart hammered in his chest. "The dome across the Slate Kingdom has fallen, and reports are that it was Queen Esmeray herself that dismantled it."

Cillian couldn't hide the surprise that raised his eyebrows. "Ardrick reported this?"

King Eamon grunted, ignoring Cillian's inquiry. "Queen Esmeray got her hands on one of *our* books. Which is, as you know, *unsuitable.*"

Cillian inhaled sharply. There was only one set of books his father obsessed over so completely that he'd personally exterminated an entire line of fae to retrieve one.

The Vessel Books.

One book for each of the four goddesses that walked earthside before the God War. The books that held wells of direct god power, only to be imbued into their Vessel of choosing.

The Book of Aella had been revered and protected for centuries by the *Vitraro,* and it took only one crumb of misplaced information on the book's whereabouts for the King to decide that the *Vitraro,* as a whole, were no longer welcomed in the Ruby Kingdom – especially after they refused to hand over the Book of Aella to him.

He killed them all - narrowly missing the singular being that smuggled out a faeling, getting her safe passage to the Slate Kingdom, and keeping her protected and invisible under a fae repelling dome that allowed her to pass as human with no activated *acat.*

Orla.

Who had, by the god's divine fuckening, ended up *right back* in the Ruby Kingdom twenty fucking years later.

"So, our musings were correct, my King?" Batair simpered, setting Cillian's teeth on edge as the gargoyle tightened his wings to his back. "Queen Esmeray is the Vessel of Death?"

"It appears so," King Eamon snarled darkly. "And now, one of the three books is completely drained of god magic."

Cillian stayed quiet, his mind buzzing. Irridessen had two books - if the Book of Aella's choppy translations were to be believed. Two books in Irridessen, two in Ingotheria.

Their searches for the fourth book, and the Book of Faune, kept coming up empty, which infuriated the King, causing him to set his sights on the Book of Phades when reports of a Queen with snow pure hair and a spell book became more than rumored whispers last year.

"What do you want to do, then, Father?" Cillian leaned back in his chair, trying to hold onto the mask he wielded in these delusional meetings with the King. His father had been too busy searching for the Vessel Books to lead his Kingdom last year, something Cillian was grateful for when he'd first begun his whispered crusade towards revolution.

The King sighed in disapproval. "Irridessen now holds a Vessel Queen with two kingdoms, *and* the Oracle. That, *son*, is an affront to Ingotheria's might. Luckily, Queen Esmeray voided the Treaty of Terramere by taking down the dome, which means we could easily retake the Slate Kingdom."

Cillian laughed hollowly, "Why would you debase yourself with a Kingdom full of humans?" His stomach twisted as his father steepled his hands against the desktop, hidden desire flashing through his features. Cillian knew if his father tried to take the Slate Kingdom by force, he'd have no choice but to challenge him for the throne immediately. A fight that could very easily end with Cillian's own soul transcending to Minmere. Shit, he needed more time.

"I don't want the Slate Kingdom," King Eamon said evenly. "And I'll be sending a diplomatic envoy to Irridessen with my demands. If the Vessel Queen is smart, she'll know any wars fought, even with god power, will ultimately end in too many Irridessen lives lost. But since I am a *benevolent* King, I'll gift her a choice. Either I march the full might of my army to the Slate Kingdom and exterminate the human leeches in full, or..." King Eamon leaned forward, his dark eyes pinning Cillian in place, "Queen Esmeray hands over what I want as a peace offering."

Cillian refused to ask, refused to take the bait, instead, raising a single brow expectantly.

Lord Batair, however, rustled his wings in impatience. "What is it you desire, my King?

King Eamon smiled. "I want the Oracle."

It was Dimas who spoke first, after the King's declaration. "My King, the Oracle is not bound to any Kingdom. It may be difficult to convince her to come live here if she has a life in Irridessen."

King Eamon turned his dark eyes to Dimas. "The Oracle should be pleased to learn that a simple move of homes on her part will avoid a lengthy war. And that, Lord Dimas, is exactly how *you* will be portraying my demands."

Cillian looked from Dimas to the King, his voice bitter, "You want *my* advisor to go to Irridessen, stand in front of a Vessel Queen, and demand the Oracle? He'd be *killed* before he even opened his mouth."

Dimas paled slightly before smoothing out a small wrinkle on his tunic, inclining his head to Cillian, his voice soft, "My Prince, I *do* serve the Ruby Kingdom, and if my King bids me to go, then I must."

King Eamon clapped sarcastically. "See? Lord Dimas is a wonderful advisor, Prince Cillian. He understands his duty. You should do the same, and mind your place as my Heir."

Loosening the tightness in his jaw, Cillian inclined his head, pushing down the panic flipping through his chest. "I meant no disrespect Father, I only wondered why you chose Lord Dimas when we have other advisors who are not as *irreplaceable*. I was hoping to heed his council to prepare for the Culling festivities."

King Eamon turned his attention to Lord Batair, giving him a slight nod. With a feral grin, Lord Batair strode to the threshold, calling in someone outside the door.

A soft scuffle and a whimper sounded as two of Lord Batair's Captains stepped into the room, a wraith thin female hanging between them. She was dirty, with stringy, dark hair that lay ratty and flat against her scalp, hanging down past her waist. Dressed in nothing but a stained brown slip, she fought against the strong grasps on her upper arms.

Neither gargoyle seem phased by her attempts to wrench herself free, jerking her to a stand as they bowed to the King. The gargoyle on the left shoved the female's neck down into a mocking bow as well, before releasing her head, keeping a firm grip on her shoulder.

"And who, pray tell, is this?" Cillian asked Lord Batair, though the barbed edged words were meant for his father.

"She's a witch," Lord Batair replied proudly. "Found 'er six months ago and threw her in the dungeon. Figured the King may have a need for her at some point."

The witch panted, though she stopped fighting long enough to stare at Cillian. Her milky pale skin was almost translucent, only broken up by the loose smock and copper chains extending from her wrists to her throat, down to her ankles.

"And need her we do," King Eamon purred, standing from the desk to approach the female. "Let her go. She won't hurt anyone in here, will you, pet?"

The witch regarded the King for a moment, before relaxing between Lord Batair's Captains in submission. Without needing to be told twice, they released her. Dimas seemed to barely be breathing as he exchanged another look with Cillian, one that read '*what the actual fuck?*' Cillian couldn't agree more.

"What is your name, witch?" King Eamon asked.

The witch looked up, her brilliantly blue eyes never leaving the King's face as she whispered, her voice raspy, "Neci, my name is Neci."

"Neci, I have need of a wonderful little witch to help keep my Kingdom safe. If you agree to assist me, I'll return you to the Jade Kingdom." The King tutted softly as the witch's eyes narrowed. "It wouldn't be too much trouble, I suppose, for you to break through witch runes?"

Neci shook her head slowly, and Cillian saw the exact moment Neci realized she was in front of the King of the Ruby Kingdom. Her back stiffened and her eyes grew wide – probably from months of hearing about the King's cruel magic from the other prisoners in the dungeon.

"I can break witch runes," she agreed quietly. "But I didn't know there were any this far south."

"Oh no, no," King Eamon chuckled, "These witch runes are in the Obsidian Palace. Do you know where the Obsidian Palace is?"

Neci nodded, her lips thinning.

"Wonderful. I have a friend stuck in some nasty witch runes, and I need your help to get her out." King Eamon straightened. "Lord Dimas will cover you while you are in the Obsidian Palace, and you're going to drain the power from the witch runes trapping our ally. Then, once you return to me with my new ally, I'll send you back to the Jade Kingdom with your weight in gold and jewels for the trouble. Is it a deal?"

A hungry look filled the witch's blue eyes. Cillian knew that look - knew that the witch either was smarter than she let on, or was easily swayed by the King's honey laced promises. But he knew his father only saw the latter, only saw the witch as nothing more than a beast to break and control.

"Put our guest in one of the royal rooms. Get her fed and clothed appropriately," King Eamon directed to the two Captains still lurking at the edge of the study. When one lunged for her, King Eamon shot a whip of air at the gargoyle's arm, and he backpedaled quickly. "None of that rough handling for our guest. Neci here will walk freely on her own accord, though she understands - *don't you, Neci* - that the shackles on your wrists must stay on until it is time for you to go to the Obsidian Kingdom?"

"Yes, your Majesty," Neci purred back, bowing low to the King before standing, tossing her sheet of black hair over her shoulder. With the same dignity as a Queen walking up the aisle to her coronation, Neci exited the room, the Captains following at a respectable distance.

Cillian waited three seconds before turning to his Father. "Who are you breaking out of witch runes?" The words came out more accusatory than he intended, but thankfully, his father was still bolstered by Neci's quick acceptance of whatever larger plans that were in play.

King Eamon rolled the sleeves of his blood red tunic up to his elbows, sighing as he sat back down into his chair. With a charming smile that didn't clear the cruelty in his eyes, he said, "Queen Adara seems rather lonely sitting in that decrepit Soul Keeper's Cell beneath the Obsidian Palace. I'm sure, with the promise of a strong alliance with Ingotheria, and our backing to place her on the thrones of Irridessen, she'll do exactly as we suggest."

"Adara murdered her own kin, almost killed Queen Esmeray, and learned some sort of magic from a Vessel Book," Cillian stated flatly, the absolute absurdity of his Father's plan settling against his shoulders. "And you think it's safe to free her?"

King Eamon cocked his head, a sneer warping his features as he leveled a bone-chilling glare at Cillian. "*Free* her? I mean to *unleash* Adara onto the twin she holds so much hate for. Queen Esmeray won't even see the blade coming until it's buried in her back."

# Part Three

---

## The FLAME

# CHAPTER FIFTY-THREE
# KEERIAN

CHILL WIND WHIPPED BETWEEN carved obsidian pillars, bringing with it the harsh scent of carrion. Keerian surveyed the mountainside from the sheer drop off of the open-air atrium, his eyes catching on the faint shimmer of dragon scales in the distance. He watched the beast drag its kill, a shaggy haired goat, into one of the many tunnels that led to the dragon's lair beneath the throne room.

With a grim smile, he glanced to the rolling fog steaming off the Pyritee Pass, the gleaming walls of black almost invisible from this high up. Keerian paced, doing his best to ignore the aura of palpating anxiety behind him.

It had been one month since Keerian and Merrick found out the spy, Jargo, was a double agent, one month since they began hunting for the last three names of King Eamon's notorious spy network that vanished without a trace from the Opal Palace. One month of dead ends and growing frustration, a festering feeling of tension sinking in its claws inch by ruthless inch.

Sparrow and Laurent continued searching for the Book of Faune, faring no better. The dried-up waterfall had been a dead end. No magical god books hid in its cave systems, no pin prickles of power or divinely sent signs pointed them in a specific direction.

Lenna had dove into the Prism again to try and narrow down the location – with no results. Not even a prophecy or a flicker of confirmation from Moirai. It was quiet on all fronts.

Too quiet.

Esmeray spent the last month doling out her own brand of divine intervention, focusing on the information revealed by Merrick, speaking with Jargo on the status of the Ruby Kingdom's growing unrest, and building a damning pile of evidence against the treasonous scum sitting on her royal council. Though no blood had been spilled, his mate grew more formidable by the day. Inheriting direct god power turned Esmeray from strong to all out lethal, and as much as it thrilled Keerian, it terrified the entirety of the council.

Which is why, when summons went out last week for the royal council of Irridessen to appear at the Obsidian Palace and meet with the Queen Absolute, every single one of them had shown up on time. Even the traitors – thinking they were in the clear, since so much time had passed. Oh, how dearly they were wrong. Esmeray gave them the rope, and they foolishly hung themselves with it.

No blood had been spilled.

*Yet*.

As if on a mental cue with Keerian's brooding monologue, gold and green light burst through the center of the atrium as Esmeray and Sparrow arrived.

Esmeray looked every bit the Vessel of Death in a sleek black gown that hugged her waist before fanning out into pools of inky fabric at her feet. Intricate black lace overlay the velvet dress, covering her moon pale throat before seeping down into long sleeves that allowed the council to view her *acat*. The back was open, her wings decorated with thin golden chains hooked and draped artfully off each polished talon. Golden paint shone at the tips of each curled horn, accentuating the crown of moonstone and twining vines that nestled between the ridges.

The six council members stood and bowed. Esmeray ignored them as she stalked to the head of the table, her eyes only meeting Keerian's.

Sparrow stepped up to the Queen's left, signifying that she was sitting in on this meeting as the Heir. Her dress was a deep emerald green, embellished with small pearls threaded into the gauzy fabric. Keerian bet that somewhere in this castle, Laurent was sporting a robe in the same color. Sparrow and Laurent had disengaged from their search for one day – just for the council meeting. They'd searched five more waterfalls over the last three and a half weeks, with no luck, and still had seven to go.

Keerian turned casually from the edge of the room, making his way to the chair on his mate's right. Esmeray waited until Keerian stood behind his seat before her gold flecked green eyes cut to the council members still standing.

"Be seated," she purred as she leaned back in her chair, her gaze settling on each advisor in turn, her expression alight with malice. Keerian could feel her magic thrumming, coiled and ready to strike.

The Opal Palace Chancellor, Lord Zorn, was the first to speak. "Queen Absolute Esmeray, forgive me, but why is Lady Sparrow still acting as Heir? I was under the impression that was a temporary arrangement due to the circumstances at Calcity."

Esmeray sized up the Chancellor, her teeth bared in a wicked smile. "Chancellor Zorn, you should've read the decree more carefully. Nowhere in that statement was Lady Sparrow's position as Heir presumptive to a specific amount of time."

Master Minzani, the Advisor of Law, inclined his head in agreement, his sky-blue wings twitching. "That is correct, Chancellor. Lady Sparrow is the Heir Apparent of Irridessen. Even if the Queen Absolute and King have a babe, the succession of Irridessen will still go to Lady Sparrow of Baryte Hill."

The Trade Advisor, Lady Belinde, made a small noise of disgust, though it was Sparrow who spoke up, her voice smooth yet barbed, "Lady Belinde, did you have something you wanted to ask?"

"It is just not *right*." Lady Belinde shook her head. "The rules of succession, agreed upon at the time of coronation, stated the King and Queen's eldest would gain the throne."

"And yet, we see rules being changed, if not outright broken, every day. Don't we, Lady Belinde?" Esmeray remarked sardonically, before leaning her palms on the tabletop. "My ruling stands, and is not up for discussion *nor* is it the purpose of this meeting."

"What we really need to decide is who'll take up the Spy Master seat." The Lord of War, Lord Orden, was as gruff and blunt as Keerian remembered from his days training for the King's Guard – when Orden was Commander. Now the gargoyle was soft, with a pudgy, thick belly, his once chestnut brown mustache swept with grey - but his clever hazel eyes still held the same attentiveness Keerian studied and thrived under.

Obsidian Palace's Chancellor, Lady Mairsile, shot Orden a glare, lamenting her own woes in leadership and explaining how they were more important. Esmeray, already bored with the bickering, was busy fashioning her nails into long, black points.

She let the council sputter into silence before she deigned to flick her eyes up.

With a wave of her hand, gold magic blasted through the room, wards flaring to life against the pillars. Keerian worked to hide the feral grin on his face as Esmeray stood slowly from her chair, her dagger edged nails dragging slowly down the tabletop. With practiced steps, Esmeray paced. "These are containment wards," she said quietly, "and they will stay up until I decide to take them down. Does anyone here have a...problem...with being trapped in these wards during the remainder of our meeting?"

"No, your Majesty," Chancellor Mairsile said firmly, steepling her tattooed fingers on the surface in front of her. "Though may I ask *why* we're warded in?"

Esmeray paused her pacing to level her steady gaze at the advisor. "Of course, Lady Chancellor. It is because, unfortunately, we have spies in Irridessen."

"Told you we needed a godsdamned Spy Master," Lord Orden huffed, leaning back in his chair to rest his hands against his protruding belly. His amber wings stretched out behind him, and with an apologetic flutter of his fingers, he added, "Apologies, your Majesty, at my informality."

Keerian inclined his head towards his old Commander, before scanning the rest of the faces in the council room. A mixture of reverence, slight concern, and confusion permeated the space as Queen Esmeray returned to the head of the table, though she didn't sit.

"I understand your grievances with the vacant Spy Master role, Orden. Trust me when I say Master Laurent will be integral in finding a candidate to fill the position. But with him soul tied to my Heir, it was purely political that he resign to minimize the danger he places himself in – and Lady Sparrow by default."

Sparrow gave the Queen a tight-lipped smile that told Keerian she was also relieved her mate was no longer infiltrating highly dangerous Kingdoms to glean information on potential threats.

Lady Belinde scowled but wisely stayed quiet.

Esmeray caught the expression, and Keerian saw the exact moment that his mate chose her move. A being appeared at the rim of the wards, and Esmeray parted them just a moment before they shut again. The likeness of the illusion was eerily uncanny - down to the same watery eyes and hue of straw-blonde hair. Lenna used Jargo as an anchor to get a good look at Ardrick, before projecting the image of the dead spy into Esmeray's mind. Esmeray formulated her plan from there.

With top-tier god magic, the illusion-Ardrick walked, breathed, and blinked with perfect replication, swaggering into the room and bowing low to Esmeray before turning to face Lady Belinde.

Lady Belinde paled slightly, her mouth hanging open as the illusion nodded towards her with familiarity.

"Lady Belinde, have you had the pleasure of meeting Sir Ardrick?" Esmeray crooned.

"I...don't believe I have," Lady Belinde simpered, before straightening and blinking twice, her facial expression shuttering as she added, "The Opal Palace is very large."

Esmeray hummed, "Well, I daresay that's confusing. You signed his recruitment papers. I thought for sure you two were formally introduced. Didn't you grow up in Shar, Belinde?"

Keerian stifled a grin, though his hand moved slowly to the dagger strapped beneath his jacket.

Lady Belinde frowned. "Any council member can approve recruits for our army. I must've signed off on the paperwork without realizing. I get correspondence on many things, your Majesty."

"So, you aren't particularly *fond* of Sir Ardrick?" Esmeray asked, as a cruel smile toyed at the edges of her red painted lips.

After Merrick killed the spy, Ardrick's body was quickly disposed of, and since he'd never shown up to an assigned fighting unit, no one knew he was missing.

Leaving Lady Belinde to believe the spy she let in the Opal Palace was alive and well.

"No. Of course not." Lady Belinde glanced sideways at the spy, the puppet strings invisible to the Trade Advisor. The illusion-Ardrick crossed his arms, shaking his head dejectedly.

*"Belinde doesn't know Ardrick is dead."* Keerian shot down his ring to Esmeray.

*"Then let's let her in on that little secret,"* Esmeray replied gleefully, though her face never wavered from the predatory stare she pinned on Lady Belinde.

Esmeray flicked her hand, pulling Goldriel out of the veil, lazily pointing the moonstone tip towards her illusion.

With a choking screech, the illusion-Ardrick fell to his knees, hands pawing at his neck, beady eyes bulging from his skull. Esmeray was behind him in a split second, her jagged nails tearing across his exposed throat, spurts of dark red blood spraying out, coating the rough-hewn stone wall of the atrium.

Lady Belinde lurched from her chair with a scream, and Keerian moved on instinct, his arm shooting out to yank the Trade Advisor away from his mate.

Master Minzani and Chancellor Mairsile rose from their chairs, though they did not dare move closer, the former doubling over as if he may puke, the latter covering her mouth with her palm in shock.

Keerian held the struggling Lady Belinde as Esmeray stalked closer, her nails dripping with blood - another part of the illusion her god magic helped her master. "Do you remember him *now?*"

"You *monster,*" Lady Belinde hissed, her demeanor falling apart rapidly as the false spy continued to bleed out and twitch on the hard ground before them. Keerian failed at keeping the pride from showing on his face. He had to hand it to Esmeray, her illusions were fascinatingly and morbidly realistic. "You killed him!"

"I know everything," Esmeray snarled, stalking closer to the pinned female. "I *know* Sir Ardrick was one of the spies sent by the Ruby Kingdom. I *know* you're getting a hefty amount of gold every month you bend to King Eamon's desires – smuggled to you directly from Ingotheria."

"You're wrong!" Lady Belinde screeched, trying to kick free of Keerian's grip on her. "I did no such thing!"

"Oh, Lady Belinde," Esmeray straightened with a scathing smile, her horns cocked as she appraised the fae. "I wasn't talking to you – I was talking to Chancellor Zorn."

With a flash, Sparrow waned behind the Chancellor, right as twin whips of gold battle magic snapped shut around his ankles. In a blink, Sparrow had the set of magic-nullifying cuffs snapped tight around his wrists. Chancellor Zorn's reddening face twisted up in a hateful snarl as he tugged against the bonds, his own magic flaring and sputtering out as quickly as it appeared. He was too powerful and slippery to directly accuse of treason, but the element of surprise worked like a godsdamned charm.

"Sorry," Sparrow sang – not sounding sorry at all as she sidled away from the enraged fae. "Witch runes are a real bitch about nullifying magic."

The Queen and Heir exchanged a knowing look as Keerian released his grip on Lady Belinde. She backpedaled until she hit the edge of the table, her breath coming in rapid bursts as she whirled to face Zorn. "You *traitor,"* she shrieked, shrill and high-pitched, "How dare you ruin the good name of this continent with your actions?"

"Give it a rest, Belinde," Chancellor Zorn yelled. "You aren't fooling anyone."

Esmeray snapped her fingers, the illusion-Ardrick disappearing along with every speck of blood. Raising her voice, she cut her eyes between Lady Belinde and Chancellor Zorn. "Whoever tells me *where* the remaining spies from the Ruby Kingdom are, and *what* they're doing on *my continent* gets to live. The other dies." Her gaze darkening, she growled low, "You have three seconds to start talking, I suggest you fill it with words."

"The spies are looking for the Vessel Book of Faune," Lady Belinde blurted out, falling to her knees, her hands twisting in her lap, "King Eamon wants it. He sent them to hunt for it – he knows it's someplace in Irridessen."

"You *bitch,*" Zorn bellowed, "you two-faced *bitch.*" The disgraced Chancellor spat on the floor.

Lord Orden continued reclining in his chair, watching the volley back and forth with minimal interest. Another advisor, Lady Spes, paled, her lips clamped shut, looking like she was two seconds away from fainting.

"Chancellor Zorn," Esmeray unfurled her wings, her eyes sparking with god magic. "Do you have anything you'd like to add?"

Zorn roared, spittle flying from his lips, "Queen Adara was a *much* better Queen than you'll *ever* be. *And -* "

Esmeray pointed Goldriel's moonstone at the Chancellor, a golden jet of power slamming straight through his chest and out the other side of the chair.

"That was going nowhere good," Esmeray muttered, as Zorn slumped over, dead.

Lady Belinde shrieked and staggered upright, attempting to run. Esmeray simply watched as Belinde smacked headfirst into the containment wards, bouncing back and falling over again.

"Belinde, give me one good reason to keep you alive," Esmeray sighed, pinching the bridge of her nose, a tone of boredom suffusing her words.

"I can give you information, whatever information you want," Lady Belinde husked immediately, crawling a foot before leaning back against her heels, her eyes wild as she tracked Esmeray's every move.

Keerian rolled his lips. Belinde barely had magic. She was a weak-powered healer, though with that, he had a feeling King Eamon hadn't deigned to fill the female in on anything of *actual* importance.

Lady Belinde held her palms out, surrendering, words spilling forth quickly, as if she believed recanting every morsel of knowledge she held would save her life. "I'll tell you King Eamon's movements - why he wants the Vessel Books."

Esmeray rolled her eyes, causing Keerian to smirk. His mate was going to play with her food before she ate it. "No thanks. I already know the King's moves, and it's pretty obvious why he wants the Vessel Books." She gestured to herself as if this was a complete affront. "*I'm* a Vessel, remember? What else?"

Stuttering, Lady Belinde's eyes shot around the room looking beseechingly at the other council members for assistance. None of them said a word. Lord Orden outright scoffed as she turned pleading eyes to him. "I – I -"

"So, you actually know nothing of interest?" Esmeray interrupted, turning to Keerian. "Maybe we should've killed her and kept Chancellor Zorn alive – he seemed to know more."

Keerian raised his eyebrows, playing the part. "Let's just kill them both and be done with it."

"Florra!" Lady Belinde screamed. "The spies are in Florra. They're tracking the Book of Faune!"

"What else," Esmeray asked darkly.

"That's it! That's all I know – I swear it."

With a shrug, Esmeray said, "I believe you." And with a flick of her wrist, Lady Belinde seized once before slumping over.

The four remaining council members sat silently as a thin trickle of blood seeped from between Lady Belinde's slightly parted lips.

"Well, now we need a Spy Master, a Chancellor, *and* a new Trade Advisor," Lord Orden grumbled, rubbing his stomach, as if this whole situation merely gave him heartburn.

Esmeray shot the Lord of War a bemused expression, flicking her wrist as the containment wards faded, before asking, "Is anyone here interested in a promotion?"

# Chapter Fifty-Four
# ESMERAY

THE THING ABOUT DREAMING is that you're never *positive* it's a dream until you wake up. And that's when you know for sure – even if the shadow of the dream follows, an echo that repeats into consciousness.

Standing in the throne room of Minmere, I knew I was dreaming. But the Goddess in front of me was very real, and *very* irritated. I breathed deep, knowing my body was safely tucked in next to my mate in Terramere, yet the fate of my subconscious mind seemed fragile as Phades clicked her jawbones, her void black robes rustling with impatience.

"You've yet to locate the Book of Faune," Phades commented.

"I do apologize, your Holiness, *especially* since you gave *such specific* details on its location," I snipped, feeling the tension spike as my words settled.

Phades leaned forward, those eyeless pits in her skull glinting with frustration. For a beat, she stared at me, before saying, "Ask your question, Queen."

"Where's the Book of Faune?"

Phades clacked her jaw again, though it was slower, more thoughtful. "That is not the question you truly seek the answer to."

I had half a mind to pinch myself, to pull me from this dream world and back into my body. But those swirling, unanswered questions taunted me from the quiet part of my mind, the part that I dared not voice aloud.

"Did you know Massis?" I felt that twinge of unease deep in my throat as I thought of Adara in the Soul Keeper's Cell. But I refused to allow the guilt to seep in, reminded myself that – sister or not – Adara deserved her punishment.

"I knew Massis very well," Phades cooed, her skull bobbing as she leaned forward in her throne of bones. "He is the only other god who found and opened a god realm separate from Aurramere. He stole away to Avamere after the God War, and stayed there throughout the Witch War, which ended with all the god realms being sealed to keep the gods out of Terramere permanently. Turns out, even gods are known to disregard a treaty. The sealing of the god realms is proof of that."

Phades chuffed, the sound hoarse, "Now, Massis is calculating and ancient, biding his time with his demon horde, locked in Avamere and brooding over his failed attempt to come to Terramere during the Witch War."

A thought struck me, then, with the way Phades spoke about Massis, making it seem as if it was not only the fae who disavowed the God of Chaos. "What was Massis's role in the Wars?"

"You are learning, Queen."

"Answer my question."

With a wave of her spindly fingers, Phades regarded me with what I could only assume was haughtiness, though reading any expression off the stark white bones of her face was a gamble. "The God War was bloody and raw, and there are many gods today that still regret their actions during that time." Phades hesitated. "Massis, however, was never one of them. The four goddesses earthside stayed in a tentative truce after returning to a god realm. And for thousands of years, there were no gods willing to break the peace."

"But that all changed during the Witch War. The silence from Avamere, from Massis, made us careless. We thought he was content in his realm." Phades shook her head. "We were wrong. And the sealing of the god realms at the culmination of the Witch War was bought about by his actions, and his actions alone. Massis used the war as an excuse to slip earthside, so he could imbue Vessels at his leisure."

The God of Chaos was written in history as the witch god who thrived on runic spell work and blood magic, though the fae knew him at a time where his siphoning gifts were rare and coveted. To be able to pull magic from other beings, nature, or from magically imbued objects, and use it in battle in the form of raw magic was deadly in times of war.

"Massis began plotting how to slip from Avamere to Terramere be-hind our backs. When the other gods, myself included, learned of his plans, we had no choice but to trap him in Avamere. If he was able to imbue a Vessel with his direct god magic..." Phades shuddered, her horns catching the soft torchlight. "But to seal him away, we were forced to close *all* the realms. Each and every god made sacrifices, some more than others, to give your realm a chance to flourish."

I frowned. "But why is his magic so feared? You imbued me with god magic."

"Because, Queen, my magic is for you and you alone – just as Faune, Aella, and Carra designed their magic – their Vessel Books. One Vessel at a time. One being holding the power of a god."

Phades growled, the sound guttural. "If Massis came earthside, he would imbue as many Vessels as he could. You know how powerful you are with god magic, Queen? Imagine an *army* of Vessels, led by a god who rules over a horde of demons, whose only goal is complete and utter decimation of every single being who doesn't kneel."

I winced, understanding. "Aella and Carra are the two other goddesses that were earthside." I felt my breath hitch. Aella, the Goddess of Destruction, gifted beings with fire. Laurent was blessed by Aella, but I knew in my soul Laurent was not the Vessel Aella would choose. And Carra...

Phades huffed in sheer irritation, "Carra has never been inclined to imbue a Vessel. She'd rather float through Aurramere bestowing soul ties with her head in the clouds. If she ever did imbue a Vessel, I fear it would simply be the most annoying creature. All doe-eyed and simpering, fawning all over itself."

"And Aella?"

The Goddess of Death cocked her head, considering my question. "Aella has wit," she said slowly. "She was always very crafty with her magic. And I wonder if you becoming my Vessel will have any pull on Aella to finally imbue her own." A purr escaped Phades's throat. "Her Vessel *would* be powerful, but she is...particular with her choosing."

"But how would Massis differ? Even if he only imbued one Vessel?" I asked, my mind frantically churning with information to bring back to my body. I doubted once Phades dismissed me from Minmere that I'd get a wink of sleep tonight.

"Massis wants to open Avamere and let his demon horde out. But the god realms cannot be unlocked from the inside – it would take an incredibly powerful outside force to unseal them for the gods to travel between realms once more. But Massis doesn't *just* want a Vessel; Massis wants to be the *only* god earthside, to *only* unseal Avamere, so he can rule two realms while the rest of the gods stay trapped, unable to do anything but watch his cruel reign. And if Massis conquered Terramere...if Massis desired more? What would stop him, with his army of Vessels and demons at his back, from challenging Minmere - Aurramere?"

I inhaled sharply. The Unmarked were bad enough with their chaos magic. If Massis unleashed the demons he ruled over, it would decimate everything in our earth realm, bringing death to every being who did not kneel. Chaos magic was wild and untamed, and if Massis was able to create a Vessel that could control demons and siphon on top of his direct god power, it would bring this world to its knees.

"Why did you imbue me now?" I asked, my heart thudding loudly in my chest.

"Because the real threat, Queen, is the following Massis is gaining in the Jade Kingdom. There are factions of witches rattling against the cage your world closed them in after the Witch War. They believe they can bring Massis earthside with blood sacrifices and runic spell work. And they are gaining the knowledge to potentially carry that out."

I swallowed.

Phades continued, with a flippant wave of her hand, "But, Queen. That fight is not yours at this time."

*What?* I paused, staring at the Goddess of Death to make sure I heard her correctly. "If Massis gets earthside, it will end up *being* my fight. I'm the only Vessel here."

"For now. But I doubt much longer." Phades inspected her palm, the bones of her jaw grinding as she lowered her skull, fixing me in place with a sightless eye.

"Who- "

Phades interrupted me with a sharp chatter. "There is someone, Queen, that I'd like you to meet."

A soft sighing of filmy fabric against the rocky floor snapped my attention to one of the depthless tunnels jutting from the throne room.

I held my breath as the clip of shoes against the ground made my body tense. Someone was coming from the peace of the afterlife to deliver a message to me.

With no magic, I was defenseless, but Phades wouldn't herald her souls attack me while she still wanted me to find the Book of Faune and do whatever other deeds I knew she was holding to surprise me with at a later time. Yet, my heartbeat hammered in my chest, the solid thumping reminding me that I was not yet dead.

As I got a glimpse of a cherub face, frozen in the roundness of youth, brilliantly blue eyes, and familiar golden waves of hair that swept behind gently pointed ears, I felt my heart stutter. The small faeling appeared from the inky blackness of the tunnel, stepping lightly into the throne room of the Goddess of Death. She pinned me in place with a look that was far too mature, far too knowing, for one as young as her.

But I knew *her*.

"Briar," I breathed.

The faeling smiled brightly at me; her face gut-wrenchingly identical to that of her twin when she first arrived to the Opal Palace's court. Sparrow's blue eyes had been glossy from crying, and tear streaks shone against her cheeks as she hid in her mother's skirts. But I understood none of that as a youngling myself and strolled right up to Sparrow to ask if she wanted to play with me in the gardens.

The memory caused tears to prick at the corners of my own eyes as I sunk to my knees, hands outstretched and trembling, my wings drooping behind me. Briar stepped into my arms, hugging me fiercely, before her small palm cupped my cheek, wiping away the first tear that fell. "Hello, Queen," Briar said sweetly, "I would like to tell you a story of two sisters who loved each other very much."

# CHAPTER FIFTY-FIVE
# ORLA

THE BAZAAR IN ARIDDEN snaked over a mile in length, with two rows of storefronts carved from the sandstone of the Palace itself. The shade thrown from the awnings separating the ground level stores from the second-floor homes acted more like a privacy screen than as a reprieve from the sun that bore down into the street.

Even though the desert lay outside the rim of thick walls surrounding the Ruby Palace, the breeze wafting overhead still managed to dump a fine layer of gritty gold sand along the ground. Multicolor flags and banners snapped in the dry air, and potted cacti flourished - nestled in metal bent window planters, bursting from chipped pots lining the walkways, hanging from intricately braided and woven nets dripping down from the railings of small porches and narrow balconies. Sun catchers threw fractures of rainbow-tinted light against the buildings, wind chimes tinkled and swayed merrily - a cheery background noise to the constant din of chatter that rose and fell along the road, diverging in different languages, accents, tones, though the bright sounds of laughter were continuous. All sorts of beings meandered leisurely through the marketplace, clutching their purchases, chatting with friends, and shopping.

It all seemed so lively, energized. So vivid in contrast to the dreary town square in Doortan where most of the stores were either closed down or on their way to meet the same, vacant, fate. But here, the street thrummed with the life blood of the Ruby Kingdom's citizens. Even vendors who couldn't afford to pay rent for a storefront pushed carts filled to the brim with their trade, shouting out prices and haggling with beings who stopped.

Orla carried a small bag slung around her hips with vials of hair oil that a lovely fae with ebony skin and a similar textured hair recommended to help combat the crisp autumn heat that dried out Orla's curls. It had been her first purchase since weaving her way through the throng of beings outside of the shop Marlo worked in but definitely wouldn't be her last.

Her head was on a constant swivel, soaking it all in as she scoured the shops in search of a being that could weave her hair into the trendy, long braids she saw other fae and gargoyles sporting, or even help her start her own locs.

Marlo walked at her side, the two of them sharing a kebab stick that boasted an assortment of charred vegetables and delectable meats that Marlo purchased at a food cart once he was able to take a break from helping customers. Orla took another bite of smoked pepper, a groan slipping out as the spices hit her tongue.

"They definitely didn't have this type of food in Doortan," Marlo said as he took another bite of roasted meat, his lids fluttering with appreciation at the hearty taste.

Orla chuckled as they wove their way down the packed street, glancing into booths filled with fabrics and shoes, assorted daggers, and apparently everything else one could desire. She stopped to admire a storefront packed with soft, flowy skirts, fingering the material of a bright yellow garment displayed outside the shop's wooden door.

"Oh, beautiful," Orla murmured as the material slipped like silk through her hand.

"Good afternoon." A female gargoyle with spun locs plaited into a braid walked through the door, smiling at Orla. Her wings were a soft brown that sparkled under the desert sun, matching her skin and delicately curved horns.

"Hi," Orla gave the female a friendly nod back, tearing her eyes from the beautiful yellow skirt.

"Are you looking for something to wear to the Ball?"

"Just looking around," Orla said. Soren had already earmarked the most scandalous dress in her closet for the occasion.

"No problem, let me know if you have any questions," the shop owner replied happily, as Marlo approached, the two exchanging greetings and chatting about their businesses.

Orla let her mind drift as she wove through the shop. It was the first afternoon she'd had off work in a week, and she was determined to spend it without her thoughts pivoting to the Prince who'd been distant over the last month. Even though she hadn't seen Cillian since that night in the desert, he still found time to sneak little notes with an array of sweet words into her room at least twice a week. And her own duties were never ending in preparation for the Equinox Ball that would begin right after the Culling.

It seemed the beings living in the Ruby Kingdom their whole lives viewed the Culling itself as little more than a tradition – since those who manifested forbidden *acatis* were few and far between. It had become more of a boring, uneventful practice than an actual barbaric ritual.

But Orla now knew better – those beings who found their lives to be in danger were whisked away in the dead of night to a safe location where they wouldn't face persecution for their gifts.

And weirdly enough, the closer the Culling approached, the more at ease Orla became, even with the added golden thread that shimmered through her soul. Seysei stayed far enough away from the Palace, though he constantly butted into her mind to voice his opinions of the Ruby Kingdom. But she found his connection welcoming – especially to know that the mighty dragon could make it to her in under ten minutes if shit really went down.

But she hadn't seen Seysei either since that night they became *kindered,* and a part of her soul longed for the dragon to meet her in the desert so she could view him again with her own eyes.

Soren knew, as well as Dimas, that she now held a connection with the beast, though neither pushed her on the subject. She hadn't told Marlo, worried he wouldn't understand how she'd changed her mind so swiftly on dragons after everything they endured in the shipwreck.

Cillian kept his distance, and Orla hated wondering if that was the Crown Prince's way of telling her that their kiss had been a mistake, even though he'd talked about kissing her again and more than one of his notes had confirmed that statement. His absence nagged at her, and she couldn't help replaying every moment of that night in her head, overthinking his words, his actions.

She glanced sidelong at Marlo, his blonde hair finally long enough for him to pull back with a small piece of leather. He'd bulked out with muscle over the last month, and between his height and his wide shoulders, more than one female had done a double take as they wandered through the bazaar. Orla had pointed it out to him, though Marlo only grunted, his cheeks reddening, and then he'd changed the subject.

Any free time Orla had away from her duties, she made it a point to visit Marlo in the bazaar or train with Soren. On that sense, she *was* getting better, and their last session even ended with quite an audience watching her and Soren shoot balls of fire at each other. She couldn't wane yet, but Soren wasn't fazed, simply telling her waning was difficult no matter how strong a fae was, and that she'd pick it up sooner or later.

In the evenings, Soren and Orla would meet in each other's rooms, sharing a bottle of wine and chatting about their day. Soren had her own duties to prepare for the Culling, both from King Eamon as well as Cillian. Orla offered her help, but Soren quickly advised Orla that her job was to lay low, and Soren's job was to keep King Eamon happy and unsuspecting that a coup was festering under his very nose. Orla never pushed Soren for specifics, but the wicked gleam of retribution that burned through Soren's bronze-hued eyes always gave Orla pause.

Orla and Marlo ventured on from the boutique of clothing, finishing the last bites of roast meat, and rounded a corner to the edge of the bazaar that lead back towards Oasees. A group of beings came into view, all clustered around what looked to be a royal notice hung against the sandstone. Two Palace guards stood on each side of the parchment, growling at anyone who got too close.

"Wonder what that says," Marlo said warily as they approached.

"Let's find out." Orla gripped Marlo's hand tightly before shoving their way through the beings until she was close enough to read the paper.

*BY ROYAL DECREE OF KING EAMON*

*The below* acatis *are forbidden in the Ruby Kingdom:*

*REANIMATION of the dead*

*BLOOD WIELDING*

*DUPLICATION*

*MIND READING and MEMORY ERASURE*

*In addition, the following heritage gifts are forbidden:*

*WITCHCRAFT of any kind, OR lineage lines tracing back to witch blood*

*DRAGONMIND*

*MANIPULATION of the MIND or EMOTIONS*

*SIPHONING*

*All beings who have manifested an* acat *within the last year MUST perform their magic before the King the night of the autumnal equinox. By appearing before His Royal Majesty, you consent to have your bloodline read and catalogued for the Royal Archives.*

*Those who can wield a separate battle magic will be required to confirm the hue of their gift.*

*Those who fail to appear will be punished, and those who are found to be hiding a cullable* acat *will be sentenced accordingly.*

Orla craned her neck past the growing crowd, seeing that more of the same decrees hung further down the hall. Heart thudding traitorously in her chest, she read the notice once more before backing up, moving away from the gathering beings, tugging Marlo with her.

"Is everything alright?" Marlo asked, worry creasing at the corners of his eyes. "That's the Culling List I was told about, right?"

"Everything's fine." Orla forced a smile on her face before pulling Marlo along the white walled corridor that separated Aridden from the entrance to Oasees. She wanted to put some space between her and the list that very obviously marked her heritage gift as forbidden.

Marlo swallowed nervously, a grin breaking out on his face as he let her drag him along the hallway. "I'm sure you're relieved; I knew fire wielding wouldn't be added. Oh, I've met a couple other fae that have your gift. I can introduce you-"

Orla tuned him out, diving into the thin golden thread inside of herself. She'd stayed connected to her dragon while walking through the bazaar, as Seysei admitted he enjoyed seeing the world through her eyes.

She'd travelled along the golden thread to see out of Seysei's gaze, but when he'd proudly shown her the corpse of a rather mangled desert elk, she had to swiftly stamp down a wave of nausea. But Orla did enjoy peering through his eyes when he took to the sky, dreaming about one day being able to climb on his back and soar through the puffy white clouds.

*"It was to be expected,"* Seysei's voice filled her head, and she knew he'd been listening and watching. *"The King believes he exterminated the entire line of* Vitraro, *but he knows* something *is causing the increase in dragon activity."*

*"What do I do?"*

Her *kindered* chuffed, the sound putting her at ease. *"You do your duties, show the King your fire wielding, and keep your head down. Running will not solve anything."*

Orla calmed her breathing, blinking her eyes and reacquainting herself with her surroundings. With a jolt she realized she was still holding onto Marlo, hauling him along the corridor.

"Fuck, sorry," she muttered, dropping his hand and wiping her sweaty palms against the loose linen pants she'd donned this morning.

"Don't worry about it." Marlo winced and rubbed life back into his fingers, shooting her a dramatic grimace. "You're strong, though. I think my fingers'll be numb for a few hours."

Orla forced a chuckle as they slowed their steps. "It's part of being fae," she explained, "You should see how fast I can run now." *Not that she'd be running, but still.*

They entered the Oasees residence corridor, coming face to face with a grim-faced Soren.

"What's going on?" Orla asked quietly as she broke from Marlo, hurrying over to the fae standing between their two doors.

Soren cut her eyes to Marlo, who paused under the all-out glare, backing up to a respectful distance before pretending to be enraptured, instead, with retying the laces on his boot.

Guiding Orla a few more feet down the hall, Soren hissed under her breath, "The Topaz Kingdom sent Princess Yin, and King Eamon called for the servants to gather in the throne room."

"Why? What?"

Soren seethed, "*Apparently*, Yin was disappointed with the help provided for her, and she wants to *choose her own*. So, you need to get dressed *super* quick and report to Nonna while I handle the dirtier side of this visit. And whatever you do, *don't* let her pick you."

Marlo awkwardly cleared his throat as he straightened, giving his boots a solemn nod of approval. Soren whipped her head towards him in a storm cloud of blonde hair, pinning him with an icy look, her teeth bared in a not-so-friendly smile. Orla pulled her key from her bag, throwing open the door to her room. "Be nice," she grumbled to Soren. "Marlo's my friend."

"Hello, Orla's very tall and handsome *friend*," Soren purred, locking Marlo in her sight. "Get lost."

"*Soren!*" Orla spat, "*Not* nice!"

At the same time, Marlo stuttered, "I'm sorry?"

Soren turned her head slowly, bronze irises blown wide as if to say, '*We absolutely do not have time for this.*'

Orla leveled a flat look back to Soren before smiling tightly at Marlo. "Thanks for today, I had a really great time. I'll come visit you this weekend?"

Marlo's gaze bounced between them before he answered, "Yeah, that sounds good. You know where to find me." He dipped his chin towards Soren, clapping his hands together. "And...okay, I'm getting lost right now."

Exactly one second after Marlo turned away, Soren hustled Orla into her room and shut the door with a flick of her hand. "You have ten minutes before you need to be in front of the throne room doors with the rest of the Oasees servants. Wear the dress I picked."

Orla cursed under her breath, quickly snatching the garment Soren laid out on her bed and hurrying to the bathroom to change.

Dressing in record time, she burst from the bathroom, quickly digging in her satchel to grab the hair oil she purchased. "Why do I need to go if I'm not supposed to be chosen?"

"Well, Princess Yin is a fucking cunt," Soren groused as she helped Orla part her hair down the middle, the pair deftly coiling and braiding each side into a neat twist. "And King Eamon won't tell her to go fuck herself. She expects her servants to be the best of the best and was *disappointed* with the two half-fae that were assigned. She wants someone...."

"She wants pure-blooded fae," Orla finished, catching where Soren was going without her expressly stating it. The longer she lived in the Ruby Kingdom, the more she picked up on the minutiae and subtleties of the ruling class. With practiced movements, she wrapped the ends of each twist with a small band of flexible silver wire.

"Yes, and King Eamon's seen you as Cillian's cupbearer. If you *don't* show up, he'll be suspicious as to why." Soren deftly cinched the ties running down the length of her muted peach dress. Long, tight sleeves, and a ruched bodice that cut high on her throat made Orla feel a bit restricted after so many months of wearing flowing, loose garments. In comparison to the rest of the outfits she wore now, this dress was ridiculously modest – even though it draped artfully over her soft curves, cutting in at her waist. "Cillian said keep your head down and hide your *acat*." Brown gloves appeared from Soren's pocket, and Orla hastily pulled them on. The silky material covered the rest of her *acat*, the color a near perfect match to her skin tone.

Unless someone looked closely, it would appear like Orla didn't have a single tattoo on her hands or fingers.

"You have five minutes." Soren turned for the door, pulling it open. "I suggest you run."

Orla ran after all.

HER FAE BODY WOULD never cease to amaze her as Orla skidded to a halt outside the throne room, quickly slipping into line without catching Nonna's wrath. Fifteen servants stood in front of her – and it took just a glance to confirm they were all fae.

Nonna stood at the closed entrance doors, her hands propped against her hips as she scowled.

"Glad you could join us, Orla Grey."

Orla winced – guess she wasn't as stealthy as she thought. She inclined her head towards the Chamber Mother before scootching out of Nonna's direct sight.

Nonna clapped, jerking the attention of every servant to her. "You will walk in one line parallel to the dais. Do *not* speak unless spoken to, remember to *bow low,* and, whatever you do, do *not* disappoint me - or you'll be sorting rubbish until this time next year."

"Yes, Nonna," the sixteen servants – Orla included – monotoned.

Nonna growled a word to the guard posted at the entrance, and he blanched before hurriedly opening the door. Orla kept her eyes lowered and her gloved hands clasped behind her back as they shuffled in silently.

Once Orla stepped into the throne room, the door shut behind them with a resounding *boom.* A tingle skittered through her as she took her place, eyes downcast, and she knew, without looking, that Cillian was watching her.

Heat rolled through her as her mind flashed back to the mind-numbing kiss they shared in her room, the feel of Cillian's lips on hers causing her breath to pitch more than any sprint through Oasees ever could. Orla bowed deeply with the other servants before rising. She kept her head lowered as instructed but couldn't help peeking up at the dais beneath her lashes.

Three thrones sat on the raised platform now, and the power radiating from them sundered heavily through Orla. She sought out Cillian, drawn to him in an instant. He sat ramrod straight, dressed in Ruby Kingdom ceremonial robes, the high neck buttoned. His locs were pulled back, revealing small, golden studs on his pointed ears. There was a hardness in his face that Orla hadn't seen before, a cruel, calculating awareness that sent a shiver through her belly. Cillian caught her eye, though he flicked his gaze away quickly, angling his head subtly towards his father.

King Eamon sat in the largest chair, dressed similarly to his son – though his robe was deep gold with blood red swirls embroidered into the thick fabric. His face curled into a jeer as Cillian purposedly sighed loudly, leaning back in his throne and settling behind his spoiled and jaded princely mask.

"Choose, Yin, and let's be done with this."

Orla clenched her teeth as her skin tingled with reckless energy, like the pressure during a lightning storm that billowed and bolstered in preparation to unleash the next white-hot strike against the earth.

Orla turned her attention to the occupant of the last throne, Princess Yin of the Topaz Kingdom. Her straight black hair was shorn chin length, swept up on both sides with golden clips that glinted like a crown atop her head. A soft yellow robe, cut to fit every curve of her body, covered most of her ivory skin, though the wide cuffs allowed Orla a glimpse at the jagged blue *acat* covering both of her hands. She was breathtaking - with soft cheekbones, full lips painted copper, and hooded eyes lined with deep black kohl that ended in sharp points below her brows.

Orla swallowed against the lump in her throat, suddenly self-conscious of her rushed make up and outfit. Now, her skin felt slightly sticky from her run through Oasees, her hair more unruly than contained. The gloves felt constricting, as if hiding away her *acat* made her uninteresting.

*"You're staring."* Seysei hummed in her mind. *"And the purpose of the gloves was to keep you from being chosen – remember?"*

Orla kept her head down. She'd never disconnected from Seysei since they spoke in the bazaar. And the dragon was prone to eavesdropping. On her thoughts *and* on the happenings around her.

The pressure in the room sparked as the female cocked her head to the side, the movement smoothly predatory.

Seysei hissed, *"I recommend keeping your distance. She makes King Eamon seem as docile and harmless as your human friend from the bazaar."*

Orla peered through her lashes. Princess Yin rose gracefully from the throne and descended the dais, her robe fanning around her slippers. That rolling power pulsed around the room as the Princess approached the first few servants, each step utterly silent against the tiled floor.

The fire inside of Orla began churning in warning as Yin stopped in front of the female to Orla's left.

"Beautiful," Yin murmured as she slowly extended her hand, tilting the servant's stare up to meet her eyes. Her voice was smooth, seductive, as she smiled prettily at the servant, who gave Yin a small, closed off smile back. With a scoff, Yin dropped her hand. "Yet utterly dull." Her voice fell flat as she glared up at Cillian, who merely narrowed his eyes back.

Orla shortened her breathing, clenching her teeth together as Yin stepped away, towards the servant Orla stood behind outside of the throne room doors. He straightened, his eyes never leaving the ground. "You look fun," Yin cooed as she trailed two fingers down the servant's chest. When the servant remained silent, Yin pulled her hand away as if his stoic demeanor burned her. She shot a mischievous grin towards the dais, before turning back to the servant.

Quicker than Orla could see, Yin drew a thin dagger from the cuff of her robe and flicked it at the male, catching him in the soft part of his shoulder. His pupils blew wide as the shock and pain hit, and he cried out, staggering back a step before falling to his knees, blood pouring out of the dagger wound and splattering the tiles in front of the Princess.

"*Yin,*" King Eamon grunted, a lackluster reprimand that had Yin smirking wickedly, twirling towards the servant, and ripping the bloodied steel out of his shoulder. The male pitched forward with a wail that echoed throughout the room.

Orla stopped breathing. None of the other servants dared move.

"*The Princess just stabbed a servant,*" Orla whispered.

"*Try not to let that happen to you,*" Seysei responded dryly.

Orla chanced a look up, shooting a wide-eyed plea towards Cillian, but he was no longer looking at her, his hands fisted in his lap as he glared at Yin.

Princess Yin turned to King Eamon and shrugged. "He won't work either, I'm afraid." She looked down her nose at the whimpering male. "Too breakable."

The other servants stood as still as possible to avoid Yin's attention. Orla prayed no one would be dumb enough to bolt. But they were all looking up now, warily watching the Princess as she strolled leisurely down the line.

The pressure palpated around Yin, right as the Princess's dark eyes locked onto Orla. Orla set her jaw in a grim line, refusing to allow a single flicker of weakness to show.

Her fire ignited in response, yanking deep inside her in a whirlwind of anger. Steeling herself, Orla kept her hands clasped behind her back, though the warming against her palm told her that flames were desperate for release. Yin smirked and took one step towards Orla –

"Enough, Yin," Cillian barked.

To Orla's complete surprise, Yin backed away, turning to look up at Cillian as he stormed off the dais, a brooding, dark expression on his handsome face.

Cillian shoved his hands in his pockets before jerking his chin towards three male servants furthest away from Orla in line. "You three, please escort the Topaz Princess towards her chambers."

Yin pouted as the servants bowed and stepped forward. "*I* wanted to pick."

"Too bad," Cillian grumbled, his brown eyes flashing with lethal...*irritation*?

"*He seems more annoyed than angry,*" Orla said into her mind, feeling the steady presence of Seysei on the other end of their shimmering golden connection.

A huff back was the dragon's only reply.

The throne room seemed to hold in a collective breath as Yin took a step towards Cillian. Orla's gaze darted between the two as her fire ebbed and banked inside of her, wavering on attacking or smoldering out. Heartbeat thudding almost painfully in her ears, she appraised Yin's movements, watched Cillian's body language, as he stood rigidly in front of the Princess, a muscle feathering through his angular jaw.

With a saccharine smile, Yin raised her hand, softly stroking Cillian's cheek. Orla felt the fire leap back up into her throat as the Princess looked up into Cillian's eyes, her body melting against his chest.

"Whatever my betrothed thinks is best," Yin amended, sliding her fingers between Cillian's locs at the base of his neck and pulling his mouth down to meet hers. She kissed him slowly before replying, "I *guess* those three will work nicely."

Orla stilled.

*What the fuck?*

# CHAPTER FIFTY-SIX
## LAURENT

THIS DEEP INTO THE cavernous tunnels behind the waterfalls of Florra, it was impossible to tell if it was night or day. Blue will-o-wisps bobbed in front of them, bathing their path forward in an eerie luminescence that threw disorienting shadows against jagged rock walls. Sparrow walked wearily at his hip; the pair silent.

They'd been travelling down this particular passageway for two full days, only stopping when Laurent's fire illuminated a stream of trickling water to refill their canteens, or to lean over and catch their breath after a steep incline.

Laurent and Sparrow searched most of the hidden caverns behind the waterfalls already, where either short tunnels dead ended into stone, or rocky, underground paths slithered and twisted for miles from one end of the thirteen waterfalls to the other, and they'd groan loudly with sheer disappointment when their boots felt that first crunch of grass. Then, Sparrow would curse – each one more creative and fouler than the last - and the two of them would trek through the Florra forest once more to find the next cave entrance.

It was furiously mind numbing.

Laurent slowed his steps and uncorked his canteen before tipping the tepid water to his lips. Sparrow paused, turning her exhausted eyes to him before pulling the stopper out of her own bottle.

"Let's walk for another hour and then set up camp. Try to get some sleep for a few hours." Laurent said quietly, his voice hoarse from unuse and dehydration. They hadn't found any water in a full day, and conserving their last canteens was growing into a new frustration. If they drained their flasks, Sparrow would be forced to wane them back out to the forest, and they'd have to do this entire walk again.

It was too dangerous to wane directly *into* an underground passageway, and Laurent was concerned even conjuring a portal could accidentally trigger a rockslide or cave in. Sparrow radiated unease that grew by the day, and Laurent knew his own emotional state fared no better.

This was fucking *disheartening*, and the lack of sun made them befuddled and irritable. Their eyes were so accustomed to the dark now that whenever they waned home to refill their supplies and rest for a few hours, they squinted against the daylight, eyes stinging and watering, before waiting until nightfall to retrace their steps.

The first few days, when their spirits were high, Sparrow and Laurent talked non-stop, swapping stories and laughter, keeping their eyes on the walls around them, hoping to spot some old runes that could point them in the right direction.

But as the days turned into weeks, and weeks began stacking up, they fell into a brooding muteness, both of them quietly losing hope that their search for the Book of Faune would be successful. Neither wanting to admit aloud that this could be a waste of time.

Their visit to the Obsidian Palace to support Esmeray in her bloody council meeting cost them two days of searching. Sparrow would've waned them back to Florra immediately after the meeting, but the

Queen took one look at the pair and decreed they were absolutely staying the night to eat something that wasn't cooked over a campfire, and sleep in a damned bed.

Sparrow sighed harshly, recapping her canteen and shoving it down the strap of her pack. The sound of her footfalls and the sighing of their leathers against sweat soaked skin were the only noises once more as Laurent forced his feet to follow Sparrow down the stone passage.

A small rock jostled loose under Laurent's steps, and he mindlessly kicked it along the path, hearing it roll and clack against the uneven ground as it disappeared into the darkness beyond.

Another few minutes of hiking in silence and the pebble was once again under his boot. Laurent shuffled his feet before spearing four weeks of exasperation into the stone. It arched into the air with his well-placed punt, the blue flame illuminating its trajectory as it sailed far into the abyss before them, the echo resounding against the rocky ground - bouncing and clattering out of sight.

The air seemed to pause.

A shudder of energy stirred around them, an unnatural gust of wind breezing through the tunnel and ruffling Sparrow's golden hair. Laurent's heart thudded as he stilled, straining his ears to pick up any sound.

A soft *tick* made him growl in warning as metallic hued flames sputtered to life in crystal sconces along the walls two hundred feet ahead of them. Sparrow gasped.

Laurent threw out an arm, chest heaving, as more small fires flared on either side of the tunnel, triggered by the rolling rock.

"Magic," Sparrow whispered, rallying green power around her hands, sending her own light probing ahead of them. With Sparrow's power weaving with Laurent's, they could make out a circular pattern of torchlight directly ahead of them.

They crept forward slowly, Laurent taking the lead, his blue flames dancing down the length of the broadsword he unstrapped from his back. Behind him, Sparrow mirrored the move, her curved blade rippling radiant green.

The tunnel widened ahead of them and Laurent sunk into the Spy Master mindset that served him well over the years. *Stay alert. Stay vigilant. Find a secondary exit.* The decades of training settled onto his shoulders as he swept his eyes quickly over the rock walls.

*Stay vigilant. Know your exits. Protect.*

*Protect Sparrow. Protect.*

He chanted it in his mind, an uneasy panic rising into his throat as his mantra warped, the thought of stepping into the unknown with his mate churning inside of his soul.

Protect. *Protect. Protect Sparrow. Stay. Vigilant.*

*What was he missing?* Laurent darted his eyes around, taking in the opening passageway, the flickering flames, the *walls.*

"Stop," Laurent breathed, raising his hand and holding his sword in front of him, the blue fire illuminating the jagged rock – and the small, carved runes that lay etched in precise lines.

"Witch runes," Sparrow muttered, leaning closer to peer at the symbols. "The runes Lenna saw in the Prism were witch runes."

"How can you tell?"

Sparrow shuddered. "I can feel their pull against my magic. If we go any further, the runes may nullify our *acatis* completely."

Laurent steadied his breathing, everything in his training screaming at him to mark the location, turn back, and wane out of here, bring more power with them on the next trip.

"We should turn back." Laurent announced, "If those are magic nullifying witch runes, we should return with gargoyle support. Maybe bring Esmeray and Keerian. They *could* be a different sort of rune, but we don't know what exactly - "

Sparrow's breath hitched. Ice coated his veins as he realized she'd taken a single step in front of him to take a closer look at the walls and the green light glimmering against the length of her sword vanished.

She whirled to face him, fear leaping into her wide blue eyes as she raised her arms and bleated, "*Don't -* "

But he was already moving, driven by the soul tie roaring inside of him at the sight of her fear, the color leeching out of her beautiful face.

Laurent lunged for her, and, as if he crossed an invisible threshold, he felt his magic die out. The flames enveloping his own blade sputtered into nothingness, bathing them in shadow, the faint torchlights flickering in the distance only emitting a sliver of light.

He gripped her hand and tugged Sparrow to his chest, pulling her back towards where the runes didn't reach – only to slam into a solid, invisible barricade.

Not only did the witch runes nullify their fae magic, but they were also trapped *in* the runic power emitting from the wall, unable to turn back.

"The runes are wards like the Soul Keeper's Cell," he hissed.

Sparrow's eyes widened as she lifted a trembling hand, her palm flattening against the invisible magic. It didn't give an inch. Laurent tried to call his magic to his fingers, but it was as if his *acat* was...gone.

"These feel different than the nullifying runes below the Obsidian Palace," Sparrow said. "They feel...older. More..." She trailed off, head swiveling, as another series of *ticks* resounded in the air around them.

The silver edged flames dotting the cavern before them intensified with a roar, funnels of fire shooting up the walls, chasing the shadows away as their surroundings came into view. Laurent blinked against the brightness, his eyes blurring and focusing against the harsh burst of light.

"Laurent." Sparrow's soft voice jarred his vision into place. "Look."

They stood at the edge of a large, circular grotto. Gleaming clusters of white gemstones dotted the high walls, and a draft of moonlight beamed down from a hundred feet above, filtered in through a narrow slit in the earth above. And in the middle of the cavern, resting against a raised podium of crystallized quartz, sat a small, golden bound book.

Laurent sucked in a harsh breath. "I would bet my favorite robe *that* is the Book of Faune."

Sparrow shot him a withering look as she lowered her sword. With expert eyes he surveyed the rest of the cave, noting that the only exit was truly the crevice high above them. Directly above the Book of Faune.

He fiddled with his ring, but with the runes carved against every inch of space, it was nothing but a pretty piece of jewelry.

No magic.

No way of telling anyone where they were.

No portal.

No waning.

Sparrow turned towards the book.

"Wait." Laurent stepped in front of his mate. "We don't know if grabbing the book will trigger anything."

"Well, do you have any other ideas?" Sparrow stalked forward. "Because I, for one, would love to grab this goddess-damned book and see if it creates some sort of magical door to get us the fuck out of here."

"Hiking has really expanded your cursing fortitude."

"I grew up with Esmeray." Sparrow waved him off as she proceeded towards the Book of Faune. "She has the filthiest mouth I've ever encountered. I just want to sleep in our own bed tonight."

Laurent agreed with that entire statement.

The pair circled the podium twice before Laurent deemed it safe. "I'll grab it," he offered. Sparrow nodded grimly, her eyes never leaving the unnaturally shimmering cover.

The Book of Faune sat in the exact center of the crystal formation. Balancing his sword in one hand, Laurent reached gingerly towards the Vessel Book, careful not to cut himself against the razor-sharp quartz that glowed in the unnatural light emitting from the torches against the stone walls.

His fingers only managed to skim the book's spine when a white-hot burst of agony lanced through his shoulder.

Sparrow screamed as the arrow struck. Laurent staggered back, blood pouring from his wound, splattering against the podium, dripping down its length to pool on the earthy floor of the grotto. Adrenaline shot through his veins to mute the nauseating wave of pain as he crouched, quickly assed the arrow shaft in his shoulder, and snapped it with his other hand, throwing the broken piece to the ground.

The arrowhead stayed embedded in the soft juncture of skin between his arm and chest but keeping it in would decrease the amount of blood loss.

"Hello, Spy Master." A female voice crooned from above them. "Thank you for finding the Book of Faune for us. King Eamon has been looking for it for a *long* time."

Laurent scrambled to his feet, cradling his injured arm to his chest, before adjusting the hilt of his sword in his good hand. Sparrow was at his side in an instant, her own sword raised, as the three missing spies from the Ruby Kingdom flew down from the crevice above.

# CHAPTER FIFTY-SEVEN
# SPARROW

They were surrounded, outnumbered, and outmatched with the witch runes nullifying access to their *acatis.*

Not to mention Laurent was bleeding profusely at her side, the hot tang of his blood invading her senses. He stood steady, but the continuous spatter of red that dripped down his arm told Sparrow that *something* was hindering his healing abilities. Either the witch runes *also* stopped their capabilities of fast healing, or that arrowhead had been coated in poison.

"Not as tough cut off from your *acatis,* are you?" The female snickered. Her dark blonde hair was shaved close to her skull, showing off a set of earthy green horns that swept up from her brows and curved slightly inward at the tips. Her keen eyes narrowed as she sniffed in disproval. "That's the problem with magic. It's nothing more than a crutch. Take it away, and what's left?"

"Let's wrap this up, Rinci." The mountain sized gargoyle standing to her right growled, his sand brown wings ruffling. "We need to get back to Ingotheria."

"Shut up, Smoth," Rinci demanded. She was much shorter than the two male spies but held an air of authority that had the other gargoyles recoiling. "King Eamon wanted the book. But what do you think he'll give us for the Book of Faune, the Heir Absolute, *and* the Spy Master?"

Smoth cocked his head, appraising Sparrow with a newfound predatory gaze. She bared her teeth. His lips curled in an unnerving smile as he said, "She's Queen Esmeray's *Heir?* But she's so small."

"Everyone's small compared to you, bonehead." Rinci snarked.

The gargoyle with dirt-brown wings standing to Rinci's left huffed a laugh. But he never took his eyes off of Laurent, a bloodthirsty glint in his yellowish eyes. Laurent flashed his fangs as he noticed the male. As if they knew each other from a previous fight. And this was where the score would be settled.

Smoth smiled gleefully, noting the yellow-eyed gargoyle's line of sight. "What a reunion for you, Hamm."

Laurent shifted in front of Sparrow, shielding her with his body.

A lump formed in her throat.

"Queen Esmeray must not trust many beings," Rinci continued casually, stepping forward slowly. "She has her *Heir* and her Heir's *mate* squatting in caves, doing her dirty work for what? What do you get for this?"

A voice murmured into Sparrow's mind, a voice that trembled as powerful as waves crashing against a rock-lined shore, as delicate as the first sprout of a flower bursting from its soil bed. *Get the Book.*

Flicking her eyes towards the Book of Faune still nestled against its podium, Sparrow swallowed, steeling herself as she stepped back from the protection of Laurent's side. Something in her soul screaming at her that this wasn't his fight.

It was hers.

Sparrow darted away, twisting around the back of the cluster of quartz to cut off the female from the book. Her sword slashed out, catching

Rinci by surprise for a single beat before she jumped back with a shout, meeting Sparrow head on with her own blade.

"Subdue the Spy Master!" Rinci shouted as Sparrow shoved her back another foot, extending the distance between Rinci and the Book of Faune, but also expanding her own distance from her mate. Her heart cried out as she caught a glimpse of the two gargoyle males launching across the grotto floor to Laurent, curved swords raised and retribution shining in their eyes. He beat them both back with a backhanded swing, his arm pouring blood with the movement.

Her quick glance at Laurent cost her. Sparrow snarled as Rinci rammed the side of her curved horn into her shoulder. Sparrow deflected the brunt of the blow as she dropped to her knees, swiping her sword out to catch Rinci in the ankle.

Rinci flared out her wings as she jumped, avoiding the blade, and kicked, catching Sparrow in the chest with her boot. The air whipped out of Sparrow's lungs at the impact, but she rolled, pushing her free hand against her sternum, taking a gasping breath of air as her vision wavered for a split second, a silvery sheen clouding the corner of her sight.

Not silver – *grey*.

And as Sparrow cried out in surprise, Merrick tucked in his wings and slammed against the cavern's floor in front of Rinci, his twin short swords unsheathed, as he snarled, *"Get the fuck away from my mate."*

# CHAPTER FIFTY-EIGHT
## ORLA

FLAMES DANCED ACROSS HER knuckles, swiftly burning away the gloves that hid her *acat*. But it was nothing compared to the inferno turning her stupid, fae heart to ash.

Unseeing, she barreled down the corridor of the Oasees residence, her mind churning as the vision of Yin kissing Cillian played on a numbingly continuous loop. She'd been a *fool* to think the fucking Crown Prince of the goddess-damned Ruby Kingdom wanted *her*. He was betrothed to a beautiful and powerful fae Princess. He didn't want Orla.

And Orla sure as fuck no longer wanted *him*.

She hadn't realized the walls around her heart crumbled until they began rebuilding themselves brick by brick. Seysei slunk around the golden thread of her *acat*, so she shoved a wall up there, too. She wanted to feel this betrayal *alone*.

Fuck. Cillian.

She flung her door open, the wood around the knob letting out a groaning sizzle upon contact with her hand. Her dress sleeves were in tatters, pieces of the fabric floating to the floor as her magic rammed through her, frustrated and backstabbed, aligned and aflame with her weeping soul.

As she tore over the threshold, a prickling sensation coated her throat like poison. Whirling around with a snarl she found Cillian backlit against the glass paned balcony door, appraising her with hard eyes, his hands shoved in his pockets, the buttons at the base of his throat undone. He took three steps towards her, stopping abruptly as golden flames shot up her fists, curling around her forearms like furious snakes.

"Get. The. *Fuck*. Out." Orla hissed, pointing at the door behind her. Embers popped, swirling in the air, turning from red to black as they hit the floor. The temperature in the room elevated until she saw heat waves shimmering between them. Or maybe that was just her temper hitting its boiling point.

Cillian raised his hands in mock surrender, though his mouth set in a grim line. His eyes darkened further as his gaze slowly roved from the churning fires spitting from Orla's clenched hands to the sneer Orla knew twisted against her lips.

They stood their ground - two sides of the room, two opposing lives. Cheery voices drifted from the oasis below, muffled and distant, though the only sounds Orla could make out was the crackling of her magic, the cracking of her heart, and the screech of betrayal ringing in her ears.

With a short curse, Cillian broke first to stalk closer, slashing his hand out as he neared. A red barrier flared to life and seeped over the walls, effectively cutting off the sounds of the Palace around them. Her bedroom door slammed shut. "What *exactly* are you going to do if I don't leave?"

The audacity caused Orla to scoff as she closed the distance between them further. "I'll go tell your *betrothed* that you're visiting my room. I'll tell her you kissed me." She cocked her head. "The Princess seems like the territorial type. I'm sure there would be a reckoning aimed directly at your throat. I only hope I'd get to watch as she ripped it out. She'd probably build you a *very* dramatic funeral pyre, too."

"And then what would you do?" Cillian growled, lowering his face an inch closer, his warm breath caressing her cheek, causing her heart to flip wildly inside her chest. "Once you push me away, destroy me, and watch my ashes blow in the wind? What would *you* do next?"

Fuck.

Orla solidified her resolve, forcing her mind to replay the scene of Yin kissing Cillian again to spark her rage further. It simmered at the surface, though the sharp edge of fury dulled - much to her annoyance as Cillian rumbled out a gruff breath.

She...may have overestimated being able to stay *that* angry at him without hearing his side.

The alarm bells pealing through her mind dimmed as she fought internally. Cillian's lips pouted as his gaze hardened into something unreadable. *He is betrothed,* she reminded herself, trying to stroke that anger again, trying to wrap her head around the male in the throne room being the same one as the male currently standing in front of her. What if he used her just as she feared? Stringing her along, offering her a life here, *kissing her* like he was starved.

But he was here. In front of her.

He smelled like cinnamon.

And he looked at her as if he wanted nothing more than to take her in his arms.

The fire at her hands banked.

"Orla," Cillian croaked, reaching out slowly to cup her chin in his hand, "I know it sounds ridiculously cliché, but Yin means *nothing* to me. We've been betrothed since we were eighteen. It's nothing more than a political alliance for my father. One I will break happily once I take the throne."

"I bet you tell that to all the other females." Orla retorted half-heartedly. She sort-of attempted to jerk her chin away, but even that was a feeble attempt as she greedily drank in the desire that flared through his eyes - the *need.*

"Only the ones that wash up on the shores of the Ruby Kingdom. And *only* the ones I am madly, overwhelmingly, annoyingly, and frustratingly drawn to," Cillian whispered, his thumb brushing her lower lip.

Orla's pulse stumbled.

The internal war was over inside of her, the walls around her heart already detonating in silence, embarrassed they'd tried to rebuild in the first place.

"I wanted to keep you out of the throne room today, but my father stated *all* servants of Oasees and if I hid you, he'd know, and then he'd dig into your life – our connection. Yin is a ruthless ruler who delights in pain and profits from tragedy. Her *acat* is the only reason no one's ever challenged her family for the throne. If she got one *whiff* of rebellion, she'd kill everyone in the general area without question."

"Soren wasn't there," Orla started, her eyes widening.

"Soren's known Yin for years." Cillian shook his head. "Unsurprisingly, they hate each other. Yin would've been affronted if Soren was even an *option* to serve her. My father thought it would be better to divert *his* personal cupbearer away since the last time Soren and Yin were in the same throne room, they almost destroyed it."

Orla narrowed her eyes, her chin still held captive in Cillian's broad hand, and tried another approach. "What did Yin do to make you hate her?"

A beat of silence stretched between them as Cillian lowered his head, breaking her gaze as if he needed a moment to collect himself. Orla winced, opening her mouth to take the question back, but Cillian answered quietly, "Yin played a very pivotal role in ensuring my mother's death. She may be a Princess in title – but don't let that fool you. *She* is the true ruler of the Topaz Kingdom. Her parents are merely puppets too terrified to reprimand her."

"I'm so sorry." Orla's throat dried out. "I should've talked to you before going all...fiery." She trailed off as Cillian's hands slid from her chin to the nape of her neck. He pulled her flush to his body.

Cillian swallowed hard. "*I'm* sorry, Orla. You don't need to apologize for how you felt. I should've considered Yin's past antics and anticipated it. I'm already adjusting plans for you while she's here, and Dimas said she's leaving immediately after the Equinox. Seven days. Then she's gone."

"You should've told me you were betrothed," Orla chastised softly, brushing her lips against the base of Cillian's throat – as a tease and as a warning - yet the warmth of his skin had the complete opposite effect. Suddenly, she was more interested in Cillian's body than her own steely resolve or list of questions. She gave in to the want, licking the column of his throat. Gods, he tasted divine. Like the deep red wine Soren smuggled from the King's personal collection.

"I should have," Cillian agreed, as his hand tightened against the nape of her neck, tilting her face up to his own.

"You should make it up to me."

"You're very much right."

"I can think of a few - "

His mouth was on hers in an instant, their lips crashing together. She couldn't get enough of him – his taste, his *feel* against her, the way he read her every thought before she even conjured it.

A moan slipped free, and she arched into his touch as he feverishly undid the laces at the back of her dress, helping her shimmy out of the burnt fabric – neither of them separating their mouths long enough to successfully get the entire layer of skirting down her legs. As the dress bunched around her waist, Orla began tugging at the buttons on his robe, wanting his chest exposed to the dim glow of her room, wanting every barrier between them eradicated.

They broke apart long enough to mutually conclude undressing each other was more of a hinderance than a productive idea. Cillian expertly untied the laces on his black pants, and Orla pulled the rest of her skirt off, flinging the gown across the room to land in a heap by the armoire.

A second later, his clothes joined her discarded garments, and he was lifting her in his arms, their kisses sloppy as their hands roved over every inch of each other's bare skin. She bracketed her legs around his waist, feeling the length of him digging against the underside of her thigh. Her gasps grew louder, more frantic, as his teeth found the sensitive flesh of her throat. She tilted her head back, baring herself to him, feeling his tongue, his lips, the coarseness of his facial hair, the graze of his fangs roving her jawline.

His fingers dug into her backside, his other palm sliding up her spine, cradling her to him, gripping the back of her neck as he kissed her harder.

And then, she hit the soft mattress and he followed her down, settling between her knees, her legs spreading to accommodate his hips. She stuttered a breath, watching him watch her through heavy lids.

Her eyes widened as she took in the blood red ink of his *acat,* a striking, masculine version of her own, with thick curves and slashes that covered his chest and travelled over his shoulder, down his left bicep, stopping at a sharp point at the crook of his arm. Orla reached out and traced the design, letting the tips of her trembling fingers travel down the lines, pausing, for a moment, over the beat of his thundering heart.

"Gods, Orla," Cillian groaned, his eyes glazed with desire and she dipped her head just slightly, daring a smirk up at him from under her lashes. His lips were red and puffy from their violent kissing, his locs undone from the leather ring that held them out of his face. She stretched her arms over her head, arching her back, feeling his eyes burn along every inch of her naked body. A strangled growl escaped his throat, and Orla's breathing accelerated as he slowly kissed up her bare leg, his strong hands kneading into her flesh as he climbed over her, holding her gently against the bed. "You are radiant. *Fuck*."

Orla playfully crinkled her nose, "Poetry isn't your strong suit I take it."

Cillian paused his ascent of her body to wink. "Poetry is for males who don't know how to fuck."

"Prove it, Prince."

His eyes flared with wicked intent as Cillian wasted no time doing just that. His hands slipped up her sides, rubbing her hips before gripping her ankle to hook around him. Orla used her legs to pull him closer, feeling the tip of his shaft brush against her. Gods, she was soaked, desperate to have him inside her, surrounding her, consuming her.

From the look of pure ache etched in the planes of Cillian's face, he felt the same, letting out a groan as he fisted the head of his cock, swiping it through her wetness.

She wriggled her hand between them, gently wrapping her fingers around his length, causing Cillian to lean down to whisper in her ear, "If you want to stop at any time, tell me. I will not take offense."

"I want you to fuck me, before I burst into flames," Orla ordered breathlessly, though Cillian's words warmed her soul. A good male that knew and understood boundaries, that carried that virtue and allowed her to be in control, while still wringing every ounce of pleasure from her... the only thing in danger was her fluttering, needy, heart.

Without missing a beat, Cillian grinned, wrapping his hand around her fingers and sinking into her an inch, and then another, and another, his lips parting, a raw groan dragging from his chest. Orla stilled at the intrusion, his overwhelming size, his girth, panting as her body adjusted. But that hunger, that instinctive urgency for all of him, had Orla squeezing her fingers around the rest of his length in a silent request for more.

Cillian's fingers threaded through hers, and he pulled her palm to his lips, pressing a gentle kiss to her feverish skin as he thrust inside her to the hilt, the two of them loosening a shuddering exhale as their bodies melded together. Slowly, he pulled out, before setting a pace that had Orla's core tightening, release coiling, driving her to the precipice of maddening delight.

She matched his rhythm, her hips rising in sync as he pounded into her, each stroke eliciting a whimpering moan to escape her lips. Their eyes locked. And when his body tensed, Orla felt hers follow, the two racing for the edge of bliss together.

As Cillian let out a hoarse shout, Orla careened over that breaking point, barreling down into the most deliciously vicious orgasm she'd ever experienced. Her vision blacked out as she threw her head back, her body bucking on its own accord as every one of her muscles locked, her rough keening muffled as Cillian's lips found hers, holding her through the throes of her climax.

When the last shivers of release cooled, leaving a sheen of sweat between them, and their breathing evened out, Cillian slowly slid out of her, padding to the bathroom and returning with a warm cloth. He wiped her down slowly, peppering kisses against her flushed skin as he worked.

"Wow," Orla whispered, her eyelids suddenly heavy as sleep tugged her down, "I'm very glad you aren't a poet."

Cillian chuckled, pulling the covers over her and tucking her. "Told you."

He headed to the bathroom, undoubtedly to wash off himself, but turned his head back once to look over at her, and Orla heard him say something softly, as if uttered under his breath, but she was already sinking into slumber, her mind too languid to process it.

As sleep rolled over her, Orla felt a smile tug at the corners of her mouth, and she decided that it may not be so bad to fall in love with the Crown Prince of the Ruby Kingdom after all.

# CHAPTER FIFTY-NINE
# SPARROW

Merrick positioned himself between Sparrow and Rinci as another gargoyle shot down from the crevice high above, a bolt snapping from the crossbow in his arms.

Smoth grunted and dove away from Laurent, narrowly missing the broad point of the projectile. With a *crack,* the arrowhead buried itself into the cavern wall, the impact spraying chunks of quartz and rock through the grotto. The gargoyle hit the ground and rolled, coming up on his knee and aiming the crossbow again in a blur of wings and wood, loosening the next bolt with deadly precision. It passed clean through Smoth's wing, causing the spy to howl and launch himself at the newcomer.

Laurent hadn't wavered from his fight with Hamm, the two trading increasingly brutal blows that looked terrifyingly evenly matched. Sparrow wavered, her panic barreling through her as Hamm dodged a slash of Laurent's sword, parrying with a downward swipe that had Laurent retreating a step before juking, sending the spy crashing into the wall horns first.

Rinci ignored the chaotic combat happening across the room to level an utterly bored look at Merrick. "I thought the Spy Master was her mate," she mused, jutting her chin towards Sparrow before shrugging. "No matter. If you're her mate also, we only need to kill one of you and the others will fall. Bringing you *all* alive seems...tedious. I'm sure you understand."

Sparrow scrambled to her feet, gripping her sword in her hand until her knuckles whitened. Her head rang with pain, a trickle of blood trailing down her temple as she fought to control her breathing. With precise steps, Merrick circled Rinci, his cooly calculating stare sizing up the female in front of them. Sparrow took a shaky step towards him, but Merrick shook his head, "Get the book, Sparrow," he said quietly, his furious glare never leaving Rinci as she dared prowl closer, "leave the trash for us to clean up."

Rinci scowled, baring her teeth as hatred flared in her eyes. Sparrow turned and bolted for the Book of Faune as it innocently glimmered on its podium, unaware of the bloody battles crashing through the grotto around it. She heard the clash of steel as Merrick and Rinci made first impact.

She skidded to a halt in front of the podium, her hands frantically grappling for purchase against the quartz to slow her momentum. Scrambling, ears ringing as the screeches of metal on metal jarred through her, she reached blindly for the book.

A hum filled the air, building in pitch, a silvery spark snapping against her outstretched fingers. Sparrow snatched her hand back with a gasp. Before her, the Book of Faune began to glow iridescent, throwing a prism of colors against the wall.

*Hello, Daughter of Life,* that voice pealed in her mind, the sound as soft as a bed of summer grass, as commanding as the gravity that controlled the ocean tides. *Have you come to me at last?*

"We do *not* have time for you to be weirdly sentient right now," Sparrow rasped through gritted teeth to the Book of Faune, steadying herself. She lashed her hand out, anticipating the quick burn, grabbing the book's spine, freeing it from its crystal podium.

The air stilled.

A thundering tremor echoed through the cavern as pure white light poured from the Book of Faune and seeped across the stone floor, swathing the room in an effervescent shine. Sparrow darted her eyes from Merrick to Laurent, but neither seemed to notice the rolling waves of ...of *magic*... spreading across the ground, pooling out in shallow ripples.

*Only you can see it, I'm afraid.*

Sparrow whirled around, coming face to face with –

"Faune," Sparrow whispered, hastily dropping into an off-balanced curtsy as the Goddess of Life smiled, inclining her head towards Sparrow in divine confirmation. The goddess was bathed in a soft glow, melding the light to her body, throwing her skin, face, and clothes in a pallor of icy silver. Faune's unbound hair fell in waves down to her bare feet as she floated above the floor. A kind expression graced the goddess's face as she extended a hand to Sparrow.

Sparrow's breath hitched as she clasped the book tighter to her chest, shooting a glance back toward Laurent and Merrick, "I – my mates -"

"They will be fine," Faune said gently, her feet gracefully touching down on the floor. "I only need to speak with you for a moment."

Sparrow opened her mouth, but no words came out. The Goddess of Life stood in front of her, that ethereal expression non blinking on her face as she waited. "Okay," Sparrow breathed, reaching her free hand out towards Faune.

There was a flare of that same, pure light, and Sparrow squeezed her eyes shut against its brilliance. With a flash, the din of fighting was gone, replaced with the trilling song of distant birds and the quiet rustle of the wildflowers that circled her, spreading for miles in every direction. Sparrow gaped as she ripped her eyes from the beautiful landscape back to the goddess standing next to her.

Now, Faune stood out in color, her golden skin flushed pink, her silvery robes replaced with a resplendent sage gown that held sentience of its own as it fluttered and danced in the sweet-smelling spring breeze. Only the goddess's hair kept the silver hue, though now it lay braided into an intricate design that wove down her back, showcasing pointed ears – longer and sharper at the tips than any ears Sparrow ever saw on a fae before.

"Are you...fae?" Sparrow asked, her fingers subconsciously tracing the shell of her own ear.

"No." Faune replied, "Gods may choose any form they wish when they cross into a different realm, though as we remain sealed in our realms, we settled into our favorites. My sister holds a very...*unique* approach to hers, as I am sure Queen Esmeray has shared with you, Sparrow."

"You know my name."

"Of course, and I would dare to assume you understand why you're here."

*Am I a Vessel?* Sparrow blocked the thought from her mind, not wanting to travel down that path. Sparrow looked around again, an uneasy feeling slithering into her gut. "Where are we?"

"The past," Faune said simply, "Though it is a memory. My book holds enough of my magic to allow me to speak with you through it, though my physical form is in Aurramere."

Sparrow tensed, warily watching the goddess as she stooped down, kneeling in a patch of wildflowers dancing in the breeze. "Sit," Faune patted the ground next to her. "I would like to tell you a story, about two sisters who loved each other very much."

Sparrow hesitated. "Esmeray told me about you and Phades, and how you came earthside. I know that story. Um..." She trailed off, praying that the goddess took no offense as she shifted her weight from one foot to the other, "I'm so sorry, and don't want to be rude, but I need to go back, I need to help my mates."

Faune beamed, as if Sparrow passed a test she didn't know existed. "Your heart is in the right place, Sparrow. But the story I want to tell you is not about my sister and I. This story is about you and *your* sister, Briar."

A crisp wind blustered past as Sparrow froze, appraising the goddess among the wildflowers with a renewed and careful apprehension. "What do you know about Briar and I? Briar passed away when I was young."

Faune only kept smiling, patting the ground next to her. Sparrow dragged her eyes around once more before her heart threatened to beat out of her chest on its own accord at the mention of Briar. Sparrow sat, the dream with Briar a month ago crossing her mind. *It was supposed to be me.* The Briar in her dream had said that. The wind whipping around Sparrow intensified.

"Gods and goddesses are not infallible," Faune started, a forlorn bleakness crossing her beautiful face. "When Briar and you were born, I *felt* the aura surrounding you two. It was strong, undimmable, unbreakable. Your family came from a long line of healers, but I saw your essence as babes, and I knew that I wanted to gift my *acat* to both of you. But it's difficult to disrupt lineage magic, to bestow onto a being when their familial line is so steadfast in a different god's power. I hadn't bestowed my gifts onto a being since the God War, and I felt a yearning to begin again, to begin anew. I begged the God of Health and Healers to allow me to gift you both my magic. After a time, Balint agreed – though he only let me to bestow my gifts onto one of you."

Faune bowed her head, a mournful expression tugging the corners of her lips down. As if the story truly upset her. "I chose Briar."

"Briar was your Vessel?" Sparrow asked, her chest tightening at the pang of loss that curled through her heart as she uttered Briar's name.

"No," Faune corrected, shaking her head, the silvery strands of hair coiling through the flowers at her sides. "I had no desire to create a Vessel. I only wished to give my gifts of plant magic, of growth and vibrancy and blossoms to Briar. The history surrounding my god power is exaggerated through retellings. I would've never survived as a young goddess earthside during the God War without Phades. My sister protected me by bolstering my own image through careful illusions and crafty magics that *seemed* to be my own power, until the other gods and goddesses backed down, cautious of my true gifts."

Sparrow ran her fingers through the flowers surrounding her, though she felt none of the energy she usually felt when she touched nature. It felt more like weaving her fingers through silk, the flowers nothing more than a backdrop to this memory.

"I didn't know Briar had been poisoned until Phades called out to me that a being was trapped in a death-sleep, her soul flickering into the halls of Minmere. Phades sensed my power coiling through Briar's unmanifested *acat* and projected herself into Aurramere as an illusion. She was curious to the importance of the faeling who'd begun following her around, unafraid of the Goddess of Death, pulling at her robes and trying to touch her horns, wanting to know what she meant to me."

Faune's shoulders sagged, as if even the goddess herself felt that weight of grief. "I was crushed, but Phades asked if I wished to take the gifts back, to bestow upon another. Phades told me the faeling would be leaving the living realm soon – that it was only a matter of time before she succumbed to the effects of poison. With her magic, Phades pulled a projection of me into Minmere, so I could ask Briar if that would be alright. When a faeling passes before their *acat* manifests, Phades will appear to that particular god, asking the same question. Typically, the god takes their piece of magic back to wait until they find another to gift it to. But I decided my gifts would stay with me again for a while, the delicate life of Briar made me less enthused to bestow upon another being."

Faune slipped into silence, staring off into the horizon, where the sun had begun to descend, throwing the field of wildflowers into hues of vibrant pinks and orange. "Briar agreed. She was so young, and *so* sweet. She only knew I was sad and wanted to help me. I plucked the unused *acat* from her soul, but before I could sever it from her and secure it back into myself, Briar froze, her eyes rolled back into her head and she began seizing, right there on the floor of Minmere. I panicked, thinking that I was hurting her by removing the *acat,* but when I went to press the magic back into Briar, it was gone."

"Earthside, you may have felt a sharp stab of pain, or a sting. But that moment, when Briar was floating on the precipice of death, you touched her, and your essence as twins confused my magic. My gift transferred to *you,* as did a sliver of Briar's own soul. The magic that was meant for Briar, then meant to be returned to me, buried in *you*. It felt your essence and slipped through my fingers, twining through the strong healer magic you were destined to inherit from Balint."

Sparrow felt hot tears gather in her eyes, slipping free quickly to coat her cheeks. She choked back a sob, remembering that moment, one hundred years ago, when she held Briar's hand for the last time, when that jolt of electricity slammed into her, when her sister finally passed.

She turned her tear-streaked face towards the Goddess, the words coming out breathless as she said, "I didn't know. For decades I thought I dreamed it – that my mind conjured up the pain because I couldn't comprehend the agony of losing Briar so young... and I gave that trauma physical form."

"No, Sparrow," Faune shook her head slowly. "You didn't imagine it. That power you felt was my magic burrowing deeply into your own not-yet-manifested *acat.*"

Confusion and guilt seeped into Sparrow as she mindlessly stroked the stems of the tall and blossoming wildflowers. She wove her fingers through the sun-warmed grass, not wanting Faune to see the tears slipping free, landing against the orange-hued petals of a poppy.

"I did not realize how vividly that piece of my magic would affect your *acat* until recently." Faune continued, her hushed tone rising and falling with the breeze. "Not until a few months ago when Phades sent an illusion of herself into Aurramere, to tell me that a soul had begun to flicker into existence in Minmere before being yanked back. She was panicked, thinking a being passed and their soul had gotten lost – or trapped – in a different god realm."

Goosebumps erupted down Sparrow's arms.

"I had not given much thought to that piece of my magic living inside you – concluding that with the healing magic you manifested from Balint being so powerful, that it would seem as insignificant as a single weed amongst a forest. Something overlooked and forgotten in a sea of mighty oak. But instead, my magic grew like wild ivy through Balint's gifts, intertwining into your *acat* so completely that one could no longer exist without the other. Your gifts...*changed.* On an ethereal level."

"But I cannot heal injured beings," Sparrow replied. Her entire lineage had been healers. Though her parents' magic was weak by comparison to other ancestors, the fact that Sparrow could not heal instigated the single crack that spiderwebbed out, affecting every facet of her upbringing.

"No, you cannot," Faune agreed, "because the piece of my magic, mixed with Balint's *acat,* created something else entirely. I knew from the moment Phades told me about the gargoyle that disappeared from Minmere's halls that you'd done the impossible. Something even the gods themselves cannot control. You, Sparrow, Daughter of Life, *stopped death*. My *acat,* mixed with Balint's very strong gift of healing, gave you the power of resurrection. You reconnected a soul with its physical body, effectively giving the gargoyle a second chance at life."

Pieces of a confusing puzzle Sparrow had silently mulled over since the night in the Opal Palace's throne room clicked into place. "I resurrected Merrick," she gasped quietly, clasping a hand over her mouth in disbelief as the words tumbled out. "I tried to heal him after Adara's blast hit him, begged my magic to do *something* to help him and – and I didn't think he was dead. I just thought he was *dying.*"

"The gargoyle *was* dead." Faune confirmed, her eyes lowering. "His soul had already crossed the threshold into Minmere. *You* pulled him back. You plucked his soul from the afterlife and shoved it back into his body."

"When Phades and I figured it out, Phades admitted to me what she knew about Massis. How she feared he was trying to come earthside and instigate a new war. She told me it was a matter of time before she'd mark Queen Esmeray as her Vessel, and she advised I do the same with you."

"I watched you for a while, saw how caring and kind you were, watched you continue to grieve for your sister a century later, felt the purity of your heart to always do the right thing. And I decided that I would ask you. To give *you* the choice. If you *want* to be my Vessel, I will allow the Book of Faune to imbue my direct god magic to you."

Sparrow swayed. All those times she'd felt a presence hovering over her...it had been the Goddess of Life.

"I admit, even I do not know what new powers, if any, will manifest if you agree. Esmeray was destined to be the Vessel of Death since Phades first felt her soul earthside. Phades imbued Esmeray with the mirror of her own magic. Every power Phades has, she passed to Esmeray. Yet, since you have both my gift and Balint's, I do not know what will happen if you take my god magic. It could merely strengthen your power of resurrection, or it may give you something new entirely."

*A choice.* A shiver wracked through Sparrow, her shoulder curving inward under a heaviness that settled like a coat of dust against an unused shelf. Sparrow never explored her magic as Esmeray had. Never felt the desire to push herself to do *more*. Sparrow swallowed tightly. Balint *had* blessed her. She should've become a healer. Briar's legacy was to inherit Faune's gifts. Not hers.

*It was supposed to be me.* Briar's words whispered through her soul.

But if she accepted Faune's offer, a piece of Briar would live on. Sparrow could do beautiful things with that god-gift. It wasn't a gift of destruction – like Esmeray's. It was the ultimate form of healing. Healing death itself.

She knew there would be limitations, knew that she'd need to carve out a strict moral compass to make sure her power was never used for ill-gain, to never be wielded as an incentive, a weapon in itself.

But Faune trusted her.

Her throat bobbed, tears welling up in her eyes with the weight of the decision. She opened her mouth to agree –

"There's one more thing," Faune interrupted, her expression turning solemn. "When you resurrected Merrick, you first poured Balint's magic into him like oil and then used my gift as the spark to light it. You shoved the ivy off the oak tree, unravelling the two gifts from each other, separating them for a short window of time.

"When the strands of your *acat* parted, the piece of Briar's soul still connected to my gift became visible for the first time after spending a century hidden away in the deepest part of yourself. And as it was a full moon, a predestined soul tie from Carra was delivered. A soul tie that was meant to wither and fade on its own accord with Briar's death. As I said, gods are not infallible. Though *some* of us *are* better than others," Faune huffed, as if the mention of Carra dredged up some...distaste.

But Sparrow only stared at the Goddess of Life, horrified as the puzzle pieces continued to find their places, eager to reveal the full picture, a picture that meant –

"Briar was supposed to be Merrick's mate," Sparrow whimpered, her heart shredding inside of her. "He was never supposed to be mine. It's why our *acatis* never changed together...right? Why we never felt any-thing other than mere attraction? Why my soul tie to Laurent is so... so...*different*?"

Faune nodded grimly, her eyes flickering and darkening. Above them, the night sky clouded over, smooth rumbles of thunder rolling through the meadow. The wildflowers around them began leaking color, pulling their petals inside of themselves, until both Sparrow and Faune were drenched in inky hues of blue and grey, the lively atmosphere morphing into a gloomy, angry storm.

"Carra decreed Merrick and Briar to be soul tied. But when Briar passed, Carra decided it was more trouble than it was worth to choose a different mate for Merrick. She gets...turbulent when her matchmaking is interrupted by something as *measly* as death." Faune scoffed, the sound slipping from her lips and wafting up to the night clouds above.

A vivid strike of lightning jumped through the star-less sky.

"If you choose to become my Vessel, my god power will imbue itself directly into your *acat*, and it will burn out the small sliver of Briar's soul that transferred with my gift. It will cause the soul tie to Merrick to evaporate. My god magic will, of course, leave you with your *correct* mate, Laurent, but it will leave Merrick with what is called a ghost soul tie."

Sparrow trembled as a gust of ice-cold wind swept over them, blowing her hair from her shoulders. She knew the shaking coursing through her body was not from the weather around them, but from the choice she needed to make.

"So, if I choose to become your Vessel, I lose my soul tie to Merrick."

"He was never meant to be yours," Faune replied gently, yet firmly, clasping Sparrow's hand in her own. "Briar was supposed to become Merrick's mate – not you. Laurent was and will *always* be the mate Carra selected for you."

Looking out beyond the horizon, beyond the night-dark sky, Sparrow placed her hand to her chest. She imagined she could feel Briar's palm against hers, silently guiding her on the winding path of life, supporting her, grieving alongside her, celebrating with her.

While tears still slipped down her cheeks, Sparrow breathed evenly, her mind calming as she turned towards the Goddess of Life. "Before I give you my answer, I need to speak with Merrick. It is only fair if you give me a choice, that I give him one as well."

A small smile graced Faune's face as she inclined her head. Around them, the storm clouds receded, leaving a clear night sky above.

"Tell the Book of Faune when you have made your decision." Faune stood slowly, holding her hand out to Sparrow. "But for now, Sparrow, know this - even the wrong decisions can lead in the right direction. The only thing that would change is the outcome itself."

A flash of pure white light swept over the meadow, and Sparrow was gone.

# CHAPTER SIXTY
# MERRICK

MERRICK HOVERED ANXIOUSLY BEHIND Laurent's kneeling back as his best friend shook Sparrow's unconscious body, pleading with her to open her eyes. Across the cavern, Jargo kicked Smoth's corpse, muttering a string of curses, before spitting on the ground where the bodies of the two gargoyle spies lay.

Rinci escaped, the damned coward. Once Smoth went down, thanks to a well-placed crossbow bolt to the throat, Laurent gained the upper hand in his duel against Hamm, and the bitch sensed the tides turning and fled before Laurent buried his sword to the hilt into Hamm's chest.

They'd turned to evaluate their surroundings, tunnel vision from engaging highly skilled opponents finally widening, to find Sparrow laying against the hard ground, the Book of Faune gripped in her hands against her chest.

And now, hearing Laurent bellow her name, his voice hoarse, Merrick lowered his eyes to the floor, scuffing a boot against the closest cluster of quartz that poked out. He felt as if he were intruding on a private moment. Merrick had spent the good part of a fortnight stomping through rock tunnels, camping in the damp forest, and generally making as much noise as possible to attract the three spies to him. Jargo volunteered to come along, blandly stating he had unfinished business with Smoth, and would be happy to spill some blood.

From the vicious way Laurent eviscerated Hamm, Merrick felt there were a lot of scores settled tonight.

Sparrow jolted, exhaling a rattling gasp as her eyelids fluttered open. Laurent shouted. Merrick rushed forward to see Sparrow's normally brilliant blue eyes were dulled, muted.

Her lids closed again, her chest rising and falling smoothly.

Alive. She was alive.

The relief coursing through Merrick paled in comparison to the heart wrenching sobs that crashed through Laurent, the fae pulling her close to cry against her hair, softly whispering to her to come back to him.

Sparrow opened her eyes with a start, panic and concern flashing over her face as she lifted her hand to lay her palm against Laurent's cheek. Merrick relaxed as her normal, blue eyes became visible.

"Are you-"

"I'm fine," Laurent assured, smoothing her hair back from her face as he helped her slowly get to her feet. Sparrow clutched the Vessel Book tightly, her gaze darting between the bodies on the floor, to Laurent's shoulder, to Merrick, to Jargo, back to Laurent, back to the bodies, before landing on the Book of Faune.

"Rinci?"

"Escaped," Merrick growled, stalking forward, finally allowing himself to sheath his swords. "And Laurent needs a healer. We need to get out of here and regroup at Obsidian. Esmeray's orders."

Jargo shoved his hands in his pockets, awkwardly trying to stay out of the conversation – which was next to impossible in this close of a setting. The spy settled on pacing the perimeter of the cavern itself, looking over the clusters of gemstone protruding from the far end of the walls with fierce intensity.

Laurent tilted her face to his. "What happened?"

"Faune wanted to chat," Sparrow muttered quietly, "I didn't know I'd be unconscious for it."

Laurent thinned his lips, gesturing to the book in her clutches. "And the Book of Faune?"

"Still very much has magic," Sparrow said shakily, "but I need to talk to you. And Merrick. I need to talk to both of you."

Merrick shot a look over to Jargo, who had returned to the corpses, kneeling down and pulling out a hooked dagger from his boot.

"Talk to Laurent first," Merrick said hastily as he turned towards Jargo. Without meeting Sparrow's eyes, he pointed towards the opposing wall. "Over there would be...best."

Sparrow knitted her eyebrows together in confusion as Laurent steered her towards the spot Merrick pointed to. Merrick strode over to Jargo, though his gaze kept flickering over to Sparrow and Laurent. They were only thirty feet away, but Laurent positioned Sparrow's back to Merrick.

"Esmeray...uhm...wants their heads." Merrick heard Laurent admit in a low voice as he held Sparrow's shoulders so she wouldn't see what was going on behind her.

Merrick couldn't see Sparrow's facial expression, but he saw her body tremble at the thought.

Jargo was having the exact opposite reaction as he merrily sawed through Smoth's spinal cord, humming to himself as he worked. Merrick swallowed, looking away for a moment as he tried, desperately, to block the sound of cracking bone from his ears.

Gore usually didn't bother him, but knowing he was about to have a serious conversation with Sparrow tipped his axis, and now his stomach felt a bit queasy. "Smoth killed my partner," Jargo explained, as he glanced up at Merrick, "I swore to him on his deathbed I'd repay the favor. It's how I ended up working for Prince Cillian."

Merrick grunted, understanding all too well that lethal rage since it had taken him to dark places when news of his mother's death reached him.

Jargo succeeded in detaching Smoth's head, holding it up to stare at it. He whistled low, pleased with his handiwork. "You want to take care of the other one?"

Merrick pressed his lips together shaking his head as his stomach pitched.

"Suit yourself." Jargo shrugged, carefully propping Smoth's head up next to him, patting its cheek. "You can watch, buddy."

Merrick closed his eyes. "Are you talking to the severed head?"

"Yeah," Jargo chuckled as the sound of sawing filled the air again.

"No wonder Esmeray likes you," Merrick huffed. "She's just as insane as you are."

"That makes me like *her* even more."

Merrick grunted, crossing his arms to sneak a glance over to Sparrow and Laurent. She was either laughing or crying, judging from the shake of her shoulders, but one look at Laurent's face and Merrick stiffened. Crying. Sparrow was definitely crying.

Thoughts buzzed around his head, each one more unsettling than the last. *What would Faune have told her to cause her to cry? Was she alright? Did the book show her something she didn't want to see?*

No answers came readily available. Merrick rolled his neck, coaxing the adrenaline that still barreled through his body to chill the fuck out.

The soft jeer from Jargo had him turning. Both heads were disconnected now, and Jargo stood above them, a shit-eating grin plastered on his face. He was covered in blood, though he looked as happy as a fish finding itself in a crystal-clear stream.

Merrick sighed.

Movement from the corner of his eye caught his attention, and Sparrow appeared at his side a second later, her eyes puffy and her face splotchy with red. Laurent mirrored Merrick's grim expression, though the fae yielded nothing as he jerked his head towards the corner of the cavern.

"Can I please talk to you?" Sparrow asked, her voice hoarse and hollow.

"Of course," Merrick replied rigidly.

He followed her over to where she'd spoken to Laurent. Her hand at his elbow shook slightly. He swallowed down his trepidation as she turned to face him.

They locked eyes, and she inhaled deeply, as if steeling herself, before gently taking his hands in hers. "I would like to tell you a story," Sparrow started sadly, "about two sisters who loved each other very much."

# CHAPTER SIXTY-ONE
## LENNA

THE CRONE SAT ACROSS from Lenna, his bony elbows propped against a long, wooden table. A blanketed hush permeated the air between them - though Lenna smiled at her predecessor. An unnatural chill seeped in from the stones at her feet, not ominous nor a threat, but as a reminder that her time speaking with the previous Oracle would be cut short, and to use every precious second before his soul disappeared to once more roam Minmere's halls.

"It is good to see you again," she said, "Though I wonder why you are here."

The crone inclined his head, a small furrow appearing between his brows, as if something troubled him. "I must admit, slipping through the veil is becoming more difficult. My visits may become much more infrequent or stop altogether. The veil around Minmere is fortifying in preparation for what is to come."

"What is coming?" Lenna asked as she settled against the hard-backed wooden chair. It niggled a part of her brain – the familiarity of this room – this chair. But she couldn't place it. Dust particles streamed down from the soft light emitting beyond heavy curtains and dark paint peeled from *the walls in strips - more severe areas sporting scars and gouge marks down to the bricked over bones of the house itself.*

*It looked as if this place had been empty for a very long time.*

*Neglected.*

*Lenna turned her attention back to the crone. "If you only have a few moments, please tell me what you know."*

*The Oracle leaned his chin against gnarled knuckles. "I cannot tell you, as I do not fully know either. As an Oracle, I will not pass along a warning based off of mere speculation. But the gods are restless, and news of a second Vessel is being whispered throughout the god realms." He gave her a hard look, staring down from his crooked nose. "All of the god realms."*

*With a wave of his hand, gesturing to the room they sat in, the Oracle asked, "Do you miss the Slate Kingdom?"*

*The odd question caused Lenna to cock her head, shooting a quizzical glance around her again.*

*The chill at her feet became ice cold as it dawned on her that this was the dining room in the Doortan Manor. And those were indeed gouges ripped into the wall – like claw marks from the aftermath of a great battle. Looking closer, she noticed the edges of the table she'd sat for breakfast almost every day for thirty years was not only in horrid disrepair – it was charred – the edges splintering off from the main slab and jutting out in every direction.*

*"I have found my home in Irridessen," she admitted after a pause, pushing aside the image around her. It was a dream. She knew that this was not the current state of the Doortan manor – only a foreboding warning for her to play her cards right. "I never felt as if I belonged in the Slate Kingdom."*

*The Oracle nodded thoughtfully, his fingers trailing absentmindedly through his beard. "And the people here. Do you think they are better or worse off now that the dome has fallen?"*

*Lenna chewed her lip, contemplating her answer. "I think there are good people and evil people in every Kingdom – dome or not it falls on each ruler to do their part and help keep the Slate Kingdom safe for humans."*

*"Though you have not spent time in the other Kingdoms. Only Irridessen."*

*Lenna opened and closed her mouth. The chiding response from her predecessor seemed...forced. Her heart started beating harder – though her physical body was safe in the Obsidian Palace, a soft voice seemed to trill in her mind to answer safe.*

*"This is not how the Doortan Manor currently looks. Why does it appear this way?*

*A curious look crossed the Oracle's face as he appraised her. "You should have learned by now, Oracle, there is a reason for everything, even if the reason itself is not quite clear. There are parts of the past that will be hidden from you – things that Moirai does not yet wish to reveal."*

*"I thought, as the Oracle, I was supposed to be able to peer into any part of the past I so wished."*

*"You are." Her predecessor nodded. "And yet you are missing important pieces of the larger picture. As I said – you have not spent time in other Kingdoms. Only the Slate Kingdom and Irridessen."*

*Leaning back in her chair Lenna surveyed her predecessor. It was clear to her now that he could not tell her what he wanted her to know – not directly anyway. But he was hinting at something...Something...*

*Something to help her prepare for what was to come.*

*Lenna blew out a rough breath as the sinking realization hit home. "I can only look into the past for the Kingdoms that I have visited."*

*A slow nod of confirmation was her only answer. She waited for him to speak but the crone only raised an eyebrow, tapping a single long finger against his temple. His eyes twinkled, as if pushing her – daring her – to ask more. To demand more information from him.*

*Her mind jumbled together as every question she had since her first steps onto Irridessen soil threatened to erupt.*

*Were there other Seers in Irridessen?*

*Who was the second Vessel?*

*Where was the second Vessel?*

*Which Kingdoms did he want her to visit?*

*Which kingdoms had he visited? All seven of them?*

*Her questions narrowed down rapidly, and she filtered through them as fast as possible, trying to find that single question he was waiting for her to ask.*

*The Oracle across from her tapped his temple again, before running his finger under his right eye, drawing it down the side of his nose. The question he wanted her to ask was about himself. That was clear enough.*

*She surveyed the Oracle again, organizing what she already knew about him and trying to figure out what to ask.*

*A silvery sheen began hazing her view as her predecessor began glowing faintly with divine light – his soul being pulled back into the afterlife.*

*"Our time is up," he said sadly, standing from the chair and clasping his hands beneath his robes. "I do hope you have everything you need, Lenna."*

*Len-na.*

*Her name.*

*Emphasized out into two drawn out syllables, by her predecessor.*

*He turned away, his body becoming translucent -*

*"Wait!" Lenna jumped from her chair, reaching across the table for him. "What is your name?"*

*The old Oracle turned and beamed at Lenna, the deep wrinkles around his eyes crinkling as he nodded in approval. "Marvin. My*

*name is Marvin Asrar. I do believe you had the pleasure of meeting
my great-great-great-grandson, Marlo."*

Lenna gasped back into consciousness, startling the six moon
crow chicks nestled beside her on top of the warm duvet. With
varying pitches of indignant screeching, the juveniles scampered off
the bed and took to the air in a frazzled fury of white feathers, aiming
back towards their aerie.

Hale lurched awake at the first shrill squawk, his panicked hands
fumbling for Lenna between the sheets. "What's wrong?" he asked,
his voice gruff with sleep and worry.

"My predecessor – the Oracle before me – did you know what
his name was?" Lenna's heart hammered in her chest. Asrar. Asrar.
Marvin Asrar, the previous Oracle, was a blood relative to *Marlo.*

Hale seemed surprised at the question as he sat up in their bed,
rubbing the sleep from his eyes. "I cannot remember off of the top of
my head – but Oracles have never been accessible to the masses. They
typically are only referred to as 'the Oracle.' Usually, only Kings and
Queens even know *where* the current Oracle lives – and maybe some
close friends but... I've lived here since I was young, and you're the
first Oracle I've met. I'd have to look up information on the previous
Oracles. Why?"

Lenna closed her eyes to calm her breathing as her mind settled
firmly back into her body. Staring up at the ceiling, she recalled every
second of the odd encounter with Oracle *Asrar.* She admitted slowly,
"I knew one of the previous Oracle's kin. It feels like there's this
invisible string that connected us long before I got activated."

Outside of the King's Chambers, blue-grey fog rolled down the
mountains, the crisp smell of rain blustered from the heavy clouds coat-

ing the night sky. The palace was dark, still, signifying dawn was a long way away. Lenna turned to Hale.

"I'm starting to think the gods have a sense of humor. Or some sort of divine plan that we think is their stab at being funny but may turn out to be a weird twist of fate. Either way, I don't think I'll be getting anymore sleep tonight."

Hale fumbled around, reaching off the side of the bed. A few moments later, he lit the three candles on his nightstand with a small match. The smell of the burning stick made Lenna think of the burnt table in her dream.

*Just a dream.* She reminded herself as Hale's face became visible in the dim light. She scooted herself closer, wrapping her arm around his bare torso, feeling his heartbeat strongly against her cheek. She inhaled deeply, his warm scent of books and the sea helping to calm her jittery feelings, soothing her abrupt crash into consciousness.

His large hand fell to her back, gently stroking her skin in long, rhythmic brushes, warming her, easing tranquility back into her tense muscles.

She nestled her head closer, feeling the soft bristles of his chest hair on her face, peppering kisses across his sternum. Her breathing steadied as his hand lazily trailed down her arm.

Her mind quieted.

"If you don't want to sleep, why don't you tell me about your dream?" Hale offered, pressing a kiss to the soft head scarf she wrapped her curls in before bed.

Lenna snuggled closer, swinging her leg over his to pull their bodies tighter together. There was so much to unpack from the dream. She committed every detail to memory, praying the minutiae would hold out to recant in the morning.

There *was* another way they could pass the time. Right now, with her predecessor's warning ringing in her ears, to fully develop her skills as an Oracle, travel would become necessary to the other Kingdoms. Kingdoms that did not have the best relationship with Irridessen.

The cozy King's chambers among the mountains suddenly felt temporary – as if there was an hourglass of sand sitting unused on Fate's desk, and her visit with Oracle Asrar caused that hourglass to flip and the sand to begin counting down towards an uncertain future.

"I have a better idea," she murmured, her voice low as she gazed up to the deep amber eyes of the male she loved. She pressed a kiss against the base of Hale's throat.

"I like it already," Hale confirmed as he captured her lips with his, tipping her head up.

A knock sounded at the door to their bedroom.

"I apologize for the intrusion." A deep voice from one of the Queen's Guards rang out. "But Queen Absolute Esmeray has requested your presence in the meeting room."

"When?" Lenna asked – her words muffled as she continued her exploration of Hale's throat. His hands twitched around the base of her neck as her mouth explored lower regions.

The guard on the other side of the door cleared their throat awkwardly. "Now."

THE OBSIDIAN PALACE WAS not as still and quiet as Lenna thought as she stepped into the hallway that led to the council room. Guards lined both sides of the narrow corridor, equipped with long spears.

Behind closed doors, Lenna could hear the rustling of book pages, low murmured voices, the clinking of glasses, and rolling laughter.

"This is the royal wing for the Ladies and Lords of court," Hale whispered as they ventured further down the hall, "but usually there aren't any guards here."

The guards seemed to be waiting for something as Lenna felt the heavy tang of magic thrumming from behind the doors at the end of the hallway. Hale gripped Lenna's hand as they neared the council room.

The door opened before they touched the handle, and a burly gargoyle with slate grey wings stepped into the hall with a rough sigh, hands deep in the pockets of his long black cloak.

"*Merrick?*" Lenna gasped as she dropped Hale's hand, rushing forward to throw her arms around Merrick's waist in a fierce hug. Merrick stiffened.

She hadn't seen Merrick since his departure from Sparrow's house after the battle against Adara, and the loss of his dry humor and sarcasm was a weight on her heart. Sparrow had told her about the whole two-mates situation, but Lenna truly missed her friend. To have him *here?* Her mind raced – maybe he and Sparrow figured out their soul tie. Maybe her first friend in Irridessen would be here to stay. She missed his company, still tried to contact him daily through their mind-speak rings.

Even though he never answered.

Merrick squeezed her in his arms, before gently removing her and stepping back. His eyes were red as if he'd been crying. His wings – usually snapped tight and held high behind his back – drooped slightly, the grey talons only held a couple inches off the floor.

"What's wrong?" Lenna whispered, fear icing her veins. She swept an assessing glance down Merrick, noting he had no visible injuries - but that he did not wear his mind-speak ring.

Her heart sunk.

Merrick shook his head, averting his eyes from her. "Later," he said gruffly, brushing past Lenna and trudging down the hall. She frowned at the abrupt dismissal, but he rounded the corner and disappeared without a backwards look.

Lenna exchanged a worried look with Hale before Hale ushered her forward and into the council chamber.

# CHAPTER SIXTY-TWO
# LAURENT

ESMERAY'S MAGIC FELT LIKE a pressurized hum, emulating the tingling feeling throughout one's blood before giving in to a surge of heady recklessness. In comparison, Sparrow's magic was a calming crackle - like the deep breath you took when you scented rain on the horizon, yet the day was still sunny.

The tension, however, was thick enough to slice through with a blade. Sparrow slumped against the chair to the left of Esmeray's seat at the head of the table, eyes bloodshot from crying, arms crossed tightly against her chest - though the paleness that had been left behind after her conversation with Merrick morphed into a healthy golden glow once the magic thrumming through the Book of Faune became infused with her own *acat*.

Her *acat* was almost as large as Esmeray's now, with deep black ink travelling from the tips of her fingers and fading out into a soft crescent shape that cupped her shoulder. Laurent wasn't even sure if Sparrow noticed.

After she spoke with Merrick in the caverns where they found the Book of Faune, Merrick had gone silent, tears flowing soundlessly into his beard, mixing, and diluting the red blood that splattered his face from their battle against the Ruby Kingdom's spies. Sparrow's hushed murmurs had been too low for even Laurent to hear, but Merrick's curt, *"Do it, then,"* had been enough for both Laurent and Jargo to ease closer to the pair.

Laurent thinned his lips, grieving over the decision Sparrow had made, stamping down the guilt that his own soul tie to Sparrow was bright and true.

Now, Sparrow radiated god magic, her aura singing and twining around Laurent's own power, though the beautiful fae herself barely glanced in Laurent's direction. They'd arrived to the Obsidian Palace in the middle of the night, bloodied and panting, and Sparrow alerted the Queen and King of their arrival through their rings.

But the royal couple was already awake and dealing with the latest fallout from the dome disappearing over the Slate Kingdom.

Esmeray had taken one look at Sparrow, nodded, and said simply, "Vessel," before tossing Sparrow a piece of parchment that had Sparrow cursing colorfully and Esmeray leading the way towards the secured-with-wards council room.

Looking between the two, Laurent rubbed his chin. They were the most powerful beings in the world – arguably as formidable as the gods themselves – yet the small note half crumpled in the middle of the table seemed more earth-shattering than the power ricocheting between the walls.

Lenna curled up on the chair next to Keerian's still-empty seat, staring at Sparrow across the table and eyeing the parchment with curiosity, her sight darting between the two as if she wasn't sure which one she wanted information on first after Laurent filled Hale and Lenna in on the events that took place in Faune's grotto.

"Did Merrick know what you taking the god magic would do?" Lenna asked, directing the question at Sparrow, an edge to her voice Laurent never heard before.

Sparrow flicked her eyes up to the Oracle before nodding slowly. "He knew."

"And he'll never be able to receive another soul tie from Carra?" Lenna's question made Sparrow flinch, and Laurent leaned over, laying a calming hand against his mate's forearm, her hand white-knuckled as she squeezed the chair's armrest.

"He will not. Though that doesn't mean he'll never love," Laurent said pointedly. "Plenty of beings go their entire lives without a soul tie from Carra, and their love is just as pure and perfect as any soul tie."

Lenna frowned but settled her gaze back to the center of the table, casting an inquisitive look at the crumpled parchment.

Hale sat next to Lenna, flipping through the pages of the drained Book of Faune, mumbling to himself as he tapped his fingers against a page here and there, only half listening to the conversation around them. His softly pointed ears pricked up, but the furrowed brows and appearance of his monocle spoke to the fact his full attention was deep in the Vessel Book.

Esmeray leaned forward with a sigh as Keerian entered the room in a cloud of rage. He stomped across the room, his golden wings high and snapped tightly to his back, plunking down into the seat at Esmeray's right, signifying that his conversation with Merrick had been about as useful as any of theirs had been. "He's lashing out," Keerian grunted, "just give him space."

Esmeray raised a single arched brow. "That's what we *all* told you before you went stalking after him."

Keerian shot the Queen a *'look'* before turning to Sparrow. "You cannot blame yourself for this – it's not your fault Merrick's soul tie is gone. Blame Carra for sitting on her moon-ass for a century instead of finding a different mate for him."

"Saying it's Carra's fault is basically blasphemy," Sparrow countered, not meeting Keerian's eyes.

"No, it's definitely just regular blasphemy," Esmeray interjected, "though it won't really get us anywhere. Besides, I hate to say this, but we have -" she reached out her hand, causing the piece of parchment to flutter off the table and into her grasp, "- more pressing matters to discuss."

Esmeray cleared her throat, causing Hale to look up from the Book of Faune, his monocle dropping from his eye and swaying at the end of its attached chain. The Dark Queen began reading aloud from the note, sneering at the paper with wrathful disgust.

*"Queen Esmeray, it is in the vested interest of Irridessen's economic and political ties that amends are made for the destruction of the dome that once protected the Slate Kingdom.*

*To look past this blatant act of war, the Ruby Kingdom demands reconciliation in the form of the Oracle. We ask Irridessen to separate ties to the Oracle so she may live within the borders of Ingotheria. The Ruby Kingdom proudly offers to provide the Oracle with every comfort and luxury available, including personal housing within the royal wing of the Ruby Palace.*

*King Eamon is pleased to send his Ambassador of Foreign Relations, Lord Dimas Citro, to the Obsidian Palace at week's end to personally escort the Oracle to the Ruby Palace, and to assure Queen Esmeray and King Consort Keerian that in war, there are no true winners.*

*With the Oracle's safe arrival, Ingotheria will continue maintaining peace and harmonious balance during this difficult time with no declarations of war."*

Hale shot Lenna a pained glance, quickly gripping her hand in his own. "What does this mean?"

Keerian seethed with fury. "The dome surrounding the Slate Kingdom is King Eamon's bargaining chip to get what he wants and threaten war. Without the fancy political bullshit, the note says, *'give us the Oracle or we'll march our army into the Slate Kingdom and take it back for ourselves.'* We just don't know *why* King Eamon decided that – out of everything – he wanted Lenna."

"So, either I go to the Ruby Kingdom, or an entire continent of defenseless humans die." Lenna stated flatly, a contemplative glint in her eyes. Sparrow growled. Laurent frowned. The Oracle looked as if she was considering it – not panicking at the thought and begging to be spared from the barbaric Ruby Kingdom.

"It's out of the question," Sparrow snapped, causing Lenna to jump, "King Eamon will have to go through all of us to get to Lenna. And Esmeray and I are both Vessels of fucking gods – he wouldn't stand a chance."

"He wouldn't," Esmeray agreed quietly, venom lacing her words. "But King Eamon isn't stupid enough to bring the fight to Irridessen. He'd do what Keerian said – take over the Slate Kingdom and kill anyone who questions his rule. We cannot forget the Ruby Kingdom has a very strong ally in the Topaz Kingdom, and our own alliance with the Larimar Islands is shaky at best."

Keerian, his face stony and devoid of emotion, read over the note again, as if the words would change, or a hidden loophole would reveal itself. "We could call his bluff. No royal can force the Oracle to live in a specific Kingdom."

"That's exactly why he worded the message as he did," Laurent grumbled. "He can't force the Oracle to move – but he *can* force Irridessen to kick the Oracle out of their continent. He told Irridessen to sever ties to the Oracle, not the other way around. If we do consider Larimar an ally, they may hesitate over our refusal to send Lenna to Ingotheria. Worst case, they could opt out of fighting altogether and announce themselves neutral."

"Can we win a war if Irridessen takes on both the Ruby and Topaz Kingdoms alone?" Sparrow asked, her new god magic whipping around the room. She took a deep breath, struggling to push the wild magic back down.

Esmeray crinkled her nose. "We *could* still win – but it would be a very slim chance considering the size and formidability of the Topaz Kingdom's standing army. And *if* we did win, it would not be without heavy tolls on lives and political relations. The Ruby Kingdom is already spreading rumors that I imprisoned Adara solely because I didn't want to share the crown."

Sparrow blew out a breath, leaning her head against the high-backed wooden chair, tilting her face towards him. Laurent stroked her hair, hating the helplessness that simmered like a veil over her features. The room buzzed with magic, spiking as Esmeray rubbed her face with her tattooed hand.

"This Ambassador of Foreign Relations," Hale said slowly. "Do you know who he is?"

Esmeray frowned and shook her head. Keerian spoke, "Dimas Citro - I only met him once, years ago, and that definitely was not his title at the time. He's cunning and slippery as fuck. I have no idea what his magic is

- but he's fae. Other than that, there's not much on him, and I hazard to believe this ambassadorship is any more real than Meer's illusions."

"Well, judging from the note, he'll be here in two days," Sparrow said. "Could we just hold him captive until King Eamon decides to relent on Lenna moving to the Ruby Kingdom?"

"I'm sure that will really help my pristine political relations," Esmeray replied dryly, her wings bristling. "I'll just chuck him in with Adara."

Keerian scowled, his gold horns lowering as he propped his chin up with his hand, his elbow thudding on the tabletop. "Our hands are tied. We can host him, feel him out, and see if we can get more out of him as to why King Eamon wants Lenna. I'm sure my lovely mate is already thinking of some ideas as to how we shall entertain his Ambassador-ness."

Esmeray's anger gave way immediately to a deranged smile that showed all her teeth as she cocked her head, drawing herself up straighter as if a whole plethora of gleefully fucked up ideas just bounced into her brain. "I have a few thoughts already. I do enjoy party planning."

"Laurent, you and I will go talk to Jargo, see what he knows about Dimas. I want Jargo to disappear while Dimas is here – I think that is the best way to keep his loyalty to Prince Cillian safe while we figure out what the Ruby Kingdom wants." Keerian leaned back and crossed his arms, though his face softened as he addressed Lenna. "At the end of the day, it's your decision. We will not force you to leave. If it comes down to the Ruby Kingdom threatening war, we can hide you and Hale until King Eamon's threats blow over. Your home is wherever you want, but I may be selfish to state I believe wholeheartedly your home is here – with us."

Lenna smiled, reaching for Keerian's hand. He extended his own, their fingers interlacing. "My home will always be here," she agreed firmly, squeezing Keerian's palm before turning to Esmeray and Sparrow. "And no one can ever take that away from me. But, if this helps Irridessen avoid war, if this saves the lives of every human in the Slate Kingdom, I will go."

Esmeray cocked her head. "Are you sure?"

Even Laurent sat, puzzled, by the calm and collected Oracle before them. His hand paused in Sparrow's hair. Sparrow turned to stare fully at Lenna. Hale swallowed before sitting up straighter.

Lenna smiled, an all-knowing smile that planted a pit of fear into Laurent's veins. She directed her focus to each of them in turn, before waving her hand in the air. "You need more information on Prince Cillian, right? To see if he would be a better ruler than King Eamon?" She chuckled heartily, patting Keerian's hand before spreading her arms out wide.

"Well, if the Prince *is* a good male, and King Eamon needs to be dethroned, then who better to infiltrate the Ruby Kingdom and take it down from within than the fucking Oracle of Terramere?"

# CHAPTER SIXTY-THREE
## ESMERAY

LORD DIMAS CITRO ARRIVED precisely when we wanted him to. As the bright red portal began flickering in the throne room of the Obsidian Palace, I took a deep breath and slipped into the role I played so well.

The Dark Queen. Queen Absolute of Irridessen. The Queen of Decimation. The Vessel of Death. The Queen who threw her own twin in the Soul Keeper's Cell.

Okay, maybe the last one wasn't an official title, but it spoke enough about my reputation.

I swept my eyes around the empty throne room, quickly confirming everything was ready for our unwanted guest. The stone pews before us were freshly polished, the glass floor looked unassuming and safe, and the skeletal handed torches along the walls glinted softly with the orange hued fires they held.

Aside from the soft whirr of the portal before us, the room was silent as a tomb. I willed my fae side to still, not allowing a single muscle in my wings to relax an inch. Keerian straightened, setting his face into a rough scowl. We wore our matching bleached bone crowns, dressed simply in garments that were neither swoon-worthy nor flashy.

My sleeveless dress was unadorned – resting loosely against my body to my ankles. Keerian wore his regular leather pants and a simple button down. Both of us wore all black. Keerian's golden wings and horns shone, the only sparkle of color atop the dais. The Ruby Kingdom prided themselves on their elaborate outfits, deeming the worth of a being based on the clothing they wore to present themselves.

And right now, Keerian and I looked...almost humble. A far cry from the richest King and Queen in Terramere. Which I was sure to remind Lord Dimas that we were.

The oval shaped portal sparked as Dimas appeared, stepping through the swirling light quickly. He was dressed in deep brown breeches paired with a bright red frock that sported gemstone buttons down the sides of the lapels. Thick gold rings sparkled against each of his fingers, some stacked atop another to wedge more wealth and opulence upon him. By comparison, Keerian and I had no jewelry on us to be seen.

I wanted Dimas off kilter, wanted him to feel out of place and over-dressed, stepping into a situation where he was firmly out of his element.

At least for the first part of this lovely game.

And as he appeared before us, oozing courtly finery, I watched a glimmer of unease flit across his face. He shot a quick look of hesitation behind him before his mouth set in a thin line.

Interesting.

It almost seemed as if Dimas didn't want to be here as much as we didn't *want* him here.

Keerian and I waited silently as Dimas turned, striding forward with his hands clasped behind his back. Dimas stopped abruptly at an appropriate distance from the dais before inclining his head and shoulders. It was a bow that stated - *I know you are a Queen, but you are not* my *Queen*.

And so, the game began.

"Lord Dimas, it has been some time since the Obsidian Palace has had the pleasure to host visitors from the Ruby Kingdom," I said, feigning interest as I stared down the fae. "Especially one with such an *esteemed* title as 'Ambassador of Foreign Relations.' Is that a new position the Ruby Kingdom decided to dole out? Your King never struck me as the type of male to truly care how others perceived him."

Dimas gave me a polite smile that did not meet the calculating look swirling through his eyes as he assessed us. "Thank you, Queen Esmeray, and King Consort Keerian, for allowing me this visit. I understand how troublesome your transition to the throne has been, and appreciate you taking the time to speak with me on behalf of King Eamon."

"Oh, my transition to Queen *Absolute* was a breeze." I waved my hand, leaning my elbow against the throne's armrest so Dimas could get a good look at my fully blacked out *acat*. "Once you're imbued with the direct power of the Goddess of Death, there isn't much that really gets in your way. Politics or...otherwise."

If he hadn't known prior to this visit that I had god magic, he hid his surprise well. But without that flicker of confusion, it meant he already knew I was the Vessel of Phades – which led me to believe the Ruby Kingdom spies definitely parroted more information back to their master before receiving due punishment.

Keerian sneered down at the Lord, leaning forward slightly to rest a hand on his knee. He looked so menacing I felt a thrill shoot down my spine. "Was this your first time traveling by portal?"

"Not my first, your Majesty, though I admit it's not my favorite means of transportation."

"Portals can be so *difficult* to get right over such a great distance," Keerian said scathingly, "though it seems King Eamon has found a strong portal master to assist with travel for his council members. Tell me, Lord

Dimas, does King Eamon provide this sort of special attention to *all* his council members? Or just you?" My mate flashed his fangs. "Do his *spies* get to travel by portal? Or does he simply stuff them onto the first ship heading to Irridessen shores?"

Dimas's answer was well-rehearsed. "I am very grateful for my King to allow me the ease of quick travel by portal. With the delicate matters at hand, it was imperative to King Eamon that I arrived safely, so we had more time to discuss our mutual interests before I'm needed back in the Ruby Kingdom for the Equinox Ball tomorrow." He hesitated for a moment before adding, "And the Ruby Kingdom has no spies in Irridessen."

I barely contained my eyeroll as I bared my teeth in a false smile, ignoring one statement in favor for the other. "The Equinox *Ball*? Is that what King Eamon is calling the Culling these days?" I clapped my hands together once. "What a *delight*. I'm sure you're needed at the *Culling,* Lord Dimas. What *would* King Eamon do without his personal bloodhound?"

Dimas stiffened.

Jargo had begrudgingly admitted that Dimas kept his *acat* a secret, and only a few trusted royals in the Ruby Palace knew the Lord had the power to find out a being's lineage and heritage magic. No wonder King Eamon kept him close.

Though Jargo told us that Dimas was Cillian's closest advisor, the double agent did seem to hold some long-suffering resentment towards the Lord. I didn't pry, though after Jargo's help, I personally packed him up with a fat sack of gold coins and sent him to lay low in Florra.

"So, you get to lurk behind King Eamon and whisper in his ear which beings need to die because their lineage god isn't *good enough* to *allow* them to live?" Keerian all but snarled the words, his green eyes glinting with fury. "And you expect us to play *nice* with your monster of a King?"

Dimas pressed his lips together before opening his mouth, a shrewd look glinting like steel in his molten eyes.

I cut him off, standing suddenly. "This conversation bores me," I said darkly before throwing my hands out wide just like Keerian and I plotted.

The throne room shimmered as my magic burst forth from my palms, flooding the space with golden light. Dimas flinched, raising his hand to cover his eyes against the brightness.

I was not casting an illusion though. Rather, I was ripping one away – the illusion of silence, of an empty throne room, of meekness and humility.

Within a beat, the room was filled with a rush of chatter, a soft melody – courtesy of a few musicians set up in the corner of the room – and the clinking of glasses. Dimas gawked at the reveal, lowering his hand slowly. Energy thrummed through the room - the very *full* throne room of beings milling about. Some held drinks while they talked with friends, others had already begun sitting at the now-visible table that spread across the throne room aisle. Not a single guest looked our way – as instructed – causing Dimas to sputter a moment before he regained his bearings.

Just in time for him to look down and realize the throne room floor was made entirely of glass, showcasing the very deep caverns below as that illusion also dissipated under my magic.

He paled, the freckles dotting his nose standing out against the ashy pallor of his skin.

I clapped once. "Let's discuss our *mutual interests* over dinner. Shall we?"

And as I stood from my throne, Keerian flanking me, our simple outfits glinted and morphed, revealing the truth behind the last of my elaborate illusions.

Keerian stepped forward with a swaggering smirk that lit his eyes with a devilish fire, his gem encrusted, ringed fingers straightening the lapels of a resplendent velvet overcoat threaded with thick gold. My plain dress was replaced with a midnight black gown that dripped with diamonds and fire opals – much more aligned with my title as Queen Absolute. The modest strapless top disappeared in favor of a plunging neckline, hugging every inch of my curves, before dramatically fanning out to the ground. My wings draped with golden chains that linked together with more opal, lest Lord Dimas forgot I ruled over two kingdoms. Black kohl lined my eyes, swept up in a striking effect and finished off with blood red lip stain.

Lastly, where our simple, bone-white crowns had sat, new ones took their place. Mine nestled between my glitter tipped horns, its palisades twisting above my head like the spires of the Obsidian Palace itself, each point adorned with a star shaped gemstone.

"That's much better." I smiled at my mate before allowing him to guide me down the stone steps towards the head seat at the dining table.

Dimas stood where he was, his eyes wide as he took in our crowns, our extravagant outfits, the lot of beings in the room, the grand table – set for fifty and complete with crystal glassware and matching plates, and the flood of servants that entered as my feet hit the last step.

As the servants came forth, the beings around us snapped their attention to me, all bowing low before taking their designated seats in a practiced effort. I hoped if Dimas took a single thing from this encounter, it was to *never* trust his instincts.

And this was only the beginning of a delightfully bedeviled evening of entertainment for him. Gods, I loved a good reason to throw a *"fuck you"* party.

The throne room was packed with hand-selected beings for such an occasion. Sparrow and Laurent gracefully rose before standing by their chairs to Keerian's left. Sparrow was dressed in a flowing white gown that shimmered with silver, Laurent in a matching robe. I caught a quick glimpse of Lady Chancellor Mairsile in a bright lilac long sleeved dress being escorted to her seat by the gruff Lord Orden who shoved his portly body into a dark emerald robe for the event. Lady Mairsile shot me a wink as our eyes met.

Captain Ballah appeared at my side a moment later, dressed in a dark tunic with matching breeches, bowing low as she offered to escort Dimas to his "seat of honor" to my right. Dimas had the good grace to keep silent as my Captain slipped into her old role of servant for one last night. Ballah had offered to play the game tonight, too. Accepting it as an honor to serve Keerian and myself while also fulfilling her duty of keeping an eye on me.

I made a mental note to see if she'd be interested in a promotion to Queen's Guard in the very near future.

Dimas hovered behind his chair, his gaze darting down the table of beings, no doubt making a note to tell his King who exactly was here. And who wasn't. I smiled again as I imagined the incredible mental gymnastics Dimas must be doing right now. If he realized some council members were missing – specifically the couple I killed for trying to sell me out to the Ruby Kingdom – he made no comment.

"What an incredible feat of magic, Queen Esmeray," Dimas commented – finally finding his voice and throwing a honeyed poison against his words.

I gave him a coy look as I raised my glass. The room fell silent.

"I want to personally thank you all for coming this evening to this very special dinner. I know it was a bit unconventional there in the beginning -" Keerian snickered as I fluttered my lashes, "- but I appreciate each and every one of you for helping *Lord* Dimas feel welcomed to the Obsidian Palace."

Everyone along the table clinked their glasses enthusiastically before I called them all to be seated. Dimas hurried into his chair, and I saw him glance oddly at the two empty seats beside him.

Keerian caught my grin, cocking his horns in Dimas's direction.

Right on cue, Lenna appeared on Hale's arm. The Oracle was dressed in a beautiful gown of ivy green, her red-gold hair curled and loose down her back. Her cheeks were flushed with a deep rosy blush and she smiled broadly as Hale escorted her across the throne room floor. Hale wore a deep charcoal robe buttoned high on his throat, embroidered with sky-blue scrollwork that patterned into large birds that lay across his chest. His locs piled high in a tight bun, decorated with blue lapis lazuli charms. With a flourish, he pulled Lenna's chair out for her, and she giggled as she dropped into the empty seat next to Dimas, kissing Hale on the cheek before bowing her head towards me – just slightly – as we practiced.

To remind Dimas that she was the Oracle – bound to no single King or Queen – and would hold King Eamon in the same regard.

Dimas appraised Lenna before catching Hale's gaze. The baker shot Dimas a look of utter loathing before taking his own seat to Lenna's left. Dimas swallowed as he lowered his gaze to the table and the empty plate before him.

"Lord Dimas," I purred, "Please meet Lenna, the Oracle of Ter-ramere."

Dimas awkwardly turned towards Lenna again, and Lenna beamed at him, holding her hand out at an angle for him to shake. He took it loosely, before giving her a returned tight smile. "It is a pleasure, Oracle. You look well."

Lenna wasted no time with pleasantries, her intense stare holding Dimas in place. "So, you're the Lord who wants to whisk me away to a Kingdom I've never set foot in before."

"I take no pleasure in it, my Lady," Dimas replied evenly. "My King only wishes to meet you, and show you the luxuries of Ingotheria."

Lenna contemplated him, her eyes roving over Dimas before replying, "I have conditions."

"I'm willing to negotiate."

"I am not a negotiation – nor am I a bargaining chip," she stated firmly, "I *will* have your full respect, or I'll set my sights on travelling to a different Kingdom. One where my choices do not appear so slim."

Hale sipped from his glass, his amber eyes flashing with contempt as he spoke, "I hear the Larimar Islands are quite nice this time of year – very tropical. And *their* King doesn't seem to take kindly to threats from Ingotherian Kings either."

Lenna gave a thoughtful hum, tapping a finger to her chin. "Gosh, I really do have my choice at Kingdoms – don't I?"

A muscle jumped in Dimas's jaw as Lenna and Hale swapped smirks. I hid my own behind my palm as Keerian nodded once to Ballah, the "servant" spinning on her heels and marching towards the throne room doors.

It was time to eat.

The servants lining the edge of the throne room stepped forward, offering refills of wine down the table as a second wave appeared, each carrying a large plate covered with a tall silver dome.

Keerian appraised Dimas like a wolf watching a doe drinking from a stream. "I do enjoy the meals our wily chef comes up with. I don't even know what the Palace kitchens prepared this evening – I was only told it was *a delicacy.*"

Lord Dimas fought a frown from his face, though he recovered quickly as he met Keerian's hate-filled eyes. "I am honored to share this meal with you, your Majesty. I foresee nothing but entertainment in the evening ahead. Though, as I must remind you, my King does expect myself and the Oracle in the Ruby Kingdom before dawn."

"How could we forget," Keerian sneered, taking a sip from his wine glass as he disregarded Dimas completely in favor of the covered silver platter that was laid before him and I. I fought the grin curling against my lips as Dimas was served third.

Ballah lay the domed plate in front of Dimas with flourish, her red eyes gleaming wickedly in the firelight flickering around the room. "Enjoy, my Lord," she murmured before slipping away to stand behind me.

I turned to Dimas, conspiratorially holding my tattooed palm against the handle atop the silver cloche. "Let's open them together," I whispered eagerly, as if this was a nightly game for us, "while the rest of the table is still getting served."

Sure enough, the beings around us were all receiving their dome-covered meals, all excitedly chattering about what the chef prepared.

Lenna thinned her lips, eyeing Dimas expectantly, and I saw Hale lean over to mutter something in her ear. Lenna swallowed tightly before shooting Hale a wide-eyed look.

Dimas bowed his head ever so slightly in my direction, as if he was merely placating my whim, his own hand wrapping around the scrolling silver handle. "As you wish, Queen Esmeray."

"On three," I replied, baring my teeth. "One, two, *three!*"

Dimas whipped his cloche off with a polite smile that fell off his face a split second later. The silver dome hit the floor with a loud *crash*, rolling and rattling across the glass, before coming to a stop near Ballah's feet. The gargoyle simply stepped on it to stop its trajectory, though the noise turned everyone's focus to Dimas and his *very* special meal.

One of the beings further down the table screamed as silence slammed through the room.

Dimas paled further, his already light skin turning ghostly as he came face to face with the severed heads of Smoth and Hamm. Their horns had been shaved down to mere pegs, a sign of disgrace within the gargoyle community, and their dead eyes stared, unseeing, towards their Lord. The chef had truly taken some liberties with my request, as each of the heads now had their jaws open and a shiny apple stuffed between their lips.

"You know, you were correct, Lord Dimas," I said in a mocking whisper, leaning closer to the fae as he winced, "The Ruby Kingdom *definitely* has no spies in Irridessen."

# CHAPTER SIXTY-FOUR
## LENNA

IT TOOK EVERY OUNCE of strength to not flinch away from the glassy eyes of the dead spies displayed against an artistic bed of kale. Lenna took a deep swallow of her wine, turning away from the gruesome display to focus on breathing and not hurling. The sweet pink wine settled in her gut, swirling, and adding a muted buzz over her senses.

Esmeray had warned her ahead of dinner what fun surprises were waiting for Lord Dimas, but knowing it was happening and *seeing it* were two very different things.

With a dramatic sigh, Esmeray stood from her chair, the chains draped over her wings twinkling as the opal links caught the firelight. She propped her hands on her hips, calling out in a loud voice filled with mirth, "Oh, Lord Dimas my *apologies!* It seems your dinner was switched with our cave dragon's snack."

Dimas shrunk back as Esmeray reached across the table, her fingers wrapping around the sand brown stumped horn of one of the severed heads. With a nonchalant toss, Esmeray threw the head over Dimas and across the glass floor as ripples appeared in the surface. The head slipped through without a sound; the apple still comically lodged between the spy's teeth. Dimas full body recoiled as a spurt of fire lit the depths of the caverns below and Resso dove from his hiding space on a ledge of rock, his silvery black wings wide as he plunged down into the cavern's darkness after the head.

The glass was still rippling as Esmeray launched the second head through the floor. Resso must have been in on the plan because curling steam appeared in his maw, less than twenty feet from the glass surface, and his silvery eyes glinted with amusement as his jaw darted out and he snapped the second head between his teeth, swallowing it whole before flipping and diving lazily out of sight.

Esmeray clapped twice to the servants standing by the throne room door. "Please bring Lord Dimas his meal, and make sure chef *checks it* this time."

Two servants hustled out of the room before reappearing a few beats later, carrying a smaller silver platter adorned with a dome. One whisked away the now-empty bed of kale as the other replaced it with the new platter. Dimas set his jaw, eyeing the new dish warily. Across from him, Keerian dug into his steak and potatoes with zest. "Not something you see everyday in the Ruby Kingdom, I'm sure," he said lightly, his mouth full of potatoes.

Dimas shuddered, wordless, as he cautiously removed the cloche from the new dish, visibly relaxing as it revealed a platter of delicately sliced fish and a bed of steaming vegetables.

Esmeray sat back in her chair, the rest of the table returning to their own conversations and meals. The room filled with laughter and the din of voices grew until it was impossible to pick out individual chatter as the beings around the table dove into their own dinners, completely unaffected by the severed heads. They'd also been warned ahead of time by their King and Queen.

Those with a queasy stomach had opted to sit out.

As had Merrick.

Lenna fought the hot tears welling behind her eyes as she picked at her meal of buttery fish, pushing a piece around before spearing it halfheartedly on her fork. She'd begged Merrick to come enjoy dinner with her before she left for the Ruby Palace.

Her bags were packed, as were Hale's, and they sat against the stone steps of the dais, still hidden by Esmeray's magic. There was no saying when she'd be back in Irridessen, but with Oracle Asrar's statement that Lenna could only see the past of the Kingdoms she visited, she knew she needed to go to the Ruby Kingdom, and travel to both the Topaz Kingdom and the Jade Kingdom while she stayed in Ingotheria.

But Merrick could have at least come to bid her goodbye. Hale's pocket watch ticked faintly in his breast pocket, counting down the seconds until Lenna departed on a new adventure. Every tick sent her heart lurching. She'd pleaded with Merrick to come, or at least to talk to her, but her friend only grunted a non-committal answer before turning away, staring blankly out of the window of his accommodations. A quick glance down the long table confirmed there were no seats open.

He wasn't coming.

She knew the ghost soul tie weighed heavy upon him, and her heart broke at the finality of Sparrow's actions. But it couldn't have been helped. It was no ordinary circumstance. Lenna felt better leaving Ir-ridessen knowing both Esmeray and Sparrow were here – and ruthlessly powerful Vessels.

The hours and courses passed as she mindlessly ate, her thoughts firmly elsewhere.

As she took small bites of a cherry filled dessert, her stomach squeezed uncomfortably against the laced corset of her dress. Sparrow and Laurent sat across from her, subdued as well, though they slipped on a mask of careful neutrality, neither engaging in conversation nor drawing attention to themselves.

Hale rubbed her thigh under the table in a comforting caress. She shot him an appreciative smile before tuning in to the conversation Dimas and Esmeray were having. The dinner had long been completed, and beings either dispersed out of the throne room to go to bed or danced to the slow songs played by the string quartet in the corner of the room. Hale leaned closer, "We should be leaving within the hour. Are you ready?"

Lenna muttered a 'yes' under her breath as she squeezed Hale's hand. At least he was coming with her. She shot another look at the throne room doors, wishing with all her might that the grey-winged gargoyle would appear with a dirty joke and booming laugh, that Merrick would be there when she left.

"- and I assure you, those spies were *not* under my jurisdiction," Dimas was saying, his fork hovering over his dessert.

"Then who sent them here?" Esmeray wondered, her sarcasm thick, as she waved a blunt-tipped dinner knife in the air before using it to cut a piece of cake, passing it to Keerian.

Dimas shook his head. "I don't know."

"Lie again," Keerian snapped. The King Consort had polished off his entire dinner in mere minutes, along with two slices of cherry pie, a few cookies, and was now scarfing down a slice of chocolate cake, glaring openly at the Ambassador the entire time.

"I – There were talks of sending spies to Irridessen, though I assure you the majority of council members vetoed the idea. For you to find spies in your lands...It must have been a covert mission that I wasn't privy to."

Esmeray leaned forward, and Lenna had to strain her ears to hear the Queen. "Lord Dimas, cut the shit. We know why the spies were here, and what they hoped to achieve. They assaulted my Heir and her mate in the Grotto of Faune. You want us to be amenable about sending the Oracle to the Ruby Kingdom? Then tell me what King Eamon knows about the Vessel Books."

Dimas shifted in his seat before shooting a glance at Sparrow. Her aquamarine eyes flared with power as she bared her teeth at Dimas.

With a swallow, Dimas muttered to Queen Esmeray, "There's a massive power imbalance between Ingotheria and Irridessen. King Eamon doesn't like that."

Esmeray gave the Lord a flat look. Sparrow hissed, silver magic coiling through her fingers, refracting against the empty crystal glass in front of her. Dimas wavered between the two Vessels, a frown marring his face as his gaze raked over Sparrow's *acat* before dropping his voice even lower. Lenna turned her head slightly, as did Hale. She locked eyes with her love, the two of them sharing a knowing-yet-tight-lipped grin. The Queen said nothing about them eavesdropping.

"Your Heir is the Vessel of Faune," Dimas breathed as his eyes widened, taking in the woosh of Sparrow's magic that pulsed through the air.

"And herein lies the issue, Dimas. You now know something that King Eamon doesn't. So, you have a choice. You can answer my questions to the best of your ability, and we can both leave this exchange harboring a dirty little secret, or you can refuse to answer my questions, and I can send my condolences to your King in regard to your tragic death." With a searing glint in her eyes, Lenna knew Queen Esmeray meant every word of that threat, and if needed, she'd follow through with it.

"King Eamon has the Book of Aella," Dimas said under his breath, with an air of defeat, "And he uses the Culling as an excuse to find and test beings blessed by the Goddess of Destruction – to see if he can imbue a Vessel with Aella's god magic. He wants his own weapon, especially in the light of you becoming a Vessel, Queen Esmeray."

Esmeray frowned. "And is my suspicion correct? Does your King know about Sparrow becoming the Vessel of Life?"

Dimas shook his head before steeling himself with a deep swallow of wine. The two paused as Ballah approached, filling the Lord's cup swiftly before disappearing again. "As far as I know, King Eamon is not aware. All I was told is he received word there was a hint of the Book of Faune in Florra, but I never heard anything else about it."

"What aren't you telling me, Lord Dimas?" Esmeray hedged, her green eyes flaring.

Keerian leaned closer, his aura imposing. "I suggest you take a more direct route with your answers, Dimas."

"The King has his sights set on the other Vessel Books," Dimas replied hastily. "More specifically, the Book of Carra. It's somewhere in Ingotheria, and the King wants to use the Oracle to track it. He wants control over the Vessel of Destruction and the Vessel of Salvation. And he wants to *weaken* Irridessen before conquering it for himself."

The way Dimas enunciated the word "*weaken*" caused a tremor to slide down Lenna's spine. It was as if Dimas was implying –

"Is King Eamon attempting to assassinate me?" Esmeray rasped low.

Dimas cocked his head, his eyes pointedly fixing on Keerian. "No, Queen Esmeray. Not you."

Keerian raised his chin, his golden horns shining. "Me, then."

The nod of Dimas's head was so slight Lenna almost missed it. "You are soul tied. Queen Esmeray is much too powerful a rival for King

Eamon to kill. But you – King Keerian – though your fierceness in battle and your legends of strength are spoken about in our Kingdom, you are not fae, you have no magic to protect yourself with if you were to be separated from Queen Esmeray. King Eamon knows if he takes you off the playing board, that it will also sweep Irridessen of a Vessel *and* their Queen Absolute. Your death would make both of the thrones in Irridessen vacant – vulnerable to conquest."

"Fuck," Esmeray exhaled. "Why are you telling us this?"

"Because, severed heads aside, I do not want to go to war, nor does Prince Cillian. And although my King has allowed me to come speak with you, there are things I cannot tell you even if I wanted. King Eamon is very powerful and wields air magic from Akash. Plus, a heritage power where he can forbid me from speaking on certain topics – to not allow me to tell you all I know. And if I tried, I die instantly." Dimas sighed heavily, "I very much enjoy living, your Majesty."

Esmeray slumped back into her chair, sharing a concerned look with her mate. Keerian looked torn between snapping Dimas's neck or throwing his wine goblet across the room in frustration. As if in answer, his knuckles tightened against the crystal. Lenna braced herself.

"Lenna," Esmeray finally said, her keen eyes scrunched, "You understand that you don't have to go to the Ruby Kingdom if you don't want in light of everything Dimas has revealed – right?"

Dimas opened his mouth to argue, but was cut off by Keerian's growl of warning.

"I do, Queen Esmeray," Lenna replied evenly. "But I will go."

"I'm going as well," Hale added, throwing a glare at Dimas that Lenna read as *'don't try and stop me.'*

Dimas gave Lenna and Hale a stiff nod before pulling a small ruby from his breast pocket. He waved a hand over the gem until it began glowing. Within moments, a portal began flickering into existence by the dais, red sparks fizzing to life against the glass floor. Lenna's heart lurched as she threw a desperate glance to the throne room doors.

Merrick did not appear.

Dimas stood, bowing lower than he had upon his arrival to the Obsidian Palace.

"You have made powerful enemies, Queen Esmeray," Dimas stated, "though I do not believe I am one of them."

Esmeray gave the Lord a saccharine smile. "I like having powerful enemies, Lord Dimas. It makes me feel important."

Dimas huffed a laugh as Esmeray flicked her fingers, Lenna and Hale's luggage appearing as the illusion slipped away. Lenna stood, moving towards Esmeray and throwing her arms around the Queen as Keerian, Sparrow and Laurent queued closer to her. She hugged each of them in turn. Keerian hugged her last as Hale exchanged a firm handshake with Laurent and Sparrow swept the baker in a tight embrace. "Keep our favorite Oracle safe for us, Hale."

Hale bowed to Sparrow. "With my life, Sparrow. Thank you for helping with the bakery while we're gone."

"You have the mind-speak ring," Keerian said under his breath as Lenna's attention pulled back to the King who still had her wrapped in his arms. "If you need anything, let us know. Keep in touch - and if you feel anything is amiss, we'll storm the Ruby Kingdom with the full force of Irridessen to get you back."

Lenna patted the King's cheek, his beard soft under her fingers. "Don't be such a worry wart," she replied with feigned brightness, more to assuage Keerian's concerns than her own. "We'll be fine."

Dimas waited patiently by the now formed portal, the blood red light thrumming with an impatient hum. Lenna shot one more look at the throne room doors, knowing that a piece of her heart would be left behind in Irridessen, wishing she could help Merrick heal from the pain of losing his chance at a true soul tie, wishing she had more time in this incredible land she called home, more time with the beings surrounding her that had become her family.

Her finger drifted over the grey stone on her ring, feeling its coolness. Merrick still had his off. She wouldn't be able to say goodbye, wouldn't be able to tell the gargoyle that ambushed her in the forest of Doortan how incredibly thankful she was for him.

With a sad smile, she gripped Hale's hand. Esmeray flicked her palm and the pile of trunks and chests floated over the floor before disappearing into the depths of the portal.

Lenna and Hale approached Dimas who gestured them forward. Lenna took a deep breath.

The throne room doors slammed open, and Lenna whipped around, her heart in her throat as Merrick appeared. His eyes still held that same red-rimmed misery, but he stalked towards the group, a small bag slung over his shoulder and his sword with the blue stone pommel strapped to his back.

"I'm going," he grunted, not meeting anyone's eyes as he closed the distance.

Keerian exchanged a look with Laurent, the surprise on their faces apparent, as Merrick approached Lenna. He looked down at her, grim determination on his face, his brown hair tied back in a leather band. His wings were snapped shut, raised high on his back. He jerked his head to Esmeray. "I'm going with them to the Ruby Kingdom."

Esmeray leveled a concerned stare to Merrick, but whatever she saw in his expression made her smile softly. The Queen reached forward, gripping Merrick's hand in her own. "Are you sure?"

"I have nothing left for me here," he said gruffly. "So, I'll go with Lenna and Hale and protect 'em."

Sparrow stepped forward, her eyes shining with tears and unspoken words, but Merrick shook his head, taking a swift step away from her. "I don't blame you, Sparrow. For any of it. I want you to know I understand." He swallowed thickly, tears shining in his own eyes. "And I hold no anger or resentment towards you. I'm happy for you and Laurent. I could imagine no better male to hold your soul tie. But I need to leave."

Tears streaked down Sparrow's face as Laurent gripped her tightly to his side, reaching his hand out to Merrick. "Be safe, brother. You'll always have a home here."

Merrick clasped Laurent's hand in his - a look of pained relief crossing his face. "Thank you, brother. Take care of things."

Keerian pulled Merrick into a hug before clapping him on the shoulder. "Keep them safe."

With a curt nod, Merrick moved over to Lenna and Hale. Lenna's heart threatened to beat out of her chest as she offered Merrick her other hand. "Thank you, Merrick," she whispered, her breathy words flooded with gratitude.

Hale smiled smugly at the gargoyle. "I knew you'd come around," he said simply.

Merrick winked at the baker before bumping Lenna affectionately with his wing. "I took Lenna from the Slate Kingdom to Irridessen. It's only right I follow her in whatever other exploits she demands to go on."

Lenna let the tears flow as she leaned her head against Merrick's arm.

Esmeray waved them forward. "I had a speech prepared, but now I just..." The Queen cleared her throat, her voice wavering with emotion. She let out a rough breath, grinning at Merrick, approval and pride shining in her eyes. "I'll keep it short and simple. Lenna and Hale, go forth and see the world. Merrick...find happiness, and go make friends."

Lenna beamed as they approached the portal, the swirling light now seeming to emit a welcoming buzz.

With a deep breath, a sense of calm swept over her. Lenna stepped through the portal and into her next adventure.

# CHAPTER SIXTY-FIVE
# ORLA

ORLA SHIFTED HER FEET ever so slightly as she stood with the rest of the Oasees residents in the throne room. King Eamon and Prince Cillian sat in their thrones, the latter looking ridiculously impassive and handsome in his deep burgundy tunic and linen pants, the thin golden crown on his head slightly askew as the minutes trickled by under a fog of silence.

A being a few pews up coughed. King Eamon twisted his face in a snarl and the being shrank back, falling silent once more. A trickle of sweat beaded down Orla's back as she shot her eyes to the Topaz Royalty, her anonymity among the teeming crowd giving her a chance to survey Princess Yin without interruption and keep her *acat* displayed.

Yin sat stick straight and alert, her lean body covered with a ridiculously modest pale-yellow, multi-layered robe that pleated and folded against her chest, covering halfway up her throat, and fanning out into wide, intricately embroidered sleeves that showcased flowers and vines in different hues of red and green.

Orla could only imagine the garment was the Princess's thickest and most formal dresswear, causing Orla's lips to quirk up in a small grin. She hoped Yin was miserably overheating.

The filmy red dress Orla wore was cut into two panels that folded and cinched around her waist, with large cutouts on each side, and just barely brushed the tops of her silky slippers. Two high slits in the skirts relieved her a fraction from the sweltering air, though it did nothing against the combined body heat of all these beings packed in the narrow sandstone pews.

The dry heat of the desert was one thing – but standing amongst the rest of Oasees, that aridness was replaced with a damp, packed warmth that had her wishing she could slip out of the throne room and draw an ice-cold bath to soak. But she couldn't imagine having to sit in one of those layered robes where the material seemed more apt for a mild or cool climate – not the scorching desert.

The King had called all of Oasees to the throne room hours ago, and the sun still hadn't risen. The Oracle was coming, and King Eamon wanted everyone in Oasees to welcome the mysterious being to Ingotheria. Orla had no idea what to expect, but with the Culling and the Equinox Ball this evening, she hoped this Oracle appeared soon so she could go back to bed for a few hours before she had to get dressed and ready herself to prove that she was a fire wielder. Then, she would have a couple hours to relax at the party before starting her duties for Nonna – which included bringing Cillian his wine while he and the council sat around waiting for the King's supposedly grand speech of the night.

She smoothed her consciousness through her mind's fingers, feeling the golden thread attaching her to Seysei. The dragon had not connected to her thoughts in two days, but it wasn't uncommon for her *kindered* to slither into a craggy desert cave to sleep off a huge meal after devouring some poor critter.

Finding the thread unconnected, Orla eased out of her strand of heritage magic, blinking up at the Prince who continued lounging on his throne as if this entire occasion was beneath him. Catching her gaze, Cillian smirked, raising a single eyebrow in her direction as his tongue licked his bottom lip sensually. Orla felt her core tighten as she shot a wink at the male from under her lashes.

Gods, maybe he could come soak in the tub *with* her...

Casting that delightful mental image aside, Orla shifted again. She lucked out getting a seat on the aisle, so when King Eamon finally released them, she could dart out of the room before the rest of the crowd and get back to her quarters without delay. Her eyes settled on Soren who stood against the side wall with the male servants assigned to take care of the Topaz Princess and King Eamon's hulking bodyguards.

Between Nonna's never-ending list of chores for Orla and the Oasees servants to prepare for the Ball, and Soren's own tasks to assist King Eamon, they were both pulling long shifts, catching odd hours of sleep when they could, and their nights of wine and gossip had been begrudgingly put on hold until after the Ball was over and the Topaz Royal fucked off back to her own Kingdom.

Orla shot a glower to Yin again. She couldn't wait for the bitch to leave. Even now, Yin continued to shoot increasingly sultry looks in Cillian's direction, causing Orla to clench her fists and teeth together. Cillian ignored Yin with an air of pure contempt.

A short fae with deep black hair and light skin scurried into the throne room, holding a glowing gemstone. He hustled up to the dais, before falling to his knees and bowing low, holding the ruby over his head and pulling all eyes to him. "Lord Dimas has activated his gemstone, my King."

King Eamon smiled, his fierce eyes darkening with a hungry gleam. "Build the portal. The Oracle will be here momentarily."

The fae rose to his feet, bowed again, and began whipping his hands above his head in erratic movements, his fingers twitching as red sparks shot out from his palms to hover in midair. The sparks conglomerated and grew as the fae pushed more of his magic into the ball of light, maintaining a look of determination as he fed the growing orb more and more.

Orla watched, fascinated, as the massive portal thrashed under the fae's control. Rivulets of perspiration ran down the portal-maker's cheeks, though he never took his eyes off his task. With a shuddering groan, the fae heaved the last bit of magic into the glowing depths before them, and the throne room was momentarily bathed in red light before he half-collapsed, half-bowed before it. King Eamon appraised the fae with a dull expression before shoo-ing him away.

The fae bowed one last time before staggering towards Soren and the other servants. Soren said something quietly to the fae before pushing a cool glass of water into his hands. The portal-maker smiled in thanks, shaking, as he tipped the cup to his lips and gulped down its contents.

Two of the three royals watched the thrumming portal expectantly, and after a few tense seconds, a *thump* sounded and a pile of bags and chests flew through the red light, skidding across the floor and bumping softly against the first steps of the dais. King Eamon tightened his mouth into a grim line, as if the sight of the Oracle's own belongings disgusted him.

Orla fought the eyeroll that threatened in favor of continuing to watch for the Oracle's arrival. Beings all around her shoved forward, craning their necks to get a glimpse of their important guest, and one being jostled her shoulder trying to practically climb over her. She twisted around, hissing darkly at the gargoyle to her left, who bared his own teeth back before noting the *acat* gracing her arms, shifting back with a tempered grunt.

With a smirk on her face, Orla peered over the fae in front of her, mentally high-fiving herself for her chosen seat. With the aisle to her right, she had an almost unobstructed view of the proceedings.

A stocky male with a thick black beard, dark skin, and long locs twisted into an intricate bun appeared, his smile wide as he took in the surroundings of the throne room. Orla raised her eyebrows as she noted the softly pointed ears of the male. She thought the Oracle had to be human, but with her limited knowledge, she could've understood wrong.

A huge gargoyle with grey wings stepped through the portal next, his eyes cutting around the room with precision, as if he was assessing any threats to the Oracle. His wings were slightly spread, and Orla noted the gargoyle seemed to be covering a being with his right wing.

Orla's eyes darted to King Eamon, whose lips had pulled back into a full grimace at the sight of the gargoyle standing before him, and Orla wondered if the gargoyle knew exactly what type of King was currently baring his teeth. Orla couldn't see more than the gargoyle's side profile, but she could see the sharp fang and knew that the gargoyle's returning smile was also more threatening than kind.

Orla rose up on her toes to see who was standing between the gargoyle and the male, but with the gargoyle's wings still raised, they blocked the Oasees residents from laying eyes on the last figure. Orla could make out a pair of brown boots and the hem of a green dress shifting between the gargoyle and the portly male but couldn't get a better look.

Dimas appeared last, stepping through the portal effortlessly, fixing the lapel of his red jacket. Orla noted Dimas looked paler than when she'd seen him a few days ago, but any information of what he saw in the Obsidian Kingdom would most likely only be shared with Prince Cillian, and a more redacted version relayed to the King.

Dimas ushered the trio forward, bowing low to King Eamon and acknowledging the rest of the royals with a dip of his head. Straightening, Dimas shot a cheery smile to the King, before saying, "King Eamon, it is my pleasure to introduce you to the Oracle of Terramere, Lady Lenna Poryadok, as well as her escorts, Hale Moyo of Florra, and Captain Merrick...from the Opal Palace." Dimas paused, chancing a glance at the gargoyle. "I apologize, I did not catch your surname."

"I didn't give it," the gargoyle – Merrick – replied gruffly.

Orla huffed a soft laugh.

King Eamon bristled.

The throne room rolled with silent tension and even Cillian shifted in his seat, though the bloodlust on Yin's face didn't match the intrigue crossing the Prince's.

Merrick shifted his wing slightly, and Orla's stomach dropped as she got a first glimpse at the Oracle. Her red-gold hair lay perfectly curled and unbound down her back as she gave King Eamon and the rest of the royals a small bow. Her stomach flipping, Orla desperately fought the tide of heads to get a look at the Oracle's face.

Could it be *her* Lenna? From the distance, she couldn't tell, but she held her breath, her mind scrambling against the slim probability.

King Eamon gave the Oracle a tight-lipped smile before standing, the rest of the royals following suit. "Oracle, it is a pleasure to welcome you to my home. I do hope you find the Ruby Kingdom to your liking. If you don't mind, I have invited the residents of Oasees, our friends and family, to welcome you as well. It has been a couple decades since we've had the pleasure of the Oracle in our midst, and I must say, our Kingdom is stronger for it." With a gesture, King Eamon waved his hand out to the throng of beings in the room, and Orla held her breath as the head of red-gold curls turned to take in the room's occupants.

It had been over half a year since Orla fled Doortan, washing up on the shores of the Ruby Kingdom, but when the Oracle turned, and Orla saw the honey-brown eyes and soft round face of Lenna, Lady of Doortan, she gasped.

Lenna's eyes immediately shot towards the noise, and Orla took a half step into the aisle, in a way where Lenna could catch sight of her, but King Eamon couldn't make Orla out from the rest of the crowd. Wide-eyed shock crossed Lenna's face, and she made a move as if she would run down the aisle to Orla. With a half shake of her head, Orla mouthed, "*I'll find you*," before darting her eyes to the King, widening them slightly in warning.

Lenna recovered quickly, smoothing the confusion and something that looked like relief off her face, before waving awkwardly around the room. The Oasees residents burst into applause, causing Lenna to blush furiously before she ducked her head, turning back to King Eamon.

"Your Palace is beautiful, King Eamon, and I am thankful for the opportunity to visit," Lenna said.

King Eamon inclined his head, "I apologize for the abrupt request, but we wanted you to be able to experience the beauty of our Equinox Ball. You will, of course, be housed in the royal wing. If you don't mind, I shall have my personal servant, Soren, direct you to your rooms. The Ball will begin this evening, and I am sure you and your...*travel companions...* would like the opportunity to rest before the festivities begin."

Dimas frowned at King Eamon's mention of Lenna's escorts, but Orla sought out Soren, who gracefully moved from her place standing by the wall and approached the dais, bowing low to King Eamon before smiling warmly at Lenna. With a murmured word, Soren gestured Lenna,

Merrick, and Hale to follow her, the four of them disappearing through one of the closed doors to the right of the dais. Once the group was out of sight, the bags and chests of Lenna's things disappeared in a plume of white magic.

King Eamon stood before his throne, addressing the beings in the room, but Orla didn't hear a word. Her eyes lay on the door where Lenna had gone, and as soon as King Eamon finished his speech and dismissed the room, Orla turned and ran down the aisle, her feet swiftly directing her towards the royal wing of the Palace and the female that ultimately saved her life.

"WHERE IS SHE?" ORLA heaved as she rounded a corner, almost bowling over Soren in the process.

Soren shot out a hand to steady her, her brows pinching. "Who? The Oracle?"

Orla nodded, struggling to regulate her breathing against the tide of emotions. She'd burst into the royal wing – thankfully finding it empty since its inhabitants were still funneling out of the throne room. But she'd already taken three rushed laps of the first level, before finding Soren after ascending the stairs to the second floor. "I know her – she's the reason I'm even here. Lenna saved my life. I – I volunteer to be her servant. Who can make that happen?"

Soren opened her mouth in shock, but pointed to a door at the end of the hall. "Lady Lenna is in there with her two escorts. I..." She hesitated a beat before snapping her fingers. "Cillian. I'll tell him you're taking over serving duties for the Oracle. I'm assuming you don't want everyone to know you've got a connection to her."

Orla shook her head rapidly. "I don't even know how she's here. I need to talk to her – if she isn't aware of what's going on..."

Soren shushed her, though Orla knew better than to add more to that statement. "Consider it done. I'll meet you back in your rooms an hour before the Culling starts."

Orla squeezed Soren in a tight hug before flying down the hall.

She didn't know what she would say – and *fuck* she should've gotten Marlo – but she couldn't easily smuggle him into the royal wing.

Without even knocking, Orla flung open the door.

Before she managed to cross the threshold, the huge gargoyle lunged forward, unsheathing a dagger from his side with a snarl, holding the curved tip millimeters from Orla's neck. She raised her hands in submission, catching her breath and choking out, *"Lady Lenna-"*

"Merrick! Put that down!" Lenna cried as she darted across the room, flapping her hands frantically. Merrick lowered the dagger, though confusion flickered across his face.

Orla crashed into Lenna with a sob, her arms wrapping tightly around her. Lenna hugged her back fiercely, and when Orla pulled away, Lenna didn't release her, merely holding her at arm's length. "You're fae?" Lenna asked shrilly, her honey eyes darting from Orla's face, to her ears, to every small and subtle difference Orla had as a human.

Orla nodded, tears breaking free from her lashes. "It was a surprise to me as well," she managed. "Especially since it means Olivera isn't my mother."

Lenna pursed her lips, a smile threatening to crack, before breaking out in laughter. "What a relief, I'm sure."

Orla buried herself in Lenna's arms once more. "How are you here? What happened? Are you truly the Oracle? How did you get away from Leon? Marlo's here, too – by the way. When did you become the Oracle? Where were you before this?" The questions spilled from her lips, but there was no helping it.

So much had happened in that six months, so much threatened to bubble up as Orla thought about everything she wanted to tell the kind female. Words that hadn't come easy when Orla and Marlo fled Doortan. She'd been no more than a shell of a being when she boarded that ship to escape, and even though the first four months of her being here were a whirlwind of fear while she adjusted to a new reality, the last two months had been spent adjusting to being fae, being *Vitraro,* meeting new friends, finding her *kindered,* and learning about her magic.

The girl she'd been in Doortan was a complete stranger to the fae female she now embraced.

Lenna sucked in a breath. "Marlo's here? How did *that* happen? I have so many questions to ask *you.*"

An awkward cough sounded behind Lenna, and the females broke apart. Lenna shot Orla a genuinely beaming smile as she gestured to the broody gargoyle who has his arms crossed, a slight frown on his face, and the dark-skinned male who was currently hopping up and down on the balls of his feet, as if he couldn't wait to meet Orla himself. There was a kind twinkle that effortlessly radiated from his eyes, and Orla immediately liked him. The gargoyle – not so much.

Lenna pointed to the gargoyle who shuffled his wings, standing up straighter as he assessed Orla and her *acat.* By the half-scowl, Orla assumed he was debating if she was a threat or a friend. Orla gave him a small nod of her head as Lenna said, "This is Merrick – he sort of ambushed me after I dropped you and Marlo off at the Doortan port. He told me I was the activated Oracle, and bought me to Irridessen."

Merrick rose his chin, surveying Orla like a hawk watching a field mouse. Orla leveled her glare right back at him. She was no mouse. She was a dragon.

"And *this* -" Lenna said happily, clasping hands with the smiling male, completely unaffected by the stare down Merrick and Orla were engaged in, "- is Hale, my love and my partner. We met shortly after my arrival to the Obsidian Kingdom."

Orla dropped her eyes from Merrick to bow her head to Hale, who wasted no time pulling her into a hug of his own. "Lenna told me *so* much about you," he gushed. "And what a surprise, I'm sure, to find out you're fae!"

"A big surprise," Orla giggled, though her eyes caught the intricate locs Hale sported. "I love your locs. I've always wanted some, but haven't found a being here that has free time to start them."

Hale's cheeks turned a deep umber as he blushed. "Thank you, Orla. I'd be happy to help you begin them if you want. Even Lenna here has learned how to retwist and tidy them up for me. Helps my old hands to have an extra pair."

It was Lenna's turn to flush as the three shared a smile. Merrick grumbled something under his breath before turning and continuing to unpack their chest of belongings.

"You said Marlo's here?" Lenna asked, her eyes shining. "Where is he?"

"He lives in the other half of the Palace, in Aridden," Orla explained. "But he has a really cool job in the bazaar and even has his own residence above the shop. We'll see him tonight at the Ball – I know he'll be thrilled to see you."

Lenna squeaked with excitement, and Hale moved away to give them some alone time to catch up. Orla and Lenna moved to the balcony of the suite, taking up seats on two of the wrought iron chairs that looked out to a lounge where beings had begun to appear, carrying silver cups of tea and relaxing against massive curved couches or nestling into large piles of pillows that dotted the ice-white floor.

Orla had never been this deep into the royal wing, its floorplan very similar to her own lodgings, though the royal wing lay beneath one of the Ruby Palace's glass-paned domes, giving the residents a courtyard of sorts that was fully separate from the elements. Lenna's room was really two rooms in one. One room was easily the size of both Orla and Soren's room combined, containing a massive bed, a much larger bathing chamber, and shelves inset into the wall around an ornately carved mantle that looked to be fully constructed from ruby.

The second room looked as if it was a smaller bedroom, but Orla only managed a quick peek to see a dark wood four-poster bed and a thin desk, before Merrick entered the room and closed the door behind him with a loud click.

"Your gargoyle escort doesn't seem very friendly," Orla commented under her breath as her *acat* flickered with flame.

"He's...been through a lot recently," Lenna exhaled, "though he is one of the greatest, most loyal friends a female could ask for." With a waggling eyebrow, Lenna shot Orla a cheeky glance. "He's normally very funny and nice. Merrick needs to make some *friends* –preferably of the female variety."

Orla groaned sarcastically, her mind drifting to her handsome Prince. "I ah, kind of have a friend of the male variety already."

Lenna inched closer, her eyes sparkling with glee. "I must meet him. Is he around?"

With a sheepish wince, Orla grinned slowly. "You already did…He's the Prince of the Ruby Kingdom. Cillian." The look on Lenna's face, with her bright eyes and surprised jaw-drop made Orla blush furiously. "But it's a secret," she amended hurriedly, "No one can know."

Lenna patted her arm. "I won't tell a soul," she promised. "There seems to be a lot of secrets in this Kingdom already, so what's one more?"

Orla huffed in agreement, and the two fell into easy conversation that spanned the length of the six months since they last saw each other, though Orla kept her *Vitraro* heritage gifts and Seysei to herself. She didn't want to implicate Lenna in anything – especially the day of the Culling.

Lenna explained her time since they last saw each other, detailing the power she received as the Oracle, before blowing into a long, sordid tale of a battle between two Queens for the thrones of Irridessen, how she used the Prism to reveal the truth of the late ruler's deaths, and recounted every event to the present.

By the end of it, Orla's mouth hung open. Lenna was *powerful* and it seemed as if Queen Esmeray wasn't the monster King Eamon believed she was. Though Orla did chuckle at the fact Dimas received two severed heads for dinner last night. No wonder he looked so pale.

The sun had fully risen and slowly began its descent into late afternoon while they talked, and Orla couldn't help the smile that stuck to her face. They laughed together, cried together, and all of the heavy, unspoken words Orla wished to tell Lenna came out in a long, jumbled mess through a sheet of tears and gratitude, but they were out – and Orla felt a weight lift from her shoulders.

"I looked for you, you know. In the Prism. You and Marlo," Lenna said softly. "I didn't understand why I couldn't see you. I feared something happened to you both, but I spoke to the late Oracle in a dream, and he told me I could only see the past for Kingdoms I've visited. That's why I'm here, though with King Eamon's threats, I'm here for purely *diplomatic* reasons." Lenna lowered her voice. "I need to stand upon the lands of both the Topaz Kingdom and the Jade Kingdom before I go back to my true Queen, Queen Esmeray."

Orla straightened. She'd yet to fly with Seysei, but the dragon was huge. She wondered if he could carry her *and* Lenna to the Topaz and Jade Kingdoms, to help Lenna's quest to visit the rest of Ingotheria.

She almost said something but thought better of it as she grasped that golden connection to Seysei, finding the thread still disconnected. Concern jittered around her mind. She was worried enough for the Culling but had felt better knowing Seysei could easily come swoop her away if anything went sideways. She pushed that aside. *You are not so easily broken,* she reminded herself. If her *kindered* felt comfortable enough to nap this evening, then Orla shouldn't be worried.

Rising to her feet, Orla embraced Lenna again.

"I asked Soren if I could be your personal servant, and she agreed. I have to go get ready to be presented at the Culling, and show King Eamon my fire magic, but after that, I'll come find you, okay? Everyone from both Oasees and Aridden will be at the Ball tonight, so we can meet up with Marlo."

Lenna agreed, releasing Orla as they reentered the bedroom. With a final wave to Hale – who was currently nose deep in a book propped up by three pillows on the bed, Orla departed and hurried from the royal wing.

Her palms lay slick with sweat, but she steeled her resolve against any intrusive thoughts that threatened to darken her mood. The only thing standing in the way of her having fun at the Equinox Ball with her friends were a few easily conjured balls of fire.

And as she slipped through the door of her own room, she wondered if Cillian would ask her to dance.

# Chapter Sixty-Six
## Cillian

Traditions were the biggest pain in the ass. Cillian propped his elbow on the armrest of his throne as the fae in front of the dais struggled to control a shakily conjured tendril of water. Dimas stood at the bottom of the steps, nodding encouragingly at the fae before writing something down in a coil bound book.

"Lineage god, Beyos. Ability, water manipulation," Dimas stated, as the "water manipulation" in question quivered and splashed into a puddle of murky liquid that seeped across the floor. The young fae male blanched before hastily drawing upon his *acat* again, carefully dissolving every drop of water into mist that threaded through the room.

King Eamon grunted, waving the fae away with an annoyed frown. The fae took the hint, bowing hastily before bolting out the door.

Cillian slumped further into his seat, relief filling his bones. They were halfway through the list of beings who manifested *acatis* this year, and though the sordid displays garnered barely more than a huff or a dismissive wave from the King, so far, no beings exhibited any gifts found on the list of cullable magics.

On the other side of his father, Yin threaded her pale fingers through her hair, shooting Cillian a doe-eyed glance that he ignored. His father invited the Princess to the Culling, but Cillian half-hoped she'd refuse simply because he didn't trust Yin to not find any powerful fae a threat – especially since Orla was yet to be presented. Last year, Yin only stayed for the first three beings before announcing she was bored and slithering off to terrorize the beings gathering for the Ball that was being held in the second-largest dome of the palace.

This year, Yin seemed more inclined to fuck with Cillian's peace of mind than she was to depart early. Even with the distance from the party that started two hours ago, Cillian could hear a soft melody merrily breeze through the throne room as the Ruby Kingdom's royal orchestra dove into an upbeat rhythmic piece that made Cillian desire to pull a certain grey-eyed female close and dance.

Three more fae came and went, each one holding slightly more magic than the fae blessed by Beyos, but none strong enough to pique royal intrigue.

Dimas continued announcing each fae in a monotonous voice, confirming with his lineage magic that they were blessed with the gifts they admitted to having. But unless a being explicitly demonstrated a cullable gift, if Dimas read something forbidden in their bloodline, he'd ignore it.

Dimas knew of Orla's *Vitraro* heritage, but Cillian's closest friend and advisor would never relay that piece of information to the sadistic King sitting beside him.

As if his thoughts alone conjured her to appear, Orla entered through the single open door, her large, stormy eyes calculating as she surveyed the room. Gods, he loved the way her brain catalogued everything, how whip-quick she was able to deduce information from tiny details.

Her gaze bounced across the empty floor to the guards posted every twenty feet along the perimeter of the throne room, their staffs held upright in one hand, the wickedly sharp blades at the top perfectly shined for the occasion.

With her lips pressed in a thin line, Orla strode forward confidently, her expression determined and her posture straight. Cillian felt his heart attempt to leap out of his chest to go to her. He couldn't tear his eyes away as he greedily drank in every curve of her body like he was famished, struggling to keep his face utterly jaded. He leaned his chin in his hand, covering his mouth and the dumbstruck grin that was forcing its way across his traitorous lips.

She wore a dark red gown with a few tiny rubies threaded into the sole strip of satin at her navel. A slit in the skirt hit above mid-thigh, giving Cillian a glimpse of her smooth, golden-brown skin. Her arms were bare, showcasing the delicate scrollwork of her *acat*.

Orla's hair was loose, fluffing around her head in an ethereal halo that begged Cillian to run his fingers through it. Thin straps at her shoulders widened into two panels that covered and hugged her perfect breasts, before dipping and twisting in the middle of her stomach, leaving her hips and waist exposed. The dress's skirts started low, a single layer of fabric that refracted a metallic glint with each step she took.

It took every bit of Cillian's willpower to hold the uninterested look on his face, because his obsession with Orla was nearing dangerous levels of infatuation, and he wanted nothing more than to throw her over his shoulder and spend the night claiming every inch of her.

He'd selfishly stuck that gown in her armoire with the small hope she'd wear it around him - but hadn't prepared himself for her to *actually wear it around him.*

Cillian's inhale hitched as his gaze narrowed onto the ruby necklace sitting perfectly in the hollow of her slim throat. A wave of relief rolled through him at the sight of the gem he'd given her, imbued with a bit of his magic that allowed Orla to move through every single one of his wards with ease, and prayed he wouldn't need to use the other safety features he'd charmed into the jewelry, prayed his paranoia was unwarranted for the imaginary situations that plagued his restless mind.

With a small flick of his fingers, Cillian conjured an invisible shield around Orla, the barricade passing unnoticed by everyone else in the room. But at least this way, if anything were to go wrong, his father wouldn't be able to kill her. Cillian's mouth dropped into a grim frown. He hated the fact that his father potentially killing Orla was *actually* something he had to account for.

Orla showed no fear as she approached the dais and curtsied low. Dimas, keeping his own features blank, asked impassively, "Orla Grey, what gift will you be displaying this evening?"

"Fire wielding," Orla said firmly.

Dimas nodded, jotting down her answer on the parchment before taking a step back. "Thank you, you may begin."

Orla stood alone in the middle of the room, taking a defensive stance as she held out her hand. Flame burst to life, coating her fingers up to her wrist in bright hues of orange, red and gold. With a small smile Orla threw the ball of pure flame up about ten feet in the air, and as it began to descend, a second, then a third ball shot out of her open palm to join the first. She caught the first, then threw it back in the air, then did the same with the second and third, adding a fourth and fifth, the fires growing in size, until she was juggling a full wheel of flames without breaking a sweat.

Cillian fought the pride from his face as she effortlessly called each ball back to herself, until only one small fire remained. With a coy smile, she threw the lone flame in the air, and it morphed into a perfect likeness of a curved sword, before it flipped on its fiery hilt and hit the floor, disappearing in a crackle of embers.

Covering his wide smile with his hand, Cillian shot Orla a wink. She'd been working hard with Soren over the past weeks to perfect this routine. Orla's *acat* covered both of her arms to her elbows and spread across her hands and palms. The swirling red ink implied that she had a lot of magic, and if the performance didn't indicate that she was truly wielding her full potential, King Eamon would think Orla was hiding something sinister.

But with Orla's magnificent performance, there should be no doubt that she merely had an impressive amount of fire control and that was that.

Dimas's eyes flickered for a moment before he called out, "Lineage god, Aella. Ability, fire wielding. Thank you, Orla."

Orla shot a smile to Dimas before turning to leave.

But King Eamon snapped his fingers. "Beings blessed by Aella with that amount of power need to stay for further study." Cillian narrowed his eyes. His father and that fucking Vessel Book. But before he had a chance to speak – to remind his father that they were going to test the book at a later time, Yin rose from her throne.

"Did you say, Aella was *her* lineage god?" Yin asked curiously.

Cillian's breath stuttered.

"I did, your Majesty," Dimas replied stiffly.

Yin crept forward, cool cunning flaring in her eyes, deep blue robes swishing as she descended the dais. "You, fae, come here," she snipped at Orla – who stopped ten feet shy of the throne room doors at the King's request. Cillian prayed Yin would sit back down as he mentally berated himself.

His father mentioned bringing the Book of Aella out of safekeeping from the royal vault to see if any beings blessed by Aella in the last year could possibly be a Vessel, but there'd already been two other fae with Aella's gifts tonight, and King Eamon hadn't stopped *them*.

Even though their lackluster *acatis* didn't scream "Vessel of Destruction."

Cillian advised strongly against testing the book tonight – stating it would be stupid to search for a Vessel while the Topaz royalty was here. He argued that if a Vessel was *here*, their alliance would suffer since King Eamon would want the Vessel to reside in the Ruby Kingdom and the Topaz would argue against that. Alliances only worked if each side believed they held the upper hand.

He'd hoped his argument was convincing, but with his father now watching Yin approach Orla, his confidence faltered further.

Orla's grey eyes glinted with pure wrath as Yin stepped lightly onto the floor of the throne room. Cillian schooled the snarl off his face, pouring more of his magic into reinforcing the shield around Orla.

"I, too, am blessed by Aella," Yin said demurely, addressing Orla like she was an old friend. But Cillian saw right past the bullshit, noting the twinge of jealousy that laced Yin's words. "Let me see your *acat.*"

Orla narrowed her eyes, though she held her arms out towards Yin stiffly, palms up. Cillian leaned forward in his seat and growled at his father, "If Yin so much as *pinches* my cupbearer, I'll knock her the fuck out."

"Quiet," King Eamon spat. "You forget your *betrothed* is also blessed by Aella. Yin could be the Vessel we're searching for. I spoke to King Wei-Li and told him we're testing all strong beings blessed by Aella tonight. That includes the Princess."

"We didn't discuss this," Cillian hissed.

"I don't discuss my plans with you, *boy*. And you would do well to remember your place. Irridessen now holds two fully activated Vessels, and Ingotheria has none. King Wei-Li and I agree that the time for Aella's Vessel to be activated is now."

Yin paused in front of Orla, the two females sizing each other up in a way that had Cillian shoving more energy into his shield. Tension crackled between the two as Yin reached forward to grip Orla's arm, but her hand collided with the barricade Cillian placed between them.

"Drop your magic, my Prince," Yin demanded, turning her head to glare at Cillian.

"I will not have you harming my cupbearer," Cillian said in what he hoped was icy indifference and not a passionate plea. "If you hurt her, I'll have to fetch my own drinks this evening, which will take time away from me dancing with you, *Princess*."

King Eamon rounded on Cillian, but Yin shrugged. "Fine. I only want to see her *acat.*"

Yin rolled up her wide sleeves, displaying jagged, deep blue tattoos that covered her hands and forearms. With a calculating eye, she swept her gaze between her own *acat* and Orla's, and Cillian knew she was mentally measuring whose was bigger.

Orla stood still, hatred coating her expression like poison as Yin ordered Orla to flip her hands over.

Yin pouted softly before turning to Dimas. "Hers extend higher on her arms, but *only* by a few inches, and *my* lines are thicker. Who is stronger?"

Dimas swallowed tightly before taking a step back. "It's difficult to say, your Highness. Since you both display the gifts from Aella differently."

Orla leveled a flat stare at Yin, before cooly replying, "You are *definitely* stronger than me, Princess."

Yin regarded Orla with pure loathing, and Orla quirked her lips up into a taunting grin, dropping her hands to her sides and stepping around the Princess, effectively dismissing Yin entirely, before staring up at King Eamon still seated on his throne. "What other test do you need me to complete, my King?"

King Eamon gave Orla a serpentine smile that did nothing to calm Cillian's rapidly fraying nerves. "Go enjoy the Equinox Ball, Orla Grey. The rest of the tests will be conducted later tonight once the rest of the Culling is complete."

Without needing to be told twice, Orla turned on her heel, her chin held high, and stalked from the room, disappearing into the hallway beyond without a single backwards glance.

# CHAPTER SIXTY-SEVEN
## ORLA

THE ADRENALINE THRUMMING THROUGH Orla's blood shot molten ire into her veins. Soren spied her the moment she stormed into the Equinox Ball, and quickly darted over, hooking a hand through her elbow, and wheeling Orla around to deposit her onto one of the low backed couches lining the perimeter of the celebration.

"Well, you aren't dead," Soren said plainly, pushing a heavy glass of wine into Orla's grasp before plunking down onto the seat next to her, adjusting the rose-pink skirts of her mostly sheer dress so her leg was suggestively revealed, her sun-kissed skin on display and immediately drawing the eyes of two males that exchanged a look before striding over. "Get lost," Soren barked menacingly before either male could open their mouth. They tripped over each other as they departed, which pulled a snorting laugh out of Orla.

"To not being dead," Orla deadpanned, raising her wine. Soren cheerily clinked her own against it before they linked arms and took a long swallow. "Even though I would've loved nothing more than to burn Yin to a crisp."

Viciousness flashed through Soren's face. "Every time I have to be near that cunt I want to rip her throat out with my teeth." The violent look morphed into a manic smile that tugged at the corners of Soren's lips. She closed her eyes, reminiscing blissfully, "I almost did once – a few years ago. Yin thought it would be funny to shock me when I was carrying an entire tray of filled wine glasses."

"What did you do?" Orla breathed, remembering how Cillian mentioned Yin and Soren's hatred spanned years.

"I dropped the tray, waned across the throne room of the Topaz Kingdom, ripped her out of her throne, got on top of her and pummeled her face with my fists. She tried to hit me with a bigger blast of lightning, but Cillian threw a barricade around me, so it bounced off his shield and hit the roof instead." Soren chuckled fondly, "Apparently, it took like...five stone wielders to fix the ceiling."

Orla blanched, staring at Soren with a mixture of intrigue and concern. "How are *you* still alive?"

Soren shrugged, patting her hair into place. "It was only Cillian, Yin, and me in the room at the time. And Cillian covered for me. The best part was Yin was so deliciously embarrassed I beat her ass that when her father showed up ten minutes later and demanded to know why her face was covered with blood and the roof was smoking, she admitted she fell down the dais stairs and accidentally shot off a bolt of lightning."

The two shared a conniving look, and Orla sighed with contentment before allowing the adrenaline to ebb from her blood and her eyes to rove around the crowded Ball.

Twelve massive chandeliers lined the dome and floated in midair, each tiered with multi-colored glass and holding individual candles that threw the entire room in a warm glow. One half of the room was decorated to mimic the royal wing's lounge, with huge poufs that easily fit two or three beings scattered around the floor, broken up by long couches. Potted plants with narrow stems and wide leaves dotted the area, and heavily patterned rugs layered atop each other, making a sitting area for the beings coming from the dance floor.

On the other side of the room, a huge, tiled dance floor dominated the space, and beings were already whirling around to the music from the full orchestra that stood on the balconies overlooking the party. Hidden rooms sectioned off with rattan partitions kept certain pleasures from view, and Orla figured morals would loosen as the night went on and the drinks kept flowing.

Orla sipped on her wine and eyed the dance floor. Soren did the same, both of them riding the high of putting Yin in her place, basking in the feeling.

A blur of red hair interrupted them as Dimas skidded to a halt in front of their couch, quickly snatching Orla's arm and hauling her up.

"What are you doing?" Orla demanded. Dimas began cursing under his breath, half shoving her towards the doors. Soren shot from her chair, eyes already darting around the room as if she was scouring for a hidden threat. Her hand flexed at her side, magic sparking to life and swirling through her fingers. It was back to the white hued battle magic she held whenever she didn't hold a mimicked *acat*.

"Is your *kindered* the red dragon from the desert?" Dimas snarled, the words quiet and rushed.

Orla attempted to rip her arm from Dimas's grasp, but he tightened his hold. She widened her eyes as Dimas faced her fully, his hands snagging her shoulders to spin her around.

Orla stuttered, but she saw fear - true fear in Dimas's eyes and her breathing ramped up. "What happened?"

Dimas crushed her to his side, practically dragging her towards the exit. Soren hovered at his back, guarding him as he pushed past the throng of beings in the hallway, darting into a shadowy alcove.

"What the fuck is going on?" Orla hissed the moment the shadows concealed the three of them from view. Dimas ignored her, instead turning his attention to Soren. "Get the bags and meet in the Aridden training ring. We have *minutes* to get the fuck out of here."

Soren nodded curtly, waning in a burst of light.

Dimas held his breath for a heart-racing second until they were once again cast in shadow. "I need to know right now, Orla. The dragon in the desert – *is he yours?*"

Orla frantically slipped through her *acat,* finding the thread connecting her to Seysei still cold, untouched. "Yes," she whispered.

Dimas cursed. "He's been captured. King Eamon has him in the Aridden training ring on display. I don't know how the fuck King Eamon got him, but if we don't release him, he'll be beheaded at midnight."

"No," Orla gasped. Her mind latched onto the thread connecting her to Seysei, and she screamed his name down their bond. There was no response. Only silence. "He isn't responding," she said, her voice cracking as sheer panic gripped her.

Not Seysei.

Not her *kindered.*

He was connected to her too deeply, and though he'd only just become hers, he was *hers* and she would never again allow something so dear to her heart be ripped away.

"They must've drugged him. You need to get to the training ring, release him, and flee until it's safe to return."

Her stomach sunk as the words crashed through her. "I have nowhere else to go," she said bitterly.

"Don't worry about that, it's already been arranged. You'll be safe."

Against the bleating terror, Orla could do nothing but focus on Dimas and the notion that she would be safe. But right now, she had to get to Seysei.

A second flash of light announced Soren's arrival, and she stood stone faced and grim, a large rucksack balanced on her back. With a cursory glance out of the alcove, she said, "Everything's ready – let's go."

"Soren's going to take you to your *kindered*," Dimas explained gently, releasing Orla with a pained expression. "I need to return to Cillian and keep an eye on King Eamon to make sure he isn't planning to move your dragon's execution up."

Orla balled her hands into fists at her side, pushing down her fear and allowing rage to sweep through her blood. Her well of fire magic rose up in a torrent of shrieks and vengeance as her soul beat a steady war drum that pulsed into her ears. Nothing else mattered right now. Not Lenna's return, or Marlo. Not her belongings, nor her private room or the full life she'd cultivated within the Ruby Palace.

Not even the handsome Prince that scaled her defensive walls and kissed her as if she was the only female in the world. Nothing mattered right now except her *kindered*. The reflection of her soul. "Take me to Seysei."

Soren stepped forward and held out her hand.

The desert air in the Aridden training ring whipped Orla's hair over her cheeks. The temperature plummeted the moment the sun sunk beyond the horizon, but the frigid wind did nothing to cool Orla's internal fire. The training ring sported a solid stone floor, with half crumbled pillars strung together with cracked archways that opened up to the star-filled night sky.

But Orla only had eyes for the thick black chains bolted into the ground, and the dragon that lay shackled within them. Seysei lay on his belly, his head held against the cold floor by additional chains that wrapped from one side of his throat to the other. A heavy muzzle clamped his jaws shut, and the sight of that alone had Orla wanted to erupt with fire until the Palace lay in ashes at her back.

Sensing her approach, Seysei cracked open one gold eye, a whimper pushing out of his throat as his dilated pupil tracked her every move.

"We're getting you out of here," Orla said softly as she rushed forward and knelt in front of her *kindered*, reaching her palm out to lay against the soft scales of his neck.

Soren squatted down, running her fingers over the first of the three sets of chains. "These aren't held in place with magic," she whispered. "We get the chains removed from his shackles but leave the cuffs themselves on his legs. We can get those off once we're safe and it'll take less time."

Orla murmured her agreement, moving to the first chain by Seysei's front legs. She gripped the thick metal in her hand at the spot closest to the ring bolted into the ground, before her mind caught up to Soren's words. "We?"

Soren glanced her way before stating, "I'm coming with you, of course. How else would you know every part of our super-secret backup plan?" Soren worked on Seysei's chain by his hind legs, eliciting a low growl of warning from the dragon.

"It's alright," Orla soothed, willing her magic to her hands to melt the link that connected the cuff to the chain. "Soren's a friend. We're going to give her a ride out of here to go someplace safe once we get you free. Is that okay?"

Her connection to Seysei was still muted, and judging by the fact the beast could barely keep his eyes open confirmed for Orla that he'd been drugged. She prayed to whatever god would listen that the dragon would still be able to fly once they got the chains unbolted.

Seysei closed his eye, a deep hum resounding from his throat. "I hope that means 'yes' in dragon," Soren muttered.

Orla forced her magic to flare hotter, and smiled in grim satisfaction as the orange flames began burning white, metal melting slowly. "I think so, but our connection is still dulled, so I can't hear him."

A heart lurching wave of relief rushed through Orla as the first of the six chains disconnected, dropping to the ground with a heavy *clank*. Soren got the second chain freed a few beats later, and they quickly rushed to the next two, Orla melting the chain holding his throat to the ground, and Soren working on the other hind leg.

Seysei's eye flew open again, and he growled louder. "Just a few more," Orla repeated. "Only a few more."

"What a *surprise*." A silvery voice purred behind them, and Orla whirled towards the source. She released her own snarl as Yin sauntered into the training arena, dressed in a deep blue cloak and a delighted expression. "Did you know, it was me who told King Eamon that if he *truly* wanted to find out if he had any dirty little *Vitraro* hiding in his Palace, all he needed to do was to catch a dragon and see who came to rescue it?"

Soren stepped to Orla's side, baring her teeth at the Princess. "Fuck off, Yin."

Yin *tisk*-ed, her blood red lips pulling back in disgust as she appraised Soren. "Hello, whore. I always hoped you'd turn out to be a traitor. It's a pity that *you* were the one being I couldn't sway King Eamon on turning against."

Orla held her hand out, stopping Soren from launching herself at Yin. "Keep working on the chains," she murmured. "We need to get Seysei free."

Soren spat at the ground at Yin's feet, before moving ever so slightly to Orla's right, her hand reaching behind her back, gripping the chain Orla half-melted. Light flared as Soren pushed her magic into the breaking link, though her eyes never left Yin's face.

Orla stood slowly, white hot funnels of flame still churning at her fists. If she could distract Yin long enough, Soren could finish freeing Seysei, and they could be airborne in seconds. Hopefully. As long as Seysei could fly. Drawing upon years of picking her battles at wild abandon, Orla sniffed, "Well, Yin, you wanted to know who between the two of us was stronger. Here's your chance to find out."

Yin's lips pulled into a nasty grin as she sank into a defensive crouch, and Orla shot a prayer to Aella, begging the goddess to at least give her a fighting chance. Orla'd been training her *acat* for two fucking months. Yin had *decades*. But she only needed to push the Princess back enough to buy Soren time to free Seysei, and Orla figured brute force could at least help her wing it for a couple minutes. Sending a last prayer skyward for a fuckton of luck, Orla shot forward, launching two bursts of fire towards Yin.

Faster than Orla could comprehend, Yin twirled and shot to the left, easily avoiding Orla's attack. The Princess slashed her clawed hand through the air, lightning bursting from her palm. Orla dove against the ground, cursing her, and barely getting out of the way in time before the lighting struck the stone floor with an ear-splitting *crack.*

Seysei struggled against his restraints, smoke pouring from his maw. But with the muzzle bolted to the ground, and four of the chains still attached to shackles, he got no traction. His tail lashed furiously, a choked roar slipping from his throat.

Orla rolled onto her knee, frantically throwing out her hand to whip a crackling tendril of fire at Yin. Yin leapt away from Orla again, waning ten feet to the right, and released a barrage of lighting - the bolts striking against the arena floor in a perfect circle around Orla.

"Is that all you can do?" Yin taunted as she danced around the ring, expertly dodging every blast of magic Orla shot at her. *Fuck* she was so fucking fast. Orla slammed a wall of fire down, but Yin merely waned to the other side. "You have such a big *acat* but absolutely no idea how to wield it."

With a wicked giggle, Yin raised her hands over her head, electricity crackling between her raised palms. "Do you even know what Aella can *do?* Have you *been* training your magic? If I knew you were this much of a novice, I would've just challenged Soren to a rematch instead."

Soren had broken the chain that held Seysei's throat to the ground, leaving only the two attached to his left legs and the muzzle that was frustratingly connected at four contact points. At Yin's words, Soren paused, her eyes flicking between the two as if she was considering taking Yin up on her offer.

*"Get the muzzle off!"* Orla screamed, right as a zap of lightning snapped against her calf. She bit down hard on her tongue, the metallic taste of blood filling her mouth. She spasmed, her muscles locking up, her breath catching in her lungs.

Yin crept closer, holding the connection to her power as she stared at Orla with a smug smirk that dripped with bloodlust. Orla felt her vision blur. She tried screaming, but the sheer power of Yin's magic made it impossible.

Every nerve in her body was on *fire*. Not the type that she'd learned to love - but the kind that had her flailing while electric currents zinged through her limbs.

Orla fought for control of her muscles, her body shaking as she writhed under the pain of Yin's lightning. Her *acat* slipped from her grasp, and Orla screamed through her consciousness, though no sound came out of her mouth.

# CHAPTER SIXTY-EIGHT
## ORLA

A BRIGHT FLASH BURST through her eyelids, and Yin screeched, losing the connection to the lightning wreaking havoc against every inch of Orla's body. Orla collapsed the moment the agony winked out, crumpling to the stones, wheezing. Breathing *hurt*. Another bolt of pure white sparked and Orla forced her eyes open, blinking against the film of haze that obstructed her sight.

Soren had gotten one of the four bolts of the muzzle free, before launching herself at Yin with a barrage of magic that made Yin stumble back a step.

Orla scrambled to her feet, staggering to Seysei's muzzle and drawing upon her *acat* with shaking fingers. Yin was powerful – but Soren was out for blood. Shot after shot of Soren's battle magic had Yin losing more ground. Yin countered with lightning arrows, but they were sucked into Soren's gift, disappearing as quickly as they materialized, jagged, blue tattoos starting to gleam and glow along Soren's forearms.

"Parasite!" Yin shrieked in fury as she switched tactics, lowering her shoulder, and driving it into Soren's stomach. Soren yelped, falling backwards, and the two went down in a pile of fangs, wild kicks, and blows that had Yin's head snapping back, and Soren cursing colorfully as Yin sucker punched her.

Orla lay a reassuring hand on Seysei's neck as she placed her palm flat on the ground, melting the bolt from his muzzle as quickly as she could. Two more bolts. Two more chains. And they were getting the fuck out of here.

A scream rendered through the night as Soren was thrown from Yin, crashing into one of the stone pillars rimming the ring. She hit the ground hard on her hands and knees, blood pouring down her face from a nasty gash cutting through her brow, splattering like morbid raindrops against the training arena floor.

She tried to rise but was forced down again as a gale of wind roared over them. Seysei thrashed under Orla's hand, the dragon bellowing his fury as King Eamon stepped into the arena, flanked by his two body-guards and fifteen warriors. The warriors fanned out around the ring, their sword staffs dropping and pointing to Soren and Orla in unison.

Orla's heart threatened to beat out of her chest. Two more bolts and Seysei could open his maw enough to breathe fire. Right now, her *kindered* could barely open his jaw enough for Orla to catch a glimpse of his teeth. But a stream of Seysei's black edged flame would improve their situation immensely. Pretending to scramble away from the guards, she moved her palm, covering the third bolt with her hand, pouring fire magic into it to melt the metal.

King Eamon cast a hate-filled glare in Soren's direction. "Grab her," he commanded, waving his personal guards forward. Soren fought as Droward yanked her up by the hair, slamming her face first into the stone pillar. Droll chuckled darkly as he watched. Droward spun Soren around, his meaty hand gripping her throat. Soren choked out a garbled curse as red magic wound around the column of her neck.

"I'm so disappointed, Soren," King Eamon said lightly, as if she'd merely shattered a glass or spoken out of turn. "But you know the punishment for disobeying me." He nodded to Droward, who grinned cruelly, his free hand hitting Soren in the chest with that same red magic. Soren's blood curling scream tore through the training ring. "And you, *Orla Grey*," King Eamon mused, rolling her name against his tongue, "what an inconvenience you've become."

Before Orla could do more than wince under the King's heavy stare, rough hands grabbed her under the arms, dragging her away from Seysei. She kicked, screaming Seysei's name as the dragon howled hoarsely in anger, struggling against the irons still holding him against the floor.

Droll cackled with malice as he stalked over to her, gripping her by the hair and snapping her head back. She snarled, spitting a mouthful of blood into the fae's face. Droll licked her blood from his lips, a feral gleam sparking in his yellow eyes. His hand began to glow red, and before Orla could even process what he was doing, he punched her in the stomach, causing her to double over, a silent cry screwing up her face.

Droll lay his hand flat against her shoulder, and Orla thrashed as his magic began slithering through her veins, dimming her connection to her *acat* until Orla gasped, feeling every ember in her soul ice over.

"That should keep you from doing anything untoward for the next few days," King Eamon chuckled as he flexed his hands, stepping closer to the restrained dragon that screeched in outrage, bucking wildly against his shackles. "Droward and Droll have the power to block access to one's *acat*. While it isn't forever, you won't be alive long enough to get your magic back."

King Eamon circled Seysei's maw, evaluating the dragon before him. "The issue with dragon activity has been unprecedented since you came to our shores. But for all the movement north from Dragon's Peak, there were multiple reports of the same beast over and over again, who seemed rather intrigued with something in the Palace. It didn't take much for me to assume a filthy *Vitraro* slinked through our gates. Though, for Lord Dimas to miss it..." King Eamon tilted his head, his mouth drawn in a frown.

Soren hissed in warning; her eye swelling rapidly. Blood dribbled from her lips and nose as she threatened the King, droplets of red embellishing a string of filthy curses. He shot her a smirk. "Seems as if my cupbearer feels rather strongly about the consequences Lord Dimas will be facing. Not to worry, pet. The two of you will be in Minmere together before the night is through. It's a shame that I'll be losing such a powerful lineage reader, but I'll find another."

Orla cried out as King Eamon's attention drifted back to Seysei, her heart ramming against her sore ribs as she fought against the guards that held her back. She struggled fruitlessly to release herself, but they only laughed, causing Orla to scream her helplessness, her voice cracking as she threw her weight to the side, fighting with every morsel of strength she had as grief wound through her preemptively.

King Eamon stood to Seysei's side, slowly tugging off his gloves and raising his hands above his head. Silver hued tendrils of air twisted between his fingers, honing into a bladed edge that hung threateningly over the base of Seysei's skull. Seysei emitted a low whirr of defeat as his beautiful eyes met Orla's. She bellowed her defiance to the stars in the sky, to the gods themselves.

"The *Vitraro* die with *you*, Orla Grey."

His hand slashed down, and the King cleaved through Seysei's neck with a razor-edged wind, beheading the great dragon in a single blow.

"*Seysei! No, no, NO!*" Her horror ripped through the training arena as she shrieked her *kindered's* name, even as blood gushed forth from Seysei's neck, his golden eye dimmed, and his life extinguished.

"I'm going to fucking *kill you.*" Orla slammed her head back into the guard behind her, catching him right in the chest. He stumbled back, though the grip on her upper arms didn't loosen. But she kept banging her head, again and again, screaming until her throat was raw and her lungs shriveled.

King Eamon chuckled as he turned, wiping his spotless hand on his black cloak before tugging his gloves back on. "Bring them," he commanded to the guards restraining Soren and Orla, "let's see how loud they yell in the dungeon. I'll have their death warrants signed right after I take care of Dimas." As Orla dug in her heels, fighting to stay rooted to the ground, her horror-struck gaze still trained on Seysei's unmoving body, Soren continued thrashing as she was dragged towards the King. King Eamon crouched down, smacking Soren lightly on the cheek. Soren bared her fangs at him. "When I find Dimas, I'll put his head on a spike for you, Soren, so you can see him one last time before you die."

Soren screamed, though King Eamon turned and waned out of the training area with Droll and Droward – who wasted no time shoving Soren into the arms of another guard.

The warrior still holding Orla pushed her forward. She locked her knees, thrashing her head. She wouldn't leave Seysei's body to cool alone.

And if they refused her of that, then she would not leave this training ring alive.

"You come willingly, or we gut you here, dragon bitch," the guard uttered in her ear, his rancid breath cloying with stale ale. "I don't care either way."

Orla opened her mouth to snarl, but before she had a chance, the guard holding Soren dropped wordlessly to his knees before pitching forward, two arrows protruding from his back. Soren tumbled out of the guard's grasp, falling onto her hands, her breathing coming in rapid pants. Orla gasped as a shadowy darkness around them closed in.

No.

Not darkness.

Beings in black cloaks silently appeared between the pillars of the arena, black masks covering their faces, leaving only their eyes visible, an assortment of weapons aimed at the retreating guards who hadn't yet noticed their arrival nor the dead guard and the now free Soren. Orla exchanged a wide-eyed look with Soren in the space between seconds.

One second, they stared at each other, Soren's mouth dropping open in disbelief.

The next second, the guard holding Orla grunted and lurched sideways, a dagger lodged in his ribs. Orla didn't question the attack, using the slackened grip to her advantage. She drove her skull back, catching the guard's nose, hearing the satisfying crack and muffled roar of pain as she ripped her arms free, diving across the stone floor and scrambling towards Seysei's body.

Their mysterious saviors garnered the attention of the remaining warriors, and with a shocked shout, they unsheathed swords and raised their long staffs, meeting the shadowy figures head on. Magic crackled through the air. Two of the black robed figures lashed vines of blue and red towards three of the guards, throwing them to the floor. The magic oozed as it spread out, covering their noses and mouths - suffocating them until their flailing stilled and their bodies stiffened with death.

The clashing of steel on steel and roars of fury drowned out Orla's wails of grief as she crawled closer to Seysei, reaching a trembling palm out to her *kindered*. His body lay inches away from his detached head, and Orla heaved against the wave of soul crushing loss. Blood and bile splattered to the ground, coating her tongue in an acidic tang that had her retching again, but she moved past it, calling Seysei's name in a horse mewl, her throat ravaged from screaming.

The ringing in her ears drowned out the chaos of the fighting around her as she sunk into numbness. Brutal battles scorched through the training ring but all she saw was the last, half-melted bolt on Seysei's muzzle, the pool of blood that stained her skirts as thoroughly as her bare and stripped heart. One bolt and his head would've been free – and he could've spewed fire at their enemies and given her the distraction to get the remaining two chains off his legs.

She had been so close to freeing him.

But it hadn't been enough.

Even though Droll's disgusting hands no longer touched her, her *acat* still felt too distant, too fragile, for her to even attempt to run her mind's fingers through. As if it was no more than spun glass, dangling precariously through her shattering sanity.

# CHAPTER SIXTY-NINE
## ORLA

His blood, the blood of her *kindered*, was on her hands. Orla stared at the glassy, golden eye of her dragon. Her body felt disconnected, as if she was standing over the fae who knelt in the pool of dragon blood from an alternate reality where Seysei had been freed, and they fled.

One bolt away.

But she failed. If she'd only let Soren fight Yin from the beginning - instead of her pride forcing Soren to stand down. If she had only trained harder, longer. If she'd only been better...

Seysei would still be alive.

Hot tears slipped down her busted chin, dropping into the blood below. Orla shuddered, a sob wracking her body as she threw her arms around Seysei's head.

A hand reached out to touch her shoulder, and Orla whipped around on instinct, shoving the mysterious figure away with a scream.

"Orla," the figure whispered roughly, "I'm so sorry."

Deep brown eyes stared back at her, filled with sorrow.

"Cillian," she choked, throwing her arms around him as another wave of grief slammed into her chest.

A quiet hum filled the arena as the rest of the cloaked figures dispersed, making sure every single one of the fifteen royal guards were truly dead. Soren was being helped to her feet by a tall, cloaked being, who bent down and murmured something to her that Orla couldn't hear. It took all of Orla's energy to incline her head toward the pair and croak, "If that's Dimas, tell him the King's trying to kill him, too."

"He's aware," Cillian replied softly, though the brittle tone of his voice ran its nails down Orla's fragile skin. "Right now, we need to get you three out of here, and we can figure the rest out as we go."

"I can't leave Seysei's body," Orla gritted out through another soul-wracking tremble.

Cillian's eyes darted above her head before he inhaled sharply. "Orla," he whispered.

"It's my fault Seysei is dead." Orla's voice broke with emotion that seemed determined to crush her into oblivion.

*"Orla."* Cillian's tone was clipped, pulling her from his chest and turning her around as a sheen of silver blanketed Seysei's body, thrumming with an expectant light that flared outwards from beneath his red scales.

As Orla watched transfixed, the light swept over Seysei's length, growing brighter – a high-pitched ringing splitting the silence around them. The rest of the cloaked figures, as well as Soren and Dimas, staggered back, shielding their eyes. Cillian shot out an arm protectively to wrap around Orla's waist. She shoved him off, lurching forward on instinct alone as the light flared, obscuring the dragon's body from view.

Orla's heart stilled alongside the air itself.

With a ground shaking roar that tore through the heavens, the luminescence sucked back into Seysei's body.

Orla gasped as the illumination faded and her *kindered* rose from the floor, now a two headed hydra a few feet longer in length than he'd been prior. His forked tail sported new, sharp spikes and he lashed it against the ground, easily ripping himself free of the remaining chains, the shackles popping apart and clattering to the floor with heavy *pings*. His wings flared out at his sides, the talons at the tops now tipped in metallic bronze, his dual heads alert, maws peeled back.

*Alive. Seysei was alive.* The thought crowed triumphant through her dumbstruck mind while the golden thread of her *acat* flared with renewed power in her soul, growing from one strand to two, coiling around each other to form a tighter, thicker cord. Her lineage magic stayed slumbering inside of her, though at the moment she didn't give a single fuck about fire wielding.

Seysei's heads shook before arching to the night sky in sync and as one let out a guttural bellow, the other opened his maw, shooting a jet of black tinged fire into the night sky.

*"Fuck,"* Cillian breathed beside her, awe coloring his curse as he stared at Seysei with reverence. "The hydras were dragons of the gods. I didn't believe they truly existed in this realm anymore."

Orla fell to her knees as Seysei stretched out his larger wings, the red sheen of his scales now tapering to that same bronzy-hue, each head sporting thicker, spiraled horns. His talons flexed against the now cold pool of blood.

Seysei turned both of his heads to Orla - one set of eyes shimmered brilliant gold, the other pair icy silver. *"Kindered."* He thundered into her mind.

*"Kindered,"* she responded as she rose from her knees, tears streaking down her face as she reached up with a shaking hand. His golden-eyed

head lowered, and she stroked his scaly maw, a deep rumble resonating from his chest.

"*How?*" Her mind wobbled as she clung desperately to their shared connection.

"*I felt a pull to stay here after death. And I chose to follow it back to you.*"

"Not to fuck up this moment," Cillian said aloud, drawing Orla out of her link to Seysei, "but we need to get you, Soren and Dimas out of here before King Eamon returns."

"*Tell the Prince I will burn the King where he stands,*" Seysei snarled as his silver-eyed head rose above the other, growling low in his throat, snaking back and forth.

"Seysei said he wants to burn King Eamon where he stands," Orla repeated dumbly, her voice still raw and hoarse. Her *kindered* stood, alive, in front of her. Her scrambled, aching brain needed a minute.

"Tell Seysei to get in line," Cillian retorted flatly. He gestured to Dimas and Soren. Dimas was practically holding Soren up as she seemed to float in and out of consciousness.

"Soren needs a healer," Dimas said urgently as he pulled her into his arms, the female going limp.

"There's one where you're headed," Cillian assured. "You know the way?"

Dimas nodded, hesitated. "I didn't expect to be leaving so soon."

"Temporary setback." Cillian grumbled, averting his narrowed gaze to the Palace at their back. "I'll see you soon. But you three need to get on Seysei and leave now. I'll handle my father."

Hearing Cillian's words, Seysei lowered his shoulder to the ground as Dimas gently adjusted Soren in his arms, curling her head into his chest. With a powerful leap, Dimas landed nimbly on Seysei's back, picking his way carefully between the large spikes that trailed the length of the hydra's spine, before sitting awkwardly at the base of Seysei's neck.

The events of the night weighed heavily against Orla's shoulders as she loosened a breath, guilt and relief warring through her, as well as the crippling realization that she was heading into the unknown, leaving Cillian behind.

He seemed to read her wavering thoughts. Cillian yanked down his mask and pulled her to him, his lips meeting hers in a desperate kiss. She melted into his hold, her hands reaching up to wrap around the back of his neck as he angled his mouth, deepening the kiss and drawing a soft whimper from her.

Sooner than she would've liked, Cillian pulled away. "Take this," he said quietly, as he dug a lumpy, drawstring bag out of his cloak and pressed it into her hands. "This isn't goodbye, Orla. I swear on my life - I'll see you soon. But you need to leave now. Dimas knows the way. Trust him and take care of yourself."

"I wanted to dance with you tonight," Orla said softly, feeling another wave of emotion prick behind her lids.

Cillian gave her an easy smile, his darkening eyes flickering as he tugged her in for another kiss, saying against her lips, "I owe you a dance, Orla Grey, last of the *Vitraro*. Hold me to that."

Before she could respond, Cillian wrapped an arm around the backs of her legs, scooping her up, and jumping from the ground to land atop Seysei's back. She yelped as the quick movement jostled her injuries, reminding her very quickly that her body was bruised all over.

He lowered her in front of Dimas, waving a hand. Red magic clamped down on her legs, securing her safely to Seysei.

"That way, you won't fall off," he chuckled tiredly, though the solemn look in his gaze pulled at Orla's heart, "and I'll be able to sleep easier tonight."

With an agile spin, Cillian dismounted Seysei, striding backwards, his eyes locked with Orla's as the hydra flared out his wings, his two heads weaving side to side. Seysei crouched low, shooting up into the sky a beat later, wings snapping wide, catching an updraft of desert wind.

Orla felt her stomach lurch with the quick ascent, her hands grappling for purchase against the short spikes in front of her, though her legs stayed tight against the hydra thanks to Cillian's magic. Dimas cursed behind her as he mirrored the move, one hand white knuckled around the base of a sharp spike, the other banded across Soren's unconscious body.

The training ring fell away as they rose higher and higher, and Seysei let out a whistling roar before streaking through the sky, flying hard and fast into the open desert. Orla craned her neck to get one last glimpse of the Ruby Palace before Seysei shot through the clouds, leaving the handsome Prince, and half her bloodied, but still beating, heart behind.

# CHAPTER SEVENTY
# SPARROW

*"IRRIDESSEN IS UNDER ATTACK."* Esmeray shouted from the wide balcony overlooking the courtyard of the Opal Palace. Sparrow drew herself up straighter, standing at Esmeray's side as the Queen continued, "Foreign Kings from Ingotheria have sent spies to our lands to steal and kill, to force our hand and attempt to bow our heads into submission."

The thousands of Irridessen citizens below cried out their fury. Esmeray held their rapt attention, her face screwed up in a grimace as she let the words ring out.

A week had passed since Lenna's departure, and Esmeray's Queen's Guard already thwarted two assassination attempts aimed at Keerian. Which meant Esmeray was out for blood, and though every assassin met a very ruthless and finite death, the threat of Irridessen's sovereignty had begun weighing heavily upon her shoulders.

Esmeray's night-black wings flared out behind her as she leaned forward, her dagger-sharp nails digging into the opal banister. Glittering green eyes darted between the beings below as she hissed, her voice amplified with magic, "Our peace and prosperity are threatened, but I will *not* allow it to stand. We will rise, as our ancestors did, and fight to death and beyond to protect what is ours. We'll beat Ingotheria back into its place beneath our heel and remind them *why* Irridessen is the strongest continent. *Who is with me?*"

At her question, the crowd below bellowed their agreement, some raising swords, others shooting off bursts of multicolored sparks.

Esmeray shot Sparrow a smirk as she spread her arms wide, fisting her hands. "In the light of King Eamon's threats to our royal line and to our allies in the Slate Kingdom, I've decided that our continent needs to divide in order to stand stronger, to change – in order to unite, and the gods have echoed that sentiment."

With an even breath, Esmeray raised her chin and said firmly, "It is with that in mind that I announce, effective *immediately*, that I, Queen Esmeray, Vessel of Phades, abdicate the throne of the Opal Kingdom to my Heir, Queen Sparrow, Vessel of Faune."

A wave of shocked silence met her words, and for a moment in the deadened quiet, Sparrow let her personal fears best her. But then, loud whoops and shrieks of delight rang out, catching quickly and spreading like wildfire, until the entire courtyard spiraled into controlled, yet thrilled, madness.

Esmeray smiled, the sheer approval apparent. "I will rule from the throne of the Obsidian Kingdom, and Queen Sparrow and I will not rest until *every threat* to Irridessen has been eradicated. We are teetering on the edge of war, but if war does find our land, Queen Sparrow and I will lead Irridessen through it, together and victoriously, as Phades and Faune did during the God War."

The crowd descended into a frenzy as every being echoed their glee, chanting and screaming, enraptured by the two Queens standing before them. Esmeray beamed as she turned, removing the solid silver crown decorated with fire opals from the small podium to her right. It was the sister to the gold and obsidian crown she wore.

With sure hands, Esmeray stepped closer to Sparrow, and Sparrow knelt one last time before her Queen. After this, they'd be equals, ruling together, fighting together. There were no titles the likes of Lesser Queen or Queen on High, no uneven tiers to their power.

Equals.

In every way.

"Sparrow, do you swear to protect Irridessen from all threats, rule just and true, and to never stray from what is right?" Esmeray's voice only managed to just barely drown out the crowd below.

"I swear it," Sparrow replied steadily, holding her hand over her heart.

Esmeray gently placed the silver and opal crown atop her head, garnering a new wave of celebration from below. "Then rise, Queen of the Opal Kingdom."

Turning, Esmeray intertwined her fingers with Sparrow's, raising their joined hands above their heads. "We will fight for the truth, for what is right, and we will not stop until Ingotheria is beaten. *Who is with us?*"

At her words, Esmeray flung her free hand up, a pillar of gold erupting from her palm and shooting skyward, bursting through the clouds in a show of power. Sparrow grinned fiercely, mirroring the move, her god magic exploding into a column of her new, vibrantly silver battle magic.

The chanting of Irridessen's citizens drifted to her ears and Sparrow's heart galloped furiously inside her as she made out the words they were repeating, louder and louder, until it seemed as if the balcony they stood upon shook.

*Long live the Vessel Queens.*

# CHAPTER SEVENTY-ONE
## SPARROW

THE MOON'S RAYS SLID and shimmered through the tall windows lining the new Queen's chambers. Prior to Merrick's departure, he'd renovated a brand-new royal wing overlooking the gardens. Though it had been built for Esmeray, Sparrow couldn't help but feel the room encapsulated all her own desires.

Pale green curtains, trimmed with silver, hung against the second story residence, and the bedroom itself was decorated with pastel hues from the gorgeous cream duvet that lay against the white birch bed, to the cushy lilac couch that sprawled along one full wall.

All she needed was to bring plants into the sprawling private library attached to the bedroom, and add bird feeders to the huge balcony. Then, maybe, just maybe, she'd feel like she belonged here.

In the Queen's Chambers.

In the Opal Palace.

Under the heavy crown that adorned her brow.

The god magic rushing through her veins still felt foreign. As if even her new *acat* knew she was nothing more than a substitute. An imposter. The tattoo of a swirling sun that now lay at the nape of her neck tingled, another addition that she hadn't fully wrapped her head around.

This was never meant to be her path. She stared hollowly out the window, her mind wending down a dark turn, picturing her twin in this crown, this life, instead of her. Wondering if their lives were wholly interchangeable, or if Sparrow was truly the right choice.

If she'd died instead of Briar, would Esmeray still be Queen? Would Laurent be haunting the halls of the Ruby Palace bowed down with the weight of a ghost soul tie instead of Merrick? Sparrow worried her lip, drifting in and out of the giddiness of her coronation, and the depression that rolled over her like a cloud, whispering in her ear that she was nothing more than a fraud.

"Whatever you're thinking about, beautiful, it isn't worth the frown on your face." Sparrow jumped, finding Laurent standing at the threshold, holding a crystal glass of wine out to her.

She cut him a tight smile. "I was just thinking of everything that happened in my life, how I got here, and debating if I truly earned it or not. You know - nothing too dramatic and upsetting."

"Well, self-depreciation makes the Queen," Keerian stated sarcastically as he strode through the door and took up a seat on the couch, his boots half unlaced and the gold crown on his head askew. "Ask Meer. She always says if she ever finds herself wallowing, then that means she's made tough decisions but still holds onto her heart. Like Adara's imprisonment for instance. It gutted Esmeray to throw her twin in the Soul Keeper's Cell, but we all know that's the best place for that raging bitch."

Sparrow cocked her head, contemplating Keerian's words. She couldn't help but agree.

The three of them were waiting on Esmeray to return from the Obsidian Palace. Apparently, after a coronation and a few glasses of strong wine, Esmeray thought the best course of action would be to go antagonize Adara before returning through the portal connecting the Opal Palace to the Obsidian Palace's caverns with a massive amount of snacks from the Obsidian Palace's kitchens because, in her words, *the chef in Obsidian is better, because Hale taught him how to bake cookies the* correct *way.*

"Does being Queen have to feel so…" Sparrow trailed off, unsure of the correct word to describe the feeling currently constricting her chest.

"Heavy? Terrifying? Stressful?" Keerian supplied unhelpfully, leaning back to stretch his wings and legs out with a groan. "Yeah, it does. But don't think it all falls on you – you have Meer, plus us King Consorts to bounce ideas off of."

Laurent smirked, straightening his pearl white robes as he puffed out his chest. His new silver crown also lay haphazard on his head, and Sparrow grinned as she saw the gleam of wicked intentions in his eye that were fully focused on her. "Keerian and I have a very difficult role," he said pointedly, holding his hand over his heart, "and that's to make sure you and Meer don't break too many laws during your reign."

"Esmeray breaks rules every day," Sparrow argued. "Literally my entire coronation was technically a law she overturned since I don't have royal blood. She argued about it with her council before telling them to either go with her idea or to get the fuck out."

"Yeah, I don't think I'm a very good King Consort," Keerian chuckled proudly. "She just looks so pretty when she gets that evil glint in her eye, and I cannot, for the life of me, tell her 'no.'"

"Plus, she did make you her Heir, so technicality or not, you are the true Queen of the Opal Kingdom now. And the citizens of Irridessen already embrace you – I daresay your coronation went a fuckton smoother than Esmeray's did." Laurent slumped against the couch next to Keerian.

"Well, Sparrow wasn't framed for any murders, so I'd concur that your rule is already off to a dazzling start." Keerian looked from Laurent to Sparrow, his brows softening. "You will both be great for Irridessen."

A real smile bloomed over Sparrow as she felt the sincerity of Keerian's words. It still felt surreal to wear a crown and be announced Queen of the Opal Kingdom with Esmeray's abdication of the throne, but the support she felt fiercely in the beings around her lifted her spirits, banishing the intrusive thoughts from her mind.

"How are the ah...assassinations attempts going?" Laurent asked Keerian as he sipped on his wine again, shooting a look of concern to the King Consort of the Obsidian Kingdom.

Keerian rolled his eyes, waving his hand in a dismissive gesture. "Unsuccessful, obviously. The Ruby Kingdom is swearing that it isn't them, but even if it's coming from the Topaz Kingdom, it's still under King Eamon's command – just semantics on who's doing the dirty work."

"We're going to need to hit back with a show of force," Laurent said quietly, placing his glass down with a clink as Sparrow felt the mood in the room shift. She'd been crowned less than twelve hours ago, and there was already bedlam and politics rippling through the continent.

"Esmeray is convinced King Wei-Li is no more than a puppet king, and that King Eamon is truly holding the loyalty of both the Ruby Kingdom and the Topaz Kingdom. It's why Lenna's visit to Ingotheria really couldn't have come at a better time. If King Eamon wants Lenna to find the Book of Carra, then she's safe there and can bluff until she *does* find the Vessel Book. Then she'll relay that to us, and we'll get to it first."

Keerian shrugged, completely at ease with the fact that a foreign King was out to kill him. "Plus, now that we have two Queens, that's two bloodlines ruling Irridessen. King Eamon's plan to kill me to conquer

Irridessen has fallen flat. And I don't believe he's willing to send a larger force to take out you *and* me, Laurent. He's not dumb enough to play out that plan now that we've called him out on it."

Laurent cocked his head, nodding at Keerian as he mused, "Dividing the power of Irridessen means he cannot take it over as easily as he anticipated."

"Divide to unite," Keerian said cheerfully.

"And Esmeray hated having to travel so much to rule both," Sparrow added. "It should be some weight off her shoulders to be able to focus on the Obsidian Kingdom solely." Sparrow crossed the room, nudging Laurent's boot with her foot until he shuffled over so she could sit down on the couch between the King Consorts. Laurent wrapped an arm around her shoulder, kissing the side of her neck delicately.

"I think she's planning on meeting with you tomorrow, Sparrow, so that the two of you can divvy up responsibilities. From an outside perspective, it'll look like Irridessen is ruled by two separate Queens, but we'll know the true power is because we're all working together. We can play to each of our strengths, rule the way this continent needs." Keerian shot Sparrow a wink before adjusting the lapels of his jacket, sitting up straighter, a dignified and solemn expression flicking into place across his face. With an air of regality, he raised his glass, eliciting a snort of laughter from Sparrow at the ridiculousness.

Laurent copied the move, arching his brow into a particularly fancy look of utter magnificence, looking every bit the part of a dignified fae King.

"To the Queens of Irridessen," Keerian boomed as he shoved his glass higher. "Long may they reign, and long may they live, because assassination attempts aside, I fucking *love* being King Consort."

Laurent barked a laugh and Sparrow giggled as they moved to clink their glasses together, awkwardly locking arms to take a sip of their wine. The bubbles seemed to float right to Sparrow's head, and she allowed herself to relax, reminding herself of her power as a Vessel, and as Queen.

With this crown, she could do so much good in the world - help the less fortunate and enact wonderful changes across the continent. She took an extra sip from her glass, a promise and a vow to herself that she would always look out for Irridessen and the best interests of its citizens.

Laurent lurched back with a shout of surprise as Esmeray waned directly into the room, Goldriel in one hand, the other fisted tightly at her side. A look of pure wrath twisted her lips into a snarl, her eyes wild and gleaming with god magic, the gown she'd worn to the coronation replaced with her black leather battle suit.

Sparrow's good cheer immediately dissipated as she took in the look of furious outrage etched across Esmeray's face.

Without waiting for anyone to speak, Esmeray unclenched her palm, displaying a small, dull, ruby – the same kind Dimas used to summon a portal back to the Ruby Kingdom.

Sparrow's breath caught in her throat as Esmeray hissed, "Adara's *gone.*"

# EPILOGUE

Dimas turned from the glowing portal that would take him to the throne room of the Obsidian Kingdom, glancing at the witch that stood beside her own portal, awaiting King Eamon's command to step through.

Barely moving his lips, Dimas muttered, "Neci, you don't have to do this. Siphon my power and wane out of here. You can go straight back to the Jade Kingdom. I'll tell King Eamon you caught me by surprise. You don't have to endanger yourself."

Neci narrowed her eyes, before raising a brow in defiance, regarding him with a viper's smile. With a shake of his head, he averted his eyes as King Eamon gave them the order to go.

Dimas turned his head towards her one last time, and she threw him an icy smirk as she disappeared through her portal.

The Prism displayed two alternate golden threads of memories to Lenna. One which would steer her to Dimas in the throne room of the Obsidian Palace, and one to follow the witch. Faintly, a thrum of a migraine swept through Lenna's temple, though her physical body seemed far away as she dove into the golden thread of the witch's memory, pushing herself onwards.

The witch stepped lightly from the portal into the caverns deep below the Obsidian Palace. In front of her lay a flat stone that pulled a soft murmur *of delight from her chest. She prowled the circumference of the Soul Keeper's Cell, her fingers delicately tracing the witch runes carved along the rim.*

*Wings rustled with indignation above her, and Neci flicked her eyes up to the Queen who stared at her with disgust. Her dress was bloodied and torn, her white wings dirty, the boning along the outer lining cracked and covered with a fine layer of grime and soot.*

*The witch's nostrils flared delicately. "Siphon," she hissed. "Massis used to gift that power to the fae long before they turned on him."*

*Adara bared her teeth. "Witch," she rasped back, spitting the word like an insult. But Neci ignored her, continuing to trail her fingers over the runes that nullified fae magic and chained a being to this stone by anchoring their very soul to the rune covered rock.*

*"Who sent you?" Adara demanded. "Esmeray?"*

*Neci scoffed, ignoring Adara as she flexed her fingers, muttering under her breath in a language Lenna never heard before. Lenna drifted closer to the witch in the memory, watching as she continued following the runes, whispering that foreign tongue.*

*With a stamp of her foot Adara snapped again, "Who sent you, witch?"*

*The witch ceased her murmuring as she shot her eyes up to Adara, a smile playing against her lips. "What would you do if I freed you?"*

*Adara stilled. "You can't free me," she said, though a waver of hope seemed to tinge her words.*

*"The Soul Keeper's Cell was never meant to be a long-term prison. My ancestors built it to cut off a fae from their power while also draining their life force. It was supposed to be a torture device – a visit to the Soul Keeper's Cell could make even the most stubborn fae spill their secrets like blood." Neci dropped her hand from the runes, crossing her arms. "I could get you out. Easily."*

"How?" Adara asked curtly, drawing herself up to stare down her nose at the witch below her.

Neci shrugged. "Only a witch can break witch runes. Fae cannot. But I could very easily pull you from that rock and set you free. But why should I? What could a fallen Queen do for me?"

Adara leveled a stare at Neci, her blue eyes narrowing. "I could give you riches beyond your wildest dreams."

Neci huffed a laugh, "I have no need for fae trinkets. King Eamon tried that already. What I want is to return home."

The two regarded each other with disgust as Lenna floated closer, watching the calculating look on Adara's face as she struggled to think of something to bribe for her freedom.

"I'll tell you what I want. And you tell me if you can make it happen," Neci finally said, breaking the tension floating through the thin air. "I want to siphon off your magic, and wane to the Slate Kingdom."

"Why? You're a witch. Why not go back to the Jade Kingdom?"

"Because the Jade Kingdom is not my home. The Slate Kingdom's dome never held power over witches like it did the fae. It is home to many covens – right under the noses of your pretentious species that believed you shoved every last witch into the Jade Kingdom. But gargoyles could still access the Slate Kingdom in their Sentry form, and witches could walk right in the front door. Our magic was never even diminished by the dome."

Adara rolled her shoulders back. "So, you would free me from the Soul Keeper's Cell just so you can siphon off my magic and flutter back to the Slate Kingdom? Why not draw off any other being with magic? Why me?"

Neci grinned then, her eyes flaring. "I need a Queen with no throne. Because in exchange for your freedom, I want you to take the throne of the Slate Kingdom. I want you to rise to power with the witches beside you to take revenge on every human, fae, and gargoyle piece of filth that looked down on the might of the Witch Kingdoms and sneered."

"Deal," Adara breathed harshly.

Neci uncrossed her arms, quickly retracing the witch runes against the lip of the Soul Keeper's Cell. The witch began chanting again in that foreign language as the runes glowed with an unnatural blue light. Adara hovered to the side, bloodlust and retribution illuminated on her face. Lenna's blood chilled as Neci inhaled sharply, her body shuddering, before the thrum in the air stilled and the magic of the Soul Keeper's Cell fractured apart.

Adara stepped from the Soul Keeper's Cell with her head held high, her opal horns glinting off the fading blue light. Neci extended her hand to Adara, and Lenna watched in utter terror as Adara took it gingerly, before another blue light flashed against Adara's palm.

"I need a lot, Queen," Neci purred as the witch drained Adara's magic, bolstering her own. Neci took and took, until Adara sagged with exhaustion, her ruined wings pitching her forward. Neci stepped back in disgust as Adara crumpled to her feet, wheezing, before staggering upright. "That should do," Neci responded with a false cheeriness, her voice dripping with venom.

Neci's eyes floated back to the slab of stone that used to be the Soul Keeper's Cell. With a dark giggle, she rooted into her pocket, pulling out a ruby, and placing it on the lip of the rock. "I won't be needing that," she announced, more to herself than to the half-conscious Adara attempting to righten herself against the drain of her magic. "But it'll give your sister the incentive she needs to declare war on the Ruby Kingdom. That should buy us time, don't you think, Queenie?"

Adara groaned as Neci reached down, gripped Adara's forearm, and waned away in a burst of blue.

Lenna pulled her consciousness from the Prism slowly, the fatigue from holding onto a memory for so long now a bone-jarring migraine. Esmeray told Lenna through their mind speak rings that Adara was missing hours ago, and Lenna had been searching the Prism ever since. But now, as the sun began cresting the horizon, she had answers.

She needed to tell Esmeray immediately before Esmeray declared war on the Ruby Kingdom. That small ruby the witch left behind was the perfect way to pin Adara's freedom on a powerful enemy – an enemy that could hold their own in a war.

All the while, a single witch was behind Adara's escape with allegiance to an entirely different continent.

A continent that was considered an ally to Irridessen.

And if Adara gained the throne of the Slate Kingdom...Lenna's blood chilled as she thought back to the vision of the burned and destroyed manor in Doortan, the image now feeling more like a seer's prophecy than a dream.

Her skull pounded, and pin-prickles of icy sweat coated her skin. She kept her eyes screwed shut, knowing that the bright light of the bedroom would only further ignite the ache in her spinning head.

She needed to lie down before she fainted. But she had to tell Esmeray first.

The *clink* of steel ripped her back to the present.

Her eyes flew open, a sharp stab of pain lanced through her temples, and her heart dropped.

King Eamon stood before her, his hands clasped behind his back. Hale and Merrick were held by hulking royal guards, daggers pressed against their throats. Hale's wide eyes shot fear straight through Lenna's soul as her migraine thrashed, causing her vision to spot and blur. Her hands began shaking so forcefully, the Prism fell from her grasp, dropping to the floor with a dull thud.

Merrick struggled against two massive fae guards with copper breastplates, their palms emitting a red light that made Merrick's face twist with pain and rage.

"Welcome back, Oracle." King Eamon said with a roll of his tongue, as if he savored the position he found her in and wanted to lengthen the torment. He jerked his head to two of the royal guards standing between Lenna and the door to the chambers they'd been assigned. "Search her."

Hale snarled at King Eamon, "Don't you lay a hand -"

One of the guards stopped in front of Hale and backhanded him, hard, across the face. Lenna screamed as Hale's head snapped to the side. Agony pulsed liquid fire through every one of her nerve endings, threatening to knock her unconscious as Hale slowly turned his neck with a panting groan, sagging against his captor's hold, a dribble of blood slipping down his lips.

Hale's eyes locked with Lenna's as the other fae guard shoved his hand, glowing with a soft red light, over Lenna's hair, her throat, past her breasts and stomach, and down each arm. "Found it," the guard crowed as he yanked the mind speak ring that connected her to Irridessen off her finger. "Queen Esmeray must've sent her with it so the Oracle could spy on you, your Majesty."

"That was not freely given," Lenna growled, with all the fury she could summon under the duress of her pounding head.

A moment later, the guard let out a howl of pain as the ring sizzled angrily, spitting boiling liquid gold down his hand, the metal bubbling as it melted. The acrid stench of burning flesh filled the room, causing Lenna to gag. The mind speak ring self-destructed, scorching away the guard's glove and searing his palm, leaving a huge, gaping blister in its wake.

The six gemstones that had been embedded in the band scattered across the floor, each jewel cracking and shattering, pinging small, sharp fragments across the room, until the mind speak ring was completely destroyed – unusable as a weapon against Irridessen.

The guard fell to his knees, screaming in agony and cradling his mangled hand to his chest. King Eamon merely glared at him, before jerking his head towards the other guard who now hovered between Lenna and Hale with a panicked look on his face. The guard blanched before jerking forward, dragging the still bellowing guard out of the room by the back of his armor.

Lenna let out a wobbly breath. Irridessen was safe. The caveat to the mind speak ring being taken against her will made it impossible to use. Keeping the connection between her friends safe and private. But now, she was fully cut-off from Irridessen.

With no way to reach anyone that could help them survive King Eamon.

Merrick hissed deep in his throat as he continued to fight against the hold of two royal guards. The King frowned as he approached Lenna. "Now, why would the Oracle have a mind speak ring connecting her to a different ruler if she *wasn't* a spy?" King Eamon mused, his gaze traveling over Lenna before he grabbed her chin in his hand, forcing her head back to meet his eyes.

"I am trying to avoid a war," Lenna whimpered, her fingers and legs tingling. It was the feeling that spiked through her limbs before she succumbed to a fainting spell. Helplessness rattled through her. She *couldn't* lose consciousness now. "For all beings in Irridessen and Ingotheria.

Irridessen believes the Ruby Kingdom freed Adara, and Irridessen will declare war on you. But you were double-crossed. The witch escaped."

King Eamon's dark gaze flickered from triumph to anger for a split second before his eyes shuttered. He released Lenna's chin, chuckling easily. "Yes, I knew the witch would disobey me. Her kind is particularly well known for being nothing more than parasitic, soulless creatures with no loyalty."

"But Irridessen thinks-"

"Irridessen will see the release of Adara as an unforgivable act. And they'll declare war on Ingotheria. But war is profitable, dear Oracle. And now that your bitch of a Queen has divided Irridessen back into two Kingdoms, I cannot hope to gain control of Irridessen as easily as I hoped. War is messy, yet it's a way for me to both weaken Irridessen and extend my grasp to...other lands."

King Eamon smirked, his gaze roving from Merrick to Hale, the latter trembling with barely leashed horror, the former still attempting to fight. "Ingotheria will decimate Irridessen easily. Irridessen has two untested Queens playing at ruling a continent. They may fight on the battlefield, they may have god magic, but they cannot be at *every* battle, at *every* turn. We'll hit them relentlessly until they're forced to realize the true might of the Ruby Kingdom. And if Adara reenters the game, who do you think she'll ally with, Oracle? Her sister who tossed her in the Soul Keeper's Cell? Or a King with the might of the world's largest standing army at his back?"

A wave of nauseousness from her migraine mixed with pure fear as King Eamon picked up the Prism with his gloved hand, placing it gently on the desk beside Lenna, though just the sound of the stone hitting the wood made Lenna wince, her head blistering and sensitive, her heartrate skittering dangerously with an impending blackout. "Now, Oracle. I have a job for you. Use the Prism and find the Book of Carra."

"No." Lenna managed, shoving as much anger into the word as she could.

King Eamon only raised a single brow, sliding the Prism closer to the edge of the table. "You will find, Oracle, that *you* are protected by ancient laws in my Kingdom. The Oracle of Terramere is a living god, and I'd never hurt you."

With a barely perceived nod from the King, the guard holding Merrick suddenly shot forward, slamming a dagger through Merrick's wing. With a roar of pain, Merrick's back bowed as the guard sneered, digging the blade deeper with a twist of his wrist.

"However, the laws that protect the Oracle, do not extend to her...*escorts*. But I'm not a monster. I understand the fear of traveling to a foreign land alone." King Eamon smiled wide as he looked down at Lenna, his cruel eyes like voids. "So, pick *one*."

Lenna's head spun, her ears now ringing with the echo of Merrick's agonized bellow, causing tears to slide from the corners of her eyes. She let out a harsh whimper in response, struggling against her now-dimming vision.

Hale, her love, the male that patiently waited for her heart to heal from decades of misery. They'd just begun building a life together. She dreamt of meeting him under the full moon, receiving a soul tie from Carra.

Merrick. Her first friend in Irridessen. The brave gargoyle that reached through Lenna's shell of a life, plucking her from the doldrums of Doortan and giving her reason to live again. The male who'd suffered so much over the last few weeks, only to willingly come to these lands with her to protect her.

"I- " Lenna stuttered, her head spinning as her migraine pulled her towards unconsciousness no matter how desperately she fought against it, her stomach rolling with a mixture of nerves and pain as the adrenaline of the moment did nothing but sharpen the agony.

But before she had the chance to beg forgiveness from the two males that meant so much to her, before she could even process the impossible question being asked of her, Merrick slammed his head back, twisting at the last second, driving the sharp tip of his horn through the eye of the leering guard holding him. The guard screeched in anguish as Merrick snarled, ripping his horn free and taking the brute's eyeball with it. The eye flung across the floor, and Lenna doubled over as a wave of sick crashed through her, her vision spotting as she heaved harder.

She was going to faint. Her heart was rushing too quickly, her head light and airy, her arms and legs suddenly heavy and immovable. Lenna slumped forward, barely keeping the crushing wave of darkness at bay, all of her energy focused on staying mostly upright.

King Eamon *tisk*-ed. "It seems the gargoyle has chosen for you, Oracle. Guards, carve him up within an inch of his life and dump him at the border of the Jade Kingdom. The witches will be more than happy to finish him off."

The King's disgusted voice, the sickening sound of steel against flesh, and a deep, guttural scream were the last things Lenna heard before everything went black.

# Acknowledgements

Well, here we are at the end of another book. How was that ending, huh? Pretty sweet, right?

I have to admit, writing a sequel to Queens of Spells and Stone was a very eye-opening experience for me because I wrote QOSAS off of literally vibes only. Up until my final edit of QOSAS, all I had was a crappy hand drawn map, a few pages of notes, and that was it. No structured timelines, no character bible, no super complex OneNote filled to the brim with every single nuanced bit and bobble that I needed to remember. (Foreshadowing)

And when I came up with the plot of Woven Fates, I realized just exactly how utterly fucked I was.

LOL.

So, while writing QOWF (again, no structured plot – just a loose basis of what I wanted plus a healthy dose of god complex) I began taking notes of my own writing from QOSAS. The reason QOWF took me over a year to write was because I was pretty much documenting how my entire fantasy world worked – while writing a brand-new story.

But, in all honesty, it set me up for success, because halfway through QOWF, I realized my originally-planned-trilogy...was actually going to span seven books. And now, I sit down and stare at my packed-to-the-brim character bible, multiple spreadsheets, chunky OneNote, and I am PROUD. Do I rigidly structure my plotting now?

Well, no. But I *am* ridiculously organized, and I think that counts for something.

But enough about me...let's get into the acknowledgements for the people who helped me make this sequel a reality.

First off – Randall. You've been there every step of the way. Thank you for celebrating with me, supporting me, and feeding me when I'm being a writing-hole goblin. You make sure I feel at peace, and you pour every ounce of your love through our life every single day. On top of being the best husband across the realms, you are also my soul mate, my best friend, and the jelly to my peanut butter. I love you forever.

To Mom & Dad – you got this book dedicated to you so you already know how much I appreciate and love you both. Thank you for always cheering me on - especially when I call multiple times over multiple days to reread and agonize over my blurb. I am so thankful that I have you both in my corner.

Carly – hmm...I just published my second book, but you are still cooler than me, so I'll check again after book #3. But in all seriousness, I love and adore you, and am so stinkin' proud of the woman you have become.

To my soul sister, Tori – thank you for making sure I don't miss any girls' day adventures and for reminding me to bring sunscreen. I couldn't do this life without you, and I appreciate your rock-solid friendship, your sarcasm, and your taste in music on top of a hundred other things that having you in my life enhances. I love you and am so blessed to have you in my corner.

Amanda – my other soul sister and my fantasy-reading-bestie. I love you and your incredible heart. Thank you for freaking out with me every time I sent you sneak peeks, for rooting for me every step of the way, and for reminding me that my parents are going to read a book that has spicy scenes in it. I am now panicked and furiously redacting their copy with a sharpie.

To Mellow, Indi, and Pig – for sharing YOUR office with lowly ol' me. Thanks for being the best pups around.

To Michelle and Tina – my ARTISTS!!! Michelle – every time I send you a description of a character, it's like you pull them directly out of my brain and give them life through your portraits. Thank you for every piece of art, and I am so thrilled to see your business thriving. It is extremely well deserved. Tina – holy bananas! THIS COVER!! I was FLOORED when I first saw the finished product, and I am SO happy that we connected. You are a total gem, and I am so excited to see how high you fly because your talent is stellar, and you are a rockstar. Seriously, you made this cover come together so quickly and so perfectly that I had to move up this release date because I am TERRIBLE at keeping secrets when it comes to my books and I needed everyone else to see this cover ASAP.

To the Indie Book Community – thank you for being so incredible! Being able to chat with so many of you, cheering each other on, and changing the publishing industry together is a joy that I am so glad to be a part of.

To my ARC readers – a massive thank you for being amazing! I am so grateful that I found each of you, that you celebrate this series alongside me, and that some of you are already asking for book #3! I am so happy you are enjoying this series, and I truly appreciate you all getting behind these books and shouting them from the rooftops!

And finally, to you, dear reader, for supporting an indie author! Thank you for choosing to read my book! I am so thankful that you read this! Yay! Every time I get a message from someone who just finished reading Queens of Spells and Stone and loved it, it warms my heart and solidifies my love for writing. I love sharing these stories with you all, and I can't wait to hear your reactions to Queens of Woven Fates!

Insider Scoop: Be on the lookout for special news that has to do with the third book of the Vessels of the Gods series...because we're heading to the Jade Kingdom next! *Softly chanting* WITCH BOOK, WITCH BOOK, WITCH BOOOOKKKK!!!

# About the Author

Katerina Stevens is a dark fantasy author who loves writing morally grey characters, creating friendly-ish beastie companions for said morally grey characters, and drinking coffee with wild abandon. She currently resides in Florida with her incredible husband, three spoiled dogs, two chunky cats, and a grumpy bearded dragon. She graduated from the University of North Florida after taking pretty much every creative writing class offered. Though she started off as a business major, she quickly discovered that math is hard, which led to her getting a bachelor's degree in Sociology. Outside of being an author, Katerina is a devout Capricorn, a tattoo collector, a Canva lover, and a OneNote enthusiast.

# CONNECT
## with me on Social Media!

*Follow Katerina on Social Media to keep up to date with  new book announcements, updates, and more!*

 @AuthorKaterinaStevens

 Katerina Stevens - Author

*Did you love this book? It would mean the world to me as an Indie Author if you would leave a review on Amazon, GoodReads, or wherever you shout your love for books to the universe!*

*Thank you so much! -Katerina*